8/13

DEATH OF KINGS

Other titles in this series:

Sleep of Death

Forthcoming:

The Pale Companion

DEATH OF KINGS

Philip Gooden

CARROLL & GRAF PUBLISHERS, INC.
New York

Carroll & Graf Publishers, Inc.
19 West 21st Street
New York
NY 10010–6805

First published in the UK by Robinson,
an imprint of Constable & Robinson Ltd 1992

First Carroll & Graf edition 2001

ISBN 0-7867-0875-1

Printed and bound in the EU

'For God's sake let us sit upon the ground
And tell sad stories of the death of kings'
                              RICHARD II, 3, ii

Historical Note

In the early months of 1601 England faced its worst crisis since the defeat of the Spanish Armada thirteen years earlier. Queen Elizabeth was in her 68th year. Most of her subjects had never known another ruler. An ageing virgin, with no direct heir, she flew into a fury if anyone even hinted at the question of succession. The last of her many flirtatious and teasing relationships with the men in her aristocratic coterie, that with Robert Devereux, Earl of Essex, had come to a bitter end.

Essex was by far the most dangerous of Elizabeth's 'courtly lovers'. Volatile and paranoid, he suspected a court faction (led by Robert Cecil, the Secretary to the Privy Council, and by his old enemy, Sir Walter Raleigh) of conspiring not only against him but against England itself. Their supposed object? To install the Spanish Infanta on the throne. Essex plotted rebellion, though whether it was to protect the Queen or to supplant her was never quite clear, perhaps even to him. Essex enjoyed immense popularity among his fellow Londoners, many of whom considered him to have been persecuted by the faction surrounding the Queen.

Essex's followers sought to capitalise on that support in various ways. One of these was to enlist the Chamberlain's Men, the acting company of Shakespeare and the Burbage brothers, to put on a performance of Shakespeare's own

Richard II at the Globe playhouse in Southwark on the afternoon of Saturday, 7 February, the day before the planned uprising. This historical play was no ordinary drama. *Richard II* climaxes with the deposition and death of a lawful monarch and his replacement by a younger and fitter (in any sense) usurper. In the circumstances of the time – with Elizabeth nearing the end of her reign, Essex perhaps ready to seize control, the people of London full of apprehension – to perform this play was to invite trouble.

Beginning

Sunday 1 February – Tuesday 3 February 1601

Though I saw nothing when I glanced over my shoulder, there could be no mistake about it this time. The man behind me might be able to rely on the night and on the shadows of the narrow street for cover, but he couldn't conceal the noise of his boots. So far he had managed to keep his steps in unison with mine. It was this whispering agreement with my own progress that first aroused my suspicions. Now, when I stopped abruptly, so did he – only he stopped a fraction too late. The sound of his heel on the icy cobbles rang in my ear. Then silence.

I looked up as if the night sky would tell me what to do next. Stars pulsed in the gap between the overhanging houses. The nipping, eager air sank its teeth into my exposed face. My breath plumed upwards. The night sky told me nothing that I didn't already know.

It was late, not long before a winter midnight. It was bitingly cold. And it was unlikely that anyone walking the streets of our capital was going about any lawful business (myself excepted, of course). What made my innards do a little dance, though, was the certainty that my friend in the shadows wanted to keep his presence a secret. Otherwise, why match his steps to mine, why stop at almost the same instant that I did? I had it in mind to call out that I was nobody, merely a poor player. He could have all of the shilling in my pocket for the asking. But a desire to avoid looking foolish prevented me.

I was unarmed, or as good as unarmed. A decorative little knife, suitable for nail-paring, lay somewhere fast asleep under my clothing. As for any representative of the law – a catchpole or a headborough – well, where are they when you need them? I might have cried out in alarm, but Mill Street, where I was standing this winter's night, though not in the first rank of turpitude, was the kind of area where doors slam shut against trouble. The only remedy lay in my feet.

Hoping that my pursuer would think that I'd stopped merely to gaze at the heavens, I started walking again. Sure enough, within two paces, the echo fell in behind me. As my boots struck the cobbles, so did his. With each step I lengthened my stride and walked a little faster. My aim, with my heart banging in my chest and clouds of breath exhaling in my wake, was to reach the corner of Hart Lane, a hundred yards or so to my right. Once there I could, perhaps, lose my pursuer in the dark warren of lanes and alleys that stretched between Mill Street and the riverbank. None of the houses and shops betrayed any sign of human life by as much as a glimmer. We might have been threading a path through a dead city. Overhead, the stars danced with cold life. Whoever was behind me seemed content to match my pace, quickening his march as I quickened mine but, as far as I could tell from the echoed steps, not attempting to gain on me.

Now I was nearing the corner of Hart Lane. And, at once, I grew frightened – I mean more frightened than before. Maybe it was the regular, remorseless tread of the being over my shoulder, a sense that I wouldn't be able to shake him off, twist and dodge as I might in any maze of alleys. Instead of walking at a steadily increasing rate towards the mouth of the Lane, I panicked. I broke into a run. But there was more than one of them. From the entrance to Hart Lane a shadow started from the darkness of the corner, as if it knew precisely the route that I intended to take.

I slowed. By instinct, I veered in the opposite direction, attempting to put space between myself and this new threat. But as I moved towards the other side of the street a *third* shape moved out from my left, and I knew that I was caught.

I stopped.

I tried to control my panting breath.

I resolved to make a good end. Why, one can do a little even with a knife that is fit only for nail-paring. Cursing the thick clothing that kept it buried, I started to fumble for the weapon.

The three figures closed around me. I couldn't see the one approaching my back but I could hear his rapidly advancing footsteps. I turned to face him, a mere shadow. He spoke. He had a soft, even voice.

"Master Revill?"

Now a different kind of fear overcame me. It was not any late passenger that these men were after, not anyone who chanced by. They were looking for someone specific, they were looking for me. I attempted to master my own tones.

"You have the advantage of me, sir."

The courtesy wasn't returned. He repeated himself, a statement now rather than a question.

"Master Nicholas Revill, the player."

His face was a darker patch in the night, a no-face.

"What do you want from me?"

I felt the presence of his two companions closing in behind me.

"Speaking for myself, nothing."

5

"That's good, because you've hit exactly on all that I possess. Nothing."

I was pleased at the steadiness in my tone.

" 'Nothing' is the usual condition of players, I believe, sir," said the other. He had a very soft voice. I had to strain to hear it and thought at the time that it was doubly insulting to have to struggle to hear an insult.

"Since you've stopped me merely to sneer at my poverty," I said, "I'll be on my way. If you want to flatter me any further you can pay your pennies at the playhouse, like everybody else, and do it there."

I made to slip aside and was not surprised to find my path blocked by one of the shapes to my rear.

"Let me pass."

"You are required," said the soft-toned man. I turned back towards him since he was evidently in command.

"Required? How so? Who are you?"

Even as I said these words, I was grasped by the upper arm on either side. The grip was firm to the point of discomfort.

"We have been instructed to take you to a place," said the shadow. The mildness of his tone contrasted with the coercion implicit in his message. "It is better for our safety – and for yours – that you don't know exactly where you are going. Accordingly, you will be blindfolded. Please don't struggle or attempt to remove it."

I almost laughed – from fear or from genuine amusement, or a mixture of both.

"For God's sake, man, it's dark."

"It is for the best, sir."

He spoke respectfully but there was a sneering quality to his words.

One of my arms was released, and the next instant the individual on that side had slipped a band of some smooth material over my head. Fumblingly, he checked to ensure that it covered my eyes before tightening the knot at the back. Then he resumed his hold on me. So I stood, pinioned, in double darkness.

"Who are you . . . thieves?"

By now I would have been relieved to discover that that was all they were. (Relieved, but also perhaps obscurely disappointed.)

"We are in authority."

"Whose authority?"

My voice broke into a kind of ignominious yelp. In any case, the question was overlooked. At once, the two men on either side began – slowly at first and then faster and faster – to spin me round in circles like a top. Instinctively, I tried to reach up with my hands to tear the cloth from my face, but my companions kept me so close that, although I could smell their breath and feel their warmth, I was unable to lift my arms. Within a few moments I was giddy enough to have fallen if they hadn't been buttressing me on each side. My wits whirled round with my body.

Then, like children at hoodman-blind, they suddenly brought me to a stop. The dark world continued to spin most unpleasantly round my head, and my ears sang. Now I was being ushered forward by my escort. Forward where? Obviously this ridiculous child's business of turning me topwise was an attempt to make me lose my bearings. They'd succeeded too. I had no idea what direction we were going in.

As I was pushed through the streets, helpless as a babe-in-arms, I had freedom to think. Oddly, I was slightly less scared now than when I'd first sensed that I was being followed. My initial assumption had been that I was the target of ruffians or rakehells – but the behaviour of this threesome (or rather of the only man to have spoken) suggested that they wanted

7

nothing so vulgar as my life or my non-existent property. 'You are required.' This had a portentous ring, as of the devil in some morality drama summoning down an overdue soul to flame and perdition. I'd have laughed at the absurdity of it if my throat hadn't been dry and my heart thudding. But it was no joke. While my feet clattered across the icy cobbles my mind wandered in a maze.

After what I supposed was about ten minutes – during which time we changed direction on several occasions and once, I am sure, merely turned round in order to go back the way we'd come – we halted. I felt dizzy and queasy. I wanted to sit down. But there was a rap on a door, there was the creak of it opening, and a wash of warmer air on the exposed part of my face.

"We have arrived. There are two steps in front of you, shallow steps. Negotiate them with care."

His advice wasn't needed for I found myself being hoist up the steps anyway. Then suddenly the arms which were pinioning me fell away. I tottered but kept my balance. Unthinkingly I made to remove the blindfold but was anticipated.

"Do keep your hands down, Master Revill."

Reluctantly, I did as I was told. I was tired of being kept in the dark.

"Before you is a doorway, only wide enough for one man at a time. Step through if you please."

"No."

I had decided, you see, that it was foolish – to say nothing of unmanly – to step into what might be a trap. It was time to take a stand. Being led along was one thing, but to cross a hostile threshhold of my own accord, this stuck in my gullet. Out on the cold, dark streets there was still a tiny measure of safety but once inside private quarters, God alone knew what might happen. Unfortunately, my 'No', intended as a curt vowel of refusal, emerged new-born and quavering into the night air. I must have been more frightened than I knew.

"No?" said the man behind me, gently but wearily as it seemed. "Well, never mind . . . I am only thinking of your dignity, sir."

Hands gripped my shoulders and half steered, half pushed me forward, as though I were a recalcitrant child. I felt wooden boards beneath my feet, and my face tingled in the comparative warmth after the night air.

"Now we are here."

The same smooth low voice at my back.

"In a moment you may remove your blindfold. When you do, you will see a flight of stairs ahead. Which you will please to climb, sir. In the room facing the head of the stairs there is a man who wishes to talk to you."

"I suppose I should count up to ten before I start looking for him," I said, trying to introduce a sneer of my own into the conversation. Perhaps the other individual was stung by the remark because he said nothing.

"Who *are* you?" I ventured now. "I demand to know before I go any further."

No answer. I sensed space around me, although if my companions had exited they must have done so as swiftly and silently as ghosts. I waited a moment longer then reached up and lifted the scarf from a corner of my eye, expecting each moment to be rebuked. But there was nobody there. I was in a bare, dimly illuminated lobby, off which several doors opened. My escort had presumably vanished behind these. I had a sense of exposure, not the agreeable feeling of being the cynosure of all eyes which one gets as a player on stage but the less pleasant impression of being spied-on through knot-holes and secret cracks in the dark woodwork. I was still holding the blindfold. In a tiny act of resistance, I dropped it on the floor.

Ahead of me was a flight of stairs, as described, leading up into darkness. I turned round and tried the main door, the one which led into the street, but it was fastened and there was no key in sight. I might have tested the two or three other exits from the room but suspected that they too would be barred against me. I thought of the quarry in a hunt, channelled to its doom by the hunters and the hounds, forced down its final path. I climbed the stairs as if in a dream. I remember that they creaked underfoot.

At the top of the stairs was a small open area and a room directly facing. The door was ajar and a faint light slipped out through the gap. I tapped timidly with my fingers' ends and a voice said 'Come in', and I did so and on the far side of a large room there sat a man at a big table. He was writing. He looked up briefly.

"There is a chair against that wall. Please be seated, Master Revill, and be easy. I shall not be a moment more on this thing." And he resumed his writing.

I did as instructed – this was a night for doing what I was told. Several candles burned on the desk or table but otherwise the room was unilluminated. I was therefore in the dark and the gentleman opposite me was in the light, available for my inspection. Perhaps he had intended this, but I do not think so. There are some men who will deliberately keep themselves writing or fiddling with their documents in order to keep you waiting, as if to say 'See how busy and important *I* am, see how little *you* matter', but it was not so with this nameless individual.

Hunched over his table, he wrote with a wide, scrawling hand, breaking off from time to time to to refresh his pen or to consult other sheets of paper spread about him. Apart from his hand nothing else of him seemed to stir, except for his feet under the table which did a little circumscribed dance of their own in time with his mobile hand. Otherwise, he did not scratch at his broad white forehead, or stroke his tapering beard; he did not stop to scrutinise his fingernails or the single golden bands which he wore on each ring-finger. He did not indulge in any of those scribbler's little delays and diversions which signify 'I am thinking' or 'I wonder what I look like when I am thinking like this'. Instead he kept on writing as if his life depended on it.

His large, pallid forehead seemed to suck in the light in the room rather than to reflect it. The candles cast shifting, contradictory patterns on the wall behind the man at the table, and there was something about his quivering shadow that did not accord properly with the solid shape in front of me – although I did not realise until later exactly what it was.

For several minutes this individual did not stop his moving, scrawling hand. Then, without any flourish, without the grin or the sigh which usually signals *finis* to our efforts on paper, he laid down his pen, clasped his hands together and rested his chin on them. His candid eyes looked at me and, in shadow though I was, I felt myself being thoroughly and rapidly assessed.

"Please, Master Revill, bring your chair forward – into the light – yes, so."

With someone else I might, I suppose, have protested at the way I'd been snatched off the street and brought to this upper room – now that I was pretty sure that I had not fallen into the hands of desperadoes, an objection or two seemed called for. But something informed me that protest was futile and that I'd be told what I needed to know when the time was ripe.

Sure enough.

"Master Nicholas Revill, of the Chamberlain's Men?"

"Yes, sir, now of the Chamberlain's. I have this very evening been at rehearsal with them."

"I know," said the man.

"We are rehearsing to play before the Queen."

"That I know too."

Evidently not a man who was easily impressed.

It was only a matter of weeks since my place in the Company of Masters Shakespeare and Burbage had been confirmed. I was still inordinately proud at securing a position with London's leading players. Dammit, any young man who has dreamed of a life in the playhouse ever since he was knee-high to a pew-step, to be precise from the moment when as a child I had first heard my parson-father thundering against plays, players and playhouses from the stage of his own pulpit – any youngster, I say, would have struggled to keep his pride within bounds when invited to join our capital's crowning glory, the Globe theatre.

"Have you seen us?" I said. "Have you watched the Chamberlain's?" It's strange how, in my eagerness to talk about my craft, I mislaid any sense of the danger I might be in, to say nothing of the insult of being lifted from the street and carried off who-knew-where. Or perhaps it was not eagerness but a player's necessary vanity.

"I have little time for the playhouse . . ." he began.

He was a puritan, then, or one of those disapproving city folk who believe that playing is the root of all evil, as well as being bad for business (because it encourages the apprentices to play truant and the common people to spend their pennies on dreams instead of worldly goods). And yet he did not look or sound like a puritan or a priggish cit.

"But I make an exception for the Chamberlain's Men."

"I am pleased to hear it, sir."

"Your Cowley, your Pope and Gough. Let me see . . . Tawyer, Sincklo and Jack Wilson too. Then there's Rice and Tyler. Fine players all. And now we must add Master Nicholas Revill to this catalogue of men."

Delighted as I was that this stranger showed such a fine awareness of our Company, I couldn't help wondering *why* he needed to know these things. It did not escape me, either, that the players he had just listed were by no means the best known or the most distinguished in the Chamberlain's – no mention of Augustine Phillips or Armin the clown or the Burbages or Master WS himself. These latter would be the only names familiar to most attenders of our little entertainments.

I grew uneasy again.

"You are asking yourself where all this leads?"

"Why you had me snatched from the street while I was going about my lawful business."

"Lawful business, indeed," he echoed in a way that suggested he doubted whether I wasn't the one at fault, and I grew uneasier still. "I must apologise for the way in which you were conveyed here. But there is no need for you to know where you are, precisely where you are, in the metropolis. In fact it is very much to my advantage—"

Sensing that I was about to interrupt, he opened, palm downward, one of the hands that still perched beneath his chin.

"—and even more than it is to my advantage, I should say it is very much for your safety's sake that you are, and remain, in ignorance of your whereabouts."

"So that when I leave I shall again be blindfolded, and so on?"

"I fear so. But if your question, Master Revill, is intended to establish that you shall leave in due course, then be assured that you will."

I made some deprecatory gesture, as if such a fear had never crossed my mind. His large, candid gaze rested on me.

"Not a hair on your head shall be touched. You are much too valuable to us."

"A poor player?" I said, thinking of the other man's comment in the street.

"Would you help yourself – and me – to some wine? There is a flask on that cupboard by the wall."

I did as he directed, noting that he had turned aside the 'poor player' remark. Even in the few moments occupied by my pouring the wine, he had returned to his paper-work so that I stood uncertainly above him while he scrawled a few words in the margin of a sheet close-written in another's hand. There was something strange about him, hunched over his work, but I could not quite put my finger on it. Then he gazed up and motioned for me to put down the glass which I held for him, all the time smiling with a candour that had me, helplessly, smiling in return.

When I'd resumed my chair, he said, "Master Revill, you are a loyal Englishman?"

"I hope I have it in me to love my country."

"And our sovereign lady, the Queen?"

"You hardly need to make *that* a question."

"But I do. Oblige me with an answer."

"She deserves respect and reverence, sir. I would not dare to talk about love . . ."

"She is lovable too, provided one be wary about it."

In another man I might have suspected that this had been said to establish a personal connection with the sovereign, yet I did not think the man opposite me was seeking to elevate himself through great associations. His comment, rather, had the air of a thrown-off observation, made half to himself. No wonder he hadn't been impressed by my saying that the

Chamberlain's had just been rehearsing for a royal performance.

"Like most of our countrymen I have known no other monarch," I said.

"Yes," he said, "you'd have to be in your fifth decade to have even a child's memory of her father."

I wondered whether *he* remembered Henry VIII. The man at the other side of the table seemed ageless – or rather he was like what I had once read of the Roman emperor Justinian, that no man could recall his ever having been young.

"While she herself is now in her seventh decade," he pursued.

Talking of the Queen's age was, somehow, disrespectful and I wished he would come to the business in hand, whatever it was.

"I find it hard to conceive that another could reign over us as she does," I said, meaning a diplomatic compliment.

"Then you are like the rest of our countrymen in that too."

"How so?"

"Unhappy."

"Unhappy?"

"In having to think of another occupying her place on the throne of England."

"I – I suppose so."

"Yet it is something that we must think of. We wouldn't be human if we didn't consider what will happen next, who will come afterwards."

"No," I said.

These were dark waters and I wasn't sure that I wanted to set sail on them.

"Come, Master Revill, let us speak more plain," he said, sipping at his glass. "The Queen must die."

"Sir, I must respectfully ask you to let me go. I did not

come here of my own free will. I never asked to be brought to this place. I have no desire to listen to treason."

"So it is treason to claim that an old woman will die?"

"No, but . . ."

"You think that I am trying to inveigle you into some trap."

"No, though . . ."

I did, and I did not. I didn't know what I thought.

"Nicholas, Nicholas, princes are as mortal as the rest of us," said the man on the far side of the table. In everything, he used a tone of sweet reason. "We know better than to believe with the Romans or the Egyptians that our rulers are gods. Our own sovereign would be the first to cry blasphemy if we did. She is nearly as pious as my own mother."

"Well then . . ." I said, for the sake of saying something.

"If I could extend our Queen's life by a year – or even a month – by giving her a year of mine in exchange, I truly believe that I would."

"Why am I here?" I said, tiring suddenly of this dangerous fiddle-faddle.

"When a king nears to the end of his reign there is fear among the populace. This is so even in the best run realms, the most orderly states. How much more do men have cause to fear when the king – or the queen – has no issue. We can't see our way clear to the future if we do not know who is to rule over us. You follow me?"

"I do not know where you are headed."

"You will soon, Nicholas. I am leading you to no place of treason or disloyalty, be assured of that. As I say, doubt over the succession breeds alarm and despondency. This is natural. With some it does more. They begin to think that it is their business to fill the vacuum which will be left at the top. Not just their business but their right and their duty."

"These are matters far above my head, sir."

"There is a certain great gentleman of this city who has recently returned from Ireland," he said, then paused. "You know who I mean?"

"It is the – the – Earl of Essex."

He tapped his forefinger against his lips. "Good. I wanted you to name him for yourself. He returned from Ireland helter-skelter, thinking to save our Queen."

"I don't know about that."

"Don't play ignorant. All of London knows his offences, and half the country besides."

True enough. Essex had been sent to that troublesome island (or had badgered the Queen and Council that he should be sent) to deal once and for all with the rebel Tyrone. I had actually seen him as he paraded through the streets with his commanders on his way northwards to embark for Ireland. The air was full of success. Victory was inevitable. But victory proved elusive. Even the expected pitched battle never took place . . . rather a meeting of the two leaders, by a river, alone . . . and rumours of an 'understanding' between Tyrone and Essex. Following which, this great gentleman conceived the idea that the Council was plotting against him and his Queen. Accordingly, he raced back to see her at her palace at Nonesuch.

"For which he was arrested and tried on a charge of treason," I said.

"And in her great mercy, our sovereign lady did not demand the extreme forfeit. You see, Nicholas, you are as familiar with the story as any citizen."

He paused and rose from the table and made his way to the cupboard against the wall to refill his glass. My drink was almost untouched. When he got up his flickering shadow seemed to swell on the plastered wall and I saw that he was a hunchback. I realised then who he was, and a great gust of fear swept across my soul. I think he understood that I had grasped his identity because he gave me time, after he'd resumed his place, to compose myself. But my hands trembled and my mouth seemed filled with sand.

"Some men are not apt for mercy," he continued. "It merely provokes them to greater disobedience. This noble gentleman we are talking of, for example. His sovereign forgave him for his disobedience, his importunacy, etc. All he had to do was to utter an appropriate declaration, to bind himself by a soothing promise, and he would have been allowed to retire to the country to meditate on the Queen's goodness. He should have struggled to bring himself within the pale. But he chose not to. We have one here who prefers to command an army rather than to command himself."

I nodded. Some strangled noise emerged from my throat. I was still too nervous to speak.

"Come, Nicholas. We are on the same side, you and I."

"Yes, Master Secretary," I managed through a tightened gorge and a sand-filled mouth.

Sir Robert Cecil, Secretary to the Council, smiled in a pleasant but slightly disdainful manner, as if he were complimenting a not overbright boy on cracking a not particularly difficult riddle.

"Now you know who I am you can surely understand why it is better that you don't know precisely where you are. This is one of several secure places that we use when we wish to conduct business away from the Argus eyes of the Court. So our guests are usually brought here as if they were playing at hoodman-blind. Ignorance is safety."

"I may not know where I am, but I can't be any use to you if I remain in ignorance about why I am . . . wherever I am," I said, neglecting in my urgency to be frightened of this great and powerful man. "*Why* have you brought me here? I am altogether in a mist."

"Well. Let me clear a little of it. I want you, Master Revill, to do some work for your Queen and your country. To the quick of the matter. I have information that, within the next couple of days, the Chamberlain's Men will be approached to put on a performance of a play."

"Saving your reverence, there is nothing special in that."

"There will be about this performance. Your Company will soon be requested to stage Master William Shakespeare's *Richard II*."

Ah, *Richard II*.

I began to see through the mist that surrounded me not so much a glimmer of light as a darker shape forming.

"You are familiar with the play?"

"It is a fusty piece, not often performed," I said.

"With good reason. It deals with the death of kings. It ends with the deposition of the lawful Richard and the triumph of the usurper Henry Bolingbroke. Anybody must see that a presentation of this play now, at this moment, would be—"

"—a nice question," I interrupted, forgetting myself.

"—a dangerous proceeding, I was going to say. But I am glad that you have such a quick apprehension, Nicholas. Yes, dangerous to all, players and spectators alike. To stage this *Richard* now is to bring fire and powder together."

"Only a play," I said.

"One spark is enough," said Sir Robert Cecil. "A fool may fire a forest. Why, you know that he wears a secret note in a little black bag tied round his neck."

"Who, sir?"

"Essex. He wears a note from James of Scotland about his neck and shows it to his intimates. He thinks his treason to be so fine that it must be displayed not once but again and again.

Well, he'll find that the cord holding that bag round his neck will be strong enough to hold up something else."

The smooth, even tones had left Sir Robert's voice. His hands no longer perched neatly under the bearded chin or lay at rest on the paper-strewn table but opened and closed in the candlelight like agitated birds.

"No matter. Essex is not your concern. He is out of your sphere. *He* will not be approaching the Chamberlain's Men with the request for *Richard*. You are to watch for a man called Cuffe or one called Merrick."

"But what do they hope to gain? Forgive me, sir, I cannot see the advantage in asking for an old play to prop up a new cause."

"Nicholas, you believe in your craft?"

"Of course."

"In fact, I have heard that you make great claims for it. Let me see—" (and he cast about among the sheets in front of him until he found the one he was looking for) "– What was it you once said? Ah I have it. You were talking of players, I believe. 'We are the voice of our age. We are the mirror of the times.' "

"No doubt I was – my tongue was carried away by liquor, perhaps."

I squirmed on my chair in embarrassment. Were those words mine?

They had a familiar ring.

"Those are the very words, the liquor-borne ones I mean, that it is worth paying attention to. *In vino veritas*," said Sir Robert. "This is beside the point. Very recently you were in the habit of making the largest claims for the players and the playhouse. Surely you haven't changed your mind?"

"I – no – I still think my profession to be an honest calling."

"No more than honest?"

"Even a noble one if it helps to cast a little light onto the benighted stage which is this world," I said defensively. "I stand by what I said."

"Very good," said Sir Robert. "Every man should esteem his trade, provided it be lawful."

But I hardly heard what he was saying. Those fine utterances about 'voices' and 'mirrors' were, no doubt, the kind of thing that I was accustomed to say too often, particularly in my early, heady days with the Chamberlain's Company (I was all of a four-month veteran now and looked back on my unfledged beginnings with amusement), but the sentences he'd quoted were precise and had the air of being reported from life. Indeed, they were from life. I now remembered a scene at supper with the Eliots, Sir Thomas, Lady Alice and young William Eliot. I remembered myself, a little flushed with drink and with the elevated company, being hoist up on my own rhetoric as I made great pronouncements on the value of plays and playing.*

But what made the sweat stand out on my brow was the realisation that this great man had before him a document which detailed some – all? – of my heedless words at a supper in a private house the previous autumn. Would you care to have recalled to you what you said last Thursday morning to your wife in the privacy of your chamber? No? Or that wordy dispute with an old school friend in the corner of a tavern? Not that neither?

Well, you may see how alarmed I began to grow as I understood that the Secretary to the Council had a record of my unconsidered words. I felt also a little anger, but that was easy enough to hold in check. Sir Robert Cecil grasped my discomfort.

* see *Sleep of Death*

"Nicholas," he said soothingly, "do not worry that I can quote you to yourself. Some men might be flattered. Anyway it is my business to know what people are thinking and saying. I agree with your words on the value of plays, by the way. I believe that Master Shakespeare has put something not dissimilar into the mouth of one of his characters."

I realised how artfully Sir Robert had gone about not only to reassure me but also to put me in my place by demonstrating that the high view which I had expressed of my profession was taken, pretty well wholesale, from our greatest playwright. I saw how quietly, how subtly, he had been able to suggest the frightening extent of his knowledge. Why, his network of informers and agents must be all-encompassing if he received reports on the high-flown words of a poor player at the supper table.

"But since you share my regard for plays," he went on, "you hardly need to ask what the value of a performance of *Richard II* is to these desperate men. They plan to use it as a fingerpost signing the way down their chosen road."

"Yes," I said.

"The road to treason is miry, and it helps to know that others have travelled that route before."

"If enough travel it, it becomes well paved," I said.

"Well," he said, looking directly at me, "that is quick of you. I believe that I have the right man in front of me. Unlike most roads, the greater the number that walk it the smoother and more even it becomes. So, Master Revill, that is why I require your help. To uproot this fingerpost before it gets firmly planted."

"Yes," I said.

"I am sorry on such a night to have kept you from your warm bed but, as you can see, these are urgent matters of state. Your mission is important . . ."

"Yes," I said. "I understand."

And what I understood was that this man must have in his service as many eyes as there were stars in the frosty sky outside.

It was under the stars that I was abandoned when the game of my arrival was reversed at the end of the interview. After telling me a little more in respect of the grandly termed 'mission', Sir Robert instructed me to return to the lobby and wait. Again, I was grasped from behind and a blind slipped over my eyes before I had an opportunity to glance round. Ushered back into the biting air, I was whirled through the streets, spun round and marched in the opposite direction, not once but several times. Eventually we halted. The same voice as in the beginning, courteous, low but firm.

"We are leaving, Master Revill. Thank you for your compliance." He spoke as if I had had a choice. His tones were soft as smoke in the night air. "Even though you might consider this a piece of child's play, I require you to count up to ten, let us say, when I give the word. After that you may remove your blind and go on your way."

"Where am I?"

"Where you were, sir. Have no fear. Now you should count."

I did as I was told and, after counting silently to ten, removed my blindfold. The dark houses rose up before me, seeming no more substantial than pasteboard against the twinkling blackness of the sky. After a moment I was able to confirm that my captor had been as good as his word and that I was standing at the very point where I had first been intercepted, by the corner of Hart Lane. The streets were empty. As far as I could tell from the position of the stars the whole episode had lasted some two hours or more. It was that dead time of the night when even the sots and ne'er-do-wells have retired or fallen down in their places, and honest, hard-working folk are not yet stirred.

The entire business might have been a dream, yet not for an instant did I consider it so. I returned to my lodgings and lay awake there, unable to stop thinking of the extraordinary events of the night and eventually falling into what seemed to be only a few minutes of strange-coloured slumber before I had to be up for rehearsal.

My mind was filled with plot and counter-plot. I had been catapaulted onto a greater stage than I was accustomed to play on. One where high and mighty conspirators disposed of whole realms, and played with crowns, as easily as you or I might crack an egg.

As I've mentioned, by chance I had once glimpsed the greatest of these conspirators.

When my lord of Essex departed for Ireland, he was sent off by the London citizenry as though he was already leading his army *home*, in triumph. Victory in the field was preordained. Only now do I see – even I, with my little knowledge of the world – that certainty as to outcomes in such affairs is rarely matched by the event. Fortune is truly a strumpet, or so she proved in this case. However, on that March day when the Earl of Essex left for the barbarous isle there was confidence, even exultation, in the air.

I made up one of the crowd that thronged the thorough-fares along which Essex and his followers paraded. I was then newly arrived in London, a stranger to the playhouse and its kingdom in Southwark. A stranger to my friend Nell and to Master WS and Burbage & Co. There is no creature greener than he who is newly come to the city from the country and who would not, for a thousand pound, wish to have that green-ness revealed. So, it was with amazement that I found myself within a day or two of my arrival tumbled into a crowd that waved and hurrahed a great general. All around us, church bells rang madly. I wondered if this were not some regular happening. Why, perhaps generals and other mighty personages rode through the streets once a fortnight! That would be something to boast about to my untravelled parents back at home in Somerset! (I forgot from time to time that I had no home, except a plague-stricken village, and no parents either who were above ground.)

Deliberately selecting a fellow member of the crowd who didn't look too quick-witted, and wouldn't therefore be inclined to mock my rusticity and ignorance, I asked him what all the to-do was about. Amid great washes of ale-breath, I was informed that a great lord called Middlesex who I could see at the head of the procession – "there, yes, 'im, that's the one!" – was about to depart for a land far away over the sea. An island beyond the place where the sun sets. Where men's heads grow out of their chests or their arses, or some such. Where they boil up their young alive and eat 'em for supper. Where they daily have congress with the beasts of the field. And what, I asked, was the lord commander Middlesex going to do when he got there? "Why, kill 'em all," said my informant, turning away from me in disgust that I'd asked such a stupid question.

Someone else standing nearby, an apparently more reliable and relatively sober individual, told me that it was the Earl of *Essex* and that he was going to subdue the Irish once and for all. It was already settled. The Queen had given him the commission. At this moment the head of the procession drew level with where we were standing and the crowd, already bubbling, went wild with pleasure. My ears were deafened with cries of approbation and screams of delight. Some of the women had tears streaming down their faces. Others held up babies, as if they expected the Earl to bless them. He turned his head and the upper part of his body from side to side and smiled benignly on the crowds but in a way that seemed to me somewhat abstracted, as if his mind were already on the other side of that sea which separates the greater island from the lesser.

And now a very unexpected thing happened, and one that augured ill too. Though it was, as I have said, a day in March when this great company set off for Ireland, the weather had been unseasonably fair. The sky over the streets of Islington was bright and clear. All at once there arose a great black cloud to the north-east, as if cast up by a giant hand. And moments later came thunder and flashes of lightning. Then a great shower of hail and rain. The parade of lords and knights on horseback, sitting so proud and erect, huddled inside their finery and tried to make themselves all small, while the honest citizenry crammed into doorways or cowered beneath the eaves of houses. I found myself sharing a nook with my drunken informant, the one who had identified the Earl of Middlesex. The mood of the crowd, which had been one of celebration, now turned to its opposite. "'tis a hominous progeny, this 'ail and thund'rin," he said, enveloping me in his reeky breath. "No, I misspeak, 'tis a hominous prodigal."

And so it was – a prodigy and ominous both. The Irish enterprise, begun with such fair expectations, was soon enveloped in its own bad weather.

So much for my introduction to the Earl of Essex.

But I couldn't spend all my waking (and sleeping) hours thinking of him and his co-conspirators, and of Secretaries of State and mysterious men who seized one off the street at midnight – I had, after all, a working life to get on with.

You might consider that the life – or at least the revenue – of a player during the winter is as pinched and bleak as the hours of daylight. Who wishes to pay for the privilege of standing in an unroofed playhouse, stamping their feet and rubbing their mittened hands against the cold? What eloquent words from the playwrights and, more importantly, what fine gestures from the players are scattered by the winter winds or sogged in the winter rains? And it is true, of course, that we are almost as governed by the seasons as those who till the soil. Nevertheless, if we stage plays, the customers come, though in diminished numbers. And since players must continue to live even when what Dick Burbage calls our 'congregations' are thin, we in the Chamberlain's must continue to play (intermittently) during the cold months. When you consider how matters stand, when you survey our principal enemies – City authorities, plague, Puritans, changes in fashion – then the vagaries of winter come limping some way in the rear.

Yet our limited performances in the playhouse are not the business that really keeps us warm in January and February before the arrival of Lent curtails our activities.

The Chamberlain's Men are the prime company in town. We are the Queen's favourites, and *that* is something to warm your hands by. Every winter the Chamberlain's are commanded to play before Her Majesty at one of her palaces, usually Whitehall. Our playwright, shareholder and occasional player, Master WS, provides the fare to put before her and we do our best to serve it up piping hot and spicy for her delectation. I say 'we' (like an old hand) but this is the first year in which I've been privileged to be a member of the Company, so I (like new hands everywhere) do my best to appear all easy and unconcerned at the terrifying prospect of appearing and *speaking* before our sovereign lady – but my heart bangs to think about it and my palms start to sweat a little. Others in the Company, however, really do seem all easy and unconcerned at the idea. To them it's just another performance, a little special perhaps, more finely honed and better dressed, but essentially no different from playing before the penny knaves on the ground and the gents and ladies in the gallery.

We have to prepare for this royal appearance. The play must be read beforehand. All plays must, in fact, be read beforehand in the office of the Master of the Revels to see whether they contain anything that might offend or undermine those in authority. The ones intended for the Queen's eyes and ears are studied with particular care. Of course, our costumes should gleam while Master WS's lines have to glitter in our mouths. This demands much more time, care and patience than we are accustomed to in rehearsal. A great room, well-lighted and well-heated, is made available to us at the old Priory of St John's in Clerkenwell where the Master of the Revels holds sway. Here, generally after dark, we prepare Master WS's *Twelfth Night* for Her Majesty. Now, the Chamberlain's had performed this before but never in the royal presence so it was most necessary to plane and polish what was well enough for the general public, plane and polish so that the grain of the play shone through for the Queen. I had been returning from a Clerkenwell rehearsal of this piece when I had been so rudely intercepted in the street and led before Sir Robert Cecil.

Nevertheless, Queen or no Queen, Secretary of Council or no Secretary of Council, life goes on, art goes on. As I've said, the play-business continues through the winter, not in full spate but with a steady trickle of new material and old matter mingled together. If there is work, we players must go to it. I was only too pleased to go to work anyway. I had the strongest reasons for being out and about during the day and, if possible, sleeping somewhere apart from my lodgings at night. This was because my lodgings were more fitted for a pig or a dog or a chicken than a human being. As it happens, they also housed representatives of those farm creatures and others besides (such as rats and bats and cats) as well as four human specimens. At least, I think they were human.

A poor player cannot be a chooser when it comes to accommodation. He needs to be close to his place of work; he is helped if he has a landlord or landlady who is not implacably hostile to the drama; but above all he requires a bed and a roof that are cheap. South of the river is almost a necessity. The climate of acceptance (or indifference) is warmer down there, the questions are fewer and, I am persuaded, the air is better. Of course, when you're searching for a place to live, a personal recommendation helps. It was someone connected with the Company who told me that he knew of four sisters who were looking for a man to share their abode off Broadwall.

So, once I'd got a fairly firm footing with the Chamberlain's, I took myself down there one autumn morning. It was a few minutes' walk from the Globe. The day was sharp but only so as to give briskness to one's stride. My head was clear and my spirits high. Who knew but that the quartet of sisters might not be youthful and limber supporters of the drama? Who knew what they might not be prepared to share with a young and, even though I say it myself, not completely unattractive player? Sisters! – and four of them, a tetrad! Of course, a moment's thought should have told me that if *that* was what was in question then my informant in the Company would hardly have passed on the location to me. He'd have kept it for himself.

The point south of Broadwall is where the town and the country fight it out for supremacy and, as usual on a battlefield, the result is somewhat messy. There were buildings but they were not particularly respectable or well-kept; there was countryside but it was not especially pure and uncluttered.

I asked a one-eyed man if he knew the whereabouts of the four sisters' residence – I'd been given no more precise information than that – and after I'd repeated the question some half dozen times he backed away from me, proceeded to make various slurping noises and then stuck out a scarecrow's arm. He was pointing at a ragged building a little further down the road. After that he crossed himself.

The house I'd been directed to seemed to have grown out of the ground. There wasn't a single straight line or clean angle in it anywhere. Rather, it humped and lumped and swelled like a monstrous dun-coloured vegetable. Weeds sprouted among the moss on the roof. The walls were pocked and blotchy. The windows squinted or leered at me. I approached the door with some trepidation. In the gaps between the boards I could see the darkness of the interior. I knocked but with no result except to roust some pigeons out of the hairy eaves. I knocked again. And again.

After a time a rustling sound approached the door. It opened a crack and a pig's snout poked out. A cat darted out beneath the snout. Then a human face peered round above the snout.

"Whadjoowant?"

"I – I – am looking for – the sisters."

"Hoosentjoo?"

"What? I'm sorry . . ."

"Izedhoosentjoo?"

"Ah, yes. I understand now. It was Master Richard Milford who told me of you."

"Hoozee?"

Another face appeared above the first one. It was this face that now asked "hoozee?"

"He's with the Chamberlain's Company. He's a playwright . . ."

My voice faltered. It did not seem as though the name of my Company was going to work its usual magic. This was obviously not a good idea. I wasn't so desperate for lodgings, was I, that I'd take anything on offer? (Yes, I was that desperate, and down to my last couple of shillings.)

"Notim . . . hoozisun?"

This was the second speaker. Then a third voice came from further down the crack in the barely open door.

"Broo?"

The face of this third speaker was as bewhiskered and carbuncled as the first two. You could not have put a hair between them for ugliness. Seeing them lined up with the pig, you might have looked from one to the other and not been entirely sure which countenances represented womankind and which the beast.

"Er . . . I . . . not sure . . ."

"Youbroo?"

"Probably not," I said. "Almost certainly I am not broo – although I *am* Nicholas Revill, player."

"Naynay," said this creature impatiently, as if it was my fault that I had no idea what she meant. "Youwantbroo?"

This was evidently a key question because the other two faces, hanging lopsided round the door-edge, regarded me with eyes that were an unappetising mixture of the milky and the blood-shot.

Then there came words from the area of the pig's snout.

"What my sister means is, do you require any of our brew?"

Jesus, a talking pig!

I looked down and saw that the snout had withdrawn from the lowest point and been replaced by a different (human) face. There they were, lined up, four heads poking out from a door ajar. All of the faces left everything to be desired. The one at the bottom, however, was the least far from the feminine.

31

"I am looking for the four sisters," I began again. "I was told that they have lodgings available. I do not know of any brew."

The expression on the bottom one's face broadened.

"Go, April and June, go, July. I will attend to this person."

The other three vanished as if they'd turned into thin air. Then the door was opened in full. The woman who'd spoken last stood there, dressed in a filthy smock.

"Forgive them, sir, they do not trust strangers and they are not used to talking. I am called May."

"Nicholas Revill."

I bowed slightly. Never let it be said that Nick Revill does not know how to comport himself before a woman, even one who is somewhat carbuncular and whiskery.

"This is the right place?" I said.

"We are the four sisters, April, May, June and July, and we are famous throughout the town," she said. "Surely you have heard of us? We were named for the spring and the first breath of summer."

"Oh yes," I said.

In the background I saw the other three fiddling around with a sort of cauldron and sipping with ladles at its contents. The fumes of something heavy and spirituous crept across the floor towards the door. I guessed that, if this unholy quartet marketed their concoctions (hence the one-eyed man's slurping sounds, hence the incomprehensible 'broo' query), they also sampled their own wares extensively.

"Lodgings, you want?"

"Only looking," I said, wondering how fast I could extricate myself from this.

"We are not dear."

"That surprises me."

"See your room?"

32

"Not mine yet," I said. But she plucked at my sleeve and led me across a filthy, uneven floor. The pig had retreated to a corner. A chicken squawked in the gloom. A dog with an interesting ancestry growled at me. One of the other sisters, April or June or July, had already succumbed to the contents of the cauldron and was lying flat out on the ground.

May urged me up a rickety staircase. At the top was a little room, amply supplied with fresh air (from the holes in the wall) and running water (down the same gappy walls). However, it had a bed.

"How much?" I said.

"Four pennies a week."

"One for each of you?"

Tapping my forefinger to my lips, I pretended to consider, but I knew that I wouldn't find anywhere cheaper south of the river. Poor players can't be choosers.

"I'll take it."

So that was how I came to lodge at the Coven, as I termed it to myself. I had some doubts about whether the foursome were genuine sisters; perhaps they were really mother and daughters or perhaps mother, daughters and grand-daughter or perhaps grandmother, etc . . . my head reeled at the possible permutations. Maybe they didn't even know how they stood in relation to each other. And however they were connected, their names had obviously been bestowed by a fantastical individual. Since they were surely barren, and neither green nor hopeful nor beautiful, no-one – not even a starry-eyed poet – could have compared them to a spring or summer's day. But, who knows, such a comparison might have been allowable once.

May was the youngest, or least raddled. She was also the most active. April and June and July appeared to do nothing except stir their noisome cauldron, sample its contents and fall into stupors. But May was out and about from time to time, no doubt doing mischief. Occasionally, furtive vagabonds came to the door and had their pots filled with some of the cauldron's contents. I was rarely there to witness any of this. I did not linger in my lodgings by day and, when I could, spent the nights elsewhere. The only virtue of my room was that it was dirt-cheap. As long as I paid my fourpence a week the sisters didn't bother me.

I was 'recommended' the sisters by Richard Milford, a journeyman dramatist who'd been hanging around the Company for some time, certainly from before the autumn when I joined them. He hoped to be commissioned to do a piece or two for the Chamberlain's but had not yet met with any success. He was an amiable fellow, a camp follower of WS, for they both came from the same county. Indeed, it was the general opinion of the Company that Master Milford of Coventry had deliberately set himself to tread in the heels of the Stratford master. He had reason to be a little grateful to me because he'd earlier pressed into my hands a copy of his unperformed play, *A Venetian Whore*, asking if I'd do him the favour of casting an eye over it.

"Why of course," I said, for it is always agreeable to a young man to have his opinion sought.

"I think my *Whore* has something to commend it," he said.

"It is a direct title," I said. "A no-nonsense title. It should draw the crowd – if it is ever put on."

"I hope so – if it is ever put on, as you say."

"You have written much else?"

I could see on Richard Milford's face a struggle between the truth, which was probably that he possessed somewhere a drawerful of creased and splotted manuscripts, and the saving lie that this was his first effort at authorship. In the end, he shrugged slightly, blushed hard and said nothing.

"Why are you asking *me*?" I asked. "Though I am willing enough, my voice is hardly the loudest in the Company."

"I would value your opinion," said Master Milford, then subtracted from the compliment by adding, "Besides the others like Master Shakespeare and Burbage are so busy and . . ."

"Great and high and mighty?"

"Not at all, or not so much," he said. "It is rather that I find myself more comfortable with someone of my own age, and someone with learning, like you, Nicholas."

Who could resist this? But I should have known that judging another's pen-work is a risky matter. Authors are touchy creatures. Like the chameleon, it may be that they can live on air but only if it is crammed with praise. And after all, hadn't I already had some experience of homicide and the dramatist?

I cast my eyes over Milford's *Whore*. The plot was a touch familiar in its outline. A wealthy young Venetian woman is unable to choose between three suitors. She has no parent to guide her, for her mother is dead and her father passes poignantly away in Act I. Which man should she take as mate for life? Is it her that they want – or her money? All her suitors, separately, proclaim undying love and the purity of their intentions. They will never pay their addresses to another woman, oh no. They will never even glance at another woman, not them. If she turns them down they will go off and live like celibates in the desert, oh yes they will. And so say all of them.

To test their sincerity, our heroine Belladonna disguises herself as a whore. That is, she dons a mask. She finds a compliant madam and keeps her soft and agreeable with money. For company she has her devoted servant Julia, also masquerading as a jade. Considering that she is an unspotted virgin – as all our heroines must be – Belladonna is highly skilled in the arts of seduction, even if she has been schooled by Julia in how to play that instrument. You can probably guess the rest. Belladonna's suitors visit the house of sale where she plies, or rather does not ply, her trade. Two of them succumb to her verbal blandishments before she removes the mask that conceals her identity. The third stands out against her, proclaiming undying love for another (what then, I ask myself, is he doing in a brothel? – while knowing the answer very well, of course). Then Belladonna lowers her mask to his stupefied gaze. She has proved his fidelity, to her own satisfaction. Meantime, Julia has been receiving the attentions of the successful suitor's servant. It is not clear whether she too merely plays the whore or becomes one for a time but with servants it hardly seems to matter. All ends well, with Belladonna and Julia contracting simultaneous marriages.

All of this – the Venetian scene, the rich heiress, the three suitors, the exposing of the false fortune-hunters and the testing of the true lover – calls to mind Master WS's *Merchant of Venice*, even if a *Merchant* without the Jew. Nevertheless if we were to banish a play because it contained a rich heiress and false suitors, on the grounds that such figures are hardly strangers to our stage, then we should find our stock of comedy sadly depleted.

Besides, Milford's *Whore* was good, surprisingly good. The scenes of love were affecting, the brothel interludes were coarse and rousing, and the whole was well observed. I said as much to him and he blushed with pleasure. He was a tall, slightly awkward young man who blushed much of the time, so that his cheeks seemed to be engaged in a perpetual rosy struggle like the war between the Yorkists and Lancastrians.

"But," I added (for there must always be a caveat in such praise, otherwise it is too easily earned), "I could not help thinking of Master Shakespeare's *Merchant of Venice* as I read your words."

"You mean that I reminded you of *him*?"

"The setting, the choice between three suitors, the rich heiress and her faithful servant – and – and—"

"—the power of my words?"

"That too," I said, though in fact I had considered his style to be a little old-fashioned.

"Master Revill – Nicholas – thank you. It comforts me, it gives me heart, to know that someone of taste approves my efforts."

"I do approve."

I felt myself to be on safe ground here since, in whatever light I considered his *Whore*, my opinion did not matter greatly.

"Since you think well of my little thing, that emboldens me to ask you another small favour."

"Well, that depends . . ."

"It seems to me that you have the ear of Master Shakespeare."

"Oh, from time to time perhaps."

"When you are next in converse with him, perhaps you would . . . perhaps you could mention my *Venetian Whore*, talk about it warmly, if you could."

All this time Richard Milford scarcely glanced at me but hung his blushing head down.

"You're a countryman of his, aren't you. I'm sure he'd look kindly on a direct request," I said, in part because I believed it to be true but in part to relieve myself of the burden of doing Master's Milford's work for him. "He is a kind man, and a courteous one."

"You mean that he'd turn me down gently."

"I am certain that he would say whatever was appropriate."

By now, such was my sageness, I felt about twice my age while Master Milford was shedding years by the second.

"Anyway, you know, Richard, that plays are approved by the senior shareholders. You must approach them yourself."

"I – I suppose so."

And away he went, clutching his precious manuscript. I wondered if he'd ever screw up the courage to approach WS directly. I wondered further why he set such store by the effusions of his pen and if he was really aware of the low standing of authors. That it was no great matter to sling a few thousand words together – because the true art lies in fleshing out those words and presenting them in front of the multitude.

He must have been sufficiently emboldened or desperate to make the direct approach I'd recommended because the next I heard was that the shareholders had read and approved *A Venetian Whore* for performance early in the spring of next year! After this there was no holding Master Milford. He became most pleased with himself and the world. Evidently he considered that I was partly responsible for his success and wanted to do me a good turn. Hearing that I was looking for cheap accommodation, he mentioned the Broadwall trio.

Afterwards, when I'd handed over my first week's rent, I asked Richard why he'd suggested the sisters.

"They will repay study," he said.

"No doubt."

"I have only one piece of advice. Keep your dealings with them strictly commercial."

Thinking that he had in mind what had originally passed through my own as I walked down Broadwall that fine autumn morning, I said, "I would struggle to imagine a bed-bound tussle with any of those four months – and then I would have to struggle to un-imagine it again."

"Four months? – oh I see, very good. But no, I did not mean dealings in that way. I meant, do not be tempted to taste their brew."

"I think I can manage not to. In fact, I wondered if that pig of theirs was an unfortunate traveller who'd drunk from the cauldron and been transformed."

"As if they were Circes," said the learned Master Milford.

"Circe was beautiful," I said, "and they are most ugly."

"Except May."

"I do not think 'except' will become 'accept' in my case, Richard."

"You should be a playwright, Nicholas, you are so sharp."

"I would rather play. I like applause. Well then, I will follow your advice and avoid their brew."

"I tried it once and . . ." he shuddered. "But they have other gifts."

"Those I have yet to see."

"They can foresee the future."

"They foresaw yours?"

Here he came over a little coy.

"They said I should be famous one day. And see, I have taken the first steps with my *Whore*. Why don't you ask them to plot your future?"

"No," I said, "I would rather carve for myself."

"I stayed several weeks with them last summer but then I considered that I required . . . more suitable lodgings."

"More suitable for a rising playwright, you mean."

He blushed when I called him 'rising'.

"I do not mean to imply that *you* are not rising, Nicholas. You, I am sure, have a fine future ahead of you."

It is extraordinary how quickly one can assume the role of patron! For this young man – to whom, only a couple of weeks earlier, I'd been giving wise words – was now assuring *me* of my 'fine future'. I almost laughed to think that all this confidence sprang from a promised play performance and the few paltry pounds which he'd receive for it. The vanity of authors!

"Thank you," I said, "but the sisters will do me for the time being – I can't expect to rise to your giddy heights."

He smiled deprecatingly, though it was easy to see that he was pleased with any compliment, however lightly meant.

"Try them for your fortune, Nicholas."

"If it comes to fortune-telling, for certain *their* future is all behind them."

"But they are cheap," he said. No man quite escapes his early penny-pinching.

The day following on my midnight meeting with the Secretary to the Council, was a busy one for us in the Chamberlain's. In the afternoon the public paying for admission to the Globe playhouse was going to enjoy *A Somerset Tragedy*, one of the first pieces I'd participated in when I joined the Company the previous autumn. And in the evening there was yet another rehearsal at Clerkenwell for *Twelfth Night*, which we were to play at court in a little over three weeks' time. So to those who consider that the player's life in between performances is like the parson's in midweek or – and this may be a more persuasive analogy, considering the low regard in which players are held by the ignorant – like the highwayman's life when snow makes the roads impassable for the traveller, that is, an existence of idle if not insolent ease, I hold up this schedule which shows *two* plays to be got through in the compass of a single day and evening.

My thoughts, however, were not directed towards these plays, in each of which I had fairly small parts. Rather I was preoccupied with my midnight meeting with one of the most powerful men in the kingdom, and with what he had asked of me. Through the day and evening of performance and then rehearsal, I found my thoughts tugged back to my conversation with the Secretary to the Council, to say nothing of the extraordinary way I'd been ushered to and from his presence. I considered that I was moving in very high circles indeed. Why, within a few weeks, I was to be seen by the Queen! And none of this conduced to my comfort. I did not wish to have greatness thrust upon me. So, at least, I thought I thought. Though a part of me delighted in being useful to great men and earning their gratitude.

Naturally I had to hold my tongue. Since my 'mission', as Sir Robert had grandly termed it, concerned the Chamberlain's Company itself I could hint at nothing to my fellow-players. Indeed, it had been impressed upon me that I might be in some danger if anyone at the Globe became aware of what I was doing. In different circumstances – in other words, where I couldn't normally confide in my fellows – I might have turned to my whore Nell, whose ear was always generously open and ready to receive whatever burdened me. But the grave secret I laboured under could not be lightened by sharing it with *anyone*. On that point the Secretary had been insistent.

It may be that she detected my distraction that night in her crib.

"Why, Nicholas, this is not like you. To go only once and then without much – much spirit."

"I have played twice today," I said.

"You are practising for the – Queen?"

There was a breathy pause before she uttered the last word. Needless to say, Nell would have kissed the ground on which her Majesty trod. I have noticed that girls like her, and those of her class in general, reverence royalty. So do I, but in an educated way if you see what I mean. Some weeks before, Nell had almost kissed the ground where I stood when I revealed that we were to present *Twelfth Night* at court. Not that I was standing at the time. Well, not entirely.

"Rehearsing for her this evening, yes we have been."

"*Her?*"

"That's what I said. Her."

But I hadn't said it with sufficient awe for Nell. Her question was a little rebuke.

Another reason I was tired was that, as on the previous night, I'd had to make my way across from Clerkenwell after the rehearsal session at the Old Priory. This meant walking to Blackfriars to take the ferry to reach the south bank and then doing another foot-slog to reach Holland's Leaguer, where Nell plied her trade. It also meant that I was constantly looking over my shoulder or keeping my ears cocked for another arrest like last night's. I jumped at the shadows. I flinched at cats and other late passengers. All this to-do – two plays, and a couple of miles paced out in the star-lit dark, and a hidden mission for the Secretary of the Council – it took it out of a man, even a young, vigorous one like myself. My head whirled and, exhausted as I was, I could not fall asleep in Nell's loving arms. For her part, Nell seemed not inclined to rest but to talk and later on, I very much feared, to another bout of night-work.

"Is this not a grand privilege, Nicholas?"

"What?" said I, deliberately obtuse.

"To play before our sovereign lady."

"The Chamberlain's are often before her. We are her men in all but name."

"Yes . . . but for you, Nicholas, it is the first time."

I had recently noticed that when Nell wanted to speak to me seriously, and particularly when she was discussing the royal performance (a subject to which she frequently adverted), she called me Nicholas. Now I was Nick only in her careless or affectionate moments. I had noticed also that there was a kind of balance – or rather, imbalance – in these things, so that as the woman's eagerness mounted higher in the scale so it behoved the man to sink down and underplay his own excitement.

"Remember, Nell, that my work is playing. Whether we have the highest in the land in our audience or the lowest, it is all one to the player. He performs his office for the love of it and regardless of anyone's regard."

"Then you don't care if no-one is watching?"

"Well, no, of course not. What I mean is that the player plays while the king is watching – or the beggar."

If I hadn't been tired I could have continued in this king-beggar vein for some time, although I would have been laughed at if I'd spoken thus in the presence of a fellow-player. Such talk would do, though, for one not initiated into the mysteries of our craft. Nell, however, was having none of it.

"I do not believe you. For one thing, the king will pay and the beggar cannot."

"You're right. I'm not sure I believe myself."

"That's better, Nick, now you are smiling."

"I am always smiling with my Nell."

"Not tonight. You have looked grim and distracted ever since you arrived."

"The light is bad in here."

We had a feeble candle to light us to bed. Nell was prudent in her housekeeping. No doubt too her customers preferred themselves in that dim way, although Nell showed to advantage in any light. (Such thoughts, to do with her and her customers, entered my mind unbidden.)

"You fool, Nick, do you think I need to see you to tell how

43

you are? I can hear it in your voice. I can feel it in you while you lie beside me. You are all stiff and uneasy."

"I am?"

"Except in the one part."

"I am tired. Two plays, a deal of walking about and . . . and . . ."

"And?"

"Other matters, which I cannot talk about."

"Very well."

I expected her to press me further. Women are bound to be curious, aren't they? I was ready to hint – in the most general terms – at large concerns, important business, sundry weighty reasons, etc. This might have afforded me some slight relief from the burden of secrecy. And I didn't altogether dislike the way Nell treated me with a new respect now that the Chamberlain's were to play before the Queen. Accordingly, I sensed I might win an even more reverential favour from her if I touched on, only *touched* on, the great affairs of state in which I was becoming entangled. This may seem to contradict the silence which had, in effect, been enjoined on me by Master Secretary Cecil but I reasoned that *hinting* was not *telling*.

"You don't want to know?" I said.

"It doesn't matter whether I want to know or not. The only thing that you want me to know is that you don't want to tell."

Perhaps it was because of the tiredness which I'd just mentioned to her, and which I hadn't much exaggerated, but I really found it a bit difficult to follow what she was saying here. I took refuge in repetition.

"I cannot speak of it."

"Very well," she said again.

I waited.

"So this is behind your absences from my bed?" she said. "This thing you cannot speak of."

I saw then the sudden use to which I might put the state business on which I was engaged. It could serve my turn too. For it was true that I had not been so frequent an occupant of her bed of late. There was – there had recently been – another matter about which I was not willing to hint at all to Nell, and I realised that I could hide it behind the larger, shadowy business.

"Yes," I said. "Forgive me, Nell. I do not willingly absent myself."

This was both true and not-true.

"I believe you do not, Nicholas."

I wasn't sure from the tone of her voice whether she did believe my words. As she had said, my friend was well able to 'read' me through my voice and attitude, even though she could neither read nor write. But I, book-learned as I was, was still so unschooled in her that I could not clearly construe her expression by the candle's feeble glimmer.

"But men will do as they please," she said. "Even as women will do everything to please them."

"It pleases me to be here with you, now," I said, stroking her warm flank.

"Here and now is easily said."

"Easily said may be heartfelt too," I said, putting well over half a heart into my words.

"Here and now," she echoed. "What about there and then?"

"I do not understand you," I said.

"I think you do," Nell said. "But it doesn't matter. Let us sleep now since you are so tired out at the hands of these things which can't be spoken of."

After that I soon fell asleep. That sleep, and the few

minutes' talk which led up to it, were the last vestiges of ordinary life which I was to enjoy for some time.

After the rigours of that day with its two plays, the next one was, for me, one of comparative ease. Or should have been. Yet it turned into one of the most difficult, and alarming, of my life.

Although I had no diversion apart from yet another rehearsal of *Twelfth Night* in the evening, habit and the love of work drew me to the Globe in the morning. There might be something for me to do. I might be useful.

I should have stayed in bed.

Sure enough, the Book-keeper of the Globe spoke to me. He was a sallow-faced gentleman named Allison who played a variety of roles in our Company. While a new play was preparing, it was his task to ensure fair copies were made from the author's foul papers, since no-one can use a splotty, scrawled and scratched-out manuscript, all warm and illegible from its creator's hand. Therefore the foul papers must be sent to the scriveners to be copied out neat and fair several times over, one of these copies being required by the Master of the Revels for allowance. Then Master Allison writes out a Plot on a piece of paper which hangs near one of the entrances to the stage, telling all when they are required to appear and with what gear (a drawn sword, a severed head, a fluttering handkerchief). And during performance Allison is our prompter. Dick Burbage and one or two others excepted, I don't suppose that anyone knew the plays we put on as well as did Master Allison, that is, knew them from paper scrawlings to their fleshly incarnation in performance.

But perhaps his chief role was to be the Company's memory and treasurer. I had heard Master Geoffrey Allison liken a play to a poor, lone boat on the high seas of this world, a little bobbing bark freighted with the author's hopes, prey to passing adventurers and pirates who might wish to possess another's work by force and pass it off as their own or, more likely, to offer it up dismasted and mutilated as sacrifice to an ignorant public. Until a play is entered at the Stationer's Hall for printing, the author's words are like the blossom that floats through the spring air: the product of Mother Nature and any man's for the sweeping up. This rather charming analogy between words and blossom was another of Master Allison's tropes. He had a taste for elaborate images. It was probably caused by hanging around poetry for too long.

Anyway, he said, it behoves a self-respecting Company of players not only to keep their own hands out of other Companies' pockets and plackets but also to ensure that what is theirs (for once the author has been paid his £5 or £6 the play becomes as much the property of the Company as are the costumes) remains safely stowed.

In the Book-keeper's office there is a locked chest. In the chest is a treasure which is the equal of the golden fleece sought by Jason in the far reaches of Colchis. This is my comparison and not Master Allison's. For the chest contains play manuscripts. I have glimpsed this treasure, or, to be more precise, the solid oak trunk which contains it, bound about with iron hoops and secured with two padlocks.

It was about this great trunk and its contents that the Book-keeper spoke to me.

"Nicholas, you have some time at leisure this morning, I believe."

"Nobody would know that better than you, Geoffrey," I said. "You are aware of all our comings and goings."

You see on what easy and familiar terms I was with the other toilers in the playhouse even if there were a few, such as the Burbages and WS, whom I addressed more formally.

"Well, since you are free for now, perhaps you would do me a little favour."

"Willingly," said I, full of helpfulness.

"I am occupied elsewhere."

"You are a busy man," said I, full of a junior's approbation.

"In fact, it should suit someone of your bookish habits and disposition. Master Shakespeare suggested that you would serve. Also I have heard that you possess a good hand and write neat."

"Then I am at your service," said I, even more pleased at being described as bookish, though I am aware that this compliment would not do for every young man, as well as being preferred for a task by WS.

"I have a chest in my office which contains fair copies of many of the pieces that we have put on."

"I know it."

"I need a master-register of what is in the chest. Even *I* do not know everything that is there. There is a mass of material in the bottom of the chest which might as well be at the bottom of the sea. Can you swim?"

"I do not like the water," I said, humouring him and his figures of speech.

"Oh well. All that I require for now is the names of plays, names of playwrights, no more."

"A catalogue you mean."

I was, for some reason, surprised by the request. I don't know what I'd been expecting but it wasn't this.

"I need someone that I can trust. Perhaps I should say *we* need someone we can trust," pursued Master Allison. "Ever since our move across the river I have been intending to catalogue what the chest contains but, like many small tasks, it continually slips just beyond one's fingers. Then Master Shakespeare, finding that this had not been done, he says

48

to me yesterday, 'Why not ask the new man, Nicholas Revill? He looks sharp and has a fair hand, and he is a lover of plays.' "

"Master Shakespeare said all that about me?"

"Indeed he did."

"How does he know I write neat and clear?"

"Oh I don't know, Nicholas, and I don't propose to enquire. You know how ready he is with a compliment. You must ask him yourself. The question is, will you make this master-list of the treasure in our chest?"

"Of course."

"Then there is no better moment to begin than now. We should seize time by the forelock."

"Undoubtedly," I said.

"I do not think there's more than a few hours' work in it. I will bring you pen and paper. Here are the keys to the locks."

He handed them over rather unceremoniously but made it all right by adding, "Be sure that I will tell Burbage and Shakespeare how happy you were to undertake this little task for the Company."

A few minutes later found me on my hands and knees – a posture of obeisance not entirely inappropriate, in view of the contents – before the great chest in Master Allison's office. Beside me were ink, pen, paper. The lid of the trunk was propped open. Inside were bundles of paper, secured with ribbon or string or cord. A certain disorder prevailed. I wondered whether the trunk had been examined since the move across the river little more than a year before, when the Chamberlain's Company secretly decamped from their site in Finsbury and established themselves here on Bankside.

I settled myself, cross-legged, on the floor. I took out a bundle of paper, undid the cord and spread out the half dozen vellum-covered scripts which it secured. I picked one up, brought it near to my eyes and flicked through the pages. I wondered whether Master Allison would begrudge me the extravagance of a candle. The play was called *Uther Pendragon*, a tale of King Arthur's father. The next was titled *Vespasian*; and the next *Vortigern*; and I was beginning to think that there was some system to Master Allison's bundling of scripts together – for these ones all dealt with the olden times in Britain or imperial Rome – when I picked up the fourth and found it was some light piece called *A Woman Hard to Please*. After that there was a play with which I was familiar, since it was one of the earliest I'd participated in at the Chamberlain's, namely *A City Pleasure*.

I examined another bundle drawn at random from the trunk and discovered a similar mix of the historical-pastoral-comical-tragical. Nor was there any unity as to authors. They were jumbled swoopstake, so that a Baxter sat next to a Rawle, a Jonson nestled with a Jackson, while Shakespeare himself bedded down with Boscombe. Indeed, some of the manuscripts were not even graced with the name of their author.

A smell now rose up from the trunk which was anything but magical. It was an unappetising, stale odour, as of things kept too long in the dark and now calling feebly for attention. I started to wonder whether my belief that this chest was the equivalent of Jason's fleece wasn't rather fanciful. Instead, the contents suggested a ewe's greasy fell, a memory I carried with me from my country days.

Confronted with all this paper, my mood suddenly changed. I would like to have shown the chest and its contents to Master Richard Milford. Even unread – especially unread – they were eloquent enough, for they spoke of the vanity of authorship, but in a different sense to that which I had originally applied to him. Oh high thoughts, oh great expectations! Here were piles of paper bound together, here was great expenditure of ink, here were all the fruits of heart and mind. And to what purpose . . . ?

But enough of melancholy! I had a job to do. I returned to my examination of the chest's contents.

I began to think that Master Allison was probably one of those men who have their own private manner of arranging things, a manner which is impenetrable to anyone else. I suspect that, if you'd requested a copy of *The World Gone Mad* or *The Tragical History of Appius and Virginia*, he would have plunged a hand into his trunk and within moments have retrieved the piece in question. Perhaps. Hadn't he said that parts of this hoard were as unglimpsed as the sea-bed?

As far as I was concerned, however, sifting and cataloguing this heap of gold, this pile of dust, seemed likely to occupy more than the promised few hours of work. I regretted the alacrity with which I'd agreed to do it. As I picked up pen and paper, I wondered how I might modestly indicate to Master Allison (to say nothing of Masters WS and Burbage) that, although this was a labour of love, it was still a *labour*.

I plunged my hand into the bottom of the chest and dragged up to the surface some mouldering manuscripts. Some of them lacked title-pages while others were no more than titles and a list of characters. I began trying to put the pieces together, and achieved a match in three or four cases. These were fusty works, perhaps deserving their sea-bed obscurity. One, however, caught my eye. It consisted of a frontispiece and only a couple of pages of dialogue. Fragments of string showed where the bulk – or the hulk – of the drama had come loose from its moorings on the title-page. I was interested to note that the characters who figured in this prefatory scene were named Belladonna and Julia, and that the former was an heiress and the latter her personal servant. So much could easily be gleaned from the expository conversation of the two. I was more interested still to register the title of this drama: *The Courtesan of Venice*. I checked the cast-list. The other characters there sounded familiar too. No author was named.

Well, there are no favourites like the old favourites. If at first you don't succeed, then go in search of someone who has and steal their work. This was, for sure, the source of Master Milford's *Venetian Whore*, the play to which I had given my faint stamp of approval and which I'd encouraged Richard to take direct to the Globe shareholders. No wonder the style of the piece had seemed a little dated to me; it was probably more than a decade old. And the hulk – or the bulk – of the drama hadn't so much come loose from its moorings on the title-page as been wrenched from them.

Strangely, I found myself blushing as furiously as Master Milford, as furiously as if I myself were the book-thief. It's odd how you can feel guilty on behalf of another.

Richard must have got hold of Allison's keys, with or (more likely) without permission. I could visualise him scrabbling round the bottom of the chest, possibly grabbing at a handful of manuscripts in his haste to find something suitable, something he might pass off as his own. Naturally he was taking a risk. Even if the play was more than ten years old, there might have been someone in the Chamberlain's who remembered it – if we had ever put on in the first place, of course. But when I thought of the hundreds of plays that must have moved into and then moved out of the Chamberlain's ken during the latter years of the last century, then Master Milford's daring began to seem quite calculated. It might even be that *The Courtesan of Venice* had strayed in from somewhere else, possibly another acting company, or that it harked back to the days when the Chamberlain's were Lord Strange's men.

After all, a whore is any man's for the asking, and the sixpence in his pocket.

Now, nobody expects a playwright to be truly original. In fact, one who fashioned his own material out of himself would rightly be regarded wth suspicion. After all there are not so many plots in the world. In any case, everyone knows it is the playwright's duty to deck the familiar and make it seem new. But what Richard Milford had done was not so much adaptation as appropriation, if the opening pages were anything to go by. And I grew hotter still to think how he had tried to use me to forward his schemes with the shareholders. I tucked the *Courtesan*'s fragments, her openings, into my shirt.

I returned to my cataloguing, but in an angry and fitful spirit, and as soon as it came to the dinner-hour I was able to justify quitting my task for a few minutes or more and break off for refreshment in the Goat & Monkey. In truth I was hoping to see my Nell there, for if she had nothing better to do she sometimes frequented the tavern in the middle of the day. At that moment I craved something familiar and wished to be taken back to her crib and diverted with a friendly tumble or, perhaps, nothing more strenuous than a friendly word. But she was either about her business elsewhere or not yet up and about in the winter world, so I had to content myself instead with a pot of ale and some words with the landlord on the subject of the weather.

As I sat over my drink in the near-empty tavern I considered Richard Milford's plagiary and decided that what grated with me wasn't so much the theft of another's words (there's nothing new under the sun, etc.) but the way he had humbly asked for my opinion and then attempted to use me as a kind of Trojan Horse to smuggle the work into the Globe playhouse. My heart rose high in indignation in my breast and then sank low to see who had just walked through the door.

"Hello, Nicholas," said Richard Milford. "I may join you?"

But he had already sat down and signalled the drawer for service. He offered to buy me a drink but I refused on the pretext that my tankard was still half full.

"I forget that you drink slow," he said. "But with me, when I look down it's usually to see an empty glass. Sometimes I wonder who's drunk it."

"Oh, the ghost of an author, I expect," I said.

He was in a good humour, and this put my back up.

"You have been working this miserable morning?"

"Doing some service for the Book-keeper."

"Indeed. I have been working too."

"On another play?"

"Since you mention it – though I do not much like to talk about my work while I am *in medias res*, if I may so express it to a learned man."

"You may," I said, hating him very much at that moment. Which could be why I added, "This is after the success of your *Whore?*"

"Well, I hope so, Nicholas, but I would not tempt fate by saying it. As you know, my play has not yet been staged and no man knows how it will be received."

"Are you sure of that?"

"Of what?"

"That *A Venetian Whore* has never been mounted before."

"Oh ha, very good – 'mounted'. I must remember to write down that piece of word-play."

I regretted giving him the opportunity for evasion. "I'm sure you will remember my joke easily enough, if only for its poverty of invention. But my question was about – what's its-name – *The Courtesan of Venice,* and whether she has appeared before."

"*She* has not, but *A Venetian Whore* will be exposed to a

wondering world at the end of this month," he said, looking at me curiously and stressing the title.

I struck my forehead lightly, as if in self-reproach at my own absence of mind.

"Of course, *A Venetian Whore*. Not *The Courtesan of Venice*. Well, what's a whore or a courtesan between friends or, come to that, a particle like 'of'? What's an 'a' or a 'the' among fellows?"

"I might have called it that, *The Whore of Venice*, I mean," said Richard, "but I wanted to distinguish my work from Master Shakespeare's *Merchant of Venice*. Not that I would dream of course – in any way – but who knows – one day—"

"After all you are both from Warwickshire," I said. "There must be some special virtue in the soil."

"It is rich ground, but how kind you are to say so, Nicholas." He had recovered his balance now. "Are you sure you have not finished your drink yet so that I could show my appreciation for your words?"

"Thank you but no. London still has to teach me how to drink deep. Tell me of your new play," I said and was glad to see a blush creep back into his features. At last! There was something unnatural about an unblushing Milford.

"I am reluctant to talk of what is only half-shaped."

"Then it does not spring from your brain fully formed?"

"No. I have to do battle with my words, like a general with mutinous soldiers. Only when I have got them into line and order are they ready for the fray."

"I respect you, Richard, for owning to a struggle. Some in your profession would say that they wrote fast, without blotting a line."

He smiled slightly at this. Both of us recognised an allusion to WS.

"In his case it is true enough, I expect."

"It must save on fair copies," I said.

I would willingly have abandoned the whole matter there and then. But the continuance of this conversation was like an itch that demands scratching. I could not stop. And besides I was still aggrieved at the way Richard Milford had tried to use me to forward 'his' play.

"Yes," said Milford thoughtfully. "Nicholas, what is it you wish to say? For sure there is something behind your kind words."

"My work for Allison this morning has been to catalogue the contents of the Book-keeper's chest. To begin cataloguing, that is. There are hundreds and hundreds of works buried there."

"And millions of words in those works. That is not surprising."

The red was fixed firmly to his cheeks and he was looking at me with an alarming intensity. For the first time I noticed that one of Richard's irises was heavily flecked with green while the other was pure blue.

"I didn't know where to start," I said, "and to be honest with you I rather regretted volunteering for the task. But I plunged my hand to the bottom of the chest and began."

"Only fusty stuff down there, I expect."

"Mostly, but some of it looked serviceable enough at first glance. A few pieces there that might bear reviving."

"But there is so much that is new," he said urgently. "Surely it is not fair to favour the past and exclude the new. Think of us playwrights that are young and tender, pushing through the dark soil of our forebears like so many shoots in spring."

"How poetical you are, Richard. You almost sound like

Master Allison. A moment earlier you were likening yourself to a general marshalling his troops of words."

"Think of us young playwrights," he repeated.

He meant, of course, *think of me*.

I made no reply but something in my look must have told him that further evasion was useless. His shoulders tensed.

"I have tried to produce something new and fresh, God knows I have tried in the past," he said, still fixing me with his parti-coloured gaze and now holding tight to my forearm with one hand. I observed that the knuckles of the other hand gripping his tankard were white. "I tried but it was poor thin stuff. I knew it even without showing it to anyone."

I still said nothing but detached my arm from his hold. There was something distasteful in his self-pity.

"What harm is there in using a dead man's words? Or an anonymous man's? It's the same thing. There was no name on the title-page. I didn't think *The Courtesan of Venice* had ever been performed. It had a neglected air. I read it and considered that it deserved to see the sunlight."

"Metamorphosed into *A Venetian Whore*. You rifled through the Book-keeper's chest, abstracted an old play, copied it off and passed it as your own work. And then you asked me to prefer it to Master Shakespeare."

"Be calm, Nicholas. *Your* conscience can be clear, for you refused to do what I should never have requested of you in the first place."

"It is your own conscience that you should be concerned with."

"There are worse things to have on it than a little plagiary."

"You were still taking a risk that the *Courtesan* – oh sorry, *Whore* – might be recognised," I said. "She has been around for some time. Perhaps you are not the only one to have fiddled with her."

"*You* didn't recognise it," he said.

"But one of the older members of the Chamberlain's, one of the shareholders . . . ?"

"I dropped one or two hints beforehand but no-one took them up. Besides . . ."

"Besides?"

"Where do you think Master Shakespeare got the idea for his *Merchant of Venice* from?"

"Are you saying that he'd read this play as well?"

"Well, it's possible. After all, you yourself commented on one or two likenesses between – my – between that piece and his. Maybe that's why he didn't say anything. Maybe your precious Shakespeare is guilty of a little plagiary too."

"Absurd," I said, but without complete conviction. Nevertheless I was angered by Milford's aspersions. "Anyway there is a difference between borrowing a few figures and ideas, and taking over another man's work wholesale. Look."

I dug out from beneath my shirt the few tattered sheets from the start of the *Courtesan*. Almost straightaway seeing what they were, he made a grab but I held them out of his reach.

"Give them me. They are not yours. I left them behind."

I was amazed at his impudence.

"Yes, you left them behind when you ransacked the trunk. Tell me, did you ask Allison for the keys – or just take them?"

"Work it out for yourself, Nicholas, since you've proved yourself so clever this far."

"It doesn't matter. But these few scraps of paper, they are the Book-keeper's. Or they belong to the Chamberlain's Company. Or even poor Master Anonymous, a greater author than you will ever be. For certain, they are not yours, Master Milford."

"What are you going to do with them?"

For a moment I savoured power. I knew that if I gave these paper fragments to Burbage or any of the seniors then Milford's budding career as a playwright with the Chamberlain's would be finished. It wasn't so much the plagiary that mattered. No doubt it happened often enough, even if not in so blatant a form. Old clothes are the most comfortable. There is nothing new under the etc . . . If he'd only presented his *Whore* – sorry, *Courtesan* – honestly, as an old piece reworked, he'd probably have got away with it. But he'd played the cony-catcher with a whole Company – or with the section of the Company which counted – and for that he was unlikely to be forgiven.

Richard's face was bright red and his eyes stared hard as he asked the question. It was fortunate that the tavern was almost empty, and that none of our Globe fraternity had wandered in to join our hushed dialogue. While I pondered my reply, I had the leisure too to wonder at the change in this hitherto quiet and reflective man. I was almost glad that we weren't alone in some isolated hole or corner for, in addition to to the fact that he was about my height, weight and age, he had the advantage of his desperation. If this is what it means to wield the writer's pen then give me the player's trumpery sword any day!

"What do you mean to do?" he repeated.

For answer, I tucked the incriminating papers inside my shirt once again. At that he broke.

"Please, Nicholas, Master Revill, say nothing. My life is in your hands. And what is more than my life, my reputation."

"You're being silly. You overstate the case," I said after a moment. "No wonder you must borrow another's words if that is the extent of your rhetoric."

Nevertheless, the pause and my words must have given him hope, for he went on, "You see, my *Whore* is about to be staged. No, very well [*seeing the demurral in my eyes*] not my

Whore but anonymous's *Courtesan*. She is about to be made an honest lady of. Surely that is an act of charity, of virtue."

"From *Courtesan* to *Whore*, that is a declension surely?"

He shrugged. "It's a blunter term, certainly."

"And for your next piece? Will that be honest and blunt too?"

Never have I felt so severe. Never have I been so uncomfortable. The role of moralist is hard to play. Hard for me, at any rate. Although I can see that one might grow into it.

"There is a strange thing, Nicholas. For you see that, when I said I had been struggling with my own words all morning, that is precisely what I have been doing. My *own* words. I promise you."

"Very well," I said, rising from the bench. "I must return to my cataloguing."

"Be sure to destroy those sheets," he said to my retreating back but I did not deign to answer him.

I returned to the Book-keeper's room, feeling that I'd acted justly in exposing to Richard Milford that I knew the secret of his 'theft', and yet unable to shake off the pulpit-taint, even the priggishness, of my words. By what right did I set myself up to judge a fellow of my own age and one who was in not altogether dissimilar circumstances? My bent was towards playing, it is true, whilst his was for words, but both of us were fired with ambition, both were hungry for recognition. Perhaps, if I'd been a word-wielder, rather than a stage-sword-shaker, and found my early efforts not yielding success, I too would have resorted to the same measures. Would have found an old, unnamed play and stamped it with my initials. To counterfeit coin is a capital crime but to arrogate another man's words is, at worst, a venial offence. Particularly if the man is dead or unknown. Where was the harm? I had to confess that most of my anger with Richard had come from the fact that he'd fooled me, had wanted *me* to commend 'his' work to WS.

I resolved to say and do nothing more. His secret was safe with me. Let the *Whore* be played before all, let him reap the small reward of a promising reputation. (For sure, he wouldn't get much money by it.) Let him go on to produce honest work. I wouldn't destroy the tell-tale title-page but I would not show it to anyone either unless directly asked about it, a thing which was not likely since nobody but he and I knew about it.

Besides, I must confess that I was a little alarmed at the fierceness of the man. His eyes had stared, his face was all inflamed when he had tried to grab at the sheets of paper.

I settled down again, cross-legged in front of the chest full of gold, of dust, of forgotten paper.

And yet that was not the end of this difficult day.

I had not been working for many minutes when there came an interruption – and one of a kind which threw into the shade the relatively trivial upsets of the morning.

"In here. We shall be private enough."

I jumped. There was a shuffling of boot on board in the room on the other side of the wall from the Book-keeper's office.

"Sit you down," said a voice which I couldn't immediately place.

A scraping of chairs, the squeak of a door closing.

"We are private?"

"No eyes but ours."

"Nor ears neither?"

"This desk is mute, and this table-book is mute. This candle too. *They* will not talk. At least they did not answer when last I spoke to them."

"This is no laughing matter."

"I believe you," said the first speaker.

"Can I believe *you*? That we are private?"

"Sure enough. I have said."

"You have locked the door?"

"No need. No one will come into Dick Burbage's room without knocking first."

"Why isn't Master Burbage here?"

"This is a quiet day for us, the winter, you know . . ."

"Why isn't Master Burbage here?" The question was sharply repeated.

"Because he has deputed me to speak for him, for the whole Company if necessary."

"I expected to see him."

"And I tell you that, just as you are trusted to speak on behalf of others, so am I."

"Very well."

There was a kind of slackening in the visitor's voice in these last words, as if he accepted and was grudgingly reassured by what he was being told. By now I had recognised the first speaker as Master Augustine Phillips, a senior share-holder in the Chamberlain's, a player and a fine musician too, a man for all occasions. He and his guest were sitting in Burbage's office, one of a cluster of small rooms back-stage and right next to the Book-keeper's quarters where I was positioned on the floor, surrounded by scattered manuscripts. As must be evident from the completeness with which I have given the foregoing exchange between the two speakers, I was able to hear each word that passed between them. These interior walls were thin lath and plaster. Furthermore, Master Phillips had a beautifully clear voice which could make even a whisper resonate through the air.

"Some refreshment?"

"Later perhaps, when our business is concluded."

While these preliminary skirmishes to conversation were going on, and even as I listened with an attent ear, I was inwardly considering what to do. It is not altogether a comfortable thing – nor an honourable one – to be an eavesdropper, even if the blame was diverted in this instance because I had neither wished nor schemed to overhear. But in the next few moments there was a choice to be made.

I might sneak out of the Book-keeper's office and creep away altogether from this area of the playhouse, and so shield my ears from whatever important matters the two men in Burbage's room intended to discuss. That they were important matters was not to be doubted: there was an anxiety, even a portentousness in the visitor's voice, which was only underlined by Master Phillips' lighter tones. On the other hand, I could draw attention to myself – by coughing, by humming a tune, by any one of a dozen bits of stage business which would alert my neighbours to my presence. This would be a polite and tactful way of signifying that the Book-room was occupied. As long as I acted now they could hardly consider that I'd overheard things of significance.

On yet another hand, I could stay precisely where I was, unmoving, silent, alert. And hear what followed.

I ask: what would you do in this situation?

I stayed (as, perhaps, you would have done). I did more than stay. Thinking of Robert Cecil's 'mission' and that it might be important to have a record of what passed between these two men, I took one of the sheets of paper meant for the task of cataloguing and during the dialogue which followed made some fragmentary jottings.

"Business before pleasure, eh, Sir Gelli?" said Augustine Phillips, referring to the other's refusal of refeshment.

And now I knew that I was in the right to remain exactly

where I was, sitting by a great box of manuscripts in the Book-keeper's room, and listening out. For, during my interview with Secretary Cecil, one of the persons he had told me to watch for was Sir Gelli Merrick, steward to the Earl of Essex. I felt the sweat break out on my brow and a strange stir in my bowels to know that I was only a feet away from an enemy to the state – if such he proved to be.

"You wish us to play for you, I understand."

"Your usual business only, or a little more."

"Come, sir, if we are to pretend that this is ordinary business, then you may make your exit now."

"To be brief," said Merrick, "our proposal is that the Chamberlain's Men should stage – a particular play – on a given afternoon. There is not much that is out of the way of your ordinary business there."

"No, not much is out of the way there."

But Master Phillips did not sound to my ears as though he was really assenting to what the other was saying.

"You are players. You are paid to perform."

"No, Sir Gelli," said Phillips. "That is not altogether right. We perform and *then* we are paid."

"The difference escapes me."

"Never mind."

"I was led to believe that I would be better received than this, that I would find myself among friends."

A note of resentment had entered Sir Gelli's voice. I almost expected him to say that he wasn't used to being talked to like this.

"You are, sir. You are among friends at the Globe."

"Then why isn't Master Burbage here or Master Shake-speare?'

My bowels gave a further lurch or twist to hear these names, especially the latter.

"Forgive me," said Augustine Phillips, "but they are busy and, as I say, I have been deputed to speak for the Company. Let me hear your proposal once more and, if you please, do not be coy about naming plays and times."

"Very well. It is Shakespeare's *Richard II* that we mean to have done."

"Ah," said the other, with no great surprise as it seemed to me. Then, echoing my own words to Sir Robert Cecil, "It is a fusty piece."

"Very fresh and to our purposes, I think," said Merrick.

"Not performed for some few years."

Again, almost the very words I had used. I shivered at the coincidence, even though it was warm in the Book-keeper's room and I was sweating with the fear of discovery – and of other things besides which I couldn't have put a name to.

"And now King Richard's time is come again. The year, the week, the very day."

In Sir Gelli's response there was a species of fervour. I had a sudden flicker of memory from my Somerset childhood and saw myself, alone, on a country track and hearing a far-off rumble of thunder, and picking up my pace to get home.

"What week, what day?"

"Master Phillips, you must surely understand that I cannot be precise here though in my opinion it will be soon."

"Because if we are to stage a play, even a fusty, time-warped piece, we must have a little warning. A morning of rehearsal at least. There may be costumes to be looked at."

"Of course. You will have sufficient time to prepare, at least a day's warning. If I cannot yet be precise it is because there are many things still uncertain, many things still to be weighed."

"This is to be a private performance?"

"Not at all, Master Phillips. It will be open to all. That is the point. You are to advertise it in your usual way, with notices and a fanfare and so on. We wish the people of London to see King Richard."

"And Henry Bolingbroke, the usurper."

"We only wish the play to be seen as it is, with nothing added, nothing omitted – that is important, nothing omitted."

"And what do we gain from this, in the Chamberlain's?"

"Oh, now you come to money. I thought that you performed and *then* were paid."

"Only a fool plays blind," said Master Phillips.

"We offer you forty shillings."

"Forty shillings extraordinary?"

"I do not understand players' talk."

"I mean, forty shillings in addition to whatever the gatherers take at the door – from the people of London who you think are so eager to see this stale piece."

"You may charge what you please at the door. You may charge whatever your audience will bear. I tell you only what you will receive from us."

"And in return, you wish for the best seats?"

"Some of them perhaps. But it may be more to the advantage of my – party – that we are scattered through the playhouse. Some in the twopenny seats, some in the threepenny ones and so on."

"And some even standing with the penny-knaves?"

"There too. We want to, ah, take the measure of things."

"Is this all that you offer the Company? Forty shillings is welcome enough but it is no great reward in itself."

"There may be other rewards to come."

"As?"

"Rewards . . . such as memory and gratitude . . . and even obligation."

"Airy rewards," said Augustine Phillips.

I could almost see the other man bristle and bridle at this. Master Phillips quickly continued, "Well, perhaps those unseen rewards may be the most valuable of all."

"They could be," said Merrick. "Time will tell, but we are confident. Have we not right and justice on our side?"

"I am not sure what you mean. You have asked us only to stage an old play about a dead king."

"Which you will do?"

"Provided we have sufficient warning, yes. I think I may speak for the Company in saying yes."

I was surprised that Augustine Phillips should agree to Sir Gelli's request. The forty shillings was not so much, and the less tangible rewards were certainly 'airy'. It was at this moment, as I was wondering at the readiness with which he'd committed the Company to what must surely be (at the least) a dubious course, that disaster struck.

I was sitting awkwardly on the floor, limbs tense, face set, ears straining at the thin partition, and attempting all the while to scribble down the secret words which came from the other side. As their dialogue seemed to be drawing to an end, so the discomfort of my position began to tell and I straightened my left leg with sufficient force to strike the treasure chest full of plays. The stick with which I had propped up the lid fell with a clatter on the floor and the lid thumped back into place.

The talking immediately ceased in the next room and there was the sound of a chair scraping on bare boards. Then came Augustine Phillips' even tones.

"Be calm, Sir Gelli."

"You said we were private."

"A rat or a cat only."

"A rat with two legs perhaps. Let me see."

The door of Burbage's office creaked open.

"Wait, Sir Gelli."

But already there were steps in the passage outside the Book-keeper's room. The latch was lifted.

"What's in here?"

"This is Master Allison's room."

"Who is he? Would you move?"

"He is our Book-keeper."

"Would you stand aside please, Master Philips." A pause, while I had time to notice Augustine Phillips' apparent reluctance to let this intruder into one of the playhouse's private rooms. Then from closer at hand, "Where is he?"

My heart near leaped out of my chest because I imagined that Merrick was looking for *me*. But the reply showed that he meant Allison. "Evidently not here," said Master Phillips. He tsk-tsk'ed. "And he has not put away his scripts, I observe."

From my position behind the great trunk I sensed, rather than saw, Phillips come forward to examine the disordered piles of paper that lay around. Surely my heart was banging loud enough to be heard by him.

"I must have a word with Master Allison. He should not leave these about."

"What is in these other rooms off here?"

"Offices of the playhouse."

"Show me."

"Sir Gelli, it was a cat or a rat."

"No doubt, but I would like to be sure."

Master Philips sighed. After a moment, the door to Allison's room was shut and I heard the other rooms in this quarter of the playhouse being opened for Merrick's inspection. I waited several minutes to see whether the two men would return to Burbage's chamber but their business was apparently concluded. Then I slid slowly out from the narrow space between the trunk and the wall. It was a wonder that Master Phillips had not seen me, even though the natural light in the Book-keeper's room was poor and the February afternoon beyond the little glazed window was all dirty and dulled over with cloud. I thanked Providence that I had not yet lit a candle to read the plays by.

After another few minutes I concluded that I was safe and that if anyone were to enter the Book-keeper's room now they would not think there was anything odd or suspicious in my presence. Therefore I lit the candle and settled to the task of sorting and listing the plays in the trunk. But my hands were unsteady and my mind distracted by the conversation between Augustine Phillips and Sir Gelli Merrick, and with what I knew I had to do next. Also, I was troubled with a strange sense that I had been abandoned by my fellows. As Master Phillips had said to his visitor, it was a quiet afternoon. It seemed that the Globe was a near-empty shell and that I huddled in one of its tiny compartments, bent over fading papers, lit by an uncertain candle. Some time later Master Allison came in to see how I was doing, and I took a little heart from that. I did not tell him of my discoveries of the morning and the afternoon.

After a time I left the Globe, freighted down with a dangerous cargo of paper. For all that it weighed next to nothing, either item was heavy enough to have driven me, and others, onto the rocks. In addition to the first few pages of *The Courtesan of Venice* by Anonymous, I had a scrawled transcription of the Phillips-Merrick talk. These were documents that I would have to guard as carefully as the playhouse scrolls which contained my parts. More carefully, in fact, for there was no playing here. Everyone – Master Richard Milford,

Master Augustine Phillips, Sir Gelli Merrick (and the horde of unseen conspirators behind him) – every one of these individuals was in deadly earnest.

My difficult day, one in which I had been privy to two unwelcome discoveries, was about to give way to a yet more troubling evening. I was making for the Bridge to cross over into Clerkenwell for another *Twelfth Night* rehearsal in the Office of the Revels and considering that one could over-rehearse a play. Passing The Knight of the Carpet ale-house, I heard an owl's forlorn hoot surprisingly close at hand. Then a voice hissed at me out of the shadows.

"Master Revill."

My instinct was to run. I was tired of night encounters in the street. Then I put the hooting and the half-familiar voice together.

"Nat, is it?"

"The very same, sir."

I was almost relieved, to have found a friend in the night. Not that Nat the Animal Man was exactly a friend, but you understand what I mean. This small, dirty, disreputable creature took halfpennies or liquor from the drinkers of the Goat and other hostelries by mimicking the cries of beasts both wild and tamed. He could do the roar of the lion or the bray of the camel, as well as the whole discourse of the farmyard. For a little more money or drink he would enact a full-scale fight from the bear-pit. I have even heard him present a panoply of grotesque creatures like the amphisbaena and the hippogriff, whose names he can scarcely pronounce but whose outlandish screams and hisses he claims to have been taught by a traveller from the East. But personally I do not believe that such a traveller ever existed.

"No custom tonight, Nat?"

I sensed rather than saw him come closer to me, a bundle of clothing, a ragged four-limbed bird.

"No, sir. No one seems interested tonight. And just when I have some animals fresh in last week."

"That old hippogriff again?"

"No sir, these are new and one of them is a beast with five heads and ten tongues, they say, and it makes a great noise. I have the sound off most infallible but the name of it has slipped my mind."

"How do you know its sound, Nat, if you have never met the beast?" I asked, as I sometimes do, to catch him out.

"A traveller who has been to far Cathay taught it me, sir," he said, as he usually does.

"And where is this far Cathay? I should like to visit it myself."

"I forget, sir. It is either three days' ride away or on the other side of this great world."

"And the rest of the animals? You said you had other fresh sounds?" I asked, to humour him.

"Only the goose in the farmyard. You may be surprised I have never done the goose in the farmyard before. And the noise of the fox too as he closes on him when the goose is least suspecting."

Something about the way Nat the Animal Man said these last words caused the hairs on the nape of my neck to bristle.

"But the fox, he makes no sound."

"You're a sharp one, sir. There are some who will pay for silence, though."

"Are you after a goose tonight?" I asked.

"Like I said, there is no custom," he said. "But I have something for you, sir, if you will open your ears."

"I am not certain that I wish to hear."

"Have you heard the bird of ill-omen, sir?"

"The bird of ill-omen? No, what sound does it make? Be-ware, be-ware, be-ware."

"Very good. You will soon supplant me in my trade, sir."

"Only if my fortunes turn Turk with me."

"This bird can talk," said Nat, "a thing sometimes found among feathered creatures. And it has a message for you."

"Watch-out, watch-out, I suppose."

There is something desperate about joking with someone you can't see, and even as I jested I had an uncomfortable idea that this conversation was heading in an unwelcome direction. Perhaps I was trying to deflect Nat from his course.

"A penny will prompt it, sir."

I held out a halfpenny and Nat's hand, doubtless dirty, seemingly taloned like a bird's, folded round it in the darkness and without acknowledgement

"The bird of ill-omen. Spell it backward, sir. Omen. Spell it back."

"I didn't know you could read, Nat."

"If a bird may talk, why should an Animal Man not read?"

"Omen backwards is nemo. That is the message?"

"That is the messenger."

I produced another halfpenny. The same palm opened and shut. Then he opened his chops and, in a kind of caw, uttered these words.

"Hartstreetmidnight – Hartstreetmidnight – Hartstreet-midnight."

"I hear you," I said.

I heard all too well, and saw also that there was no limit to the net that Robert Cecil or his minions were able to weave about the honest citizens of London.

We were in the great chamber at the Office of the Master of the Revels. The February night was kept at bay with a roaring fire, and a blaze of candles, lamps and candelabra, but the warmest item of all was the buzz of human activity. We were in the midst of our preparations for the royal *Twelfth Night*. All was ordered bustle. Sir Edmund Tilney, the Revel Master in person, was darting about, consulting with the Burbage brothers, with Master Shakespeare, with Master Phillips and other senior members of the Company. Old Heminges, who was responsible for the financial side of such performances, was much in request. We lesser figures of the Chamberlain's waited on the pleasure of our elders, studying the scrolls which contained our parts and which by this time we knew backwards, talking quietly and joking, straightening seams and brushing imagined motes and flecks off our clothing.

Every so often the Tire-man or one of his assistants would separate himself from the principal players and wander over to look us up and down, then press back a fold here or tighten a loose point there, and all the while with pursed lips as if to say, "For God's sake, man, don't you know that the Queen's real interest is in our costumes?" And then Master Allison would come among us and check for the twentieth time that we knew our exits and entrances and what (if anything) we were supposed to carry on or take off stage with us. All of this worked well enough when we played at what I might term our home, the Globe Theatre. But now that we were transplanted to the grander surroundings of the Clerkenwell Priory in anticipation of the even greater grandeur of Whitehall Palace, everything which was plain and straight before had to be crumpled and rumpled – if only in order to be smoothed out once more.

The one man who did not seem troubled with the forth-coming performance was Master WS. Though he was acting as the 'guider' for this production, *he* did not come over and tell us how to stand and how to deliver our lines. *He* did not appear to worry himself over whether we had memorised the words but took it for granted that, as proper proud players, we would do our duty. And yet there were other matters weighing on Master Shakespeare's mind, as I was soon to discover.

Meantime I should say a little about my own role in *Twelfth Night*, and about the play in general.

This comedy is a light and happy piece but also a sad one in places – and indeed there can be no true comedy without some heaviness. As it is in the beginning, when shipwrecked Viola is cast up on the coast of Illyria, believing that her twin brother Sebastian is drowned. Where Illyria is I am not sure but it is not so far from Messina, for that is the birthplace of Viola and Sebastian. And Messina is in the Kingdom of Sicily. And the Kingdom of Sicily is . . .

Enough geography! Back to the story.

Viola takes man's disguise and the name Cesario for protection (but really in order that Master WS may make the most of the confusion which inevitably follows). Our disguised Viola joins the court of Duke Orsino, ruler of Illyria and would-be lover of the Countess Olivia. The Duke sends disguised Cesario to woo the Countess on his behalf – all too successfully. Olivia falls for a him who is not a he. Meanwhile, Cesario, the he who is a she, has fallen in love with Orsino. Each of these three loves another and is loved in turn by the third. How to satisfy the sexes? How to resolve this iron triangle and make it into a pliant square? Master WS, conjurer that he is, now calls up Viola's twin brother Sebastian, who has after all survived the shipwreck and the surges. This gentleman is easily confused – of course! – with his sister in her male disguise. Eventually all is well: Orsino is paired off with Viola, now out of man's attire and her adopted name, while Sebastian is delighted with the beauteous Olivia. We end with weddings in abundance.

But on the margins of this happy tale are some discontented and unhappy folk. There is no maker of melancholy like a wedding, your funeral is nothing to it. The steward Malvolio, like Narcissus, loves only his own self and image. Feste the clown (played by Robert Armin), though he sings of love, seems not to seek it for himself. There is a knight, Sir Andrew Aguecheek, who is a fool whether he is in or out of love. And then there is poor Antonio, who has rescued Sebastian from the ocean billows and who now companions his new friend with a dogged, selfless devotion. He is sloughed off at the end when Sebastian finds a more attractive prospect in the shape of the fair Olivia. Who should blame Sebastian? Who would feel for Antonio?

Well, Antonio was my part, and I was determined to make something of it and him, not in a noisy passionate way, but quietly and modestly, which I considered to be the fellow's nature.

I had three or four scenes to play, first with Sebastian and afterwards with Viola-Cesario, whom I mistake for her twin brother. Then I am arrested as an enemy to the state of Illyria; and, although all is made straight again at the end, the happy amity between Antonio and Sebastian will never come again, for it has served its turn.

In the gaps and the intervals and nothingnesses that fill up a large part of any rehearsal – and, since these intervals are so much longer than the action, it seems as if the play is an interruption of one's leisure rather than the other way about – in such pauses, I say, I fell to talking, or arguing, about friendship with my fellow-player Jack Horner, he who had the role of Sebastian.

Jack was a Londoner born and bred yet had the air of the country about him, being fresh-faced and flaxen-haired and guileless, as it appeared to me. Four years or so older than I,

Jack possessed a wife who was his reverse or antipodes (closed, secretive, dark-haired).

"Why don't you think that this friendship can be disinterested, Jack?" I said, referring not to ourselves but to the relationship between the two individuals that we played. "Doesn't Antonio save and befriend Sebastian with no end in view, no end at all?"

"It is not a friendship between equals," said Jack. "And so it is no true friendship."

"You mean, because your Sebastian is well-born and my Antonio wears a sea-cap and is no gentleman, perhaps. Your definition is too narrow."

"I mean that, in this case, the advantage is all to Sebastian. He is the only gainer. Antonio saves his life, Antonio gives Sebastian money and so on, and he receives nothing in return."

"Then it is more like love, which seeks for no reward," I said. "After all, [*speaking in my character*] 'Come what may, I do adore thee so.'"

"Love is not friendship."

"Though each may speak the language of the other?"

"Those are fine words no doubt, Nick, whatever they mean. All I know is that I have a wife . . ."

(This I knew. Her I knew.)

"Yes, and so?" I said.

"I am not friends with my wife, I think. Indeed, I am not sure that a man can be friends with a woman in the way that men may be with each other. Though I suppose I love her – love her not always or constantly, but sometimes."

(This I also knew.)

"Yes," I said, growing a little uncomfortable where we sat on the benches by the side of the great chamber, watching the bustle of activity and waiting for our cues.

"Love flares up, like that fire over there, and like a fire it will die down, it must die down," said Jack. "But if you come to friendship, oh that is a much more even-handed and steady business. Look at us, Nick. We are friends because neither of us has anything to offer or to take from the other. There is no advantage, you see."

"Let us ask young Martin Hancock for his opinion," I said, very glad of the interruption when the lad playing Viola-Cesario came to sit down next to us. This would be Martin Hancock's last season playing women's parts. He was growing too tall and his voice was near to cracking in the ring, as Master WS puts it. In appearance he owned very few touches of his 'brother' Sebastian, having dark locks and looks. They were easily received as twins, however, by the audience, who will accept whatever they're told to accept, good-natured credulous creatures that they are. In short, Jack and Martin appeared quite dissimilar, sharing only a certain openness in expression. Even this, however, proceeded from different sources, for Jack's was a frank innocence and Martin's was the calculated freshness of one who plays the boy. For though he was but a boy in years – and though in *Twelfth Night* he played the chaste heroine – he was quick and ribald in his own attire, as it were. At the moment this boy player was wearing male disguise in order that might penetrate (as he would most likely express it) Orsino and his court. He settled himself quite close to me on the bench.

"Well, Martin," I said. "You may be able to help us in a question here."

"At your pleasure, masters," said Martin Hancock. "How can I serve you?"

"Jack Horner and I were talking about friendship. What is the nature of the friendship between Sebastian and Antonio? Can you speak from what you know of your twin brother in the play?"

I must confess that I was talking to no particular purpose and only to prevent Jack reverting to the subject of his wife. That I addressed Martin more or less as an adult is not to be wondered at. Keeping company with us all the day, sharing in our comedies, our tragedies and our bawdry, these boy apprentices grew up faster than ordinary lads. Also, the fact that they played above their years and out of their sex – and were frequently the dealers-out or the recipients of the most impassioned words and gestures on stage – could not help but spill over into our daily intercourse. Nevertheless, I should say here and now that we of the Chamberlain's Company largely kept ourselves free from the dangerous taint of sodomy and those other unnatural practices which the enemies of the stage charged us with. It is perhaps as well that this be made clear before you hear the clever quibbles of Master Martin, for they might lead you to think otherwise.

"It is plain as a pikestaff," answered the knowing young Martin to my question about the two friends in *Twelfth Night*. "Antonio wishes to bolster with my 'brother' here."

"Bolster? What kind of word is that?" said Jack.

"A perfectly good one," said Martin. "As good a word as your name, Master Jack *Horner*."

Like the boy that he still was in some ways, Martin delighted in naughty terms and general rudery. When he was not playing honest girls and chaste heroines he spent much time giggling with the other Company boys. The fact that our fellow-player had a name, Horner, expressive of a capacity to make holes in other men's best coats – in brief, to cuckold them – was to young Master Martin a constant, sniggering pleasure. Believe me when I say that the irony of Jack Horner's last name was not lost on me at that moment.

"Now justify yourself," I said, severe as a schoolmaster, "in this business of Sebastian and Antonio, that is, him and me."

"He gives Sebastian a purse full of crowns and ducats but it is not the purse – or the crowns – or the ducats – that he wishes the other to dandle with, I think."

"Horrid boy," said Jack Horner, between splutters of laughter.

"Mere supposition," I said with disapproval. I could sense my late father the parson peeping his head out at this point.

"And when he draws to defend me," continued the boy, pleased with the reaction that he was getting, "when Antonio draws believing that he is protecting his beloved Sebastian, do you think that it is really his *sword* he wants to unsheathe? After all, does not Sir Toby Belch later tell me to strip my sword 'stark naked', and we all know what *he* means – even though I am but a poor unfurnished girl in this department."

"Hypothesis only, this business of the sword," I said pointedly, feeling even more like a schoolmaster, one who has discovered a bright boy doing adept but crude drawings at the back of the class.

"Horrid and clever boy," said Jack. But in his voice there was a note of admiration that a mere lad should be so forward and fluent in filth.

"Oh very clever, Martin, but I do not like your construction of this matter," I said. "I prefer you as the virginal Viola, thinking well of all men – and women too. I'm sure Sebastian here prefers you in that way too."

Jack said nothing so I assumed that he agreed. For myself, I found it hard to square the sweet-mouthed and courageous Viola with this naughty lad beside me. But then I should not have done; after all, we are all players.

"Well, Nick," said Jack, "out of the mouths of babes and lads . . . This love between my Sebastian and your Antonio is not as disinterested as you pretend. True, I get money from you, to say nothing of being rescued from a stormy sea in the first place, but you . . . all the time you do have an end in view."

"Your end, Master Jack," said nasty Martin, "your . . . bottom."

"Not so," I said, feeling faintly indignant, and wanting Jack to object to this familiar handling. But still he said nothing. Perhaps I felt more indignant than the occasion warranted because I noticed Master WS hoving into view. "It is higher than this. You must raise your eyes, both of you, and stop grubbing on the ground. With Antonio and Sebastian, I see it as being like the friendship between Damon and Pythias in the old story. The one, you know, risked death for the other."

"Good old Nick," said Jack. "Ever ready to think well of us, and to clothe our lower impulses in a cleaner garb."

Not so again, I thought rather than said, and I turned slightly away from him in shame as he clasped a fraternal arm about my shoulder. Fortunately, by this time Martin was required once more as Viola-Cesario and so left us. Shortly afterwards Jack and I were due to appear together for our first scene.

As I have said, Master Shakespeare was the guider during rehearsals for this royal performance. He took no player's part in the production (indeed, the last role I had seen him in had been as the Ghost in *Hamlet*) but as the author he was obviously in the best position to oversee the fleshing-out of his words.

If I were asked about Master WS's method in guiding us Chamberlain's men in one of his own plays, I would find it difficult to answer. With someone like Dick Burbage, the business of guiding – or, as one might term it, the direction – was firm and emphatic. If he was the tillerman and the players the vessel, then Burbage kept a strong, steady hand on the boat's progress. You would always be aware of his presence, sitting up aloft in the stern, one eye on the crew, the other on the waters ahead. But with Master WS it was different. To maintain the analogy: if he was the tillerman, then he was one who did not make an exhibition of himself up there; indeed, he might sometimes seem to be absent altogether from his post (though I do not mean to imply by this that he was negligent). Tiny, infrequent touches on the tiller seemed to suffice. And yet all went sailingly enough. I did not understand the trick of it.

After I had delivered my first lines as Antonio and had promised to follow Sebastian to the court of Duke Orsino of Illyria, perilous as it might be, because

> *come what may, I do adore thee so,*
> *That danger shall seem sport, and I will go*

Master WS drew me to one side as I exited from the playing area, which was marked out in chalk on the uneven boards of the great chamber.

"Nicholas, you have a moment?"

His large, open face tilted confidingly towards me as he placed a cupped hand under my right elbow. He ushered me towards a clear corner. I thought that he was going to say something about the quality of my playing, either in compliment or complaint (though with Master WS the balance was always tilted most indulgently in favour of the former).

Anyone observing us must have thought that we were discussing something to do with the play. But it was not so, or at least only in the beginning.

"Nicholas, I heard what you said just now about friendship, about Damon and Pythias."

"Oh, you did," I said, as though half regretful at being overheard – when really I was not. In fact, I own up to wanting him to overhear me.

"I have often thought that the history of those two would make a good argument for a play. *The Two Friends from Syracuse*. What do you think? Or simply *Damon and Pythias*. The one stood surety for the other and was ready to die in his place, when the tyrant Dionysius demanded it. Is that not true friendship?"

"But it ended happily, did it not?"

"Yes," said WS. "Dionysius was so struck by Pythias's readiness to lay down his life for his friend that he pardoned both of them."

"Would that all rulers showed a like mercy," I said piously – and emptily.

"We would surely say *merci* if they did," said WS.

"What? Oh yes," I said, catching the pun before it disappeared round the corner and out of sight. Even by WS's standards it was a particularly feeble one – and, had I been inclined to contest with him, I would have pointed out that one should not trespass outside one's own tongue to make a play on words.

"In that case," he continued, "a ruler's mercy was prompted by the honourable friendship of two young men. Even a tyrant may be infected by goodness – though he must catch it by stealth. It will not do to have designs on him."

I said nothing, because I could think of nothing to say. When Master WS talked, one generally listened.

"I have always been moved by these ancient tales of friendship," he said.

"Like Antonio and Sebastian in your *Twelfth Night*?" I said.

"Friendship as between Palamon and Arcite," continued WS almost wistfully, and appearing not to notice that I had said anything. "Or Aeneas and Achates from Troy. 'Fidus' Achates, as Vergil calls him. Faithful Achates."

"Yes . . ."

"I ask you whether that steady-burning friendship is not a truer emblem of that eternal and stainless love which we are enjoined to believe in, I mean the love which dwells above – a truer emblem than the passion of Aeneas for Dido, and hers for him, which ended in all the fury of the funeral pyre."

I wondered to hear WS make a comparison like Jack Horner had made, between man-and-woman's love and a violent fire.

"In the olden times, such friendship between men was no doubt possible," he continued.

"But no longer?" I said.

"Olden times become golden times to men's eyes, but our own age is always leaden. Or iron. Heavy, hard."

"But ready to be transmuted?" I said.

"Why yes, Nick," said WS, appearing to notice me again. "Everything can somehow be transmuted, the base metal turned to gold. Or if not, we can make it seem so."

He motioned with his hand at the room, in which lights flared and business-like yet excited activity and talk flowed around us.

"Still, Nick, this is not exactly what I wanted to say to you. In the beaten way of friendship. I have a particular request to make . . ."

Friendship! The word rang in my mind . . .

And while we're on the subject of friendship I might as well tell the tale of my dealings with Mistress Isabella Horner. No, not might as well but must. It's connected with what you've just heard, it has to do with what follows. And I'm finding it increasingly difficult to keep quiet about it. Guilt, I suppose, the need to get it off my chest.

So before I reach my midnight rendezvous in Hart Street with Nemo, here is what we players call . . .

An Interlude

It started one afternoon in the late autumn in the tiring-house. Or, to be precise, it started earlier that day. I was going about my lawful business walking riverwards up Long Southwark. Ahead I could glimpse Great Stone Gate framing the entrance to the Bridge. On either side was a parade of houses and shops which were well enough on this side of the Thames – that is, they were without the airs and graces which might have afflicted them on the other bank. I was glancing vacantly at one when I noticed Master WS slipping out of a doorway. By 'slipping' I don't necessarily mean to imply stealth. Quietness and unobtrusiveness characterised Shakespeare's gait and manner.

I was about to wave or cry out in greeting when I saw that the playwright wasn't alone. A woman followed him close at heels out of the door. She was small and dark-haired. In complexion she was almost swarthy. The two stood together for a moment in the entrance before the woman closed the door behind her. Even then I might have called out but something about the way Master WS inclined his head to catch the words coming from her lips made me think that they would rather not be interrupted at this moment. Not that there was anything secretive about the occasion. I didn't get the impression that either WS or the dark lady was anxious to avoid being seen; neither so much as glanced up or down the thinly peopled street. It was more the easiness that each appeared to have in the other's company, the mutual famil-iarity, which suggested that any third party was bound to be an intruder.

I picked up all this in a long sideways glance and a few forward paces. (Perhaps it is the player's training which imparts to one the ability to read posture and attitude so quickly.) Afraid of being caught out in curiosity, I did not look back to see which direction they were moving in or whether they were even walking together. But as I continued up Long Southwark the image of the two – William Shakespeare and the unknown dark lady – floated through my mind, together with the inevitable questions: Who was she? Whose house where they coming out of (not Master WS's, for I happened to know he lodged in the Liberty of the Clink a few streets off)? And the inevitable question that slips through your mind whenever you see a man and a woman together, close together, easy together – you know the question that I mean.

Then I put them out of mind until that afternoon's performance at the Globe. Or rather after the performance, when we were changing from our costumes into our day-clothes. When players are disrobing in the tiring-house after a presentation, some of us have no greater delight than in picking over performances and comparing them with the previous day's or week's. Once we've looked at ourselves in the glass, as it were, we turn to the audience. You, mere (but dear) spectators or attenders at the event, may be surprised to learn that *your* performance too is assessed and weighed by the players. Like us, you can be good, or bad or indifferent. You might have been quick to understand things that afternoon or, perhaps, especially slow-witted. You will be judged on your attentiveness, your readiness to be distracted, your promptness in laughter, your capacity for tears. Individual members of the crowd will be selected for praise and dispraise: the man who laughed loud and long, the woman who was showing a lot of tit.

As you might expect, it was the younger members of the company who tended to hang around. The older, sensible ones, who had other business or homes to attend to, usually disappeared after a few comradely insults, observations and pleasantries. On the margins of this scene hovered the Tire-man and his assistant, receiving the discarded costumes before lovingly placing them back in store. We'd been playing something not bad in its own way, a madcap piece called *A Merry Old World, My Masters*.

It was the boy-player Martin Hancock who twitted me about a woman he'd noticed among the audience standing next to the stage.

"I tell you, Nicholas, she was much moved by your plight as Quentin. She was all eyes for you, deserted by your lover in favour of that rich old man."

While I was pleased enough to be told that I had touched a member of the audience, I did not quite believe young Master Hancock, particularly because it was he who'd played the faithless young Zanche in our *Merry Old World*.

"You mean she was not looking at you," I said.

"Oh, her eye was for you and it was open," said Hancock, deadpan in his double meanings.

"The one in a scarlet dress, you mean?"

"No, the one *I* mean was in something dark."

"Describe her more exactly."

"She was about my height," he said, "and my colouring but deeper."

"Not fair then?"

"No but certainly not foul neither."

"Well, Martin, I must thank you for seeking out opportunities for me, though I am well enough furnished already."

I was thinking of my Nell.

"Then here comes another piece of furniture, Nick."

"What? Where?"

"The woman I was talking about, the one who was ogling you."

I turned round and glimpsed through the backs and shoulders of my fellows a slight figure making her way across the Tiring-house. It was the same woman I'd seen coming out of the Southwark doorway with WS that morning. This individual was no stranger to some of our company, however. She seemed to be handing out what looked like sweetmeats or confectionary, almost with the air of a mother rewarding good children. Then she approached Jack Horner and clasped him in a quite companionable way. Jack looked a little uncomfortable, as men sometimes do when they are accosted by a loved one at their place of work.

"She is already spoken for, I think," I said to Martin Hancock.

Before he could think up some indecent reply we were interrupted by Jack, still in his costume. The dark woman followed him at heels.

"Nick, Martin, my wife here is eager to meet Quentin and his Zanche."

Master Hancock affected a coy look while I bowed my head slightly, concealing my surprise that this dark-complexioned woman was his spouse. This added another, uh, layer to my glimpse of her and Master WS together.

"Oh Zanche I know well enough, but I haven't seen you before, have I?" she said to me.

"I am newly with the Chamberlain's . . . Mistress . . . Horner," I said, wondering why Martin had pretended to me not to know who she was. "A matter of weeks only."

"I thought so. I would have remembered."

Her voice was not quite English. Thick and sweet, it seemed to come from down in her dark throat.

"I hope you approved of our performance," I said, meaning (naturally) *my* performance and wondering if it was true that this woman had been looking at me on stage in the manner which Martin had described.

"Yes, although I am no great lover of comedy," she said.

"Isabella prefers the blood and guts and rhyming couplets of the old school," said Jack, beginning to unfasten the points of his doublet.

"Women often do," I said airily, at the same time as the name of Isabella jingled in my head like a bell on a horse's bridle. Is-a-bell-a. "It is the men who like true love and happy endings."

"And the players, what do you prefer?"

"You should ask your husband. He's been at this game longer than I have."

"It is quite straightforward. There is only one thing that players prefer, and that is whatever brings them profit," said Jack Horner, now half out of his doublet. He moved away to complete his undressing and to hand his costume to the Tire-man. I had already surrendered my playing clothes. The tiring-house was thinning out. I gazed at Mistress Isabella Horner and she gazed at me. She had a closed, somehow elfish face, with a narrow chin and short, tangled locks of hair. There was something feline about her. Her eyes were as unreadable as a cat's. Master Hancock had been right: she was about his height and colour. I was conscious of young Martin now, standing a little to one side of us and regarding us both. He had said nothing since Jack introduced his wife, but I had the uneasy feeling that he was storing up every word he heard, every glance he glimpsed between us, probably so as to disgorge them later with appropriate commentary among his ribald young peers.

"But I ask you now . . . Nick . . . ?"

"Revill. Ask me what?"

"Master Revill, what is it *you* prefer? Blood and guts? Or happy endings?"

"Happy endings are harder to play," I said. "And I have noticed that the audience is sometimes more cheerful at the end of a tragedy than they are at a comedy."

"That is because the misery of others is often good to behold," she said.

"While their pleasure can be hard to watch," I responded (since we were talking aphoristically).

But now her fresh-faced, uncostumed husband returned.

"Well, Nick, are you going to join us? Martin, you will for sure?"

"That depends on where you're drinking."

We younger players often repaired to one of the many ale-houses of Southwark after a performance.

"No tavern, but the pit instead. My wife wishes to be taken there. In fact, I think she came to see the play today only so that we might go to the pit afterwards."

"Just as she is no great lover of comedy," I said, conscious of sounding slightly priggish, "I do not much like the pit."

"Then you are no true Londoner, Master Revill," said Mistress Horner.

This might have been true but it still stung slightly.

"It is Sackerson today," said Jack. "Or is it Harry Hunks? I forget which."

"No matter," said Mistress Horner, all eager to see some blood and guts. "Let's hurry or they will begin without us."

So I and Martin Hancock together with the Horners made up the foursome that now left the Globe tiring-house. It was a fine late afternoon with a couple of hours of daylight left. The playhouse-goers had dispersed in their various directions; many eastwards to the Bridge or straight up to Bank End to catch a boat to the other side. Some were headed westward like us, and probably with the same destination in mind. The day's pleasures were not yet exhausted; the night's delights twinkled in the distance.

The area around the theatre was criss-crossed with ditches, the contents of which – whether liquid or solid or something in between – rose and fell in languid agreement with the river. Because the bridges across them were narrow, hardly more than a few pieces of planking, we were compelled to travel single file.

Jack Horner led the way across one such bridge with Martin in his wake. As Mistress Horner went ahead of me she slipped, or appeared to do so, and reached back to grasp hold of me. Instinctively, my own hand shot out to save her from the turdy trench. She fell back involuntarily, or seemed to do so, into my chest. At the same time her hands clasped tight hold of both of mine and brought them sharp up against her chest and – to speak a little more pointedly – into the direct region of a nice if diminutive pair of tits. Or so it seemed to me. At the same time, I couldn't help – simply could not help, you understand – wondering whether Shakespeare had ever felt what I had just felt. Not Master Horner, for he obviously must have done, but Master WS.

"Pardon, Master Revill," she said, her voice deep and resonant in her throat. I said nothing. She took some time to regain her balance, and continued to cling close as we made our way across the tiny little bridge. Up ahead of us Master Horner was deep in conversation with young Hancock and hadn't noticed how close to grief his wife had nearly come.

"Thank you, Master Revill," she said when we reached the safety of the far bank of the ditch (all of eight feet away from the other side). Her way of speaking was quite formal, at odds with the apparent familiarity of her movements. Perhaps I'd

been mistaken in thinking that she had stumbled deliberately.
But she was slow to disengage herself from my grasp and,
naturally, I was slow too to relinquish her. She might, after all,
have been about to lose her footing once again and I did not
want to put myself to the trouble of saving her twice.

Our proximity emboldened me to say, "I have seen you
before."

"I dare say you have," she said, "although you've only been
with the Chamberlain's a few weeks."

"It was this very morning."

"Was it indeed?"

"In Long Southwark."

"I know it."

I waited for some further comment, but none came (and
indeed she owed me nothing).

"You were with . . . a . . ."

"A bear?" she said. "An ape I was with?"

"No, neither of those," I said. "Forgive me for prying."

The wooden walls of the Bankside bear-pit loomed up
ahead of us. As usual, there was a crowd of loiterers and ne'er-
do-wells milling about the entrance. I have always looked
down on the crowd that attends the pit, considering that they
are drawn by baser motives than the refined men and women
who frequent the playhouse. This is high-minded and silly,
because often they are one and the same, these men and
women. I might also have remembered that the playhouses are
recent settlers on these southern shores while the animal-
baiting pits are so old as to be native to the ground. Why, the
Bankside had been erected before the days of our Queen's
father!

I hadn't been exaggerating when I said to Mistress Horner
that I had no great liking for the bear-pit or bear-garden. Yes,
I'm aware this puts me in the same camp as the Puritans, who

loathe everything which brings simple pleasure and excitement into the lives of Londoners. Even so, it can't be helped. I don't like the pit, and that's that. I was keeping company with Jack and Martin for friendship, not for the delight of watching Sackerson or Harry Hunks or whichever beast happened to be bear of the day. And I was keeping company with my fellows to keep company with Mistress Horner, if you understand.

When I ask myself why it is that I don't like the sight and sound of the bears and bulls and other animals being tormented, I am forced to conclude that the reason lies with my narrow upbringing in the country. For this taught me that while the beasts of the field are ordained to suffer and endure for the good of humankind – did not God Himself give Adam dominion over them – they are not bound to die for our mere gratification. I know how green and squeamish this must sound. Even so, and you may call me soft-hearted if that's your pleasure, I have detected in the narrow, pink eye of the bear, as it glances at the next wave of dogs to be unleashed against it, a kind of fear, a species of long-suffering, which would almost persuade one that it had feelings not so far removed from our own. And to see the crowd whoop and laugh and revel in the animal's discomfiture, you might be forgiven for wondering sometimes which was the baser of God's creations.

We paid our pennies and climbed up two storeys into one of the galleries. I kept close behind Mistress Horner in case she should choose to tumble back down the stairs and into my arms. Once in the gallery we pushed forward, while Jack and Martin delayed to place their wagers. The blood and guts which the lady had been afraid we might miss hadn't yet been spilled. The fights were often timed to begin soon after the end of the playhouse performances. There's no sense, after all, in offering your audience simultaneous distractions.

There was a deal of stinky, garlicky breath in the gallery, and much pushing and shoving and cursing. To my hostile eye the people here were definitely inferior to the quick, appreciative individuals who applauded us at the Globe. (Mind you, we were in the cheaper part of the bear-garden.) Even the golden air over the arena seemed to have taken on a reddish tinge, as if it had sucked up some of blood and slaver spilled there over the years.

Mistress Horner was the most forward of our little group and reached the front first. In her eagerness to get there she pushed and cursed with the best of them. Once she'd gained the wooden barrier overlooking the pit, she grasped it as if fearful that someone was going to play the usurper on her. I was close at her heels. Gazing out and down from our high vantage point I saw rows of hungry, gaping faces. The beaten earth floor of the arena was stained dark in places. In the centre was a scarred wooden stake, well set into the solid ground. Mounds of rubbish lay against the brick walls at the base of the viewing galleries. Thick clouds of flies wove dirty nets around these mounds. Above all, there was the stench of the pit: a compound of blood and sweat, sun-heated fur and tobacco smoke, shit and fear and excitement.

When the bear-wards led out the great brown beast to the stake in the centre of the ring, a mighty, deep-throated roar rose from the crowd. They were greeting an old friend. His name – "Stubbes!" – was called out with affection, with acclaim. Some of this same crowd would doubtless weep if he were to be mauled to death in the coming engagement. The muzzled Stubbes, secured round the neck by cords which were held firm on either side by two of the bear-wards, shambled on all fours towards the middle of the arena. A long chain also hung down from his neck and trailed clankingly along the ground with him. Stubbes was obviously an old hand at this business, knowing where he was meant to go, and taking the crowd's cheers and shouts as no more than his due. On his flanks and shoulders were patches of lighter fur and even of exposed, raw-looking flesh which marked the wounds of earlier engagements.

Once at the stake he was swiftly fastened to it by the chain. The muzzle remained in place. The bear-wards backed away. The crowd fell silent. My mouth was dry and I could feel my heart thudding in my chest. The bear stayed down on all four limbs, casting his head about a little from side to side. I could see his small eyes. He seemed to be scenting out the direction from which his danger might come.

There was a yowling and yelping, then all at once four great dogs bounded out from a gate on the opposite side of the ring from where we were standing. This is the number that is usually loosed at the beginning of a baiting, the sport being to see how the bear will deal with an attack in force . . .

Forgive me if I have not the appetite to describe the fight to you now. (It is, anyway outside my purpose here, which is to recount my early encounters with Isabella Horner.) Perhaps I will return to the pit on another occasion, and satisfy the desire that some of you no doubt possess to hear a bloody report.

I will simply say that at the end of this engagement there lay five dogs, the original four having been reinforced; five dogs still or twitching in a rough circle about the bear and his stake. Two or three other curs slunk around the perimeter of the pit, their fighting mettle quite cowed by Stubbes the bear's prowess and skill. Nothing – not words or blows, not the sticks or taunts of the bear-wards – could induce them to try their luck once more against the brown foe. Doubtless they might expect a good whipping that night to prepare them for the next session of baiting. Eventually they were called off.

As for Stubbes . . . he was bloody and only a little bowed. He would live to fight another day. He would be carefully tended by the bear-wards, his wounds given time to heal, while word of his skill and ferocity was allowed to spread more widely through the liberties and suburbs in order that the crowd, and the money wagered, would be even greater next time.

As for our little party . . . it was obvious that both Martin Hancock and Jack Horner had taken a little tumble on the outcome of the fight. Mistress Isabella Horner wasn't interested in the wager or, perhaps fortunately for him, in how much money her husband might have thrown away. No, she was interested in the fight. Or, more precisely, she was interested in the blood and gore and slaver of it. As the battle progressed – as Stubbes slashed and tore at the flanks and bellies and muzzles of his persecutors – as they sometimes succeeded, against the odds, in leaving their teeth or claw marks on him – as the howling and the roaring of men, women and beasts rose to new heights – so too did Mistress Horner's enthusiasm for what she was witnessing scale fresh peaks. I knew this because, as I have said, I was crushed in from behind by the weight of the gallery crowd and so was pressed against the dark lady, willy nilly.

This I did not wholly object to, for although she was quite short in stature, she was well-formed in a sinewy fashion. In the crush all were pressed against all. Nevertheless the lady shoved backwards in order to return my, as it were, involuntary push and continued to shove in a manner that was somehow both soft and hard. She was wearing a dark dress of some thin stuff. With that instantaneous and infallible instinct which Mother Nature has given us in such matters, I realised that she could feel and was responding to my own excitement. Not only my excitement at the mounting carnage down below in the arena but the stiffening of my member as she rubbed her buttocks against and around it in a churning motion.

And all this while her husband and the boy-player were right next to us. But then the whole mob in our gallery was utterly distracted. Like every other compartment in the ring, they were intent on the bloody business among the beasts and were anyway shifting, shoving and shouting so much that they would probably have considered the last trump to be the tooting of a penny whistle. I have no doubt, either, that other encounters like that between Mistress Horner and myself were going on round the ring. In the crush of people and the oblivion of spilled blood (as long as it belongs to another) there is something which inflames the baser senses.

Or so I persuaded myself afterwards, in the evening. I was not afflicted with the heart-heaviness that normally comes over me after a visit to a baiting. Instead I felt . . . well . . . full, even engorged. Luckily, Nell was keeping me company that night and I remember that she commented approvingly on my energy. Then, as Nell innocently slept, I penned a note to Isabella Horner, having already established as we left the bear-pit that she, unlike Nell, was able to read. What else would you expect of a lady who is to be seen in the company of William Shakespeare? Actually, if it hadn't been for the way she had conducted herself towards me in the bear-garden I would have left her well alone, judging that she was most likely meat for greater men's tables as well as being the spouse of a fellow-player.

I tucked the note about my person and waited for the opportunity to pass it privily to Mistress Isabella. I was confident she would return to the playhouse; had in fact already learned that that was her intention in the same dialogue in which I had ascertained her skill at letters. Sure enough, she did pay us a return visit in a day or two. And when she repaired to the tiring-house after the performance I slipped her my little epistle, the product of my own little pen. I think she was half expecting such a move. Certainly there was no flinch of surprise when I thrust the folded-up square of paper into her hand. Instead, I noted that it closed round the paper, and round my own hand, with a most promising alacrity.

What was on the paper? Well . . . a poem, and a subscribed suggestion that we should find a mutually convenient time to continue the dialogue which had begun so agreeably at the Bankside bear-pit. I wrote a poem because . . . dare I say it? . . . I was emulating the probable approach of my high-browed fellow, WS. For sure, he wooed whole audiences with words, and ladies in particular would be sure to tumble to his honey tongue. Not that I knew any of this for fact but I presupposed it, clinging to that little fragment of evidence of seeing WS and Isabella Horner emerging together from the house in Long Southwark.

As I say, she clutched at my own little poetic offering. Here was a lady who did not waste time. Her actions spoke not just louder, but instead of, words. As I chatted with my co-players, I noticed her surreptitiously reading my message. When I next glanced in her direction she'd gone. This was disappointing. For a moment I wondered whether I'd offended her.

But not so. For, as I was walking in my street costume down the narrow passage that led away from the tiring-house and out of the Globe, I felt a tug at my sleeve, almost as if it had snagged on a handle. I was in the rearward of a small group, including Jack Horner, as it happened. We were on our way to an ale-house, The Goat & Monkey or The Knight of the Carpet, most likely. I looked round and there, through the crack of a door slightly ajar, shone the dark eyes of Mistress Horner. I hardly had time to take in the sight of her face before the door closed. I made my mumbled excuses to the company – forgotten something – scroll for next day's performance, ring that must've dropped on tiring-house floor, word that had to be exchanged with the Tire-man about my costume – made my excuses, catch up with you later, dropped back, counted twenty, rapped soft on door – and was admitted, in every sense.

It was dark. This was one of those tiny interior rooms, and one which I hadn't come across before, more like a press or a closet, probably used for storage. I realised afterwards that Mistress Horner must know the Playhouse well, either that or she had found this corner by chance. There was something material on the floor to take off its hardness, but not by much. Mistress Horner and I, we tussled in the dark and I was soon underneath and she on top, where she impaled herself most gladly. She was as lithe and slippery as a weasel and it was soon finished.

So it began.

A closet may be a good enough place to commence an amour but it is not necessarily appropriate for its continuance. I have to admit also that I was unhappy about taking my pleasure at my place of work. I suppose there may have been an element of guilt or shame in this. I did not like the idea of the Globe playhouse, the seat of so much that was admirable and refined, becoming the cistern of our lust. I was also a little uneasy at the prospect of being seen with Isabella by Master WS (and to a lesser extent by Jack Horner). For though I was perhaps emulating our playwright in my pursuit of this dark lady, I did not care to let him see this.

On one of our early occasions together I said, "You have been careful with that note I sent you?"

I really wanted her to comment on the poem I had penned. The accompanying note, about continuing a 'dialogue', did not give much away. But the poem, with its talk of flashing orbs, coral lips and dark locks, was much more revealing. I considered it one of my best effusions. Not that I'd ever claim to be a poet.

"Note?"

"Before our first . . . you know."

"I have it somewhere about the place. You are not the first to send me notes."

"Or poems?"

"Or poems."

My heart beat a little quicker because, you see, I had not yet dared to approach the subject of her connection to WS. I was most eager to discover whether I was indeed following the playwright's trail. Indeed, I wondered whether it was not in some sense because I believed that *he* had been in this position with Isabella – viz. bed – that I wasn't here too, now. That, and her brisk and avid seduction of me conjoined, had put me where I was.

"Does Jack send you poems?"

"A husband does not send his wife poems," she said. "Besides, does he look like a poet?"

"What does a poet look like?" I said, hoping that she would make some affectionate and flattering reply. Instead, she looked thoughtful as though my question was a real one.

"It is more what he looks *at*, or *how* he looks, that makes him a poet," she said somewhat cryptically.

She was similarly unforthcoming on my attempts to find out where she came from. There was something unEnglish, unstolid, about Isabella. I wondered if there was some gypsy in her; that, or a strain of something hot and southern. She had decided strong appetites that needed satisfying and brooked no obstacles.

We required somewhere to meet and she did not consider

my Coven-quarters adequate, once I'd given her a brief description of them. She encouraged me on a handful of occasions to come to the place she shared with Jack, claiming that her husband was often out in the evenings. These lodgings were indeed a part of the house in Long Southwark where I'd first glimpsed her. I fell in with this proposal somewhat unwillingly but always supposing her to have more to lose by the arrangement than I, if things went wrong.

Mistress Isabella generally knew if Master Jack was going to be absent on a particular evening – where he went I never enquired, nor did she seem inclined to volunteer the information (if she ever knew in the first place) – and she contrived an ingenious way of signalling to me whether she expected to be 'unoccupied' for a few hours.

She was in the habit of bringing to the playhouse some little gift of comestibles for the players – or at least for those, like Martin Hancock and now myself, who were close to her husband. This was the avowed reason she had come to the tiring-house on the first occasion we'd met. She was a good cook, producing excellent comfits and sweetmeats and other confectionery. Now our secret signal was this: if her little cakes contained raisins, then the coast was clear for that night, the gates unguarded and her portals open. If, on the other hand, the cakes contained no raisins then it signified that she expected her husband to be at home that evening.

You may imagine with what appetite I bit each time into one of her sweeetmeats, sometimes proferred direct by her if she was attending a performance but more often conveyed to the playhouse by husband Jack. Little did he suspect that, as he was passing around this tasty evidence of his wife's skill at grinding, mixing and baking, he was actually sending a stealthy love-message. About all this I felt a curious exultation, but one admixed with some guilt and discomfiture. In the end, the guilt and discomfiture gained the upper hand. For might it not have been said as I eagerly looked out for those cakes containing raisins, that I was actually looking out to 'raise sin' with Mistress Horner. (Forgive the pun, which I consider to be bad enough for Master William Shakespeare himself.) But the joke masks a serious face. I am sufficiently my parson-father's son to know what a sin is. Oddly, the times I spent with Nell had a kind of openness and harmlessness to them, compared with the dark weasel-y hours in Mistress Horner's company.

On another of our bed-encounters together I asked her, "Do you know Master Shakespeare?"

"Master Shakespeare?"

"Our playwright and shareholder in the Chamberlain's."

"Oh, you know that I know some of you."

"Like this?"

"There are too many lovers of boys in the playhouses for much of this."

"Not in the Chamberlain's," I said indignantly.

She rolled her cat-eyes.

"Your question is an impertinent one in any case."

"Then it is as well you haven't answered it."

I was obviously going to discover very little about her. Not the least of the mysteries surrounding her was how she'd inveigled Jack into marriage – for some reason, this was how I put it to myself. Jack was open and guileless while she was dark and secretive, and passionate.

However, I did not feel happy or at ease with her. There was an itch scratched, an urge blunted, but nothing more. I felt somehow to one side of Isabella, not central as I was with my Nell. And this was perhaps not unfair, since my own interest in Mistress Horner had first been provoked by seeing her in the playwright's company.

Accordingly, after only a few exchanges – and I promise those of you who worry about my behaviour, it was only a few exchanges – well, not *that* many – in her (and Jack's) bed, I steeled myself to declare that I no longer wished to enjoy her company in this fashion.

"Why is this?" she said, turning on me. We were not yet lying down and, if I had my unwicked way with her, we never would be again. For I had determined on this little scene and speech before we descended bedwards, considering that my virtuous edge would be blunted by any other course.

"I am Jack's friend," I said, "and I cannot continue to be his and your friend – in this fashion."

I gestured at the bed which lay between us.

"Admit that this is nothing to do with friendship, this is because I do not satisfy your curiosity, your endless questions about Master Shakespeare – and others."

"I don't know what you mean," I said (though I did).

"I will not be left," she said, advancing round the bed to stand near me.

"I'm sure there are many – I mean, there must be—"

She slapped me across the face. Water started to my eyes. "You shall not leave me. *Me.*"

I backed away as she advanced with both hands raised and fingers crooked, ready to rake my cheeks. My brimming eyes made her image wobble.

I thought I heard her hiss but it was probably imagination.

"This began at the pit," I said, my breath coming short, "but it is not necessary that it should end with a fight too."

I ducked as she swung a hooked arm across my head.

"We may still be friends – in other ways," I said, absurdly in the circumstances. "Please."

The other arm raked at me from the opposite direction.

102

I almost vaulted across the bed and with it once again between us secured a breathing-space. I am no expert in close combat. I was, in truth, afraid of her. I might grab her round the middle but unless I could control her flailing claws I feared that my face would be marked.

"Look," I said, "I have an idea – which I will tell – as long as you keep your distance."

"And I tell you I will not be left, Master Revill," she said.

"But I tell you that you may leave *me*," I said, having an inkling of what this was about. "I tell you that you should leave me."

"Why?"

Her hands dropped to her side. She gazed at me across the field of battle and pleasure, the deferred field, its surface slightly dented by my vault.

"Because – because – I am no real lover of women."

"Say you so?"

"Yes."

"Your body seemed to say otherwise."

"Then my body belies my heart. My true taste is for others of my own sex. I am guilty of that sin which the ancient Greeks approved of."

I regretted these words almost as soon as they were out of my mouth. They were hostages to fortune. To confess to what I was confessing to, even perhaps to a friend, was to take a risk. To confess it to a possible enemy was foolhardy. I saw suddenly that a lie can be as dangerous as the truth.

"You are a filthy pederast."

I bridled at this, almost as if I were genuinely what I was claiming to be and yet wanted to distinguish myself from the worst of the caste.

"No, no, I have no ingles."

"Ingles?"

"No catamites, no attendant boys . . . those I am not interested in, but grown men only."

"Like my husband?"

"Well, I . . ."

"You said you could not be friends with him and me."

Now that she asked this, I was forced to consider an answer, and my hesitation perhaps testified to a momentary doubt in my own mind – hadn't I been drawn towards Jack Horner pretty well ever since joining the Chamberlain's? Were I so inclined, he might well be my bent. On the other hand, my hesitation could be ascribed to tact, a natural unwillingness to confess to the wife a shared partiality for the husband.

"Yes, so I said . . ."

I hung my head down in mock-acknowledgement of what she'd suggested. She stood, still on the far side of the bed, gazing at me with an expression that I read as being somewhere between amusement and amazement. At least her claws were sheathed.

"You're joking, Master Revill."

"No joke."

"I do not believe you."

"Whether you do or not, it is so."

"So, you are determined that we shall not encounter each other here again?"

"Yes," I said, mustering firmness. "Since I am travelling on a different route, Mistress Horner."

"What did I say about players? You're all the same."

"We are not," I began, then remembered that it would be better to agree with her. "Well, obviously some of us are . . ."

"But *you* think you can travel on two roads at once, do you, Master Revill?"

"This has been a deflection from my true course," I said,

glancing down at the unrumpled bed and then across at her. "A pleasant deflection, naturally," I added quickly, seeing her eyes narrow.

"Unnaturally, you had rather say," she said.

I shrugged rather than be drawn further down the road of metaphor. She, however, had more to deliver in this vein.

"You will not be reformed?"

"If anyone could have reformed me, it would have been *you*, Mistress Isabella."

For the first time it occurred to me that she had, in her litheness and hardness, something of the boy.

"Then if you still wish to be reformed, you will accept something which can put you on the correct path and take you away from those filthy by-ways that you tread."

"Very well," I said, not having the least idea what she was proposing.

She bent down and rummaged in a little box that sat on the floor. From it she withdrew a small green glass bottle.

"There. Go on, take it. It has no teeth. It is a potion to put your heart in order – if you wish."

For the sake of quietness, I accepted the proffered phial.

"You have tasted my cakes and raisins. You know that I am an expert maker and blender. Now, when you tire of treading your boys' by-paths, you should drink from my little bottle, and you will find yourself restored to the highway of women."

"Why didn't you give it to me straight without saying anything?" I asked. "If it is so potent."

"I had no idea of your leanings before. And now our skirmish is over, Master Revill. Come back when you have tasted my potion."

I almost feared her calmness as much as her fury; certainly I trusted it less. However, I promised to keep the bottle safe and sound, and to drink it if I felt the wind changing direction and my weathercock swinging accordingly. Of course, the first thing I did when I got back to my lodgings was to put the green bottle in a safe place. I was about as likely to drink my own piss as taste the contents of Mistress Horner's potion. More likely, actually.

Middle

Wednesday 4 February – Sunday 8 February 1601

Just after midnight I made my way to the corner of Hart Street, as instructed by Nat the Animal Man. The February night was again crisp, clear, cold. The close-set houses clustered about me, all dark and inquisitive. My heart thudding, I waited to be surprised, as on the earlier evening – and learned, incidentally, that waiting to be surprised is more troubling to one's well-being and tranquillity of mind than simply being surprised. Would I be taken off, blindfolded, to be addressed by Robert Cecil once more? Would I have to hop and dance through the dark streets again?

I have to say that I already felt dizzy and benighted. So many people seemed to be making demands of me, and insinuating that on my compliance hinged the welfare of the state. So much was obscure and likely to remain so. One demand clashed with another. Loyalty to my sovereign lady the Queen was one thing, loyalty to the Chamberlain's Company was another, and it did not seem as though the two loyalties were destined to meet and shake hands. Apart from this, there was my respect and, dare I say it?, affection for Messrs Burbage, Shakespeare, Phillips, etc. which was a thing almost apart from my allegiance to the Company. Yet there

107

could be no doubt from what what Sir Robert had told me – and from what I had overheard for myself in the Book-keeper's office during the morning – that some very grave matter was at hand.

I remembered once again that rumble of thunder heard by a child walking on a country track.

"Master Revill?"

This time the figure seemed to rise up in front of me like a column of dirty smoke. The voice, soft, pervasive, was that of my conductor of the other evening. He was a darker figure against a dark night. And now he owned a name. Nemo: nobody.

"Follow me, sir."

I heard his footsteps clacking on the cobbles. No supporter emerged to usher me by the arms. I was trusted to follow. But I was certain that if I failed to follow him voluntarily I would be compelled to do so. We were heading down towards the black, glittering river. A shivering draught blew off the water as if a door had been left open to a cold world that lay even beyond the night.

The sound of the feet in front changed from striking on stone to the hollower thud of board. A moment later I was treading on a little wooden jetty. A torch burned forlornly at the end. It was low-tide. The head of a ladder led down into darkness. Of my guide there was no sign.

"Oh step down."

The voice came from below.

I do not like being told where to go. More, I do not like boats. I've never glimpsed the wide open sea, and see no reason to – the Bristol Channel was enough for me. I will not willingly exchange the firm-set earth for the slipperiness of water. Nevertheless I turned about and clambered down the ladder. The deck rocked very slightly as if in confirmation of my arrival. Nemo must have had others to assist him because the torch was suddenly withdrawn from the head of the jetty and, at either end of the boat, I felt rather than saw oars or poles thrust against the wooden piles. With a little lurch we were pushed off from the land and launched out onto the dark current.

All around was pitch black. I was afraid to move in case I stumbled over a coil of rope or other maritime lumber and toppled head-first into the river. Beside me stood my companion, his breath coming in soft sighs. Then he grasped me by the arm and ushered me through a gap in some thick fabric which seemed to serve as the entrance to one of the low little huts on deck. It was smoky inside this makeshift room. A slight light came from a couple of candles in the corners and – for heat on this sharp midnight – a tripod of glowing charcoal stood to one side. There were no seats; instead, large cushions were scattered about in apparent invitation to recline. I thought of a Roman general on campaign against some tribe of barbarians. The motion of the boat could be felt underfoot and there was the occasional muffled movement of an oar or the slop of water against the side.

"Lay yourself down, sir, make yourself at ease."

Nemo's voice came from close over my right shoulder. I made an abrupt shift around, spinning on my heel, for I wanted to get him full in the face, to take the measure of the man. I was tired of secrecy and subterfuge. I turned rapidly, intending to give my guide a small surprise. He turned his own face quickly away but the precaution was unnecessary. The light in the cabin was very dim and, anyway, he had smeared his countenance with some blacking substance. His eyes alone glittered.

"I prefer to remain obscure. It is better so."

So saying, keeping his face averted, he touched me lightly

on the breast with his fingertips (I shrank slightly from him) and I almost fell back on one of the cushions littering the tiny cabin. Then this strange being, clad in nondescript grey or black, tall enough to have to stoop as he moved across from me, settled himself on the far side of the room. The tripod of hot charcoal caused the dusky air to shimmer and I had the sensation that I was looking into a dream, or a nightmare, in which all identity became an unknown or shifting question.

"Have we stopped moving? We are no longer moving, are we? Where are we?"

I was no longer conscious of any motion from the boat, nor was there any sound from outside.

"We are somewhere off-shore, anchored in mid-stream."

"Safe from either bank," I said.

"You speak more wisely than you know, sir. The walls of this cabin are well-quilted, as you may see. Sounds are deadened. We are away from prying eyes and ears."

For all the contact I felt with reality, we might as well have been floating through the empty air in our little sealed, tent-like chamber.

"Is the world so curious to know what you do?" I said.

"The world is a curious place and a perilous one," he said. "There is much to guard against."

"I do not understand . . ." I began. "I do not understand what you do, what the part you play is."

"I am like the night watchman. I work while others sleep," said Nemo. "Indeed, I work so that others *may* sleep. I walk the streets and, seeing a flame creeping from the corner of your house, I shout 'Fire!'" – he delivered the exclamation without raising his soft voice – "and so save lives and goods. Or I grab hold of that rogue who is now, even now, making his stealthy way towards the casement which your foolish housewife has left ajar. There are outbreaks of fire in the great ship of state. There are always windows left carelessly ajar."

"We live in troubled times," I said, trying to match my interlocutor's portentousness.

"These are indeed troubled times," Nemo echoed. "There are mad plots that you would scarcely credit. For instance, there is a certain gentleman who is planning to dry up the river that we are floating on at this present moment."

"Dry it up – how?"

"With a species of burning-glass. And then there is another individual who lives in Finsbury and who is in the pay of Spain."

"I suppose he intends to extinguish the sun."

"No. He is training up an ape in the art of assassination. Him we have not moved against yet, but the moment the ape shows signs of being able to wield a knife proficiently we will arrest the both of them."

"The ape too?"

"Would you leave a murderous ape at large, sir?"

I said nothing. The little chamber that we sat in might have been the product of an addled brain.

"And there are deeper, more perilous currents. Men who are to be taken more seriously. I believe you know who I am referring to. There is a man has a house on the Strand."

"The Earl of—"

"Shh. No names. Though I must tell you that there is more than one earl in question. And then there is another man. A commoner. William Shakespeare."

"Shakespeare," I said. "I seem to recognise the name."

I struggled in the gloom of the cabin to make out the ash-coloured face of my interlocutor as he nestled in a mound of cushions on the other side of the cabin. But his countenance, his whole form, wavered in the close, stuffy air. His voice remained soft, even when describing absurd conspiracies, even when uttering threats.

"Tell me your dealings with Shakespeare."

"He is my employer. He and Master Burbage and the other shareholders in the Chamberlain's."

"I do not mean in the way of ordinary business."

"I am not sure what business you mean, then."

"Let us leave that for the moment," said Nemo. "First tell me about the dialogue between Master Phillips and Sir Gelli Merrick."

The reference did not take me by surprise.

"If you know of it already, why do you need to ask?"

"This is not a test of them, sir. It is a test of you."

"I wish to speak to Master Secretary."

"You were fortunate to be granted one interview with him. Even he cannot be everywhere at once or available to all. Come, tell me what passed between Phillips and Merrick. If everything is above board, you are doing no disservice to your company of players."

"We are asked to perform a play, no more," I said.

"That I know. And to be paid forty shillings and so on."

"What more is there to say?"

"Most of the tale is in the telling. I want to know what *you* made of the scene. I want to know how you construed it."

So I told this strange, dirty-faced man what I had overheard in the Book-keeper's office, although first I had to explain the circumstances under which I came to be there. Then I described how Master Augustine Phillips had seemed suspicious or sceptical of the request made by Sir Gelli. How he had fingered it first, before giving assent.

"How did he give assent?" said Nemo. "Willingly? With understanding?"

"As far as I could tell, it seemed to be be no more than a matter of business," I said.

"Like your dealings with Master Shakespeare and the others?"

"Not at all," I said. "That is a business tempered with shared aims, shared pleasures and hopes. But this thing with Merrick, if that is his name—"

"That is his name."

"It was a transaction only."

"Simply business?"

"We all have to earn a living. Those of us who are unlucky enough not to be born earls."

"I think it may be lucky you mean – before this is concluded."

"Should I really call you Nemo?" I said, trying to wrest some advantage from him.

"That is how I am known here."

"So on this boat you are Captain Nemo, and when you seize innocent men from the street you are . . . what are you then?"

The figure facing me seemed to dissolve into the smoky air, so ill-lit, so hazy was the tiny cabin.

"I am nobody. Be content not to know, sir."

"I have no choice," I said.

"What you have said is half a story. Now tell me what transpired with Master Shakespeare. You were seen talking with him alone in a corner of the Revels Office for a good quarter of an hour."

I did not register surprise that he knew about my recent dialogue with WS at the *Twelfth Night* rehearsal. To be honest, I would not have been surprised if he'd informed me of the exact colour of my stool that morning.

"Yes, we did speak," I said.

It occurred to me, in a little burst of scruple, that what had passed between Master WS and me was privileged conversation, unlike that between Phillips and Merrick at which I had been an unacknowledged and unwilling third. This distinction stood out very clear in my mind and I tried to explain it to the dark figure on the other side of the cabin, hoping, I suppose, that he might release me of the necessity of informing on Master WS. For I could well see that what I had been asked to do cast the great playwright in no very favourable light. Foolishly, I muttered something about loyalty.

But it was futile.

"This is no light matter, sir," said Nemo. "I can see well that you are actuated by loyalty to your Company, and to the individuals who compose it. No bad thing. But there are other, greater loyalties."

He paused.

"Besides . . . if you want to turn to loyalties now . . ."

"Yes?" I said, half knowing what was coming.

"There is the question of your friendship with Mistress Isabella Horner."

Something curled and puckered inside me.

"Yes – I – what has that . . . ?"

"Loyalty is not divisible, I think," said Nemo. "What would your friend Jack Horner say if he knew how his wife was occupied? And who was occupying her."

"It is finished," I said then added, "but although he is a peaceful man he would not be pleased, I think."

"Beware those mild men," said Nemo mildly. "Worse still, what would the senior men of your Company say, Shakespeare and the Burbages and the rest?"

"They are men of the world . . . anyway Master Shakespeare himself . . ."

"Yes?"

"Never mind."

"Of course they are men of the world, as you say. This is not a moral question. But you are a newcomer to the Chamberlain's, are you not, with your three months' experience?"

"Rather more than four," I said, aware that to quibble about such a detail was already to admit defeat. Nemo didn't even bother to acknowledge my correction. For a moment I wished that I was being confronted with Master Secretary Cecil. Perhaps naively, I imagined that he would have been more understanding.

"They would not applaud the cuckolding of one member of the Company by another?"

"Perhaps not," I replied, aware – as Nemo must have been aware – that companies of players, like other small groups of men with a common purpose, are held together by multitudinous, almost invisible threads of duty, mutual need and obligation. Confused by lust, I had carelessly slashed at some of those threads. My earlier conversation with Jack Horner had hinted at my discomfort, even my shame.

"But my lips are tight shut on this matter," said Nemo.

"Provided I am open about what Master Shakespeare requested of me?"

"Just so."

I was exasperated, less with Nemo and the secret machinery that lay behind him, than with myself. I had been trapped with all my high-minded talk of loyalty.

So I told Master Secretary's grey-faced agent what had been requested of me by England's leading playwright. Even if *I* didn't properly grasp what Master WS meant by the words I was expected to convey, it was evident that they had meaning for others. He made me repeat Shakespeare's words several times over, I mean the words that I had to pass on.

"You are sure that was what he said?" said Nemo. "That *that* is what he wants you to say?"

"His very words," I said.

"No more?"

"No more."

"You were seen to talk together for several minutes. And all for these few words?"

"Men may talk together."

"Men should not talk quiet and private in the public gaze. It invites speculation."

"We talked of friendship."

"His and yours?"

"I would be proud to count him as a friend, but we talked in, ah, more general terms. Of the friendships of antiquity. Of Damon and Pythias. Of Aeneas and Achates."

"You know that he and . . . this gentleman you have mentioned . . . the Earl of Southampton . . . were once friends."

"I do not know it."

"And are so still perhaps?"

"I do not know that either."

"That is what we have to determine, whether they are still friends."

"You could do so without my help."

"No, sir. You are very essential in this matter. You are our man in this matter."

"I am nobody's man," I said indignantly.

"Not even Mistress Horner's?" he said.

"Not hers neither, no more."

"Well, well, we shall see," he said. "In the meantime we ask you to do no more than Master Shakespeare requests of you. That is, to deliver this message to his old friend."

"And . . . ?"

"To observe how it is received and, if occasion demands, to report it to me."

"I am no tell-tale."

"It is a tell-*truth* that we require. You think that you are betraying your fellows but I say that you are not. You are defending the realm and you are defending them too. It is for their well-being and their protection that as much as possible be known. In knowledge lies safety."

With these words and other similar ones this man shuffled me off. At some stage in our conversation the boat must have been directed back to the shore for when grey-face uncoiled himself to signify that we had finished and then ushered me out of his close, quilted cabin, I found that we were again in the shadow of a pier. The tide had risen while we were talking and I had fewer rungs of the ladder to climb. When I regained the wooden jetty I turned about. But already the boat was being pushed off by unseen hands and of Nemo there was no sign.

I was getting too old for these late nights. serving the state. I made my way back to the Coven. Now, I am not usually troubled about crossing my home patch, by day or night. It is true that Southwark is commonly regarded by those superior folk who live on the other bank as a lawless waste (though I've observed that that doesn't stop them coming across in boat-loads to take their pleasure). But if you're native to an area, even if you're a recent native like me, you discount their well-bred fears and fables, at the same time as taking a bit of pride in them. A finely jewelled lady, a gentleman decked out in valuables, yes, such people would be fools if they strolled our streets after dark. But indigence is its own protection. Why attack a poor player? He's left the most valuable item he's ever worn – his costume – behind him at the playhouse. The most precious thing about his person is likely to be the scroll from the Book-man containing his part for the next day's performance, and unless I'm much mistaken the renegades of Southwark do not assail a man for a pennyworth of verse or a cupful of prose.

So I considered myself safe.

Tonight, however, walking away from Nemo's strange river-craft and stranger words, I felt myself the object of a thousand eyes and half as many dagger- or club-wielding hands. Lurking behind every bush or tree or wall, tucked into every hole and corner, creviced in the night, were shadows who were waiting for me. And there were many, many shadows on that star-riddled night. There was something in the air. I remembered Nemo's talk about plots. Well, the razor-sharp air was certainly infected tonight. With suspicion and unease and plain mischief.

There! What was the shape shifting stealthily out from behind the bole of that tree? Something rubbed its hands in the bottom of the ditch I'd just leapt over. A cough scraped the night. A portion of wall detached itself from its surroundings, dusted itself down and set off into the dark. My breath plumed out in front of me. I started to run. The cold air had already seized on the muddy ruts and puddles in the path so that they were slippery and brittle underfoot. Over the sound of my own panting I heard behind me a wheezing that could have been exhaled breath. In fact, I was near certain I could hear a twin pumping of breath – so there were at least two of them! I glanced over my shoulder – a double mistake, because I could see nothing anyway and because I skidded and almost fell. My home the Coven – ha! home – was a couple of hundred yards away. Despite the cold, beads of sweat were running down my forehead and into my eyes. The straggle of buildings on either side jumped and blurred to my sight.

As my feet thudded and slithered over the ground, my

mind ran too. Ran not rationally, but frantically, as I considered the possible identity and purpose of my pursuers. Was it Captain Nemo and his invisible minions, come to catch me and haul me back to the boat? Perhaps it was my own fellows from the Chamberlain's who thought that I was betraying them to Sir Robert Cecil, and who were running after me to tell me that they no longer wished me in their Company?

There was something dream-like, or rather nighmarish, in this jumble of thoughts – and nightmarish too in my panicky, skidding progress along the hard, muddy road that lead to the Coven. Finally I reached my ramshackle house, fell against the door, fumbled for the key, scrabbled for the hole, pushed the key home and twisted it violently. The door fell open under my weight and I tumbled through and slammed it shut with myself safe on the other side. After a moment, I peeped through one of the many cracks in the door. The road outside lay quiet. The frost and fresh ice glittered under the half-moon and the starlight. I waited. And waited. But no shape or shadow passed along the way. After a time my breathing calmed and my heart stopped banging.

Someone coughed behind me and I near shed my skin in fright. But it was only one of the sisters, curled up in a corner. I couldn't tell whether she was awake or not but I bade her goodnight anyway and tottered up the rickety stairs to bed.

The morning after my midnight encounter with Captain Nemo was as shadowed as my mind. Dirty clouds were draped low across the town. Everything felt enclosed, as if the streets, even the wide river, were roofed over. Here we stood at that moment in winter when you think warm days will never come again; it was the very antipodes of summer, not winter's midpoint by the calendar, perhaps, but by that inward almanac which men keep in their minds.

It was the Strand which I was making my way along. Now this is the thoroughfare which has some claim to be the grandest and most important in our capital for it links Whitehall to Temple Bar, and might be said to be the axis on which the metropolis turns. Lining this route are some of the finest houses – or at least their roofs and chimneys – you could ever hope to glimpse over high garden walls. Yet the road here was full of water-filled holes and pitfalls, in urgent need of repair, while rubbish lay piled amply against walls and in corners. It was hardly surprising that discerning or hurried travellers preferred the river to the streets.

Yet neither the weather nor the parlous state of the London highways occupied my mind. I was on my way to one of the greatest of the Strand mansions at the request of one of the greatest – no, the very greatest – authors of our age. For Master William Shakespeare, no less, had entrusted me with a message, which, to be truthful, I did not completely under-stand (did not in fact understand at all), to be delivered to a certain gentleman who was temporarily residing there. Usually I would be pleased enough to run an errand for our playwright for, quite apart from my natural regard for him, I considered that I owed my position with the Chamberlain's Men to his and Burbage's influence. Nevertheless this was no common errand, such as visiting a printer or passing a word to a lady. There was an element of danger in it.

'I have many enemies in Orsino's court.' Ever alert to the similitudes between art and life, I could not but think of the part I played in Master WS's *Twelfth Night*, that of Sebastian's loving saviour, Antonio. When Sebastian (Jack Horner) sets off for the capital of Illyria, he bids farewell to the sea-captain (Nick Revill) who has rescued him from the ocean, thinking that he will never encounter him again. Antonio would like to accompany his friend but Sebastian prefers solitude, claiming that he doesn't want his bad luck to affect Antonio too. Nevertheless, Antonio is so drawn by love that he resolves to tread in his departing friend's footsteps. I could not say that I was drawn by *love*, exactly, to do WS's bidding. Respect, yes; gratitude, yes; and that hope of standing well in the eyes of men whom we like. Still, whatever urged me on, here I was, walking into a nest of malcontents. Little wonder that Antonio's words circled round in my head – 'I have many enemies in Orsino's court'. Despite that danger, despite the enemies, Antonio goes there to protect a friend. Was this what I was doing? Or was I helping to damn him?

And who was I working for?

I had hardly entered into this affair, yet already I felt myself to be in a labyrinth. Still thinking of the two scenes of the previous night, the rehearsal in the Revels Office and then the boat-bound encounter with Nemo, I was wrapped up in uncertainty, so wrapped up that I almost fell headlong into an extensive water-filled cavity in the middle of the Strand. I was only saved from a soaking and, no doubt, stinking arrival at my destination by the shout of a carter whose plodding nag was about to butt me in the back. Nimbly sidestepping the stem-and-stern hazards of pond and cart – to the evident disappointment of a clutch of loiterers and loungers who seemed gathered at this spot in the hope of seeing their betters take a tumble – I looked around with more attention and realised that I had indeed reached my goal.

The mansion of the Earl of Essex is grand enough to be styled, simply, Essex House. It draws back from the street some way behind its high walls, and its ample upper storey looks down on us common folk in the common thoroughfare. The main gates were tight shut but there was a postern to one side. About this little entrance clustered another knot of loiterers and I realised that the presence of so many idlers in this part of the Strand was not solely in the hope of seeing passengers fall down into holes. Rather, they were drawn like flies to decaying meat, or carrion to a battlefield. No one knew what was going to happen; but *something* was surely going to happen, some stir and disturbance perhaps involving more than the few cracked heads and snapped limbs of your usual street broil. No one knew when it was going to happen either; but there was in the air the same charged anticipation that presages a thunderstorm. It was, if I may compare great things with small, like the ripple of expectation that traverses our audience just before we begin proceedings at the Globe. Except that here was no innocent playing of the pulling down of old kings and the elevation of new ones. Here was, perhaps, the thing itself. The idea was enough to make my heart beat painfully loud in my ears.

Dry-mouthed and short-breathed, I moved towards the little gateway. I have to say that I was tempted to turn about and make again for my lodgings. But a combination of the trust which WS had reposed in me and the veiled threats and persuasion applied by Nemo, and his master Sir Robert Cecil, were just adequate to propel my unwilling limbs towards my lord of Essex's domain.

The little band of men near the door parted slowly and in an aggrieved fashion, reluctant to let by a newcomer who, from his costume, could not be anybody of great significance. One roused himself to spit near my feet. Far from being mere idlers, they plainly regarded themselves as custodians of the doorway. Nevertheless I reached and crossed the threshold, beyond which was a large court. To one side was the door-keeper's hutch. Now, these fellows are often surly, and as reluctant to admit anyone as St Peter. They are bred for the purpose, thick-set and short-tempered. They look for reasons to turn visitors away.

But the Essex House doorkeeper was different.

He was finely dressed, by contrast with the majority of those occupying this post, who affect a costume that suggests they are newly returned from the wars. But my friend here, lounging against the door-jamb of his lodging, was a picture.

His dark hair was worn in love-locks, hanging down like curtains on either side of his face and coming to rest in a curl on each shoulder. It is a fashion I have briefly considered (and rejected) for myself, my hair not being fine or abundant enough for the task. He had a little pencil beard but a luxuriant moustache which stuck out cockily. His eyes were hard and his nose exact. His doublet was richly embroidered, with a lace-edged ruffle peeping out; and all the rest of him was cut from the same fine cloth. I would have set him down as harmless enough and only describe him at a little length here to show how one may be misled by appearances.

He looked a query at me but did not deign to open his small mouth.

"My name is Revill. I come with a message for a gentleman who, I believe, is staying here."

He said nothing.

"I have to convey the message in person," I said. "I cannot give it to any third party."

He still said nothing, but continued to regard me through his sceptical optics.

"Come, sir, will you admit me?"

No response, but a slight pout of the lips showed what he thought of me and my message.

I made to go past him, in search of some more receptive individual. But before I had moved a couple of paces I was seized by the upper left arm while a hand darted over my right shoulder. I felt a sharp jab under the chin.

"Do not move. Or I push zis *daga sotto vostra lingua*. Tong-ee – *capisce?*"

His voice, I noted in my distraction, was surprisingly deep. As he threatened, I could feel it resonate against my backbone. And I wondered why he was using a foreign tongue. His hot breath puffed at my ear and his moustache tickled the back of my head. He smelled foreign and garlicky.

"Be easy," I said. He surely would not do me damage here, in broad daylight, in the open court of Essex House. Why, the yard was crowded with gallants and others wandering about, though they did not seem much troubled by the to-do at the gate. Perhaps it was customary to greet unrecognised visitors in this way.

For answer he jabbed harder under my chin, and I felt myself rising involuntarily on tiptoe to accommodate his point.

"I am not, 'ow you say, eezy," he said. "You are not eezy neither until you tell me your buzz – your bizz – *gli affari.*"

"I – tell you – I—"

It was hard to get the words out through an overstretched throat. Fear was drying me up too. I had a sudden vision of my gorge, naked to his naked steel. He must have realised that I was hardly able to speak because his grip on my upper arm relaxed slightly while the pressure of the dagger point was eased.

"I am only a messenger," I swallowed. "I have a message."

"*La parola.* Give me *la parola.*"

"I – I do not know—"

"*Parola.* You say watchword, be a good boy," he hissed hotly to my ear. "I give you 'ow it start, and you have to finish. It start: 'God save – '."

Utter those words to any Englishman and by instinct he will add 'the Queen'. I just stopped myself from adding them, aware that I was in a place where men did not hold the Queen in high regard.

"—the King. God save the King, I say," I said.

I had no doubt that, if this foreigner was representative of the strange band gathered together in Essex House, then they intended to displace our divinely appointed sovereign with one of their own creation, viz, the Scottish James, or even my lord of Essex himself. So much had Secretary Cecil hinted to me. So much, indeed, was the whispered gossip of the town. Therefore I considered that saying 'the King' was the least dangerous thing in a perilous situation. It might be enough to indicate that I was of *their* party. Pray God it might be. Pray God he understood me.

(Yet even in this extremity I had given a jesuitical, tergi-versating answer – one which might not satisfy any inquisitors if I were put to the question but which nevertheless satisfied me in the depths of my conscience. I had heard that our Elizabeth often referred to herself as 'King', perhaps in tribute to her long-dead father, perhaps in the desire to arrogate masculine qualities to herself. Therefore, to avoid the sacrilege of wishing another set up in her place, I brought her image to my mind's eye even as I uttered the words, 'God save the King'.)

This answer, whether it was the watchword or no, appeared partly to satisfy my assailant too. His grip relaxed further and the steel point was altogether withdrawn from under my chin. I sensed it still hovering however. At the edge of my vision I discerned a little nose-gay of gallants making their indolent progress towards us.

"Ze King, yes. Now you be good boy again and say why you 'ere."

But, though I might have saved myself by complying with his command, I was more afraid that the simple phrases which

Master WS had requested me to transmit would serve as further provocation to this violent man.

"I have a message – words – but they are for Mr HW alone, the words that I have."

Reluctant to name the individual, I took refuge in the flimsy shelter of his initials.

"HW? Who izz HW? I do not know HW. Give me ze words."

"They are for one man alone. I have been strictly instructed."

This, by the by, was true. Master WS had been most insistent that his words were intended for one pair of ears only.

But it was my own ears that now received the hot, smelly, ticklish and breathy attention of the well-dressed door-keeper, as he once more tightened his hold on my upper arm and brought his dagger into play around the throat region.

"Your words or I kill you."

His voice resonated down my spine.

"Only to Mr HW."

I was perhaps encouraged to refuse him by the arrival of the group of gentlemen whose bright costumes now flared in the corner of my eye. The presence of these others would surely deter my assailant from further violence. But I was deluded, for the man at my back jabbed at the underside of my chin hard enough – as I discovered an instant later – to draw blood. He would certainly have gone on to do worse if one of the bystanders had not spoken out, quietly but authoritatively.

"What has this person done?"

" 'E as words, words to say."

"Do you mean to cut them out of him?"

There was a ripple of laughter from the knot of gents.

" 'E *far la spia*," said my assailant. " 'E spy." I could feel wetness trickling down my upturned throat and soaking into my ruff (for I had dressed up to enter such a grand house, even a house so full of knaves).

"What is your name?" said the man who appeared to be the leader of the gallants. To be asked one's name is a step on the road of civility, even if the other's voice betrayed no great friendliness towards me.

"Nicholas Revill."

"Are you a spy, Master Revill?"

Well, the uncomfortable truth was that I was, in some manner, a spy. In addition to the blood running down my throat, I felt my armpits and sides spouting sweat.

"I am a player, sir."

"Spies may be players too, I suppose."

There was another little ripple of laughter from his group at this sally. Nevertheless, he signalled with his eyes to the man holding me and I was released. Instinctively, my hand sprang to the cut in my throat.

"With the Chamberlain's, I am with the Chamberlain's Company," I said, following up this advantage.

I sensed an alteration, a more attentive spirit, in the group when I thus placed myself.

"And I have a message for a gentleman who is staying here."

"I will take you to him," said the speaker in the group. "But first Signor Noti there will give you something so that you may staunch the wound he has inflicted – which, by the by, does not appear to be very grave. I suggest that you surrender one of your fine handkerchiefs, Signor Noti. *Vostro fazzolo*, Signor Noti, *per favore*."

There was no question who was in command here. I realised that the speaker was not only exerting his authority but also making some kind of amends for the hostile reception which I had received. While the well-dressed 'door-keeper' pretended to search his person for a handkerchief, I studied my rescuer.

Like the others, he wore his dark hair long but in his case it was arranged in a tress on one side. The rest was brushed back, uncovering a high forehead which gave him a pensive appearance. His face, regarding me with mild curiosity, seemed too refined for any desperate action. A fine pair of gauntlets dangled languidly in one hand. He waited until the 'door-keeper' Noti finally pushed into my hand a small square of embroidered silk, fine material which I had pleasure in spoiling with some of the blood from the nick his knife had caused.

"With me, please, Master Revill. You will doubtless need privacy."

He turned about as if there was no question that I'd follow him. It occurred to me that he had not asked for whom my message was intended. Presumably he'd overheard those cryptic initials, HW. The other gentlemen, almost as polished as their leader, formed a loose circle about us as we made our way across the flagged courtyard and towards the entrance to the house itself.

For the first time I had leisure to look about me. And to consider more than ever the pertinency of that line of mine (and Master WS's), 'I have many enemies in Orsino's court'. This was a great town-house but it had, at the moment, something of the air of an armed camp. Mingled incongruously among the gents and gallants, there were grizzled captains and superannuated ensigns. My lord of Essex's campaign in Ireland had concluded over a year earlier but these veterans looked, as it were, fresh in their weariness. As if they had stepped straight from foreign bog to boat to homeland again, without an interval to change clothes or even to wipe their begrimed faces, let alone lay down their weapons. They moved about the courtyard purposefully, and not with the resentful expressions with which unemployed soldiers customarily equip themselves on the public streets. They clotted together or strode briskly between groups, clapping each other on the shoulders, admiring each other's swords and the girdles and hangers which supported them, all the while laughing or talking loudly. Either these hardened soldiers did not care who saw and heard them or they presumed that each person here was of like mind. This was indeed a dangerous place for he who was not an Essexite.

If I had earlier thought that the charged air was similar to that in the playhouse before a performance, now it seemed more like the heady, blood-seeking mood of the crowd in the bear-pit. Everywhere, there was a happy, brawny buzz which betokened action – and action soon. It was plain that they expected trouble. It was equally plain that they were looking forward to trouble.

The man who had directed me to accompany him kept a little ahead but did not look round or address any more words to me. We entered through the grand central portal of the house. Inside, there was an even greater press and ferment than outside. In a large, tiled entrance hall men were crowded shoulder to jostled shoulder. After the chill of the February morning it was warm and stuffy with breath and tobacco smoke. The obscurity was dimly alleviated by the winter morning coming through the mullioned lights in the north wall above the entrance. What I could see suggested that the crowd was the same mixture of gallants and military veterans as in the open air, but with a sprinkling of more ruffianly types. I was surprised, however, to see one or two individuals in Puritan garb. I should not have been, I suppose. Malcontents will wear any costume.

Motioning to me, my companion made his way round the edge of the hall. The others with him were absorbed into the crowd. I kept faithfully at his heels. I was, in truth, a little alarmed at the possibility of losing sight of him. There was small sign here of the privacy which he had promised. Those who saw us cleared a small passage, sometimes urging others to get out of the way, but frequently we had to tug at sleeves or push shoulders to pass through. Consequently, it took several minutes to travel a matter of yards. We were further delayed because the crowd was distracted. Moments after we'd started, a hush fell over the hall which, for an instant, I attributed to our arrival. But then a figure seemed to rise up out of the crush, swaying unsteadily at the far end of the hall. At first I thought he was being hoist aloft by the arms and shoulders of the crowd. But as he found his footing it was evident that he had been placed on some sort of dais. He was dressed in the black-and-white of the Puritan preacher. He stood there, a thin dark candle of a man topped by a thin white face which was lit up with zeal. His mouth gaped. He was all a-fire to speak.

My late father was a preacher. I am well disposed towards them as a species. The best of them have few equals . . . and as for the rest, well, they are mostly no worse than our fallen fellows. But the Puritans or square-toes are different. If we theatre folk are cats, then the Puritans are dogs to us; we instinctively arch our backs and spit, or experience a sudden sharp desire to flee from their fluting tones and narrow condemnation. They loathe the playhouse and all its works, and many other things as well, with a passion that far exceeds their love for God and His saints. It is true that my father also hated plays and players but I ascribed this to his ignorance and his innocence, for he had never attended a playhouse in his life. In himself, away from the church, he was a mild man.

Were he alive, he would long ago have forgiven me for my disreputable way of life. Or so I choose to believe.

I wondered again what this being, this Puritan spouter, was doing in such motley company. Among gallants who whored and gambled and captains who drank and swore, as well as, most probably, ruffians who stole and did worse. Necessity makes strange bedfellows. When the crowd was properly quiet, this individual started to orate in a reedy but powerful voice. I listened, I had no choice but to listen, even as we pushed and shoved our path through the crush. The gentleman who had intervened to help me by the gate was still leading the way.

"My brothers in Christ," the speaker began, "oh, dear brothers in Christ, I am moved in spirit to be here this day and to speak before you, to raise my voice in protest against the foul face of these times. The houses of the unholy – the settlements of Satan – the tents of the wicked – we see that they are pitched not a quarter of a mile from where we stand. There sits a woman and her crooked councillors—"

There were murmurs at this, not of anger or shock but, as it seemed, of assent. If I could have clapped my hands over my ears without drawing attention to the gesture, I would have done it, so alarmed was I at the preacher's words. To hear treason uttered, even against one's wishes, is to feel contaminated by it. I was conscious too of the dreadful risk this preacher man was running, and wondered at his impudence and daring. If caught and tried, he might well have lost his ears for abusing those of others by speaking ill of her majesty. Yet this evidently did not weigh with him for, pleased with the reception of his treasonous words, he repeated them with yet more force.

"—a woman and her crooked councillors, I say. One in particular has a body which is as twisted as his mind and spirit and so all may see that he bears the mark of the beast [*I supposed it was Sir Robert Cecil, with his hunch-back, whom he meant*]. And what do these profane councillors of corruption – these Satanic suggesters who crawl on their bellies the better to raise their heads in pride – what is it that they seek? What is their infernal quest? Why, to persuade our sovereign lady [*but the sneering way that he uttered the phrase indicated that he considered our Queen to be neither sovereign nor a lady*] that the safety of the realm lies across the water. With a foreign bastard wrapped in the robes of Rome. We shall be sold to the whore of Babylon, I tell you. We shall be strangled in the bands of the Antichrist."

At this, the murmurs rose to groans and oaths and shrieks of – of outrage, approval, indignation, I could not tell. From the point of view of a player, I could not but admire the skill with which this preacher was working on his congregation. In fact, I was a little affected by his words myself and with difficulty stopped myself mouthing quiet assent, despite my abhorrence of treason.

All this time I continued to squeeze my way though the press of men round the perimeter of the hall of Essex House, dogging my protector's heels, and presuming we should soon arrive at some place of privacy. So it proved, for a moment later he ducked through a doorway to his left, glancing over his shoulder to ensure that I was still behind him. Before we got safely shut away from the hall and the ranting, however, I heard the speaker's voice rising and strengthening as he reached some kind of peroration.

"Brothers in Christ, there comes a time in the affairs of this vale of tears when it is needful for men to follow the dictates of their consciences. This tells us that compulsion is lawful, yes, compulsion even against the highest in the land."

Cries of agreement, gestures of assent.

"Oh compulsion, my brothers. Sweet word, compulsion. On such occasions it is God Himself thrusts the arms into our hands and bids us use them."

Then the door was shut behind us.

We were in a small closet. From beyond the walls came the preacher's urging, but muffled, together with the sussuration of the crowd, like the wind playing through a stand of tall trees.

There was a table in the room and a couple of chairs. It was dark-panelled, with only a modicum of light coming through a small high window. The room might have been designed for close conversation. I attempted to study my companion, who took up his station on the far side of the table, but the gloom made this difficult. Even so, it seemed to me that a slight smile hovered about his face. His broad brow glimmered. He motioned towards a chair on one side of the table and reclined gracefully in the other. I dabbed at the underside of my chin with the door-keeper's silken scrap. The blood no longer trickled. My ruff would require laundering.

"Master Busy is in his element. He is good for another hour yet."

He gestured slightly towards the hall in which the reedy voice still sounded. I was glad I didn't have to listen to such seditious material for an hour.

"The smoke and the oaths remind me of the playhouse," I said, "and that is one place where you would not expect to find a Puritan divine. He is not really Master Busy?"

"That is what I call him," said the other.

"And what is his element?"

"Dissent is his element. That is what he is drawn to."

"He is a Thunderer," I said.

"Is that a sect?"

"Oh no. I mean that he is a Thunderer to my mind. I catalogue preachers as Thunderers, Reasoners or Shepherds."

133

"And whiners and pedants," said the man on the other side of the table. "Or rabble-rousers." His eyes moved door-wards.

I was puzzled by the detached nature of these remarks, as if the speaker was removing himself from the words and activities on the far side of the closet wall.

"And what is *your* element, Master Revill?"

"I'm just a poor player, sir, entrusted with a message."

"The defence of ignorance and simplicity, eh? You'll be telling me next you didn't understand what Busy was saying, about the crooked councillors and the foreign bastard in Roman garb."

"I – don't – well, not—"

It is strange how reluctant one is to own up to ignorance, even about disreputable matters.

"Come. It is well known, is it not, that there is a plot?"

"A plot? Yes, there is always a plot." (This seemed the safest thing to say. And true too.)

"A plot involving Cecil and Cobham and Raleigh."

"Oh their plot, yes."

"You may pretend not to know, Master Revill, but I tell you that your playing does not convince me."

In another's mouth, these words might have been a threat but with this gentleman they conveyed passing amusement. His voice, too, was peculiarly dulcet and lulling. One could have listened to it without searching for meaning, as one listens to birdsong or the gentle purl of a stream.

I shrugged helplessly, as if he had seen right through me, while all the time I hadn't the faintest notion what he was talking about.

"They are plotting – Cecil and Cobham and Raleigh . . ."

He paused, as if he expected me to finish the sentence for him. Evidently he still thought I was feigning ignorance. I shrugged again, placatingly. In the gap while neither of us said anything, I had leisure to reflect on the irony of a player's being accused of acting when he was merely being his innocent, simple self. When the other man finally realised I wasn't going to break my silence, he spoke up.

"They are plotting to make the Spanish Infanta the successor to the English throne. That is what Cecil and Cobham and Raleigh intend. You must surely know that, Master Revill? Everybody knows that."

As if to confirm his words, there was another burst of shouting and groaning from the far side of the door.

"I – well, now you say so – I—"

"It is the talk of the town, from tavern to palace."

"The talk of the town, yes."

I realised now that in the hot and fevered air of Essex House all sorts of wild notions and strange conceits might grip the minds and fancies of those who filled its precincts. What appeared to this gentleman to be 'the talk of the town' was no more than the discontented delirium of the Essexites. Why, the Spanish Infanta . . . successor to the throne . . . ridiculous! Cecil, Cobham and Raleigh plotting to this end . . . absurd!

Yet, although this was my instinctive response, a tiny doubt crept into my mind. Perhaps this gentleman was in possession of facts – of secrets – which were hidden from ordinary mortals like me. He looked as though he might be, for he was obviously well connected. In addition, he spoke with a quiet assurance and, as I have described, his tone had a peculiar, ears-enchanting quality. As my eyes grew accustomed to the closet's gloom, and I had more leisure for study, I saw too that he was not merely well dressed but finely dressed. His doublet was of white silk and his purple trunks and knee breeches were gold-encrusted. The flower-embroidered gauntlets he had been carrying were now laid between us on the table. I wondered whether he decked himself out every day as though he might be going to sit for his portrait.

"Now, Master Revill, you have a message?"

He gazed direct at me and I saw that his eyes possessed a particular brilliance.

"Not for all ears. For . . . HW only."

"You are speaking to him. I am HW, Henry Wriothesley."

This was as I had half suspected. Even so, I was jolted by the realisation that I was talking to the Earl of Southampton.

"I – I guessed as much."

"Then let me guess a little in return." The same mild smile played around his lips. I wondered what this easy-going man was doing in a nest of rebels and malcontents, indulging in fantasies or nightmares about Cecil and Raleigh and the Spanish Infanta. Outside in the hall, the preacher's reedy tones rose and fell, with crowd's noises as a ground-bass.

The Earl pursed his lips and pretended to be puzzled. "Let me guess. As to the identity of the person who has entrusted you with a message, now. Would his first initial be a W and his last one be an S, so that the two being put together make WS?"

"Yes," I said tersely, feeling that he was mocking me for my coyness in not naming him outright.

"William Shakespeare?"

"Yes. Our author."

"Our?"

For some reason he seemed put out by my description. I was quite pleased to see this.

"I mean our author at the Chamberlain's. He is a shareholder – and sometimes a player too."

"I know this," said Wriothesley. "Now tell me something I don't know. What is the message that you have brought?'

"It doesn't make much sense to me," I said.

"It doesn't have to. After all, you yourself said you were only a poor player. Out with it now, man."

I hesitated. There is a difference between calling oneself 'a poor player' and being so described by another. But the larger reason for my hesitating was the nature of the message I had to pass on. It really did not make much sense, and I suddenly became self-conscious about speaking the words in front of this great nobleman.

"Very well. I was asked to say this to you (clearing my throat and taking a deep breath like some journeyman actor):

'For shame deny that thou bear'st love to any
Who for thy self art so unprovident.' "

After I'd recited these two lines there was a pause. I feared that there was some covert insult in them.

"And that was all," I said.

A change had come over the face of the man lounging opposite me. The playful, half-mocking look had gone to be replaced by an expression that was almost wistful. The brilliant eyes seemed dimmed.

"No more is necessary," he said. "Tell me, how is Master Shakespeare – and Burbage and the others?"

I was about to say something to the effect that he should know, since one of his party (to wit, Sir Gelli Merrick) had visited the Globe playhouse only the day before, when I realised that the visit had been *sub rosa* – certainly intended to be concealed from a poor player like Nick Revill and possibly not even known to a great player like the Earl of Southampton.

"The winter is a lean period for all playhouses," I said.

"Yet you have the Queen's favour, and that must take some of the edge off the chills and rain of winter."

Was it my imagination or was there a sharpness to his comment? For it was universally known that the individual in whose mansion we were sitting, the Earl of Essex, had until recently been the Queen's favourite, indeed her chiefest favourite. But now, like Icarus, he had tumbled down as low as he had once flown high. The sun of the Queen's favour had turned to ice. As with other great men at court, Southampton's fortunes too could rise and fall. Since he had hitched his wagon to Essex's train, those fortunes must of necessity have been on the wane. Still, it must be galling in the extreme to have basked in the Queen's favour once and then to watch others warming themselves in the same place now – even if it was only a company of players.

"We are to perform soon in her presence," I said, hoping that a simple statement of fact would not offend or provoke him.

"God willing, you will perform – and she will watch it," he said mysteriously, then fell silent. Outside, the preacher continued to pipe his tune. Henry Wriothesley seemed to gather himself to say more. "Though I am glad enough that your company prospers, I meant to ask after particular individuals in it rather than the collective."

"Master Shakespeare?"

I thought of Nemo's words – 'he and . . . this gentleman you have mentioned . . . were once friends'.

"Yes, it is him I mean," said Southampton. "He is well?"

"I have no reason to think otherwise," I said – rather formally perhaps.

"As well as the indifferent children of the earth?"

"What? Oh, yes," I said, picking up the allusion to WS's own *Hamlet*.

"Happy in that he is not over-happy, you mean."

"On Fortune's cap he is not the very button."

"No player – or author – can be that, I think. There are no great fortunes to be made in the playhouse, in any sense."

"You are better off so. Fortune gives only to take away."

"What she takes she can restore," I said, with matching sententiousness.

"Perhaps, but she is truly a strumpet and no man should depend on her favours."

The image of Nell flashed across my mind.

"He was very particular that I should speak to you in person."

"Who?"

"Master Shakespeare."

"Return my greetings to him. You do not mind being a messenger, Master Revill? A Mercury?"

"Not in the least."

And at that moment I did not. Listening to this graceful, slightly melancholy man, I had already fallen under the spell of his voice and his manner. I could understand how WS might have picked him out for a friend, or the other way about. Although he was perhaps only a year or two older than I was, he seemed far ahead of me in experience.

"Thank him for his words. They are like him. They are his own words too, of course."

"I – I assumed so."

"I should reply in kind. Let me see."

This time the pause and puzzlement on Henry Wriothesley's face was genuine. He was evidently searching his memory.

"Ah, yes. I have it. Tell him this."

The Earl of Southampton straightened himself slightly in his seat. Without the preamble of throat clearing, he said:

" *'Lo in the orient when the gracious light*
Lifts up his burning head, each under eye
Doth homage to his new-appearing sight,

Serving with looks his sacred majesty . . .'"

"You should have been a player, my lord," I said, when it was evident he was going to say no more. "Your voice would have brought in a thousand."

The compliment, untainted by flattery, slipped out. In fact it was the kind of remark which might easily be taken amiss. There are many men – and not all of them well-born either – who would be happy to take offence at having the low trade of the stage suggested to them. Yet Henry Wriothesley appeared the true gentleman when he inclined his head in acknowledgement of my words, used though he must have been to hearing his praises sung. Furthermore, he returned my compliment winged.

"*Experto crede*, Master Revill. When the expert speaks we must believe him."

Now it was my turn to nod gracefully. And so we might have continued throughout the live-long day to pay each other compliment and counter-compliment. But I sensed that the interview was drawing to an end.

"Kindly pass on those lines to Master Shakespeare, Mercury Revill," he said. "I would not insult your powers of memory by asking you to repeat them to me now."

"No need," I said. "But he will understand them?"

"He should do. They are his own as well."

He rose and went towards the door. Holding it open, he said over his shoulder.

"I will escort you safely out of the gate, in case our hot-headed Italian friend gets it into his head to attack you again."

I was about to make some remark to the effect that I could deal with a mere door-keeper, when our attention was distracted by what was happening outside in the hall of Essex House.

The Puritan preacher had finished or, perhaps, had been

interrupted in mid-spout (for once they have got their feet on a dais or their finger-ends over a pulpit they are most reluctant to let go). But now across the hallway a figure was sweeping from the main door towards the grand staircase. The crowd parted to let him by. He had a group of men at his heels and seemed to be both talking and listening to several of them simultaneously. He moved with a queer gait, with strange long steps. His head was thrust forward, as if in eagerness to meet whatever was coming towards him. His speed and the string of companions behind him made me think of an old picture in one of my father's books, the image of a comet blazing across the heavens, attended by its train.

I knew, without being told, that this rushing individual was Robert Devereux, the Earl of Essex. I knew without being told because I had seen him before in the streets of Islington when he had set out, in all high hopes, for Ireland in the spring of 1599.

The leader of that ill-omened expedition now swept past me in the hall of Essex House. A cape was flung over his shoulders in such a careless, unstudied fashion that it suggested he dressed – or, rather, was dressed – with the same swiftness with which he moved. I was reminded of his passage through London, for he looked to right and left with an equally vague, abstracted air, all the while seeming both to speak and to listen to the men in his train.

"That is Cuffe," said a voice in my ear, and I started for I had momentarily forgotten the presence of the Earl of Southampton at my elbow. "Henry Cuffe, he is his secretary. There is Sir Charles Danvers. And that man struggling to keep up is Sir Gelli Merrick."

I recognised the individual who had been with Augustine Phillips and whom I had glimpsed from my hiding place behind the great trunk when they entered the Book-keeper's room.

"I am glad to know some of the, ah, *dramatis personae*," I said.

By this time the company had reached the foot of the stairs. The preacher had been forgotten in the great glare and hum which accompanied the return of the Earl of Essex.

"I would make a good chorus, if you ever have an opening in the Chamberlain's," said my Earl. "Would I fit in? Every man should be a master of two trades, in case one turn Turk with him."

"Do you want me to pass on so much to Master Shakespeare?"

For some reason I whispered this, whispered it into his uncovered ear, the other being concealed by a great tress of dark hair.

"Oh, there is a man who is master of more trades than I can count . . ." said Henry Wriothesley. "No, my Mercury, I do not seriously look for employment with the Chamberlain's. I have enough to do here. Forgive me if I don't after all accompany you to the gate. I will be required upstairs."

He tilted his head in the direction which the group surrounding Essex had taken. He placed his hand briefly on my upper arm and then entered the crowd which, further excitement being unavailable after the transit of their leader, was now splitting into smaller, chattering groups.

I made my way out across the courtyard and through the postern gate. The man who had pricked me in the throat was nowhere to be seen. In fact, the door was unattended and I wondered at the laxness of this band of desperate men. Nevertheless, as I navigated the ponds and sloughs of the Strand, what I chiefly thought of was not the little injury which had been done to me at the gate – nor the ranting of the square-toes preacher (even though I wondered how Robert Cecil and the Council could tolerate such sedition being uttered so close to home) – nor the verse message which Master WS had contracted me to deliver to Master HW; no, what stayed with me was the touch of the Earl on my upper arm, his touch and his brilliant gaze.

This was my first association, fleeting as it might have been, with the world of the high and mighty. It was not my last.

It was a strange season, those few months of winter in London, taking them all in all. The figure of Rumour, painted with a thousand tongues and each one of them wagging a different tale, passed through our streets and chambers, sometimes whispering, sometimes roaring. Naturally, whatever Rumour said never served to inform, only to excite and confuse. One day you might hear that our beloved Queen was dead; the next that, in her sixty-plus year, she had miraculously been delivered of a baby boy who was the very image in little of his maternal grandfather.

I was told on good authority that a whale had beached itself at Gravesend and that this signified the wreck of the great enterprise of England. Someone else, telling me of what was (presumably) the same whale, was most certain that this entailed the destruction of all those foreign enemies who would tread on our shores. A little while afterwards, a third person informed me in strictest confidence that there never was a whale, but rather that a great eagle had been sighted over Whitehall which had, suddenly and unaccountably, tumbled from the sky and smashed into the ground. Yet the onlookers, rushing to examine the spot, had been unable to find any trace of the mighty bird. What did this portend?

A little before the mighty Julius Caesar fell, they say, strange sights and sounds were witnessed in Rome. The graves stood tenantless; the sheeted dead did squeak and gibber in the streets. In London, the graves retained their guests, as far as I know, but one strange thing I can confirm from my own experience. Shortly before the Christmas of 1600, we were shaken by an earth-tremor. Awoken by some dreadful combination of noise and motion, I was in my own indifferent quarters, and not with Nell (or Mistress Horner). It was early in the morning, barely light. Almost as soon as it had started, the grinding noise and the motion – a kind of slight shrugging which brought down a few tiles and chimneys, nothing more – ceased. People rushed from their lodgings, some still in night-attire and all equipped with white, terror-struck faces. Even the Coven seemed alarmed. No doubt I looked as frightened as my fellow citizens. Certainly, I could not leave off shaking for an hour after, and all day felt cold and hungry. The rumbling or grinding, which can have lasted only moments, seemed to resound in my ears. I was reminded of the area beneath our playhouse stage which is entered by a trap-door and which, during the action, serves as a grave or as a portal to Hell or Purgatory. This is the dark cellarage from where the ghost of Prince Hamlet's father begins his stalk. It surely follows that underneath our firm-set earth there must be some great, fearful machinery to produce such sound and motion.

This tremor was, naturally, taken for a prodigy – or as my street informant would have said, a progeny-prodigal. Like the sudden black cloud which had flown up into the Earl of Essex's way as he had departed for Ireland over a year earlier, it plainly had significance – and not of a hopeful sort. I too couldn't help wondering what all this meant.

But we none of us had long to wait before we discovered what it did mean: whales and earth-tremors, falling eagles, black clouds *et al.* We Londoners were shortly to see over-weening pride and towering ambition brought low. So perhaps the story of the eagle was true in the end.

*　　　*　　　*

"How is my Nell?"

"Why, Nick, it's a long time since I've heard you say that."

"You have been in my thoughts."

"But not in my bed."

"It's not grown cold on that account, I'm sure."

"Come and warm it now."

"I . . ."

"You're surely not going to claim that you have pressing business elsewhere at this time of night?"

"No. But an early start, you know . . ."

"That never used to trouble you. Nor did your brow used to furrow like that. Come here and let Nell smooth it for you."

"Very well, but for a moment only."

"I know I should be grateful for a morsel of your time. You must be much in demand."

"Ah . . . that's better."

"You have not forgotten what strange power I have in my hands and fingers."

"It's good to be reminded."

"Power to soothe and smooth – and to swell."

"Yes, that is better."

"Only you must submit to me entirely to feel its full effects. Lie back now—"

"For a moment only."

"Of course. And as I work you shall tell me a little of your day. You have been rehearsing to see the Queen again."

"We do not rehearse to *see* her but to play before her. She sees us."

"But you will still be in Her presence."

"I have been in the presence of other great ones today instead."

"There is none so great as our sovereign lady."

"There are some would be."

"Are you sure that these are things which you are supposed to talk of, Nicholas? Are you sure that this news is for your peace of mind? Last time we met you played the mute. Lie still and attend to what I am doing."

"One day I shall tell you all."

"No, you will tell me *nearly* all. But look now, I have put you into a state where you need say nothing further. See. Feel."

"Ah yes."

"Nothing except a few words of love, if you wish."

I left Nell's crib a little less heavy in body and mind. Once again, it was a frosty night. The trees stood gaunt by the roadside. The moon, growing towards fullness, was suspended low above the ground, looking pale and sickly. Maybe I was on the alert for signs but I saw several meteors tracing out their mischievous paths among the stars and recalled the heavenly omens which were reported in Rome before Julius's fall. Who was our Caesar? The rushing man in Essex House or our solitary sovereign in Whitehall Palace? For certain, London could not contain them both for much longer, no more than England had been able to bear the weight of Henry Bolingbroke and Richard together on her soil.

Arrived at the Coven, I almost stumbled over April and June and July bundled up together near the entrance, like cubs in a litter. They appeared to have fallen asleep where they fell. I could have got drunk on the fumes that ascended from their huddled shapes. I assumed it was those three, and that May was absent, because the others acted as a kind of monstrous conjoined body, never, as far as I could see, parting more than a few feet from each other's company. I wondered where the more limber May was. Out about her business, no doubt, spreading alarm and despondency like the meteors. I felt my way up the perilous stairs and so into my room. There were so many chinks, rents and unadorned holes in the fabric of the walls that I might almost have seen to read by starfall.

My room was spare. It contained a bed. And to enhance the homeliness of my quarters, I had imported a small chest in which I kept my valuables – or would have done had I possessed any. Nevertheless, it guarded two or three things of significance to me, like the agreement I'd signed when invited to become a member of the Chamberlain's (never have I appended my signature so eagerly to anything), my father's signet ring, a cambric handkerchief which Nell presented to me when first we met, as well as a few other items.

In short, there were only two objects of furniture in the room. Now, by the faint light that filtered through the gaps, I could see that I was the owner of a third. A carpet had been delivered and left rolled up in the middle of the uneven floor. My first thought was that the Coven had suddenly grown mindful of the comfort of their lodger and, as a gesture of their interest in his welfare, had spontaneously decided that his room required an additional domestic touch. My second thought was that, since the sisters were content to live like pigs in shit, there was no reason for them to be remotely concerned with the well-being of a mere lodger.

My third thought was straightforward enough.

It was: Jesus!

For, when I bent over to examine it, the rolled-up bundle on the floor turned into a huddled human body. I coughed to clear the phlegm which had suddenly gathered in my throat. There was a roaring in my ears. The loudest sound – the only sound – in the room was the banging of my heart. I tried to say something, to say anything, but only a squeak emerged. Then I put my hand out and felt the other's stiff arm. I darted my fingertips into the area of the face, paler than the rest of the mound, and encountered a rough, razorable cheek, all of it quite cold. My scalp prickled and I broke out into goose-flesh.

I'd been squatting on my haunches and now sat down heavily on the floor. For a moment I hoped – hoped! – that the body in my room was May's, the fourth member of the Coven. If the other three were in a stupor downstairs, then perhaps it did not stretch belief that she might be dead drunk on my upper floor. Perhaps she'd swallowed too much of her own concoction. However, a second's reflection showed it couldn't be May. The rough and razorable cheek I'd felt would not have been a disqualification with April and the others, because they were patchily whiskered, but the more feminine May approached a sort of smoothness. It wasn't her. And I'd already glimpsed the other three downstairs, far gone but not over the other side of death's borne.

So, who was this person in my room?

I would have preferred not to look, would rather have leapt into bed and pulled the stinking covers about me, would just as soon have fled the house altogether. But there was a body in my room, and fear and curiosity and anger combined to make me want to discover its identity (for some reason I assumed that I would know him).

With shaking hands I lit my carefully conserved candle. The flame flickered and swooped as I held it over the dead man's countenance. It was poor Nat the Animal Man, as I think I already half suspected it would be. His face tilted to one side and his mouth stretched to expose raggedy teeth. His scarecrow rags were pulled about him, as if to cover up what had proved mortal enough. He'd paid his debt, but everything about him – his expression, his huddled posture, even his very presence in my chamber – signified that it had been a forced settlement.

Carefully, very carefully, I placed the candle on the floor, for I was afraid that otherwise it might drop from my trembling hand. I closed my eyes for a moment and, as I sometimes did before walking out on stage, tried to steady my breathing and calm my heart. I wasn't certain what I felt: anger, fear, grief. Or rather, I experienced all these emotions but in varying quantities at different instants, so that at one moment I was frightened for my own life and at the next furious that someone had taken away the life of a fellow human. And in my little room! Then I would think how old Nat was really a harmless individual, and not so old either, trying to scrape a penny-living with his gallery of unhuman noises, and a tear would start to my eye. Yet all of this occurred in little more than the blink of that same eye.

I strove to control my feelings, with some success. It was important to draw what conclusions I could from this event. To discover, for example, how Nat had met his death; to think of reasons why his death should be necessary. I started to study the body. He was lying upon his side, his thin legs pulled up. Both of his hands were clenched and drawn tight against his chest. Both of them were clutching at something. I opened the cage of his fingers, not yet gone stiff, and recovered what was inside them.

One of the items was a balled-up scrap of paper. I unfolded it, saw some writing and put the fragment to one side, intending to examine it later. The other item was a small bottle made of dark glass. The bottle felt empty. I tilted it and a single tear of clear liquid fell to the floor, catching the light from my candle. I sniffed at the bottle's lip. A sweetish smell, quite pleasant, not unlike the aroma of sack. I leaned forward and sniffed briefly at Nat's gaping mouth. My gorge rose but even as I struggled to control my nausea I thought that I detected that same smell on his cold lips. So, I tried to reason coolly, it was possible that he had drunk from this little bottle and then died. But had he died *because* of the bottle or, rather, because of its contents? And, supposing that it had contained poison, why should Nat have been carrying with him a vial of envenomed liquor?

Still kneeling, I brought the bottle closer to the candle flame. It was made of green glass, a worthless little container so shoddy that there was a bulge on one side near the base. Then all my fears, which had been slightly allayed by the attempt to apply reason to the corpse's presence, returned in full force. As I've mentioned, my bare room contained only two movables: bed and chest. I shuffled on my knees towards the latter. Besides that I possessed nothing of true value to keep from the world's prying eyes, the lock on the chest had long since been broken. I retrieved the candle, opened the lid and took an inventory of my goods. Yes, there tucked in one corner was my Chamberlain's contract. In another was my spare shirt and, beneath that, Nell's cambric handkerchief with my father's ring safely folded inside it. There were a couple of books too and other things besides.

But what was missing from the chest in which I'd put it for safe-keeping was the bottled concoction which Mistress Isabella Horner had presented to me not long ago, the concoction which, she'd claimed, would restore me to the straight and narrow highway of women when I tired of the by-ways of men and boys. The bottle was absent from the chest because it was presently clasped by the defunct Nat. Isabella Horner had hoped to work a cure on me. But her cure was to be a permanent one. It was evident enough, was it not, that if I'd sipped at Mistress Horner's preparation then it would have been Nick lying down, lying clenched and curled in the place where Nat was now.

I thought of Mistress Horner's skill at compounding and

combining. I remembered her raisin-fraught cakes; and then, her cat-like fury when I'd announced that I wished to see her no more. I thought that her culinary art might stretch to the ingredients for murder. I thought of her gypsyish, un-English background. Certainly I believed that she had the will to kill. I had left her on the pretext of preferring my own sex to hers, and for that I would pay. They say that there are some who like their revenge piping-hot while others prefer it cold (there is a third class who eschew revenge altogether, but we are not concerned with saints here). Isabella Horner had presented me with the poisonous bottle, knowing that I would one day – sooner or later – out of curiosity or need – go and taste it. Then, from a distance, she would be gratified to hear of the death of that rising young player Nicholas Revill in his obscure Broadwall lodgings, and she would hug to herself the secret of how she was responsible for his demise. Even were the bottle and its contents to be blamed, there would be no evidence as to who had given it to me. That knowledge would have perished with my person.

She was the real witch in the case, Isabella Horner. April, May, June and July were as nothing to her.

Still hunched over my chest, I attempted to work out the likely sequence of events. Old Nat had come to see me, with or without the knowledge of the Coven. It wouldn't have been difficult for him to creep up the rickety stairs without their being aware of it. In fact, the periods when they were drunk-asleep far exceeded the times when they were wakeful. In any case, they would have cared little if the raggedy animal man announced that he had business with me. Why did he come calling? To deliver a message, the piece of paper balled up in his other hand. No doubt he was acting on behalf of Nemo, as when he'd intercepted me the previous evening. Perhaps he'd been hanging around as I whiled away the hours most pleasantly in Nell's crib (so much for the brief moments I'd planned to spend there). Then, knowing I must come back in the end to my hovel-home, he had stationed himself in my room, awaiting my return.

Growing thirsty – more or less a permanent condition with Nat – he had rummaged through my sparse possessions in search of liquid refreshment. There, at the bottom of my chest, by bad fortune he had chanced on Horner's bottle. How he'd have seized on it! In the same quick, grasping style as his hand-claw closed around the halfpennies one proferred him for his animal sounds. He'd unstoppered the green bottle, lifted it to his quivering beak, liked the faintly sack-like smell, upturned the thing and sluiced its contents down his ever-open gullet.

And died.

I remembered that Nat was never too particular about where or what he drank. His life was largely dedicated to raising the pennies that would enable him to slurp away his waking hours in various ale-houses. I remembered too that green, the colour of Horner's bottle, was also the colour of jealousy.

Definitely, Isabella Horner was one who preferred her vengeance cold, so cold that it was almost iced over. I shivered. I suppose I should have been sorry for poor Nat lying huddled there but it was of myself I was chiefly thinking, and how a fellow human being felt murderous towards me.

My first instinct was to run to the authorities with my information, and I had half risen from my position by the chest to do so. But I quickly checked myself. To whom should this outrage be reported? The local constable? There were none on this side of the river. Besides, most of them were dolts, more likely to congratulate themselves on letting a knave go by than to risk trouble in the attempt to apprehend him. A magistrate? Well, yes, that gentleman might have the wit to grasp the crime which had occurred in my room. Might think as well that the possessor of the poison-bottle was also the individual who'd administered the dose. To be accused of a murder plot originally directed against oneself, and then to hang for it, would be like painting the lily, as Master WS has said in a different context. Everything was complicated by the connection that had existed between me and Mistress Horner. And how could I be really sure that Nat had died by her hand? So sure that I wanted the affairs of the Chamberlain's Company – or at least of two of its players and a wife – to be aired abroad, which would most certainly be the result if the death were reported to those in authority.

In this way I argued myself into a less uncomfortable position, one where no action was necessary, or not straightaway. Besides, I reminded myself, I was at present engaged on important affairs of state and could not afford the distraction of magistrates and investigations into what was essentially a question of domestic jealousy. When the Essex storm had blown itself out, when my own slight role in it was concluded, then I might make a move against Mistress Isabella Horner (though what sort of move I hadn't the faintest idea).

However, one thing was clear. I could not sleep with Nat's corpse in my room. It was not conducive to my health, in any sense. Guided by the candle's flickering flame, I tugged at his body. It came easily. Underneath his scarecrow rags, Nat was small-boned, as thinly nourished as a bird in winter. My room opened directly onto the stair-head so I paused there to hoist him over my shoulders rather than risk a noisy, bumping progress down the rickety treads. With some difficulty I positioned his arms so that they flopped past my ears, then held him pickaback fashion. He did not seem so light and pitiable now, and the cold mask of his countenance pressed on the nape of my neck. I swallowed hard then listened. From the lower floor came human and animal snores.

I put one foot tentatively out in search of the first downward step. I usually took great care in going to and from my room. Like Jacob's ladder, the Coven flight could well have led you straight to heaven (or, more likely, to the other place), so uneven and rotten were the stairs and so high the risk of tumbling from or through them. Now with a body on my back, I proceeded with extra caution, fearful of waking the slumbering sisters or their familiars. The steps creaked and groaned as, swaying, we made our way down. I was glad that Nat had earned only pennies, that most of what he'd earned must have been pissed away in drink, that he was, no heavier than a great shrunk starling – for even as he was, he was a big enough burden for me.

We reached the floor of the sty in safety. The fire under the cauldron hadn't quite died away and it cast a dim red glow across the rough floor. As usual, a haze of smoke filled the room. The humped shapes near the entrance were April, June, July and the pig. One of them farted, another sighed, a third muttered some incomprehensible syllable, while a fourth grunted, but I could not have apportioned any sound to any particular origin. I do not think it was the pig which grunted. All at once I was seized with the desire to laugh. With a dead man on my back, and an uncertain future to the front, I shook with suppressed laughter until my eyes watered. Nat's draped arms shook with me.

Then, after my little fit, I moved towards the door as softly as if I were walking on eggshells. I threaded my way between the sleeping lumps. By the entrance I fumbled for the key with one hand, keeping Nat hoist in position with the other. The door opened creakily inwards and, while stepping back, I trod on a cat's tail. At least I think it was a cat. There was a hissing and a scrabbling in the darkness. I almost dropped my burden in fright. More rumblings and grumblings from the sleeping forms but no one rose up to challenge me.

Through door and into road, turn round with body on back, pull door closed, no need to lock it, am not going far, where am I going?

Don't know.

The night air was like a bucket of cold water thrown in my face after the fug of the Coven. I was sweating from the exertion of carrying Nat and from fear. My breath feathered forth. Now I was out in the open I had to do something, to dispose of Nat's body somewhere. Even in a dubious area like Broadwall it would not do to hang around with a dead man on your back. The longer I spent over it the more likely it was that I would be seen by someone, even in the middle of the night. I remembered the other evening when I ran back to the Coven, convinced that I was being pursued. Who knew that there were not eyes out there now in the darkness, watching this strange, double-backed, nocturnal beast?

I turned southwards, away from the scatter of buildings and towards the more open country. I hunched forward to keep balance. Nat's head bumped against the back of my head while the rest of his body slipped and slid behind as I attempted to keep him in position by grasping tight hold of his shrunk shanks. I picked up speed on the frosty track. I had the weird sensation that he had come back to life and was breathing down my neck, urging me to make haste. It was like a childish game of pickaback when boys play at being knights in the lists and race around trying to unseat each other. But it was also most unlike, horribly unlike, such a game.

Above us was the great arc of a starry night. On either side stretched the flat fields of London, fenced by naked hedgerows and skeletal trees, their line interrupted by the occasional dwelling-place. The moon, now higher and smaller in the heavens, looked down indifferently. To my right one of the many streams that debouched into the river ran more or less parallel to the rutted road. I still had no idea what to do with the man clinging to my back. I suppose my intention was to put as many furlongs as possible between where I'd found him and wherever I would leave him. At the same time, I had to balance the danger of discovery with the need to go a distance. And it is hard to think straight if you are bumping down a slippery track on a cold night with a murdered man around your neck.

In the end, after I'd gone perhaps half a mile and the sweat was pouring into my eyes and my breath coming in great wheezes, the problem of how far to travel was solved. I skidded on an icy patch and fell sideways, losing touch with Nat. I rolled onto my back, surprised, the breath knocked out of me, for an instant forgetting where I was, what I'd been doing. Then I recalled my fellow-traveller. Unwilling to get up, I merely turned my head to one side. How wide the road seemed when you were lying right down among its frost-bound ruts! Wide and empty too. Nat had disappeared. After a time it occurred to me that I should look to my other side. There, seemingly at a great distance, across a veritable land-scape of ridges and furrows, lay a huddled shape that was probably the animal man. He must have rolled there after we fell together.

Well, he could rest in that spot for a while. He was in no hurry to move. He wouldn't get cold, he wouldn't get hungry, wouldn't get thirsty (always the real consideration with Nat), wouldn't get anything ever again. He was beyond harm. The stars over my head started to blur and shimmer in my eyes as I thought of these matters. Then I sat up like a man invigorated. It was myself I was really sorry for, or sorry for as much as I was for him. The difference was that I was alive and Nat was not. He might have been beyond harm but Nick Revill most certainly wasn't. It behoves every man to protect himself from danger.

I stood up and walked the few paces to the body. He had landed on the opposite side of the road to where the stream ran. This half, the left hand, was bounded by a ditch beyond which was a bank overtopped with a row of trees.

I had to leave the body somewhere and I might as well leave it here. Not out on the open road but in the decent obscurity of the ditch. This was hardly Christian burial but I could do no other, and I consoled myself with the thought that God will surely judge us according to the circumstances and conditions which He has laid on us.

Once again I took hold of Nat, this time tugging him by the shoulders towards his final destination. I slid down into the ditch and he followed me close and willing. The sides and bottom were full of fallen leaves, the ungathered waste of many autumns. They rustled and crackled under our weight. Although it was less sharp down here than out on the open road, the frost had already begun to crisp the leaves. If I'd had a digging implement of any kind I could have attempted to burrow right into the flank of the ditch and given Nat at least a thin crust of earth for cover. But I had nothing more than my bare hands, so I scraped and scooped at a mixture of leaf and sticky soil until I'd made a sort of elongated nest.

I pushed Nat into the area I'd hollowed out near the base of the ditch. I covered him as best I could, piling up the leaves again and laying some fallen branches and stems athwart the corpse. I didn't delude myself that it would lie there for long undisturbed. The beasts and scavengers of the London fields would scent Nat soon enough and have him out of his covert. I suppose there was a certain appositeness in this: that he, who had scraped a living through imitating their wild cries, would now find himself supplementing their meagre winter pantries. Better such a fate, unchristian though it might seem, than that he should be uncovered by human scavengers, who'd simply strip his body of its rags and leave him Adam-naked. Much better than that he should be found by someone with the authority to question and investigate his death. (Not that this was likely, I told myself, for he'd most probably be taken for one of the many vagabonds who died outdoors in the winter months through cold and hunger and exhaustion.)

As I put the final branches on his resting-place I promised Nat – I promised myself – that I would avenge his death. That I would extract a confession from Mistress Isabella of how she had planned to kill me and how, her schemes going awry, she had destroyed an innocent and harmless man whose cries and barks and whinnies had given an equally innocent pleasure to tavern-drinkers the length and breadth of the town. A cold fury rose up in me but I mastered it with effort, and said a short prayer over Nat's ill-concealed remains, such as I had often heard my father intone over the dead in our village of Miching.

I clambered out of the ditch and set my face northwards back to the Coven. As I neared my lodgings I saw a figure approaching from the opposite direction. We met at the entrance.

"Master Nicholas, is it not?"

"May?"

"The very same."

On another occasion I might have made some light-hearted remark on seeing her, like "Where have you been? Out and about killing swine?", since we were on quite easy terms, but I was not in the mood now.

"I have something to tell you," she said.

"And I have nothing to tell you," I said, taking slight fright at her tone and wondering if she'd seen anything. "I am tired now and on my way to my hole."

So I did not question her on her night's activities and she did not have the chance to question me on mine. This was perhaps a mistake, though I did not see it at the time. Once inside, she went off to join her sleeping sisters on the floor and I climbed my weary way up the rickety flight of stairs.

The room was as I had left it. No more bodies, thank God! I was surprised at how little of the candle – which I had carelessly left lit – was burned out. The night might have seemed endless but, in reality, not so much time had elapsed. I carefully replaced the empty green bottle in my trunk, thinking to confront Mistress Isabella at some point with her killing machine. Casting about my quarters I caught sight of the ball of paper which Nat had been clutching. I unfolded it.

As I'd half expected it was a message, a message written in plain English and from Nemo, if I was to believe the four letters appended at the end.

It said:

For the eyes of Nicholas Revill alone. You are to go to Essex House on Sunday morning by nine of the clock. You will be my eyes and ears there and report to me what you see and hear. You are in a position to do the state some service. Your compliance is required; do so, and then your loyalty will be rewarded and your Company protected from the misfortune that might otherwise overtake it for foul play. Do not doubt that I am the author of this that you are reading. Remember that I know of the trunk-work between you and a certain married lady.

Read and digest. Destroy this note. Eat my words now.

Nemo

I read this several times over but was none the wiser. In fact, I was significantly more confused. The note raised a host of questions and answered none. Why should I go back to Essex House? And why on the Sunday morning? What was supposed to happen then, happen there? How did he – Nemo – know what was likely to transpire in the enemy camp when he was in Cecil's employ? What did the reference to my Company and their 'foul play' mean? Was it a joke? If so, it wasn't one that I was privy to. And how could I, a humble player, protect the Chamberlain's? Was this scrap of paper, found in a dead man's hand, really from Nemo? This was about the only point that I was able to answer with a degree of assurance. Probably it was his; the tone, half jocular, half threatening (that reference to 'trunk-work'), seemed typical of the man. And I already had experience of how he employed Nat as a messenger.

It was evident that matters were coming to a head. Of course, Cecil and the Council were desperate to be kept informed, but why should *I* act as their agent? Because I had a foot in both camps, a little voice whispered inside my head. I was a player – and there was obviously a faction among the players which was not ill-disposed towards the Essex cause – but I was also a true Englishman, loyal to my sovereign and mindful of the commonwealth. That was the lever which they were using to get me to act as a spy, that and my fatal intimacy with Mistress Horner.

Anyway, all this was pretty much beside the point. They'd got me in a corner, had tied me to a stake like Stubbes the bear. If I had a foot in both camps I was also caught between them. If I didn't do as Nemo's note instructed, then it looked as though the Chamberlain's Company might suffer. Perhaps it was arrogance to think so, but if I was able to safeguard the Company by making a return visit to Essex House, this was surely a small task to undertake. I toyed for a moment with the notion of running and telling all I knew to Dick Burbage or Master WS, there and then. I trusted them much more than I trusted the ash-complexioned, soft-mouthed Nemo. Him I trusted not at all.

But I could easily be painted as a government spy in the Globe, someone who had voluntarily agreed to work for the authorities. Had I not already betrayed the Company in some small sense by cuckolding one of my fellows? The taste of that double-dealing was not pleasant in the mouth, although it had been overtaken by the terrible discovery that Mistress Horner wanted to do away with me. And how could I explain *that* to anyone? Go up to Jack Horner and say, "Oh by the way your wife nearly succeeded in poisoning me the other night. Matter of fact, she did manage to do someone in, you might remember him, old Nat the Animal Man. Pity. Shame. Oh, why did she want to see me dead? Well, you see, I was fucking her – sorry about that but she did start it in a way and I don't think I'm the only one, if that's any consolation . . . it's not, oh well – and then I told her I'd rather be fucking a man, men rather, because that's my true taste you see, my real bent, well not my true taste, I just said it to get out of . . . oh never mind. Anyway, she was so pissed off with me when I said this thing about men, that she gave me a green bottle full of poison and told me to drink it when I wanted to go back to the straight and narrow of womankind. No, no, of course she didn't tell me that she'd put poison in the bottle . . ."

I mean, would *you* believe a word of it? I wouldn't.

I went round in circles, with my allegiances and obligations tangled together so tight that it would have taken a smarter head than mine to unravel them. The only thing that was clear was that I was expected to call at Essex House on the next Sunday morning. Perhaps it would be a quiet day in the old hotbed, just the odd Puritan spouting and the occasional malcontent ranting but no one actually *doing* anything. But what was to be my pretext? Nemo hadn't told me that. I'd have to trust to luck and quick wits if I was once again stopped at the postern by Signor Noti.

I blew out the candle and lay down on my lumpy bed. It was freezing. I shivered and pulled over my head the mixture of blankets and stinking animal skins (no doubt the remains of their sacrificial rites) which the Coven had thoughtfully provided for my nocturnal comfort. After a while I realised that I was still clutching Nemo's note. It was a perilous piece of paper, too perilous to be seen by the eye of morning. If the candle had been alight I would have burned it to ashes. As it wasn't, I had to obey Nemo's final injunction and eat his words. They tasted as bitter as ashes and for some time after I'd swallowed his secrets I seemed to feel them, a mushy bolus, lodged in my windpipe.

We rarely held meetings in the Chamberlain's. We were, in a sense, meeting all the time, we ordinary players. The day-to-day business of the Company was in the hands of the Burbage brothers and the major shareholders such as Shakespeare and Phillips and Heminges. They commissioned or bought new work and decided what plays would be put on and when, they handled negotiations with the Office of the Revels and dealt with licences and, most important, with the finances. Individuals such as the Tire-man or the Book-keeper had their little kingdoms, with that inclination towards tyrannous rule which seems to characterise small rulers, but the management of the Globe in all its fullness and roundness was firmly in the hands of a few.

It was something of a surprise therefore when word came through from Dick Burbage that he wanted to speak to the entire company at the ungodly hour of nine on a February Friday morning. This was a couple of days after my excursion to Essex House and the dire events of that night. In my imagination, I repeated and re-repeated my walk in the dark down Broadwall. And when I thought about it, which was much of the time, I could feel still the weight and form of a dead man hanging on my back. So, in a way, I welcomed any distraction, including an early morning meeting.

It was too cold to assemble in the open on the stage and since the only room large enough to hold all the members of the company was the tire-house, it was there that we were summoned. There was a queer expectation in the air, half excitement, half apprehension. I was standing with the two Jacks – Horner and Wilson – and our boy-player Martin Hancock. Needless to say, I had said nothing to Jack about his wife's behaviour. In fact, I would have gone to great lengths to protect my friend from the knowledge of Isabella's vicious duplicity. I was dreading another visit by her to the Globe, although they had been infrequent of late. How does one converse with someone who has attempted by violent stealth to cut one's mortal thread? The ordinary small change of discourse seems somehow inadequate. Therefore I hoped not to see her again, or at least not see her until our current crisis had passed and I could turn my mind to how best to deal with Mistress Horner. Glancing round the tire-house now, I saw the faces that had become familiar over the last few months, the senior men like Cowley and Pope and the more junior ones such as Cook and Rice.

That this was a significant occasion was indicated by the presence on a make-shift platform at the end of the room of the Burbage brothers, Richard and Cuthbert, together with the senior players William Shakepeare and Augustine Phillips. Seeing Master WS reminded me that I hadn't passed on to him the message from Henry Wriothesley. I hadn't really had the opportunity but neither had I sought for one. This playing at Mercury was becoming wearisome – and probably danger-ous, if recent nights were anything to go by.

I had never before attended a meeting at which the Chamberlain's Company had been so formally called to-gether. After a moment, and without a signal from anyone, the buzz of conversation died down. Dick Burbage, who had been deep in dialogue with WS, turned towards us and began to speak. They always said that Dick was a Proteus, able to take on any role – able to *become* any role – someone who submerged himself in his part before the play began and surfaced for air only when disrobing after the action was finished. I would not have dared to approach him while he was off-stage during a performance, and I'd noticed that even the more important members of the Company had only the briefest exchanges with him at such times. To every part that he played he brought a physical attack, hard or insinuating, as if he would make it his by seizure or seduction. Now he played at being the responsible manager and shareholder, always conscious that the well-being of his beloved Company rested in his hands. Or perhaps he really *was* the responsible manager, etc. It's easy enough when an actor's on stage because you *know* he must be playing but when he's off, how can you tell what he's feeling?

"Friends and fellow players," Burbage began, perhaps in deliberate echo of Mark Antony's opening words in WS's *Julius Caesar* as he speaks to the crowd over the corpse of his precious Caesar, "friends . . . I have summoned you here this early in the morning for no idle purpose. I say 'I' but I mean, of course, Cuthbert and William and Augustine and the rest of the shareholders. *We* have called this unusual meeting. Now, we may be mere players, but we are players near the heart of things. In the last few years we have played at the royal court more than twice as often as another company which I will not name [*he meant Henslowe's Admiral's men*]. Our sovereign has been pleased not merely to grace our performances but to compliment us on them in the warmest terms. We are *her* men in all but name."

So far, so unexceptionable. Around me I sensed the beginnings of bewilderment: why have they called us together? Surely not just to say that we're the Queen's favourites? We know *that*. Stale news. As if sensing the mood of the Company, Dick Burbage continued:

"This you know well. Long may we continue to be the favourites of Queen Elizabeth. Long may she continue to reign over us! [*A few murmurs of assent at this point, but for form's sake only.*] However, if it behoves every man to think of the future, how much more does it behove every group of men allied together for mutual benefit – as we are allied – to arm itself against 'the slings and arrows of outrageous fortune' [*here he nodded slightly at Master WS in acknowledgement of his words*]. In short, we have to look out for ourselves. To be on the watch for new patrons and friends. I do not have to tell you, my friends, how precarious is the life of the player.

"We have only recently attained respectability. And always our enemies, Puritans and the like, are seeking to thrust us back onto the high-roads and inn-yards, if not into the ditch where they think we belong. We have other enemies too that I scarcely need to enumerate. A cold spell keeps people indoors, the bear-baiting draws away their pennies, while an outbreak of the plague closes us down altogether. And even when we do succeed in gathering a congregation [*this was Dick Burbage's preferred term for the playhouse audience*], gathering them in sufficient numbers, we must keep them diverted. If we fail to amuse them, my friends, then we too will shortly fail – fail to eat, fail to pay our rent, fail to feed our families. Ah, how precarious is the life of the player!"

None of this was exactly new to the Company. I glanced at my companions, the Jacks and Martin. All of us were well aware of just how unstable our trade was, even in the finest, best-established of acting companies. Yet, such was Dick Burbage's oratorical skill, that we listened to his words as if he were telling us great, unuttered truths. At the back of my mind, though, was the certainty that we hadn't yet reached the heart of his speech, the real reason we'd been summoned to the tiring-house on a cold winter's morning. Everything he'd said so far was a preparation for something that when it came wasn't, I suspected, going to be entirely welcome. Otherwise, why was Dick making such a business of selling it to us?

It came, sure enough:

"As players we must look with favour on those who would favour *us*. We cannot afford to turn a cavilling, carping face to the world; rather we must show welcome both in eye and tongue. We have been requested to stage a special performance this Saturday afternoon, which will be advertised as usual and open to our public as usual, but for which we have been offered the sum of forty shillings extraordinary."

He paused. There were no gasps or whistles of amazement at this sum, for although it might have been 'forty shillings extraordinary' – that is, in addition to whatever receipts we might take at the door – it was hardly an extraordinary sum in itself. In fact, I calculated that it would have kept me going for less than two months in London, and that would be by living sparely. So, if it was to be shared out among the Company, forty shillings represented a thoroughly modest disbursement.

"What's this play then, Dick?" said someone, Thomas Pope I think. "It must be very special that we cannot just be told our parts but need to meet about it beforehand."

"It is one of our own," said Burbage, again inclining his head in the direction of Master WS. "It is William's *Richard II* that I am talking about."

"That old piece," Jack Horner muttered next to me. His feeling was obviously shared by the majority of the Company, to judge by the shifting and stirring and muttering around us. I would probably have felt the same way, had I not been privy to the conversation between Sir Gelli Merrick and Augustine Phillips. That, together with Robert Cecil's warning, had alerted me not only to the title of the play but also to its significance. In truth, this latter point was nothing very arcane. Very soon my fellows in the Company, or the quicker-witted among them, had grasped the meaning of a request for *Richard II*. I glanced at WS to see whether he was offended by comments about the fustiness or dustiness of his work; I wondered whether he would speak up on his own account. But he did nothing other than wear his usual bland expression.

"A practical point, Dick," said Pope, again. "You say that we're being offered forty shillings extraordinary to put on a piece which – not to put too fine a point on it and saving your reverence, William – is a little musty. But in my view we're likely to *lose* more than forty shillings when our regular customers stay away in droves. Why don't we do something new, or at least do something not quite so old?"

"Yes, and it may be more than the forty shillings we'll lose," said someone on the opposite side of the room. There was an agitated flurry at this point, since a consideration that most of us had been uneasily aware of was pushed to the forefront of our minds. Yes, we could lose in several ways: it would be bad enough to forfeit money rather than to make it, if we were fined by the Council; it would be yet worse if some of us lost our liberty, as a result of putting on a play which the Council would certainly frown at; and worse still, if some lost more than liberty . . .

Several people turned in the direction of the last speaker, as if they expected him to enlarge on his remark. Dick Burbage was also looking towards him, giving him the chance to have his say. It was Richard Sincklo, a quiet and rather formal man.

"Master Burbage, we all know that there are . . . reasons why this play of *Richard* should be requested at this time."

"Tell us them, Richard," said Dick Burbage kindly but firmly, like a master to a pupil.

"It deals with the . . . the death of kings. It shows a throne usurped, and the usurper triumphant. It shows that a sovereign may be deposed and then put to a violent death. These are nice subjects at this time. I think I do not have to expatiate further."

Now Master WS, he nodded slightly at Dick Burbage and stepped forward on the makeshift platform. This was his right – after all, it was *his* play that we were talking about. Who better to defend it? Unlike Burbage with his overmastering 'attack', WS had a softer approach. His voice and intonation still carried traces of country sweetness and simplicity. Or perhaps it was all an act.

"Richard Sincklo, thank you for dealing so plain, as usual. No, you do not need to expatiate further. [*I noticed that he did not take the opportunity to mock Richard Sincklo's slightly formal 'expatiate', something a lesser man might have done. As ever, Master WS paid grave and good-humoured attention to what he heard.*] We all know what you are talking about, and these matters should be aired. You say that my *Richard* shows 'a throne usurped', you say it shows a 'usurper triumphant'. So it does – or rather, so our History does. What I have recorded is what happened, happened once. And I ask you what became of the usurper, Henry Bolingbroke? For that is History too. Why, he lived as King Henry IV, and not so long after he ascended the throne he died of a sickness, and during his reign our kingdom was torn apart by inland wars and civil strife. This too I have recorded, as I think you know. [*Appreciative laughter, for it was WS's Henry IV that first offered to the world the indestructible figure of Falstaff and other riotous fellows.*] Those plays about a usurper met with no little success, I think, even though I showed him dying in defeat and disillusion. The lessons that History teaches are not simple. Those who would treat them as an A-B-C primer may be fools. What I am saying, my friends, is that we must not think of our audience as fools."

Shakespeare paused here.

"We are afraid of trouble now if we show a play about the death of a king. But I say to you: we are players first and foremost. Let those who wish to construe what they watch in a bad sense, do so. We are not guilty of their false assumptions and constructions. We are guilty of nothing, only of holding the mirror up to nature. If a man looks in the glass and doesn't like what he sees, then the fault – and the remedy – lies with him."

"What if he goes and smashes the glass, William?" shouted out Thomas Pope. "What then? You know how costly a glass is, how difficult it may be to replace."

"More fool him," said WS, easily equal to this elaboration of his original 'glass' metaphor; in fact, comfortably able to top it. "Each piece of shattered glass will tell him just the same story again when he looks at it, but this time it will be multiplied a hundredfold. I say once more, we are players. Players are bold and truthful, or they are nothing. *We* are nothing."

There were murmurs of assent at this. Jack Wilson nudged me and I nodded at Jack Horner. We were all infused with a sense of the dignity of our trade. Later, in a cooler moment, I was able to see that Burbage and Shakespeare had presented a kind of double act here: while Dick stressed the insecurity of the player's life (and the consequent requirement to accept just about anything that was on the table), William showed himself an adept at stiffening our sinews and summoning up the blood. We were players; we should be proud; we ought to fear no man. I wondered whether the two shareholders had worked out beforehand who was to say what, or whether they knew each other's methods so well that they simply fell into this kind of pattern without consulting over it. I wondered too why they were going to all this trouble about a performance for which the Company would receive only forty shillings. We got five times as much for a performance at Court – and got it with royal thanks and without the danger of treason.

Dick Burbage stepped forward once more. This time he spoke briskly, as if everything were settled. Again he showed his shrewdness here. A pause for more questioning would have allowed for protest, objection.

"Now we must proceed. Gentleman, please collect your scrolls from the Book-man. Robert Gough will be playing the King and I will be taking the part of Bolingbroke. We begin rehearsing in an hour."

The debate was over. It had been over before it began, since I noted that the roles must have been allotted and the scrolls prepared in advance of the meeting. We trooped off to see what Master Allison had for us in the way of parts. Looking round, I found Master WS at my elbow.

"Oh Nicholas," he said as if it was a chance encounter. It was only much later that I wondered whether anything, *anything*, occurred by chance in those strange days.

"Sir," I said, then, "William."

As you can see, I was still thrown into a slight state of confusion in my encounters with WS. He smiled vaguely but his mind seemed elsewhere.

"You have seen our friend, as I asked?"

"Yes. In another man's house, as you asked," I replied, thinking how easy it was to fall into the cryptic mode.

"And passed on the words I gave?"

"Yes," I said, reflecting now that Master WS must be in an unusually unquiet state of mind to be seeking confirmation that his requests to me had been complied with.

"Thank you," said WS.

"He gave me something for you."

"Something?"

"Four lines."

"Lines?" said WS, for all the world as though verse was a foreign language to him.

"Of verse. They are:
'Lo in the orient when the gracious light
Lifts up his burning head, each under eye
Doth homage to his new-appearing sight,
Serving with looks his sacred majesty . . .'"

"These I know well," said WS. "What does he mean by 'sacred majesty'? Is it reassurance or warning?"

"They are your lines, are they not?"

"Must we be held accountable for all our words?" he said wearily. "I suppose so. Do you think we shall be required to listen to everything we have ever said and written, when the day of judgement comes? Or do you think that a mere abstract will suffice?"

"I don't know," I said, because I truly didn't. Master WS was unaccustomedly grave and, well, abstracted. Then he reverted to the Earl of Southampton.

"But he said nothing else? No further message?"

"No," I said, "but he was mindful of . . . of your welfare."

I wished I could communicate to WS the tone in which his friend HW had enquired after him, for in the latter's questions there had been much more gentleness and warmth and interest than my own rather bald description would indicate. Master Shakespeare seemed satisfied, however.

"He should rather be mindful for his own. Tell me, Nick, you also saw the inside of . . . the other man's house, when you saw my friend?"

"We had an interview within its walls, yes."

"And your impressions?"

"Of the house?"

"Of its occupants."

I hesitated, partly from uncertainty as to what to say, partly from uncertainty as to what he wanted to hear.

"I heard some wild and whirling words there. A Puritan was up on his hind-legs, spouting stuff that it would be unwise to repeat."

"He was preaching to the unconverted in that place," said WS.

"And I saw – saw Devereux himself."

"What was my lord of Essex doing – cutting a caper?"

"In a manner, yes. He moved so very fast across the hallway, he might have been dancing."

"Leading others a dance."

"Nothing so light," I said, deliberately misunderstanding

the comment. "It seemed to me a place of swearers and desperate men."

"I fear so," said the playwright. "I fear there will be many wrecked on the Essex coast before this is finished."

I had never seen him in so quiet a mood, almost a despondent one. The resolve and the steel which he had showed on the platform so recently had all gone. I would have almost welcomed a pun from him.

"Then why . . . ?" I began.

"Yes, why, Nicholas. Go on, complete your question please."

"Just now, when you were speaking to us all, you seemed to be saying that we should not concern ourselves with the bad construction placed on our words – your words, I should say . Or on our actions either. That players should be true to themselves and so on."

"So we should."

"Well then?"

I was surprised at myself for the directness, almost the impertinence of the question. But really I did not understand how Master Shakespeare could at one moment counsel that we of the Chamberlain's ought to play whatever we pleased and the devil take the hindmost, and the next that he should express the utmost apprehension about the enterprise presently unfolding at Essex House. For, if his prognostications were correct about many being wrecked on the Essex coast, then what were *we* doing staging a play at the behest of a bunch of malcontents and renegades?

I did not voice this question in so many words but it was the one that Master WS chose to hear and to answer.

"You ask yourself what we're doing," he said, and I almost jumped because he had echoed my thoughts. By this time we were snugged in a corner. The rest of the company were queuing for their parts and costumes.

"What Dick Burbage said was right," said Shakespeare. "We can't afford to pick and choose, and play only what we feel like playing."

"But you said – your grand words about holding the mirrror up to nature – not caring what people think," I said, feeling disappointed (and a little angry as well).

"Well, grand words are true too – in their place. On stage or in the pulpit. Your father was a parson, wasn't he, Nick?"

"Yes," I said, now irritated at what I thought was WS's attempt to divert the conversation.

"You are a traditional man, Nicholas?"

"Perhaps," I said warily, wondering what this had to do with anything.

"You like a story with a beginning, a middle and an end," said WS.

"And an epilogue," I added.

"Well, life is not always so neat," said the playwright. "Sometimes we must trim and compromise."

"I suppose so. Next thing you'll say is that I'll learn."

Master WS almost smiled.

"Let me tell you, in confidence, Nicholas, that there is a design behind what we are doing . . . even though it may not at first appear. It is the case."

"In this case?" I pressed him.

Compelled to justify my persistence, my importunity, I suppose I'd have argued that William Shakespeare having employed me to run an errand to his friend Henry Wriothesley gave me the right to an answer. I considered myself to be, on all sides, a man freighted with secret knowledge. A privileged man. A man in danger.

"The weather may turn, Nick. In such situations, anybody with sense provides himself with as many burrows as possible. Do you understand me now?"

"I – I am not sure."

"Or, to vary the figure, it is the foolish gambler who risks everything on one throw."

"Gamblers are foolish by nature."

"Says the parson's son," said WS, looking closely at me and smiling slightly to rob the words of any offence. "You are probably right and it was a poor analogy. But sometimes we have to gamble."

At that point he was beckoned across by Dick Burbage on the far side of the room. He clapped me round the shoulder and walked away without another word. As I waited my moment with the Book-keeper, to see what little role I'd been allotted in *Richard II*, in my mind I turned round and round WS's words. When he'd talked about having more than a single 'burrow', I presumed that he meant that he and Burbage and the rest of the senior men had agreed to put on a performance of *Richard* at Merrick's request (and, behind him, the Earl of Essex) because there was a possibility – a slight possibility – that Essex might find himself once more a power in the land. It would not do to alienate such an influential figure.

Yet, even as it occurred to me, this explanation didn't really answer. There was no chance of Essex's scrabbling his way back into favour with our Elizabeth. Even I, who was no politician or court-leech, knew that Devereux had crossed his Rubicon when he stormed back from Ireland. He'd been lucky to escape with his head still fastened to his shoulders on that occasion – and if what I'd witnessed in his house was anything to go by, he could not long avoid a fatal appointment in the Tower yard. No, I was forced to conclude that the real reason why Shakespeare & Company were staging *Richard* was that they considered the Essexites might *win* if they raised a head. In other and blunter words, they believed our sovereign lady might be deposed by force and insurrection . . . and another elevated to her place.

This was not – let it be whispered – impossible. Kings have been compulsorily unseated before now and usurpers have taken their place. WS's own *Richard* and then his sequel of *Henry IV* showed this very thing. But if the Chamberlain's senior men were really throwing in their lot with a wild bunch on the Strand, then I had to question their judgement. It may be that history is a series of improbable chances and unlikely outcomes, but it did not seem to me that the Essexites had it in them to replace a divinely appointed sovereign with one of their own choosing. What I'd sensed in that hall in Essex House had been dangerous and unpredictable, but also wavering and uncertain in its aim. Could it really be that we of the Chamberlain's had hitched our fortunes to such a rickety wagon?

Enough of this speculation. I didn't really know what it was all about. They say that history might have different if Cleopatra's nose had been a bit longer – or a bit shorter (I forget which) – so perhaps very great alterations may proceed from very small causes. Perhaps all it takes to shift the ship of state in its course is a bunch of wild men. After all, they only have to overpower one individual and seize the wheel, to drive us all onto the rocks.

I was hastening away from the Globe at the end of our Friday morning rehearsal of *Richard II*, confirmed in my impression that this play of WS's was the worst of both worlds, paradoxically fusty and current and therefore (for us) dangerous to perform, when I heard shouts from behind. I looked round and there was another troubled Richard running up to keep me company.

Like King Richard when he begins to realise that his throne

may be forfeit, Richard Milford wore a somewhat anguished expression, a beseeching countenance. The would-be playwright's face was even redder than usual from the morning's cold and from his pursuit of me.

"Nicholas, may I join you?"

"You already have."

"You are going back to your lodgings?"

In fact, I was going to nowhere in particular, but rather wishing to get *away* from the uneasy atmosphere of the playhouse rehearsal. No one, however, likes to admit to being without a destination and so I simply nodded.

"How do you find the four sisters? Are they still mixing their brews and potions."

"They were well enough when I left them," I said, irritated by Milford's attempt to make casual conversation when it was obvious that he'd approached me for a deeper reason. I was far from forgetting – more important, so was he – the scraps of manuscript which I'd found in the bottom of the book-room trunk, the few tattered sheets which gave me an unwished-for power over the playwright's professional fortunes.

"And your room . . . which once was mine? I always found it a little cold in the winter."

So cold, I almost said, that a man died in it the other night. However, what I actually said was, "Master Milford, it is generous of you to be concerned about my welfare, particularly now that you have moved up in the world . . . on the expectation of success."

"You have hit on the very thing I wished to speak to you about."

"I can guess it."

"Master . . . Nicholas . . . you are an educated man. You know the story of Damocles and his sword?"

"Yes," I said. "He flattered Dionysius of Syracuse by saying that the king must be the most fortunate of men. Dionysius invited him to experience royal happiness. The king placed him at a banquet. Looking up, Damocles saw a naked sword hanging over his head by a single hair."

"You are an educated man, as I said," said Milford.

"And this was the happiness of a monarch, this was his security."

As I spoke, I wondered at Milford's drift.

"Would you be surprised if I said that I see myself as Damocles?"

Although I could suddenly see where he was headed I nevertheless said, "No doubt you can enlighten me."

"Damocles lived in fear and trembling that at any moment the thread might snap and the sword plunge into his head. Believe me, Nicholas, when I say that my own state is not too far from Damocles's."

"I am no Dionysius," I said, half indignant, half amused, and remembering that Master Shakespeare had recently alluded to the tyrant of Sicily as well. "I am no tyrant, and if I didn't find the imputation funny I might be angry."

"No, of course you're not – but at any moment I fear that a word from you will bring to an end my burgeoning career in the playhouse. That the sword of imputed plagiary will dash my brains out. And my *Whore* is soon to be staged, you know. It is her beginning – and mine too."

"Really, Richard, you should save all this stuff for the stage. I don't know why you had to borrow another man's words. You've quite enough of your own, and a fine sense of your own drama too."

"Each man stands on his own piece of earth," he said stiffly.

I glanced at him. His face was turned earnestly towards me, perhaps reddened by cold rather than embarrassment. The eye which was flecked with green had a peculiar liveliness to it while the other stared bluely. We were heading, willy nilly, in the direction of Broadwall and the Coven. Again the thought recurred of the fate of poor Nat, ill-covered by leaves and strewn with branches in a ditch not far south of here. There was a real case of foul play. I wondered whether the corpse had yet been disturbed in its resting-place by the foxes and the crows. For sure, I would not be walking that way again for some time. All of a sudden, I grew impatient with Master Milford's maunderings. For God's sake! He wanted reassurance that I would not 'betray' him, that I would not run like some schoolboy to inform on him and his play-thieving to Messrs Burbage and Shakespeare. With all his talk about the sword of Damocles, he wanted me to be sorry for him, he wanted to be forgiven, to be absolved by the parson's son.

Well, I would not 'betray' him to our seniors – even though part of me urged that this was what he richly deserved – but nor would I tell him this, since his anxiety was not unpleasant to me. Indeed, I regarded it as penitential. And, for certain, I would not absolve him of his fault. Oddly enough, if he'd freely owned up to carelessness, even dishonesty, in appropriating another's work, and then laughed it off, I think I'd have done the same. But as it was, he wriggled and squirmed on the hook of his own self-pity and self-importance, and I could not find it in myself to release him.

"You know, Richard," I said, "when you started to talk about Damocles and his sword, I thought that you had rather greater matters in mind."

He looked astonishment at me, as though there could be any greater business than his own concerns.

"I mean this matter of the drama of Richard, *Richard II*, that is, and not Richard Milford. There *is* actual foul play. There may be a sword hanging over our heads by a thread and some may stand to lose more than their reputations if it falls."

I added a note of grimness to my speech. It was not feigned. For the phrase 'foul play', which had been floating around in my mind and which had already attached itself to Nat's demise, now became linked with our presentation of *Richard*. Just as the deposition of the King was foul play, so would be – in certain eyes – the agreement of the Chamberlain's to enact it on the Globe stage. And this was the very phrase that Nemo had used in his message to me. Which suggested that he already knew of the decision of our shareholders as soon as they had taken it; we were to put on a play which could be construed as 'foul'; he was making a sardonic joke out of it. Was Nemo aware of what was planned before it had been announced to the rest of us that Friday morning. What was going on?

If I was in the dark, a dangerous dark, it was apparent that Richard Milford had little notion of what I was talking about either. What was Essex or Richard to him? There had been no reason for him to attend that morning's tire-house meeting. His association with the Chamberlain's was still tenuous. I questioned whether he was even aware of the bubbling, distracted state of London and her inhabitants. Probably not. After all he was merely the author stuck up in a garret somewhere, cut off from the real world.

"I do . . . do not know much about these things," he said.

"No, well, believe me there is much pressing on our minds and hearts at this moment."

"Of course," he said in the tone of one who does not quite believe. "But for me . . . Milford's mind and heart . . . Nicholas?"

"Oh I promise nothing," I said, and strode off, feeling almost as much anger and irritation as I played at showing.

I've taken part in some pretty odd dramatic presentations in my time, and one or two dangerous ones too, but I don't suppose any of them were as odd or dangerous as our Saturday afternoon performance of *Richard II* – even though that paled in comparison with the doings of the next day.

Some of the danger came from the play itself because of its story but more of the danger came from our audience. Now, normally, the worst that we players expect to receive as a mark of the spectators' disapprobation is a catcall or a nutshell tossed in our direction. Occasionally a fight breaks out among the groundlings, when one man slights another's trollop or attempts to snip his purse-strings. In general, however, our congregations are happy enough to leave the fighting and the fury to the experts on stage.

This audience for *Richard* though was a different kettle of fish – and, if it hadn't been for the quantity of well-born and noble citizens in our playhouse that afternoon, I'd be tempted to call it a *stinking* kettle of fish. Not that anybody threw anything at us or made an adverse comment on our performances. I rather wished they had. Of course they weren't really interested in us as players; we might just as well have been apes dressed up or parrots mouthing Master WS's words. Give me a normal riotous assembly any day.

Never have I seen such a bunch of swaggerers and swearers, such a pile of saucy fellows and silly fops as the Essexites. These gentlemen were quite distinct from our usual attenders. Oh, they were present too, a few of them. Those in our Company who'd claimed that the play wouldn't be a great draw because of its fustiness, or for some other reason, seemed to be in the right. If I'd been an Essexite and had my wits about me (probably a contradiction in terms in those dizzy days) I might have taken note of the thin sprinkling of ordinary folk in the playhouse and seen it as an omen. However, the wild boys in the audience were having none of that. They were oblivious to everything except each other and the cause.

Watching the playhouse fill up on that dull-skied afternoon was like watching a witches' cauldron over a blazing fire. The crowd seethed and bubbled away, not in pleasurable anticipation of the action about to unfold on stage, but in mad delight at its own motion. And, as in a witches' cauldron, some very unpalatable stuff was bobbing about on the surface. I even thought that I caught a glimpse in the audience of the Puritan divine, Master Busy, the one who'd been ranting on about 'compulsion' when I visited Essex House. If so, it must the first occasion when one of his breed has swallowed his hatred of the drama for the sake of his hatred of the state. This shows that they can swallow anything if they gape wide enough. But in all this action, this milling about, we players were secondary. No, not even that. We were scarcely a sideshow.

Before I tell you about the reception of *Richard* and its aftermath I'd better explain what I said a moment ago about the play being dangerous. I'd never seen it myself until I appeared in it (and then of course I only saw the action in fragments). All I'd heard were the hints and disagreements about it beforehand. Perhaps I'd considered them a little overstated – after all, we were only talking about a *play*, for goodness' sake. However, when the piece was actually presented by the Chamberlain's on that Saturday afternoon a dead text became a living animal. I understood why some of our fellows were uneasy. I grew uneasy myself, particularly after witnessing the nature of our audience. The play was like an instrument that is being used to probe a wound. The wound was the sad condition of our realm, with an ageing, childless Queen and no immediate heir to her throne. The question was whether this was a mortal wound; and whether our play-probe would worsen an already grave situation.

In the unfolding of WS's drama, Richard may be a poor king but he is still a divinely appointed one. Henry Bolingbroke is banished by Richard, who is his cousin, and his lands are seized. Henry forces his way back from exile, to general acclaim. Almost all of King Richard's followers desert the falling star for the rising sun. Richard abdicates but, in truth, he is shoved from his throne by the usurper. He is murdered in Pomfret Castle. The manner of his death is affecting, for Richard in his fall from grace has acquired a new humility. Meanwhile, Bolingbroke rides high in triumph through London on his coronation day. He rides on Richard's horse, Barbary.

But Bolingbroke's moment of triumph is short-lived for, as WS has shown us in his plays of Hal and Falstaff, the new King pays dearly for seizing the throne. His land is torn apart by inward wars even as his own body is sapped by sickness. He has taught treason and his followers have followed him in that too. I have always considered our playwrights to be as stern moralists as our preachers. My father could not have delivered so strict a lesson on the vanity of human ambition as did Master Shakespeare in his plays of Richard and Henry. Far from being at odds, playwright and parson should make common cause! For the only thing that we are sure of down here on earth, king and commoner alike, is our own mortality. While all that we need to learn is that, as we sow, so surely shall we reap.

But I fear that the lessons drawn from this piece were not to do with grace and humility. The simple lesson for the Essexites was that divinely appointed sovereigns may be thrust from their thrones, if a fitter ruler come among them. It has happened once in our history; there is precedent. Now, our

Elizabeth was not a weak ruler like WS's Richard. She was a strong woman – stronger in heart and spirit than most men, I would think, though able to use her feminine parts when it would advantage her or her country. Nevertheless, she was in a – if I might so put it without disrespect – thrust-able situation. Like ripe fruit, our Queen could be loosened. And the looseners were out there in the pit and the galleries of the Globe playhouse.

My part in this play was small. King Richard has a trio of favourites named Bushy, Bagot and Green. They are cater-pillars of the commonwealth, preying off the land and giving nothing in return. It may be that the King prefers their company to that of his Queen. It may be that together these men are guilty of the sin that is named for one of the cities of the plain, the unnatural practice which outsiders often believe players to be guilty of with their boys and which I had unwisely imputed to myself in order to get rid of Mistress Horner. It *may* be that Bushy, Bagot and Green are of that bent; but it would be unwise to be too open about such things on stage, even more unwise perhaps than showing how to procure the downfall of kings. Nevertheless one may mince and strut just a little to show one's mettle. I was one of Richard's favourites, you see: I was Bushy (together with some even smaller part). Halfway through I lose my head, as does Green.

We players were not the ones losing our heads that after-noon. That could safely be left to the audience. I observed them through the spy-holes which were provided back-stage. Indeed, there was a more than normal interest in the specta-tors' response and, for the duration of the play, those members of the Chamberlain's who weren't out front could be found clustered round the little chinks which afforded a view of the pit and galleries. Even Master Shakespeare was concerned to watch how his words were being received. I saw Thomas Pope, who played the part of John of Gaunt, look most uncomfortable with what he was witnessing, as if he had indeed stepped into that old nobleman's shoes and was in despair at the condition of his beloved England.

This was no occasion for refined playing. The small touches and flourishes that I brought to my Bushy and the other attendant lord went for nothing. At times indeed the Essexites seemed almost impatient with the happenings on stage, and these were usually the melting moments when Richard bids farewell to his Queen or when the poor, abandoned King is alone, philosophising in his Pomfret cell. Then I sensed more than impatience – almost a contempt – with much nudging, laughter and shifting among our watchers. They seemed to be giving vent to their hatred for this enfeebled and impotent king. When he was murdered there was an instant of hush, as if even they appreciated the gravity, the sacrilege, of what had occurred on stage. But this was succeeded by muted cheers and other marks of approbation at his death.

Their real enthusiasm was reserved for those scenes in which Bolingbroke stretches the sinews of his new-found power. As when he confronts Richard for the first time after his return from exile and kneels down, in fair pretence of loyalty and meekness, saying that he has come back only to reclaim what is his own. Richard the King says, 'Your own is yours and I am yours and all.' It is the moment at which power is transferred from king to claimant. Once that door is opened it can never be shut again. This exchange was greeted with a great shout from one of the noble Essexites in the galleries and in seconds it was taken up by the whole crowd. Undoubtedly they saw their darling in Bolingbroke's place. I dreaded to imagine what Cecil's agents would think, for it was certain that there must be some among the audience and that they would hot-foot it back to their master to report this disgraceful response. Even worse was to come later when the Duke of York told his Duchess how Bolingbroke was greeted by the people in his triumphal progress through London. Master WS paints a picture in words, he does not show it. However, it was enough to move the Essexites to almost uncontainable excitement.

Whilst all tongues cried "God save thee, Bolingbroke!"
You would have thought the very windows spake:
So many greedy looks of young and old
Through casements darted their desiring eyes
Upon his visage; and that all the walls
With painted imagery had said at once
"Jesu preserve thee! Welcome, Bolingbroke!"

Through our peepholes we watched the bubbling crowd, unprompted, act out the scene, mouthing 'Essex' instead of 'Bolingbroke', and darting their eyes hither and thither as if they were standing at London's casements and watching their leader parade through the streets. You would have thought that Essex himself was in the audience – and in a sense he was, for he was present to their minds' eye almost more vividly than if he had been there in the flesh. The crowd was shifting and jabbering so much that they missed the sequel to this description of Henry Bolingbroke. In the Duke of York's utterance, Master WS has offered two pictures, telling us to look upon a victorious usurper and then upon a dejected king, for the latter rides at the heels of his dispossessor. Disloyal Londoners scowl at him and throw dust upon that sacred head. Yet all this was lost upon the Essexites, so excited were they by the vision of their conquering hero.

I remembered my own first glimpse of the man, how he had turned his head and the upper part of his body from side to side and smiled benignly on the crowd. I remembered too the sudden up-rush of the black cloud which had been rightly taken for an omen; how everyone had scrabbled for shelter. Now, the waving arms and bobbing heads and agitated noises of the Globe audience seemed like tree-tops readying themselves to be shaken by a storm.

So much for *Richard II*.

After the performance was over, we made our bows but did not finish with the customary jig. However, despite the lateness of the February afternoon, the audience did not disperse to their homes or the usual healthy diversions like the stews or the bear-pit. Rather, wanting to prolong the thrill of what they'd just gone through, they seemed most reluctant to shift from their seats or standing places though a few stepped up onto the stage. Some of the players were intercepted before they could reach the tiring-room.

Now, we players are used to acclaim. (A carping critic might say that this, the desire to be in the public eye and to be praised for it, is the main reason – no, the *only* reason – why some of us put on motley. And the carpers may be partly in the right.) Some are more accustomed to acclaim than others, it's true, and I hope one day to rise to the dizzy heights of a Burbage or a Phillips. But the kind of attention that the chief players were getting now was different.

Still in costume, there stood the late King Richard in the person of Robert Gough and the living Bolingbroke in the shape of Dick Burbage. Around these two in particular clustered the Essexites. Voices were raised; gesticulations became sharper. I recognised the dark figure of Signor Noti. He shook his fist at Gough before seizing hold of him by the shoulders and shaking him violently. When Dick Burbage, who was being fawned over as if he were a real usurper, noticed what was happening to Gough he walked over and put a restraining hand on Noti. The Italian spun round, mentally reaching for his dagger no doubt, but when he saw it was the 'king' (for Dick still wore the crown he sported in his final appearance), Noti bowed and withdrew. Eventually, we were allowed to proceed unhindered to the tiring-room.

Without the evidence of my own eyes, I shouldn't have believed such a scene possible. It was apparent that the passions of the Essexites were running so high that they wanted to mistake the sham for the real. For them, the man who played the usurper-king was a king in fact, while the player who personated poor Richard was a despised, feeble creature, to be bullied and crowed over. And yet here we were dealing with kings and queens, dukes and lords, who had been dead these many, many years. I do not think that the Essexites who clambered onto the Globe stage genuinely believed Gough or Burbage to *be* Richard or Bolingbroke – though who can penetrate the wilder recesses of the human mind? Rather, they were so transported by their own visions that they wished to applaud the victor and exult over the loser, even in play, even in effigy.

It made little sense to me. It frightened me too. To judge by the faces and manner of my fellows in the Company, none of us was pleased by the performance, even though one might say that it had been a triumph in terms of its reception. It is a good instance of the notion that one can do too well.

As I made my way back to the tiring-house, I saw Master WS deep in conversation with a finely dressed man. They were standing together at the end of one of the galleries closest to the stage. The man had his back to me but I knew him instantly for Henry Wriothesley. I had time to be surprised that he should deign to attend our performance (for certain, his master the Earl of Essex had not been present) before he noticed me as I passed.

"Mercury," he said.

He turned on me his brilliant gaze, and I felt myself come alive again after the turmoil of the performance and its conclusion. He and WS were standing a little above me but within an arm's distance.

"I hope that you enjoyed the play, my lord," I said.

"I was much affected by the troubles of the king," he said.

"Which one?" I said, greatly daring.

"Of the kings, you mean," said Master WS, looking at his companion with a gaze that seemed to combine a mild warning with – something or other. I really couldn't fathom what was between these two men. I couldn't fathom either what the Earl was doing at this Saturday performance. Essexite he might have been, but it all seemed a bit, well, crude for a man of his sensibility. He would not have cheered the downfall of a philosopher-king surely, even though part of him might have supported a Bolingbroke?

"Of the kings, I mean," said Wriothesley. "Thank you, William. As you always do, you put me right."

There was a mixture of compliment and pointedness in this reply and Shakespeare did not look particularly pleased. I sensed that he would have gone on to make some retort had I not been there. The despondent look that had hung about him the previous morning had cleared somewhat but he was still preoccupied. I wanted to ask him if he held to yesterday's opinion, that we players weren't in a position to pick and choose what we presented. For it seemed to me that we had stored up a mass of trouble for ourselves with our *Richard*, and all for forty shillings extraordinary! But this was not an opportune moment to ask questions of our chief playwright and shareholder, even had he been willing to answer them, and so, excusing myself, I went off to change. Before I'd moved a pace or two, the two men had resumed their private colloquy.

189

The rest of that Saturday was quiet, almost dead. Customers seemed to melt away from the Southwark amusements. I heard afterwards from Nell that she and the other women in Holland's Leaguer had never known such an absence of trade on the day before the Sabbath. The taverns and ale-houses were almost empty. It was as if the city authorities had rung a curfew. I loafed around the cold, inward-looking streets for a time, unwilling to return to the Coven and not sure of what reception I'd get from Nell if I tried her. My fellows in the Chamberlain's had mostly repaired to their homes and lodgings. It was an evening for each man to seek the shelter of the familiar.

For the second time within a few days I made my way along the Strand early in the morning. The pocky street was less populous than previously, but then it was a Sunday and all good citizens ought to have been preparing for their devotions at church. I wondered whether, if I was ever called up and fined for non-attendance myself, I'd be able to plead affairs of state. A wintry sun threw my shadow ahead of me. As I approached Essex House a rumbling noise grew louder. It was like water rushing over a weir. If it seemed to be drawing me on, it was doing the same for a few other fellows. They were trickling through the little postern gate. I noticed that they were armed.

I hoped to make an entrance in their wake for it was apparent that there was a greater crowd than ever in the courtyard; it was they who were responsible for the continual rumbling, a sound which had a curiously even and insistent quality to it. I fell in behind a gigantic, heavily bearded man who was waiting his turn to slip through the narrow entrance. He turned to me.

"We are summoned," he said in a surprisingly slight voice.

"Yes," I said

"Our hour has come."

"As you say," I said.

"At last."

Fortunately, I was saved from any more of these unsatisfactory utterances by his passing through the door from where he was immediately absorbed into the throng on the other side. On the other side also was Signor Noti. But there was a change in him from my last encounter.

"Ah, Signor Revill, the *commediante*."

"Signor Noti," I said, almost relieved to see a familiar if unfriendly face. I might have offered him his handkerchief back if I'd had it on me. He cast a quick eye up and down my form.

"You are not – how you say? – quipped?"

"Equipped?"

"Where is your weapon? *Vostro gladio*?"

"My weapon is well hidden," I said, thinking of the little blade I kept concealed, more suited for peeling fruit than anything else. Indeed, I'd never used it for any more life-threatening activity than nail-paring and cutting up food. "It is sharp and I am prepared," I added, falling into the prevailing style of threat and ambiguity.

"Sharp. *Bene*. Is good," said Noti, his moustache twitching and eyes already flicking to the next entrant through the gate. "*I grandissimi sono arrivati*."

"And our hour has come," I said, thinking that – insofar as I could understand him and his foreigner's tongue – he was wildly overestimating the importance of Nick Revill if he identified him as one of the great ones.

"*Si finalmente*, ower hower," said Noti in his Italian fashion.

I found myself pushed forward into the great yard. At first

glance, it contained the same mixture of men as before, a confused rabble of superannuated soldiers and reckless ne'er-do-wells. But whereas last time they'd looked smudged and dirty, as if newly landed from some foreign campaign or freshly scraped up from the streets, everyone now wore bright looks and clothes – well, brightish and rather gaudy. It was as if they were indeed dressing for their Sunday devotions, but devotions of no very holy sort. The noise in the yard, which I'd first heard from a distance, maintained its subdued but insistent note, seeming to come from nowhere in particular. Strangely, the sound was similar to the hopeful susurration of a playhouse congregation; whereas on the previous afternoon those attending our performance of *Richard* had sounded (and behaved) much more like a mob. This audible steadiness, this even buzz, suggested a seriousness of purpose which convinced me that I had walked into real danger, perhaps a trap.

Another feature reminiscent of the playhouse was the way in which most of the men in the yard were directing their attention at the raised area before the main entrance to the house. Unoccupied at the moment, it had the expectant air of an empty stage just before a performance. And just as it can sometimes be in an audience, each man was disposed to pass the time of day with his neighbour so it wasn't long before I found out from those around me enough information to make me want to take to my heels.

Noti's remark about '*i grandissimi*' hadn't been an ironic or flattering joke when I and one or two others passed through the postern. For there were genuine grandees inside Essex House at this moment. Someone said that the Lord Chief Justice was of the party. Another that it included the Lord Keeper. These great titles were uttered in no great tones of respect. Essex's official visitors had been ushered through the main entrance of his mansion only minutes before. No wonder all eyes were fastened to the spot before the porch.

The 'great ones' were come hot-foot from the Court and the Council, and for why? . . . to proclaim the Earl of Essex heir to the English throne – to arrest him on a charge of high treason – to restore him as his sovereign's favourite – to kneel down at his feet – to make him kneel down at *their* feet – to have his head – to follow his lead – and so on. Everybody knew why they were there and no one had the faintest idea.

So this wasn't going to be just another regular day at Essex House, after all, a day of ultimately peaceful turmoil and wild but swallowed words. Most likely, there'd be a few fiery adjectives thrown about before dark but there would also be an abundance of furious action. What I was witnessing here was the final throw of a desperate enterprise. It wasn't surprising the Essexites were dressed-up. If they were going to succeed they wanted to be well-scrubbed and attired for the occasion. But if it all went wrong, they planned to go to their deaths, as smug as bridegrooms. The trouble was that they might drag me down with them.

Instinct told me to run. I turned round to look at the postern gate by which I'd entered. But escape that way was already blocked. The door was tight shut, barred and guarded. Signor Noti had been joined by a couple of other exquisites, although whether they were stopping anyone else getting in or preventing them getting out was a question I didn't want to put to the test.

The impressive main gates to the courtyard were guarded by a detachment of halberdiers. We were sealed in, cribbed, cabined and confined. More to the point, I was sealed in.

While I waited on the event, I reckoned it would be less dangerous if I seemed to know what I was doing there. Accordingly, I cast my eyes about with a quietly purposive air, nodding or shaking my head with fervour when addressed and, in general, furrowing my brow while looking grim. There was not much play-acting involved in this pose. I estimated the numbers in the courtyard to be around three hundred or so – as a player, you get used to assessing the size of audiences. And an audience is what we were at this moment, waiting on the main players. There was even a kind of viewing gallery. Above the plumed or bonneted or helmeted or bare or bandaged heads in the courtyard, I saw faces, mostly women's, crowded at all the windows on the front of the house.

Then a rippling movement passed across the crowd, like a breeze through a field of corn. At the same time the faces at the windows craned forward and downwards to see what was occurring under their noses. There was a stir at the top of the steps which fronted onto the main entrance. A gentleman emerged, followed by a handful of others. They too were in their high-day finery but it was the genuine article, rather than the trumpery items and gaudy apparel worn by most of the crowd below. Among the men on the steps I recognised Henry Wriothesley. But the principal player was Robert Devereux, the Earl of Essex himself. Standing a little to his rear was a group of grey beards and white heads, whom I presumed to be the emissaries from Court and Council. For an instant I was gripped by the extravagant hope that these noble individuals had come to an accommodation indoors, so that we might all go home again with swords undrawn and harsh words kept in their sheaths. But a glance at their faces was enough to show that the parley which had taken place inside had, if anything, made the situation worse.

Even from a distance I could see that Essex's visage was white and taut with strain. His head was thrust forward, with one ear cocked in the direction of a tall, dark man by his side and his eyes scanning a piece of paper which he held in his hand. This was the third time I'd seen Robert Devereux and once again I had the impression of a man who was somehow part-abstracted from his surroundings, for all the drama of the occasion. He reminded me of a player who is going through his motions and mouthing his lines but whose mind is elsewhere – with his wife or his mistress, or distracted by debts and other dolours.

Essex handed the paper to the tall man and then raised his arms, half for quiet, half in acknowledgement. When he started to speak I was surprised by the moderate, almost mild tone of his voice. His words carried to the corner of the yard where I stood but would not have travelled much further. I suppose I'd been expecting a firebrand, a ranter, like the Puritans to whom he gave house room. Of course he'd been sick for much of the previous year, sick in body (and, I could not help thinking, perhaps in mind). Now he appealed to the crowd in the courtyard for help. He said that they, his friends, had been summoned there that morning because he was in grave danger. At this there were murmurs of assent and sympathy, together with some deeper-throated growlings.

Essex continued, more in sorrow than in anger as it seemed to me. "I have been sent for by the Council . . ." Here he paused, almost to encourage the cries of "Refuse them!" and "They betray you!" which swelled up from the crowd. I saw how adeptly he was acting the persecuted man, with his moderate tone and injured words. I started to revise my view of him; if he was a player, then he wasn't such a bad one. ". . . sent for by the Council, I say. But I mean with the help of my friends to defend myself. It is no offence if a man defend himself with the help of his friends."

There were cries of "aye!" and "no offence, none".

"But, my friends, it is only right that you should listen to Lord Keeper Egerton too. He has come with a message for me but I think it right to share it with you."

There were loud murmurs at this, of which one made not far from me – "He can be the Lord Keeper of my arse" – seemed representative. Essex moved to the side of the little platform at the top of the steps while one of the greybeards stepped forward. I had to remind myself that this individual was a very great man indeed, one of the most powerful in the kingdom. I had to remind myself that this was no playhouse stage, and that these events were being enacted on the stage of the world, where the blood that may flow is real enough (and not the sheep's blood that we employ in the playhouse), where men's wounds are often fatal and their words scarcely less dangerous.

When the Lord Keeper spoke, it was with one eye on the crowd. Doubtless he was tailoring his words for us almost as much as he was shaping them for Essex, Southampton and the other principals. This perhaps made him more politic than he would have been in private. Certainly the short dialogue which followed had an almost 'stagey' rehearsed quality to it. These men were speaking *at* each other and *to* an audience.

"My lord," Egerton began graciously, "our gracious lady the Queen has sent us to know the causes of your discontents and why you have assembled these men here today."

"My lord," Essex replied, "you may tell our gracious lady the Queen that the causes of my discontents and the cause why my friends are assembled here today are so close together that you might not put an hair between them. My discontents are theirs also – and these 'discontents', as you please to term them, I think you and the rest of the Council know well."

"Then you must also know that you have the promise of the Council for a full hearing and justice for any grievances."

"I know only that my life has been sought by the Council and that I should have been murdered in my bed."

Essex now spoke in a loud, unsteady voice that was at odds

with his earlier more-in-sorrow-than anger speech to us. Lord Keeper Egerton seemed taken aback by the vehemence of the Earl's words. It was as if Devereux had departed from a play text. Now Egerton repeated the promise that the other's grievances would be attended to. But Essex's outburst had broken the relative calm of the beginning of the encounter, and there was a general stirring on the stage at the top of the steps as well as renewed murmuring in the crowd. Another of the greybeards – even more reverend than the Lord Keeper, if that was possible – now took centre stage in an attempt to restore order to the scene. Some wag identified him in my hearing as Popham, "the Lord Chief Injustice". I couldn't hear what Popham said but his gesturing was sufficient to show that he meant for all the great ones to step inside the house once again and confer in private. This was too much for many members of the crowd. They'd had enough talk; they craved action. There was some outright shouting, including some from my Italian gateman.

"They will abuse you!"

"They betray you!"

"*Cattivi! Cani!*"

"You will be undone, my lord!"

"You lose time."

The Lord Keeper must have realised that the crowd was entirely hostile to him and the other Councillors, and that nothing was to be gained by reason or argument, for then he did a brave thing. He turned to face us and placed his hat back on his head. This seemed to signify that he was no longer making way for little courtesies but was acting now with the full weight of his office. He cried out:

"I command you all upon your allegiance to lay down your weapons and to depart."

Speaking for myself, I was so willing to comply with the

command that I would happily have burrowed in my clothing and laid my little knife at his feet, as if to say "Look at me, a loyal subject of her majesty." But my companions in the courtyard, after taking a moment to taste the seriousness of Egerton's words and not liking their flavour, proceeded to spit them out again. At the same time Essex replaced *his* hat on his head (as if this was a signal that hostilities were now to be resumed), spun round on his heel and marched back into his house. He was followed by the others, both the emissaries of the Queen and his own group. From the yard came cries of "Kill them!" and "Throw them out the window!" Signor Noti was particularly vocal in demanding instant death, as befitted his nation and his temperament.

Well, I thought, this will make a fine tale to tell my grandchildren one day – of how I once kept distant company with Earls and Keepers of the Great Seal and the like, and was present at the unfolding of great affairs of state – that's to say, if I lived long enough to sire the children who'd produce the grandchildren. At the moment this appeared doubtful. The mood in the courtyard was grim. Rapiers were being flexed, fingers pricked with dagger points.

I was right in my belief that no further indoors parley was intended for, within the space of a few minutes, Essex and Southampton reappeared on the steps in the company of some of his own gentlemen but without the Queen's men. At first I thought that they might have been murdered inside the house but, although there was a look of resolution on the rebels' faces, there was as yet no mark of bloody desperation about them. Whatever had happened to the Keeper and the Chief Injustice was probably no worse than involuntary confinement. The first shots had still to be fired in this battle. What had occurred so far was a shadow-play, a dumb-show.

Now everything happened very fast. Essex made a sign to

the commander of the halberdiers and then he and Southampton with their retinue made towards the main gates. The
crowd didn't know whether to accompany them or to make
way for them and, in the ensuing confusion, I found myself
carried forward and then almost thrown against Henry
Wriothesley.

"Mercury, you are here," he said, grasping at my arm in the
middle of the press. Absurdly, he sounded to my ears pleased
to see me.

"My lord," I said equally absurdly, as if we were meeting
back-stage.

We were forced forward together by the squeezing of the
crowd at our heels and shoulders. By this time the main gates had
been opened and the whole company gushed out into the
Strand. I'm not a military man but if there was an instant when
the Essexites were vulnerable it was surely as they – we – were
pouring into the public highway, confined between the gate-
posts and in disarray. But when I looked round the Strand, across
which fell the thin sun of a winter morning, I saw only a few
stragglers and a more disciplined group dressed in livery who
were, I presumed, the abandoned attendants of the Lord Keeper.

I began to think that, if the authorities were so remiss as to
despatch their greatest emissaries with only a handful of
unarmed servants, then they were too sleepy, too secure.
Where was Robert Cecil's famous foreknowledge? What price
Nemo's machinations now?

I was still next to the Earl of Southampton.

"Is this your fight, Mercury, or do you come with another
message from the playwright?"

"Neither," I said, unthinking – or not wanting to be
associated with this dangerous tide of men. In fact, I planned
to take to my heels as soon as I spotted a convenient bend or
corner.

"Then what are you doing here? This is a dangerous place, a dangerous time."

He looked hard at me as he said these words, with the Essexites milling all about us, shouting and crying, clasping each others' hands, leaning against one another like drunkards, brandishing swords and daggers so that they flashed in the sun. For some reason I felt disinclined to lie to Southampton – or maybe it was that I simply couldn't think of anything else to say.

"I – I am here as a witness."

"Yes," he said, seeming to accept what I said (which was, after all, a version of the truth and preferable to saying I was a spy). "A witness. We shall have need of those. In how many ages hence will this scene be acted over? How often shall we be called the restorers of our country's liberty? Yes, we shall have need of witnesses."

It was alarming that my innocent fragment of truth was being taken so seriously.

"Keep close to me, Mercury. I may need you during the day."

This was the last thing I wanted to hear. It would make slipping away more difficult. It would make slipping away look like desertion or betrayal. Then I thought that if I lived through this tumultuous day, if I survived this fraught hour, I would indeed have something to report to those grandchildren of mine. More to the point, I would have a great deal to tell Nemo and so earn his eternal gratitude – or at least gratitude enough to get me out of the hole I appeared to have dug for myself in this respect, and maybe enough to help protect the Chamberlain's into the bargain.

On the other hand, if fickle fortune favoured Essex and his followers, I'd be well placed to do . . . who knew what? Just well placed.

I'm faintly ashamed now to confess to these thoughts, which flashed through my mind incoherently, and in a fraction of the time it takes to read them. My main idea was still to get away, or if that was impossible to keep my head well down.

Where was the Earl of Essex during this period? He must have been at the edge of the group because there was a sudden surge to the right – that is to the east. Southampton moved through the press to rejoin his leader, urging me to accompany him. I might have broken away altogether at this point but it isn't easy to extricate yourself from a moving mass, or at least to move in the opposite direction. Besides, I felt a strange reluctance to abandon Wriothesley. I reasoned that we had not yet come to harm, and that it would be prudent to float on this stream for the time being – or if not prudent then less dangerous than attempting to swim against it. I tried to make my way after Southampton but without being in any great hurry to catch him up, if you see what I mean.

Thus we moved eastwards down the Strand and past Temple Bar, tramping and swinging all the while through mud and puddles with the indifference of children who have their minds on greater things and who forget their mothers' scoldings. While we were in the early stages of our march, Signor Noti strode along the edges of the company, urging us on with extravagant gestures and shouts of "Avanti!" and other incomprehensible foreignisms. I could not rid my mind of the thought: so this is what it is to be part (albeit an unwilling part) of a head, a rising, an insurrection! History's smithy was hot. Great works were being beaten out in her forge, were they not? I wondered whether these scenes would be enacted, as Henry Wriothesley had claimed, in centuries yet to come. I wondered whether other great happenings – such as the assassination of Julius Caesar, or the fall of the noble town of Troy – had proceeded in this lame-brain, rag-tag, half-meant fashion. Somehow I doubted it.

Now it was not so far from mid-morning and the sun beat on our heads with an unseasonable fierceness. There were some questions, shouted and whispered, about our destination. We were heading for the City but no one seemed to know exactly where we were going. And where were the cheering crowds, the faces packed at the windows, the supporters waiting to be picked up on the way? All the noise and the eagerness were coming from the few hundred of us who were streaming along, and not from the bystanders, of whom there were only a few – and those few seeming rather to be baffled than enthusiastic. As we passed between St Dunstan's and Temple Church, the number of watchers was swelled by men and women exiting the churches. But, as far as I could judge from my position at the edge of the throng, they were gazing at us with surprise or shock, as if we were a party of apprentice boys. Believe me when I say that I took care to shout or at least to talk loud in support of the rowdy company in which I found myself, at the same time as holding in reserve an expression of scepticism, of distance, should it be required.

This was the strangest journey I'd ever been on, I thought. Then I remembered that only a couple of days earlier I'd walked half a mile with a dead man on my back.

There were more people on the street at the bottom of Ludgate Hill, where the slope had the effect of compressing and slowing us down, but they avoided meeting our eyes or, if they did, regarded us with outright fear and hostility. I noticed one or two mothers actually snatched up their little children and cradled them to their breasts or turned their faces to the wall. I glimpsed doors being hastily shut. If the Essexites hadn't been so wrapped up in their own cause, if they hadn't still been making a fair amount of noise about it, they might have noticed the dead silence of the streets.

Once we'd penetrated the City walls through Lud Gate it became known by some strange, unspoken process that our destination was St Pauls. The great churchyard is the heart, or navel, of the City, and on weekdays is crowded with humanity of all shapes, mostly crooked ones. Fertile ground for the rearing of a head, perhaps. But on the Sabbath a pallid respectability establishes itself briefly over the area. If Essex's hope was that he would find the Sunday congregation just emerging and rather more ready to listen to his address than to a sermon, he was almost certainly too late. The morning service must have been finished some time since. In any case the silent streets and the barred doors smacked to me of the hand of the authorities.

I confess to a wish that someone should have stepped in at that point, likely a stern but kindly parent, and stopped us in our tracks, or turned us gently aside, or told us to disperse to our lodgings. Sunday is for home or church. This was not my fight. Even so I was quite unable to shift away from the tag-rag parade, partly from the shame of being seen to break ranks, partly through our hapless forward motion. I wondered whether it was in this spirit that men entered battle, willy nilly.

St Paul's churchyard was emptier than I'd ever seen it. Our low army milled about in the middle while the sun pondered us at a slant and Essex strode about, declaiming that there was a plot to murder him and a plot to sell the crown to the Spanish Infanta. I wasn't sure whether he was addressing us, or the handful of bystanders (who looked petrified or perplexed, as men will in the presence of the mad), or merely talking to himself. Sweat stood out on his white brow and his face was contorted. Much of the fire had gone out of the party.

There were as yet no murmurings of dissent but the few weapons in view were carried at a somewhat depressed angle and the cries were more muted. I caught the eye of the gigantic gentleman, the one who'd told me in a small voice as we entered Essex's courtyard that our hour had come. He looked away.

After St Paul's the next port of call on our mad, sun-lit progress was the house of Sheriff Smyth in Fenchurch Street. The Sheriff was waiting on his doorstep like the good host. His demeanour, however, looked to me not like one ready to receive visitors but rather of one who would bar them from his premises. I don't know why we were there. You might have thought it was to lay our hands on some arms, since Sheriff Smyth was known to be half an Essexite (although, until the moment when they were actually called on, many Londoners were half-Essexites). What we actually received from him was a drink. Perhaps to buy time, perhaps out of pity for us dry, sweaty rebels, he sent out his servants with tankards and cups of beer. When the liquor and the containers ran out, he ordered some of his fellows to fetch supplies from the nearest ale-house. The beer was most welcome but I could not help thinking it was beside our purpose, a digression on our journey. As we swilled and sweated in the sun, we watched our leaders conferring with the Sheriff. Then Essex entered his house and the Sheriff closed the door.

Then the moment came which told me that they – we – were defeated, when they'd barely started. No, to be precise, there were two such moments. Someone said that Devereux had repaired to Smyth's house not to discuss strategy or ask for support, but to request a change of shirt. Now, it was true that the day was unwontedly hot and that, as I'd already seen for myself, Essex had worked himself up into a lather. Nevertheless, just as one shouldn't change horses in midstream, one shouldn't, I suspect, change shirts in mid-rebellion. It reveals a lack of . . . some essential requirement for a successful uprising.

The second moment was this: to while away the time while his seniors were shut up with the Sheriff, shirt-hunting or otherwise, one of the Essex leaders high-handedly ordered a neighbouring armourer to surrender some half dozen halberds which were sunning themselves in the window of his shop. These weapons were triumphantly seized upon and bandied about as if they were genuine spoils of battle. Then I overheard the armourer, a stout tradesman and no whit abashed, ask the Essexite when he might expect payment for his goods. I didn't hear what answer was made, but it was at this moment – when a fat, phlegmatic shop-keeper enquired of a tall rebel when his bill would be settled – that I suspected our uprising was likely to fall flat on its face.

I didn't hear the response, if indeed one was given at all, because at that instant there came trotting up Fenchurch Street a detachment of horsemen. Some of the Essexites threw down their tankards and plucked out their swords, but the riders stopped well out of range. From their midst rode a brightly caparisoned figure. His costume was of a flashing richness, reds and golds and blues catching the sun. The ostrich feathers on his hat would have kept Icarus aloft. His horse, nearly as well decked out as the rider, skittered on the cobbles.

Slowly, deliberately, he extracted from his gorgeous garments a scroll which he unfurled with the same deliberation. No one uttered a word while this was going on. We watched as breathlessly as I have seen an audience hang on through one of Burbage's masterly pauses. Then the herald, as his subsequent words proved him to be, cast his eyes over the mass of men gathered in the street. I wondered what he saw through his case of eyes. A gathering of discontented individuals, some holding tankards, others with swords at half-port, sweat trickling off their brows, their Sunday finery looking not of the freshest. Though the herald had the advantage which a mounted man always possesses over grounded humanity, I noticed that he still kept a prudent distance. Arrayed behind him was his escort.

Then he spoke. His voice carried; it was clear and firm; sufficient prerequisites for a herald, I suppose.

"Hear you the proclamation of our most blessed sovereign, her majesty Queen Elizabeth, the defender of the faith, a prince anointed by God, the empress of England and Ireland. All good and loyal citizens are required to listen to her proclamation. Her most excellent Majesty and our gracious Queen hereby declares Robert Devereux, Earl of Essex, to be a traitor to her and to her realm. Moreover, she proclaims that all those who give aid, comfort and succour to the said Earl of Essex by word or deed are equally with him proclaimed traitors and no true subjects of her majesty. Furthermore, our most excellent sovereign declares that all good and loyal citizens are bound by their allegiance to give to her and to her realm any and all such assistance as shall be required to defeat the malice of treason and the impiety of rebellion. Long live the Queen!"

All around me there was silence as the import of the herald's words struck home. It was as if the Essexites had embarked on this enterprise in a reckless moment, or in holiday mood, and not realised until this very instant the gravity of their situation. For myself, I felt relieved that we had been, as it were, called to order. Surely now everyone would turn their faces homeward and do their best to bury this unhappy day.

The herald did not deign to gaze at us for more than a few moments after he'd delivered his proclamation. Perhaps he had our measure; or perhaps it was merely that he was commissioned to pronounce, not to parley. He wheeled his horse around and, surrounded by his entourage, trotted off down Fenchurch Street. There were odd abusive cries from Essex's company, but they lacked force or heart. Someone in the vanguard launched off a halberd – perhaps one of those which had just been appropriated – at the retreating troop. It was a gesture; a halberd is not designed to be thrown. It clattered harmlessly on the cobbles. That was all.

There was a sudden burst of conversation around me. "It's a trick," one said, and a second, "We are undone," while a third contented himself with muttering "Treachery" several times over in a pensive tone. The crowd moved uncertainly in one direction, then in another. If it had a mind, it was unable to make it up. Then Essex and the rest emerged from the Sheriff's house. The door was closed firm behind them as if to shut off assistance or retreat that way. He didn't appear to have got anything from the Sheriff, not even a change of shirt. I wondered whether Devereux had been sheltering indoors until the herald departed but quickly dismissed that notion. Foolish he might have been; a hothead for sure; not altogether in his right mind then (and perhaps for many months previously); but he was no coward.

Soon apprised of what had occurred – that he was now officially denounced as a traitor, and that all those who hitched their fortunes to his wagon would be similarly regarded – he tried to stiffen his followers' sinews by proclaiming that he alone stood for the good of the Queen and, mindful of his hearers, the good of London too. That if they searched for traitors now, they should be looking in other directions. His voice came wavering over the men strung out along the street.

But it was too late. Too late to indulge in argument and

definitions of treason. Essex's day might have been saved if the citizens of London had risen in his wake, as their forebears had massed behind the swaggering Henry Bolingbroke. But our mother city, she had stayed quiet – and thus had London spoken, in her own fashion. Now Essex, having failed to acquire new followers, started to lose command of those he already had. The company was fraying at the edges. One man near me made off down Mincing Lane. Another strode rapidly up the street, as if he'd just remembered an urgent, unperformed task. I spied the little-voiced giant edging his way with delicacy through the crowd; evidently he'd decided that, for him, the hour had come and gone.

Strangely, now that it was possible to make an unobtrusive escape from this unhappy scene, I found myself rooted to the spot. It was simple enough for any man to save himself by slipping down one of the many narrow streets and alleys which lead off Fenchurch Street, and this is what many were now doing. Some even discarded their weapons, either by leaning them carefully against the walls of houses (perhaps they thought to retrieve them later) or by letting them drop to the ground from nerveless fingers. If I'd earlier thought we were like an army marching, helplessly, towards a battle, I now saw the scene as a bloodless rout. It was the more shaming because there was no sign of an enemy, no smoke, no cannon, no sword or lance. We were self-driven from the field.

I don't know why I should have felt the shame of their defeat as if it were my own. Such a reaction was absurd too, because I had no interest in the Earl of Essex's success and ought to have invested every hope in his failure. Nevertheless, I was somehow sorry that events had taken this turn.

I must have fallen into a kind of reverie because the next thing I was aware of was Henry Wriothesley once again at my side.

"Come, Mercury, it will not do to stand here like a lame-brain in the middle of the road. We are all departing."

"Where?"

"Our day is not done. We have not finished."

He gestured in the direction of a mass of men beginning to move off in a westerly direction down Fenchurch Street. They were returning along the way we'd come not so long before. A glance sufficed to show that the Essexites were a depleted force, probably a spent one. I've seen mobs of apprentices almost as numerous. The difference was that these men – the ones that had chosen not to slide away down the alleys and side-streets – were the desperate and the dangerous ones. Or the ones with absolute conviction as to the rightness of their cause. Perhaps it comes to the same thing. They were still armed; and now, even though on the move, they were surely cornered. Among their number were several distinguished individuals. Knights and lords of the realm. Commanders, generals and other men of worth. Men who at other times had done the state some service.

None of these thoughts occurred to me at the time, of course. But later, when I tried to account for the peculiar sadness which the event threw over me, these were the terms in which I explained it to myself. It was my first experience of the waste – I can think of no better word – the waste, I say, that sometimes seems to lie at the heart of all our striving.

But such reflections were far from my mind now, as I looked at the Earl of Southampton.

"You understand, Mercury. We have not finished."

"If you say so," I said dully.

"But you are not with us. You never were."

While the stragglers of the group flowed past us, I struggled to remember our earlier conversation outside Essex House.

"A witness only," I said, finally recalling a talk that seemed to have taken place centuries before. "A witness."

"Like the playwright," said Wriothesley.

I thought I knew whom he alluded to, but for some reason did not want enlightenment.

"I'm a player, when all is said and done."

"A player," he repeated, and I wondered that he could find the leisure to echo my words.

"Nothing more than that," I said thankfully.

"What did I say?" he said. "I mean the first time that we met. Happy in that you are not over-happy."

"Though you did not apply the words to me, I accept them willingly."

"Do not become over-happy, Mercury," he said, clasping my shoulder. "Now make your escape. Do not travel in our direction."

"You too, my lord? It isn't too late to change course."

"That is the first foolish remark I have heard from your lips," he said. He half-smiled, turned on his heel and ran to join the vanishing troop.

Comes a time when every man must consider his own preservation. Instinctively I headed for the river and started off down Rood Lane. It was deserted. All good citizens had locked themselves up safe from the taint of insurrection, while those Essexites who considered discretion the better part of valour had already taken advantage of the few minutes since the herald's proclamation to put a space between themselves and their erstwhile leader.

I ran and ran, my feet thudding on the rough cobbles and trying to avoid the kennel which bisected the narrow street and whose contents, not touched by the direct hand of the sun, were nevertheless beginning to loosen in the warmth of the day and to grow slippery and noxious. Sweat poured down my face and trickled into my eyes, making my passage harder. All I was concerned to do was to reach the river, catch a ferry to the other side and go to ground in my home territory. Though normally accounted the most lawless region of our great city, Southwark seemed to me now, after the perils of the northern shores, a positive haven.

It was then that I heard behind me a familiar voice.

"Signor Revill! Signor Revill!"

I slackened and looked round, although I knew what I'd see. Sure enough there was our Italian exquisite in hot pursuit. At first I thought he was chasing after me in order to drag me back to the Essexites but a glance was enough to establish that he too was running away. His neat features were drawn tight, and I was pleased to note a disorder in his dress and a droop in his moustache. He drew level.

"Signor Revill. *Mio amico.*"

I made no reply but continued to move at something between a walk and a run.

"*Dove vai?*" he half shouted, keeping pace.

Without understanding his words I could guess at his meaning. He grasped me by the upper arm even as we were proceeding rapidly side by side.

"I say, where you go?"

I tried to shake him off but he had a strong, insistent grip. I wanted to rid myself of Signor Noti's company not only because I instinctively disliked – and feared – the man but also because I considered that he was not safe to be with. If they were looking for the leaders of the insurrection, then this loud-mouthed, finely dressed foreigner who had kept the postern-gate at Essex House would surely not escape their notice.

So I halted, meaning to disengage myself from his grasp even if I had to prise off his fingers one by one. Then, as we were gazing at each other like angry lovers, we heard a swelling sound, like many voices rising together and carried aloft on the wind. Then a sharper, more unmistakable noise: the rattle of pistol fire from a few streets away. It was coming from the quarter in which the remaining Essexites had departed. I guessed that they'd encountered some opposition, perhaps as they were trying to exit the city by one of the gates.

Signor Noti turned to look in the direction of the gunfire, releasing my arm as he did so. Then, with one accord, we made off down Rood Lane with renewed urgency. My impulse was still to get to the river; his impulse, evidently, was to stick by my side. I deferred the problem of escaping from him. As we crossed Thames Street I slowed down slightly, thinking that to be seen running in a more populous thoroughfare might be to draw attention to oneself, might be construed as the gait of guilt. I needn't have worried. The houses in this street too were firm shut. There was that air of fear and withdrawal which I have observed when the plague strikes.

I turned smart down St Mary Hill. I was breathing hard and, in between my own gasps, heard at my back the panting of my unwished-for companion. Moments later I – we – had reached the river. The February sun glinted off the water. It looked calm, reassuring. But our Thames is like the vulgar mob, never to be trusted, capable of changing its face from one instant to the next. There was a scatter of keys and landing points along this stretch below the Bridge and usually one found a ferry soon enough. A boatman, sometimes two or three, would be waiting at Billingsgate or Somar Key, or on his way across with a fare from the other bank.

As my feet clattered on the wooden platform which jettied out over the water, I shaded my eyes and cast about for a ferryman. The river returned my gaze with its blank glitter.

There didn't appear to be a boat, or at least not a boat in motion, anywhere. I wondered whether the ferrymen too had been seized by the prevailing alarm and had scuttled for shelter until this storm should have blown itself out.

To my right was the solid wooden cliff of London Bridge, to my left the wider expanses of the river. My home was on the other bank but it might as well have been in far Cathay, or in Elysium, for all the chance there seemed of reaching it at this moment. Of course, I could have walked the few hundred yards to the Bridge and thus made shift to cross the water. But the sound of gunfire still rung in my mind, if not my ears. I was convinced that 'they', the authorities, would have closed up the entrance on this side or, at the least, would be stopping and interrogating all those who wanted to cross from north to south. It was what I would have done in their position. Though no voluntary participant in the Essex uprising, though only present at this morning's turmoil because of the written instructions of an agent of the state, I was by no means certain that this guaranteed my safety. At worst, I might come within range of a careless pistol. At best, I could be seized and shut up. Then questioned and threatened. And afterwards tortured.

Not far along the northern bank is that Tower of London which men say was erected by Julius Caesar. I could see it from where I stood. There is a gate that leads straight from the river into the bowels of that grim building, through which traitors can pass direct and from which they may never emerge again. I was a small and unwilling player in this business, but who knew what sweepings-up of small players 'they' would authorise. My predicament would grow even more parlous when it was discovered that I was a member of the Chamberlain's, that notorious Company which only the preceding day had fomented public discord by staging the dangerous drama of *Richard II*. In my mind's eye, I saw the crouched instruments of agony and persuasion. I heard myself crying out all those answers which they will ease from you.

I shivered in the brisk air from the river.

It is strange how rapidly the scroll of disaster – of discovery, trial and penalty – can unfurl inside one's head.

During this brief space I'd almost forgotten my unwanted companion, Signor Noti. Now this gentleman tugged at my arm in his excitable fashion and gestured with his other hand at the open water, as if to demand that I personally produce a ferryboat, perhaps out of the sleeve that he was clutching. Why wasn't Captain Nemo here now, with his mysterious craft? He'd got me into this, with his persuasion and threats. Where was that stealthy nightboat? Why wasn't it waiting to rescue me? I was in this predicament because of a man with an ashen face, an individual who rejoiced in the name of Nemo, the title which Odysseus had chosen to escape detection in the cave of the Cyclops.

Then Noti pulled at my sleeve again and I saw that he was alerting me to the sudden appearance of a ferryboat virtually at our feet. Why, all this while, a boat had been tucked almost out of sight below the jetty! Now the boatman propelled himself into view and looked a query at us.

In his eagerness to get away, Noti jumped down into its cushioned stern and almost capsized boat and boatman.

"What the fuck do you think you're doing, you stupid cunt!" said the boatman, in tones that were (by the standards of Thames boatmen) comparatively mild.

"*Scusi, scusi,*" said Noti, holding his arms aloft, either in a penitential display or to counter the violent rocking of the boat. "*Non capisco, non capisco. Scusi, scusi.*"

"I'll fucking skoozi you if you do that again."

The boatman looked up to where I stood as if he suspected

me of being foreign as well. Indeed, in many English eyes, the act of being foreign is a grave crime, and one altogether without extenuation. If there'd been more than one boat I would have left Signor Noti to his own devices. With any luck the Italian might have so upset the boatman (metaphorically) – or the boat (literally) – that he would not have made it across the river. But there was only the one boat. So I smiled placatingly at the boatman and asked him in good, clear English to bring his craft nearer the ladder that was fixed to the end of the jetty. Then I clambered down the ladder and hopped nimbly into the boat in what I hoped was a mariner's manner, as if to say 'We Englishmen know a thing or two about boats and the water, we laugh at foreigners and their clumsiness.'

But I should have known that it is almost impossible to impress a Thames boatman. In fact, try to impress one and his mouth curves down in contempt while the rest of his face turns to stone. Which was the expression that now fastened itself to the bearded individual sitting opposite. The unattractive quality of his countenance was exacerbated by deep scars which furrowed one of his whiskery cheeks. As I settled down unwillingly next to the Italian fugitive, the boatman dug his oars into the glinting current and we moved away from the north shore.

Noti kept on looking round at the bank we'd left behind, as if he was expecting trouble or pursuit from that quarter. I pretended that I was nothing to do with the Essexite, that we were two men sharing a ferry by chance. But the boatman caught Signor Noti's anxiety, and probably mine as well. It did not require much perception.

"Trouble?" he asked slyly.

"Not at all," I said.

"There's been a stirring and rumbling on the north bank all morning."

"Has there?"

"What's the matter with him then?"

"He is foreign."

"I thought I heard the sound of shots a short time since," said the boatman, jerking his head. "In the direction you come from."

"Did you?" I said.

"Fucking strange how sound carries across water."

"I expect so," I said.

"What are you, a fucking parrot?"

He pulled in the oars and rested them on his broad and begrimed lap.

"No further until you tell me what's going on."

"Is it money you want?"

"Maybe. Depends on what you've got to say."

I reached into my doublet. I didn't have much on me but it might be sufficient to persuade the boatman to carry us to the far shore. I was aware of Noti, sitting close by on the thin, spray-spattered cushions and glancing uneasily from the boatman to me and back again. He must have had enough English to work out that we were being threatened. Expression and intonation alone would have been sufficient. I wondered what had happened to all his fine and dangerous airs. Why didn't he get out that narrow little dagger with which he'd pricked me on my first visit to Essex House? Why didn't he try to exercise a portion of his menace on this surly ferryman? Instead he sat, silent and seemingly unsure of himself, in the stern.

While the boatman waited on my answer, our boat was being carried remorselessly downstream by the current, which was more powerful at this point because of our proximity to the Bridge. Not liking the idea of ending up in the deserts of Surrey or, much worse, of being swept out into the open estuary, not liking the idea of staying on this pirate's craft a moment longer than I had to, I drew out a handful of coins and made some appropriate gesture. Reluctantly, our ferryman dug in his oars once more and waggled them about a bit, but only so as to arrest our drift, not to transport us to the south bank. When we were more or less back where we'd first halted in mid-stream he again ported his blades. Not before I'd handed over sixpence though.

"Now then," he said.

I'd decided that a measure of honesty would be the speediest way of rescuing us from this predicament.

"You're right," I said. "There is trouble in the city. We were unlucky enough to get caught up in it, innocent bystanders though we are, and . . . we had to run . . . for our lives."

"My arse," said my interlocutor.

"If you say so."

"Don't you start fucking parroting with me again," said this deeply unpleasant man. "You were right in the middle of it. I can see it on your fucking face. Admit it."

So much for my skills as a player.

"All right, yes, we were. I was anyway."

"This is to do with Essex."

This was not a question. The boatman was sure of his ground (or water).

Oh God, I thought. Just my luck to have stumbled across the only well-informed boatman in London town. This bearded being, with his downturned mouth, scarred cheek and contemptuous stare, who held our lives arrested and in mid-river, was probably one of those ordinary working men who consider themselves experts in statecraft. No doubt we'd now be treated to his views on a variety of subjects.

"With him or against him?"

"Who?"

"Essex, the fucking Earl of. With him or against him? Simple question, isn't it?"

I paused. Then said tentatively, "With . . . I was marching with the Earl . . ."

"And him?" said the boatman, nodding at Noti.

"Him too."

"*Si, si,*" said Noti, his little mouth working earnestly. He seemed to have been able to follow the rudiments of what we'd been talking about. "Earl of Essex – 'e is *uomo di guerra, uomo di cuore, uomo bravo, uomo—*"

"You get the drift," I said quickly to the boatman. "The gentleman beside me is a supporter of Essex."

"He takes all fucking sorts, the Earl, don't he."

"*Per molto variare la natura e bella,* " said Noti. I didn't know what he meant but I couldn't help contrasting the musicality of his tones with the guttural, oath-strewn harshness of the boatman's language. Even so I was eager for my Italian to keep his teeth together. If being foreign is crime enough in many English eyes, then speaking in another tongue is, to those same English ears, a dangerous aggravation of an already serious offence.

"With the Earl then?" said our boatman.

"Yes."

There was another pause. Then a strange transformation occurred in the boatman's grim visage. The down-turned mouth creased upwards in a species of smile. His tangled beard seemed to catch the sun, and the spray-sprinkled whiskers sparkled with light. Even the angry scars on his cheek looked to be glowing with approval.

Evidently I'd jumped the right way in claiming to be on Essex's side. (In truth, the gamble wasn't as great as it might appear. For one thing, many Londoners were supporters of the Earl – or at least they had been until he called on them to take up arms. For another, boatmen as a class were notoriously hostile to the authorities and so would have instinctive sympathy with any rebel. And for a third, the way in which the boatman had phrased the question, "With him or against him?", suggested to me his own leanings in this affair. I also thought I'd detected a near-tenderness in the way he'd mentioned the Earl by his title, even if he'd appended a 'fucking' to it. This, in a boatman's mouth, is not necessarily a mark of disapprobation. So for all these reasons, which flashed across my mind like lightning, I'd felt on fairly safe ground when claiming to be of the Essex party. Even so, it was a relief to see our ferryman responding as he did.)

He now reached across and patted me approvingly on the shoulder. He almost brought himself to do the same for Signor Noti, who grew visibly brighter at this turn in our fortunes.

"Why didn't you say so?" he said.

"Not all of London is a friend to the Earl."

"Not in my boat, they're not fucking not," said the ferryman, tying himself up, sailor-wise, in his nots.

"Essex, 'e good man, 'e *uomo di corte*, 'e *uomo d'onore*, 'e—" began Noti vigorously before I cut him off.

"Could you ferry us to the other bank now?"

The boatman planted his oars firmly into the current and we made good progress towards land. As we travelled on, we were honoured with his maritime reminiscences.

"I was with him, see, in the Islands voyage. With the Earl in the A-zores. In '97. Where I got these." He tilted the scarred side of his face.

"A great campaign," I said, groping in the cupboard of memory to discover whether this was one of Essex's victories. Unfortunately, the cupboard was bare.

"A great *commander*," said the boatman. "Not his fault if the fucking dagos cheated us."

"They're foreigners, what else do you expect," I said, but the boatman was now well launched on his private stream of memory and required no prompting or agreement.

"They knew we were lying in wait for them off the A-zores, and so did not send their treasure fleet that way from the Americas. Those bastard sods, those devious dagos. So we did not get our chance to crack their skulls and seize their golden plate that year."

I pulled a commiserating face. By now we were only yards from a key on the south bank.

"Is he a dago?" he asked, meaning Noti, who had been pursing his little mouth in puzzlement over the boatman's words.

"Oh no, he's not Spanish, no," I said quickly.

The boatman's curiosity as to the race of my fellow-passenger went no further. "They are fucking duplicitous," he said, "and do not play fair. Not sending their treasure boats past where we were lying in wait for them. Still, never let it be said that it was the fault of fucking Essex, though there were some back home – over there [*he jerked his head sideways in the vague direction of Whitehall upriver*] – who sought to blame him."

We bumped up against the jetty. I made to pay the ferryman for the crossing but he shook his head.

"Answer me this one thing."

"If I can."

"He's lost, hasn't he?"

"This time, yes," I said.

"It's his last campaign, his last fucking campaign, isn't it?"

"I fear so," I said.

"I knew it," said this pirate, sniffing loudly and waggling his oars about.

Sensing my moment, I again made a gesture of payment. "Any friend of Essex's a fucking friend . . ."

He grasped me feelingly by the shoulder once again and his eyes glistened with moisture – incipient tears, or perhaps no more than flecks of Thames water. Now that this boatman and I were firm friends, I briefly considered whether it was worth asking him for the return of the sixpence which he'd extorted from me midstream (sixpence is sixpence) but decided against it (sixpence is only sixpence, after all). He might be a man of feeling but he was also a pirate.

While I paused, Signor Noti had hopped onto the jetty ladder with surprising nimbleness. Now he hung there by one arm and, half smiling under a moustache which had regained some of its exuberance, reached out with his right hand to facilitate my own passage from ship to shore. It's hard to turn down an outstretched hand. As I made to clasp it, thinking that I had misjudged this slippery foreigner, Noti must have lost his own footing on the slimy rungs. He managed to keep clinging onto the ladder with his left arm but his right jerked sideways, almost seeming to consign me to the water. At the same time the boat swung away from the jetty so that I was straddling a watery abyss.

I went down.

I do not like water or boats (or boatmen). Nothing that happened in the next few seconds caused me to change my mind. Some of the murky Thames blurred past my descending eyes, some entered my gaping mouth, while the rest of it sogged my clothes and boots so as to pull me down into the dark depths. The entire river was my enemy. The water was freezing.

I flailed wildly. My head shot clear of the water and I spluttered and tried to call out. How big water is when you are immersed in it! In my panic I was aware of the side of the ferryman's boat and of him waving his oar about before I went down for a second time.

This time I seemed to be sinking faster and further. Yet, such is the celerity of one's thoughts in these drastic moments, that I also had time to remember how I'd once seen some men of fashion swimming in these very waters, using bladders to stay afloat. Ridiculous! If God had intended humankind to take to the waves He would have furnished us with fins.

Then I resurfaced. Only to see the boatman waving his oar about as if he wanted to strike me over the head. As I sank for the second time, I considered that he must be a very unfeeling pirate to lash out at a drowning man. I thought we were friends, fellow Essexites.

Struggling, kicking. trying to push out sounds through a water-logged gullet, I came to the surface for a third time and there was that same fucking stupid fellow still attempting to smash me about the ears. Only I suddenly realised that what he was actually doing was holding out the oar for me to catch hold of and once I'd seen that he meant me no harm I reached out my hands and clasped gratefully at my salvation and was pulled towards the side of the ferry and with much puffing and oath-making was hauled and tugged and manhandled until I was landed on the bottom of his boat where I lay gasping, breathless, thankful.

After a time, I sat up and he pulled in towards the jetty. In truth we had never drifted very far from it – but what of that? A man may drown in a bucket, let alone a portion of river. My ferryman, now my saviour too, looked at me with a mixture of concern and mild amusement.

"Foreign?"

He didn't have to say who he was referring to. The ladder leading up to the jetty was empty. I nodded, scattering water droplets about me.

"What did I say?" said the boatman triumphantly. "Fucking duplicitous is what I said."

"You were right, my friend," I said, suddenly aware of a nasty river taste in my mouth. "Thank you for . . . for saving . . . my . . . you know . . ."

The boatman's awkwardness matched my own. His scars blushed, he looked away.

"Would've been fucking otherwise if you weren't an Essex man. Then you'd've got this over your pate."

He clattered one of his oars. Smiling weakly and waterily, I hoisted my water-logged self up the slimy ladder and once atop the jetty waved farewell to my preserver. He was already on his way back to the other bank. Then I looked about me. The platform was deserted. There was no sound apart from the soft patter of my dripping clothes.

Signor Noti had vanished. The sensible Italian. Because, if he'd still been there, I would have thrown him into the water, moustache, finery and all.

Well, I thought to myself, I'm well out of that. Little did I know.

As I learned later, the second act of the Essex uprising was a short-lived affair. The shots that Noti and I had heard as we sped down Rood Lane were indeed the result of a skirmish between the retreating band of the Earl's men and a detachment of pikemen and halberdiers by Ludgate. The tattered remnant of the rebels had then, like us, fled in the direction of the river. At about the same time as I was heading hot-foot (and also wet-foot) for my lodgings at the Coven, the leaders of this lost cause must have been boarding boats at Queenhythe. From there they made their frantic way back to Essex House. God knows why. Perhaps the Earl thought to use his great hostages to bargain with; perhaps by then he was beyond thought.

The last scene of this strange, eventful history occurred when the Lord High Admiral brought up cannon and threatened to blow Essex House and its occupants into the next world. Surrender soon followed. The Earl together with Southampton and some of their lesser fellows were brought to that same mighty Tower which I'd glimpsed and shivered at on the north bank.

Essex had raised a head in order to save his own. Now he looked most certain to lose it. Southampton too perhaps, and I could not help but regret the likely execution of a man with whom I'd passed a few pleasant minutes. I wondered at Master WS's reaction too. If I knew a little more about these things than the common man in the Strand it was because we in the Chamberlain's were deeply interested in the uprising and its aftermath. Not only because of our minor role in mounting *Richard* on the Saturday afternoon. Now Master Augustine Phillips had been summoned before the Council to explain why we had gone ahead with such a dangerous production. Others in the Company might have to follow him and explain themselves as well.

For my own part, I was glad that there was such a bulwark of older, more experienced men to bear the brunt of the world's quizzing and disapproval, and possibly worse. It did not seem likely that the Council's attention would be directed towards an insignificant young player. In any case, I told myself, I was working for the agents of that Council. Had I not enjoyed a midnight meeting with Secretary Cecil? Was I not a dutiful spy for the mysterious Nemo? These connections would provide protection – surely?

Nevertheless I also took a small measure to safeguard myself. In my chest in my room at the Coven were the notes I'd made of the conversation between Sir Gelli and Augustine Phillips. Although Captain Nemo knew that I'd eavesdropped on the scene, having heard my account of it on his dark boat, no one but I knew of the existence of a *written* record. Hadn't I seen in the case of Richard Milford how incriminating a few sheets of paper could be? The moment I got back to my lodgings after quitting the Essex boatman and being quit by the Essex Italian, I went anxiously to my chest.

Now, in the way of such things, it may be that I expected to find it gone. After all, Nat had already tampered with my unlockable chest with fatal results. Were this a story, the papers would most certainly have disappeared, filched by persons unknown. But no, the dangerous document was still there, tucked up close to my Chamberlain's contract. Be sure that I speedily set it alight and watched with satisfaction as the sheets containing Merrick's and Phillips' sentences curled and blackened. I ground the ashes thoroughly into my filthy, uneven floor. As a way of disposing of compromising words, it was preferable to eating them.

End

Friday 13 February – Tuesday 24 February 1601

fter all this excitement, I could now get back to
worrying about minor domestic matters, such as the
aftermath of my amour with the murderous Isabella
Horner. And in order to describe what happened next I am
going to introduce:

Another Interlude

Scene: The Goat & Monkey Tavern
Time: One morning a few days after the events described on
the preceding pages. In fact an ominous day, Friday the
Thirteenth. Whatever its number, Friday is an unlucky day
anyway, they say, particularly in matters of the heart.
Characters: Jack Wilson, Jack Horner, Martin Hancock,
myself and a handful of other men of the Company.
Theme: There was only one theme to our conversation in
those days: the uprising, and the role which we in the
Chamberlain's had played on the borders of Essex and his
business; what was going to happen to the rebels; what might
happen to us players.
(Mind you, we kept our opinions pretty much to ourselves.
We talked low in taverns; we spoke in asides in the tiring-

house. On this occasion I was only half listening to the conversation that was flying to and fro between Wilson and Horner and the rest. Normally, I'd have been willing enough to throw in my groatsworth, though always mindful that I harboured great secrets of state. But I was distracted. For when we arrived at the Goat & Monkey who should be there but Mistress Isabella Horner, drinking hard on a bench and all the while looking displeased and dark. Strangely – considering that she'd tried to poison me – I felt a little stab of desire. Her husband greeted her without much surprise but with the abstracted air which I'd seen him use before, as if to say 'What are *you* doing here?' He was more interested in pursuing the debate about *Richard II* with his fellows. That left Mistress Horner to me, so the following talk ensued when I'd got a drink and positioned myself next to her. I suppose I intended to . . . have it out with her. Recklessly, I would accuse her of being a reckless homicide. We spoke in urgent but subdued tones. My heart beat hard in my chest. Here sat the wicked woman who was responsible for the death of a poor innocent, Nat the Animal Man. And almost responsible for the death of another poor innocent, Nick Revill, player.)

Nick Revill: Well, Mistress Horner, you must be surprised to see me.
Isabella Horner. Why?
NR (*remembering that Isabella's poison had been, as it were, dateless. If her plans had gone a-right, I would only have known the secret of the fatal bottle when I woke up to find myself dead*): Er.
IH: Let us turn the tables. *You* seem surprised to see me.
NR (*behaving like a player who has lost his prompt*): Um.
IH: I suppose I may be here sometimes.
NR: Alone?

IH: I suppose I may drink alone, Master Revill.

NR: To be sure. But a woman alone in a place like this might easily be mistaken . . .

IH: Mistaken?

NR: . . . for a whore.

JH: That must be why so many of you playhouse fellows frequent a place like this. To mistake women. To mis-take women, whether we want it or no.

NR: I cannot speak for the others.

IH: And when you speak for yourself it is to tell me that your bent is in a different direction.

NR: If you say so.

IH: Come, Master Revill, it was you that told me so and told me most clear, the last time we met.

NR: Perhaps I am cured or reformed by now.

IH: I thought you liked travelling on your by-ways of vice.

NR: *Unnatural* by-ways, according to you.

IH: But ones that are in *your* nature. Tell me, can nature deviate from herself so quick?

NR: What if I had taken some of the liquor that you prepared for me? You remember? The liquor in the little green bottle that was to restore me to the highway of women.

IH: Have you?

NR: Yes.

IH: Good.

NR: You sound – surprised.

IH: And you seem to be detecting surprise everywhere today, Master Revill. You have swallowed some of my concoction and I say good. That is all.

NR: And I ask you what my inclination should be now, after I've swallowed your concoction.

IH: That is for you to tell me, surely.

NR: Oh I will tell you what my inclination is – or what it should be. It should be a dead man's inclination. I should be lying flat.

IH: You mean . . . in a bed?

NR: I mean in a grave.

IH: I do not understand you.

NR: Oh you do.

IH: It is no good growing angry. Besides, you are attracting the attention of the others. Calm yourself. I say, I do not understand you.

NR: Come, Mistress Isabella, enough evasion.

IH: How can I evade something if I don't know what it is I'm meant to be evading? This is about my concoction, is it?

NR: Say poison rather.

IH: Poison!

NR: It was my word, lady.

IH: I – I – still don't understand . . .

NR: Then let me put it plain. You gave me a preparation which you pretended would cure me of my preference for men. It would have cured me of more than my preference, it would have cured me of my life.

IH: You say you tried it, and yet you are here.

NR: I said that to lead you on.

IH: Lead me on? And I suppose you said that you preferred men to women to lead me on too?

NR (*realising that this conversation was not going in the direction I'd planned*): Not to lead you on, no . . . but rather to lead you off.

IH: Master Revill, did you drink deep before you came to the tavern this morning? Very deep? You are making no sense. You have told me two stories and now you are denying them.

NR: What did you put in that concoction?

IH: No more than a compound of a few simples and . . . and . . . something of my bodily self.

NR: What thing?

IH: That is my secret. But it was a kind of love potion – to win you back.

NR: I thought we were finished

IH: *You* finished it with your talk of men and unnatural vice.

NR: I did not mean that. It was all pretence.

IH: And what is all this about poison? Is that pretence too? Do you not mean that either?

NR: Forgive me, Mistress Horner, I'm not sure what I do mean any longer. I think I may have made a terrible mistake.

IH: As when you said I might be taken for a whore?

NR: That was a joke.

IH: Oh ha.

NR (*blushing as furiously as Richard Milford*): I'm sorry.

IH: But let me treat your nonsense seriously. How would I be taken for a whore? Instruct me.

NR (*hoping to divert the dialogue onto less dangerous territory*): A piece of advice then, you need a brighter costume – something – something flame-coloured.

IH: Like that woman over there?

NR: Who? Where? Oh her. Oh Jesus.

(*Across the Goat & Monkey came my friend Nell. There wasn't much doubt about the nature of her trade, considering the flame-coloured dress she wore and the fair bit of tit she was showing, for all the coldness of the season. At any other time I'd have been quite pleased to see her but she was arriving at a most inopportune moment, just after I realised that I'd made a gross error in accusing my ex-mistress of being a poisoner.*)

NELL: Nick!

NR: Nell.

NELL: What are you doing here?

NR: Finishing a drink. I think I must be getting back to the playhouse now. We are rehearsing for tomorrow afternoon.

NELL: No, stay a moment. Who is your friend?

NR: This is Mistress Horner. And that is her husband over there.

NELL: Yes, I know him, Nicholas. I know most of you, you know.

IH: And who is this lady, Master Revill?

NR: This is a – Nell.

IH: Oh, a Nell . . . one of the tribe of Nell.

NELL: Shove up, Nicholas, there's room for me between the two of you. And now tell me what was making you smile when I saw you from the other side of the room.

IH: Well, Nell, Master Revill here has been instructing me in how to recognise a whore by certain signs and tokens.

NELL: Nicholas is a good teacher, so listen to him. He knows much about the sacking law.

IH: Sacking law?

NELL: Whoredom.

NR: I protest I know nothing about it, next to nothing. Truly, I don't.

IH: You protest too much, I think.

NELL: What signs and tokens, Nicholas?

NR: I . . . er . . .

NELL: I will tell you. A red dress like this one I am wearing, and cut so as this one is cut, and an inviting look like this one I am giving you now, Nicholas. You see it? These are your signs and tokens.

IH: Ah yes, Nell, I understand that I am a novice here.

NELL: I am not coy about my trade, Mistress. Why should I be?

IH: No reason at all. We are not the coy ones here. We are not engaged in a mysterious business. Leave that to the men. They will make up stories until your head spins. Master Revill has been talking in a most peculiar way.

NR (*making to rise*): Look, my companions are going. I must return to the Globe. Important rehearsal.
NELL: Go, Nicholas, if you must. Leave me to enjoy Mistress Horner's company.
IH: Yes, Master Revill. There is obviously much for me to learn from this lady . . .

So I went off, uncomfortably, after my fellows. I noticed that Jack hardly acknowledged his wife Isabella, just as I'd noticed that she had never taken up Nell's hint about knowing her husband. I wondered what the women were going to talk about behind my back and was afraid enough that their subject would be me. (At the same time, though, if I'd been told by a little bird that neither breathed a word about me after my departure, I'd have been disappointed.)

But the main thought that whirled around in my head was: how could I have been so foolish as to brand Mistress Isabella Horner with the mark of Cain? A strange, dark and passionate woman she might have been, but that did not turn her into a murderess. It was not unlikely that she had harboured the odd homicidal prompting towards me – for certain, she was most indignant when I announced that I wished to terminate our amour – but which of us has not occasionally harboured such promptings?

I had been misled by my alarm at Mistress Horner's manner when we parted, her raging temper coupled with her gift of the bottled potion which would put my heart in order. Then came the discovery in the Coven garret of Nat's body, with his hand clawed round the little green bottle, drained of its contents. What more natural than to assume that his demise was linked to Horner's concoction? And that, in accomplishing his death, she had really intended to procure mine? In a peculiar way, it underlined my importance to her;

that she would give me a poison to take in my own good time – rather say, in my bad time. How much more likely, though, that a woman would give me a love potion compounded of some few simples . . . and something of herself (naturally, I wondered from whereabouts that tantalising something had emanated). So in the same way that I had leaped to the premature conclusion that she was a murderess, now I jumped in the opposite direction and became convinced of her innocence. Far from meaning harm, she had genuinely intended reform. She really did wish to win me away from the by-ways of vice, and perhaps to usher me back towards her bed.

Remained the question: what had Nat the Animal Man died of? That was not so hard to answer either, even if the cause of his death might never be known for sure. Hadn't I thought to myself as I tucked his body into the leaf-strewn ditch beside the road that, if found, he'd be taken for one of the many vagabonds who died outdoors in the winter months through cold and hunger? The only difference was that Nat'd died indoors, my indoors. But his life was essentially no different from a vagrant's. Whether he had anywhere regular to lay his withered poll was doubtful. What little money he earned from his stock of beastly sounds and from running little errands for individuals such as Nemo, he pissed away in ale. He must have been tough to defer death for so long. Perhaps he'd succumbed to a sudden apoplexy, a fatal fit (I remembered his stretched mouth, his raggedy teeth, his huddled posture on the floor). Perhaps in some final agony or confusion of mind, he'd ransacked my chest, found the bottle and swallowed its contents to the last drop. Perhaps, as I'd originally thought, he'd simply been rummaging through my sparse belongings in search of liquid refreshment as he awaited my return.

Drank and died. *Post hoc sed non propter hoc.* After but not on account of. Nat died natural. So I settled it. So I thought.

These weren't easy days for us at the Chamberlain's. The ordinary business of February persisted but it was thin enough fare at the Globe, practically lenten fare, and we were reduced to a couple of performances a week. Of course, we were still rehearsing for our presentation of *Twelfth Night* at Whitehall some days hence.

The strange aspect to this was that, even while we were mouthing Master WS's words for the twelfth time and having our costumes checked for the twentieth – and all so that we might shine bright in the presence of Her Majesty – we were apparently suspected of being enemies to her person and her realm. Although the Burbage brothers and Shakespeare and the other seniors continued to attend to their duties both in the playhouse and at the Clerkenwell Revels Office, they did so with the air of men who were distracted. This was under-standable for we all knew that, from time to time during the days that followed on Essex's failed rising, one or other of our shareholders was being hauled before some members of the Council or their agents to give an account of the Company's participation in the rebellion.

To wit: why had we agreed to stage *Richard II*, knowing the state of things, having regard to the pressures of time and place, being aware of the dangerous condition of London, indeed of England?

Augustine Phillips, he was summoned on at least two or three occasions. This was perhaps not altogether surprising since, as I knew from my eavesdropping in the book-room, he had taken on the principal role in negotiating with Merrick the Essexite, a knight who now found himself incarcerated in the Tower. It's a measure of the closeness of our Company that the report of what Phillips said in his – our – defence should have been so soon spread among the rest of us. According to Company talk, Master Phillips claimed that the play of King Richard was so old and so long out of use that the Chamberlain's Company had small expectations of an audience. Why then did they play it? Persuaded by the inducement of forty shillings, was his answer.

Now, if I'd been a member of the Council, this would not have convinced me. Why, had I not heard Master Phillips make the very same points to Merrick on their first meeting? That the play was fusty and dusty. Identical objections had been raised at the general meeting of the Company. That Richard was indeed an old piece. That we might fail to draw an audience. That this was a giddy moment to stage this particular play.

All true. Except perhaps for the point about the audience; although, even in this respect, the congregation on that Saturday had been mostly made up of devout Essexites, renegades who would have watched the rain fall if their leader had instructed them to.

So the mystery remained: why had we staged this play?

And another mystery: why did the Council accept, or seem to accept, the reasons which Augustine Phillips and the other shareholders gave? Reasons? Excuses rather. I repeat: had I been a member of the Council, or one of their agents, I would have probed further. They had, after all, sufficient instruments for probing at their disposal.

Don't get me wrong.

I was relieved, I was delighted, that they – we – escaped unscathed from this dangerous pass. And if we were ever in real disfavour, which I doubt, it was very short-lived. The proof of this? Well, we did indeed perform before Her Majesty on Shrove Tuesday, 24 February. You shall hear about that performance and its aftermath soon enough.

What puzzles me is how we – they – got away with it.

Only now do I have an inkling (and you'll hear about that soon enough too).

The fortunes of the Chamberlain's, and whether one or two of its senior members might be cast into gaol, was pretty small beer to anyone outside the playhouse. The eyes of London were firmly fixed on the fate of the Earl of Essex. Within a few days, indictments were laid against him and Southampton and others. The trial of the two Earls followed hard at heels, and it was clear to all that there could be only one sequel to this.

These things didn't weigh very greatly on my mind, except for the passing regret about Wriothesley which I've already mentioned. Even here, I felt it greatly daring and presumptuous to be concerned at the fortunes of a nobleman. I was slightly surprised not to have been summoned by Nemo to another midnight meeting. It was he, after all, who had instructed me to be a spy in the house of Essex in the first place and who had then conveyed, via the unfortunate Nat, a message commanding me to attend an uprising. Except, of course, Nemo couldn't have known that that Sunday morning had been chosen as rebellion's glorious dawn, could he? Any more than he should have been aware that the Chamberlain's were going to stage the 'foul play' of *Richard* on the Saturday. Why, we hadn't decided on this ourselves until the company meeting which I'd attended *after* receiving Nemo's note (and eating his words, literally).

I say 'we hadn't decided' but of course the decision had already been made by the shareholders, baffling though it might have been to us common players. Now, Nemo's note suggested prior knowledge of which way we were going to jump. Which suggested, in turn, collusion – or, at the least, an understanding – between the authorities and the senior

Chamberlain's, the very gentlemen who were now being quizzed by those same authorities. Which suggested . . . I didn't know what. My poor brain reeled as it had when I'd been blindfolded and led a dance through the dark streets to meet Cecil. All I knew was that I wanted nothing more to do with the world of spies and affairs of state.

Such thoughts ran in my head as I returned to my lodgings after a morning rehearsal for Richard Milford's *A Venetian Whore*. In this comedy I played one of the three suitors for Belladonna's hand. She is, you will recall, the heroine of the piece, a lady who, to test her would-be lovers' sincerity and purity, takes to a whore's life, or to a whore's garb and manners at any rate. I was a nobleman – the Duke of Argal – come to woo the wealthy Belladonna with the prospect of an extensive champaign, with fertile meads and rich forests. Unfortunately, during my return to the Dukedom of Argal I decide to drop into a brothel and there I take a fancy to a new woman. Who, just before she succumbs to my blandishments (viz. money), reveals herself to be . . . the disguised Belladonna! No fit husband-to-be, I slink back to Argal.

It was a nice role, somewhere between small and large, and I played the nobleman with one or two touches of grace and ease which I'd picked up in my brief encounters with (whisper it soft) the Earl of Southampton. And *A Venetian Whore* had the great advantage for us at this moment of being a light, frothy piece, nothing to do with kings, depositions or deaths. However, the play isn't the thing here. I mention it and my part in it merely to report on the behaviour of Richard Milford during rehearsals.

I'd already observed the manner of a handful of authors during my short association with the Chamberlain's, and before that with the Admiral's. They are strange creatures, not seeming to realise their own strangeness. I except Master

Shakespeare here. Though not indifferent to his own words, he showed a kind of casualness about their application. I have occasionally watched him step forward so as to moderate a player's delivery, to temper his gestures and motions, but I have not otherwise seen him seek to interfere in the player's craft. This is perhaps because he himself is a player, and understands how each man must be left to find not only his own voice, but his own stance and gait. With other authors it can be different.

Master Milford was an extreme case of fret and worry. Fitfully watching as we mouthed his lines (not really his, of course), he could hardly keep still. He strode around in the groundlings' area, casting sidelong glances at the stage. Then he would materialise backstage, ear pressed to the panelling, checking that we were sticking to his precious text – as if he had actually written it! A moment later and there he was hanging about on the edge of the platform, biting his nails to the quick and getting in everyone's way. He had something of the quality of the ghost in *Hamlet*, able to be everywhere at once, *hic et ubique*. At one point, Heminges had to ask Milford to kindly leave the stage, which he did, blushing furiously.

Now, I do not know whether Richard Milford would have been so restless and troubled if he had been the genuine and only begetter of *A Venetian Whore*. Was he agitated as an author or as a plagiarist? I alone knew that he was the guardian of another man's words, even if that other was an anon. And he knew that I knew. This perhaps explained why I often noticed him observing me during his perambulations about the fringes of the stage. Even during the ragged attendance at a rehearsal, a player soon learns not to fix his eye on any single member of the audience; it can be disconcerting for the one so picked out, and besides it seems somehow discourteous to all those others who have paid their pennies. So I did not return

Master Milford's stare but it seemed to combine two contradictory qualities: a kind of brazenness and a species of shame. As if to say, 'Shog off, Master Revill, I care not what you think' and 'Please, Nicholas, do not give me away at this point – just as my play is about to be given to the public.'

Perhaps Master Milford intended to convey no such mixed message to me. Perhaps it was merely that, in his shoes, shoes which had been borrowed (or stolen) off another, I would have felt the same compound of guilt and defiance. Those two are old bedfellows. In the matter of Milford, I thought too of his odd parti-coloured eye and remembered his excited talk about the sword of Damocles. Then I tried to put him out of my mind and enjoy my stroll back to the Coven.

It was one of those February mornings when Spring haunts the air. The air was soft and balmy. There was still the stench of the city underlying all, but if you walked this stretch of Southwark between the bear-garden and Broadwall with your nostrils closed and your eyes cast upwards you might have imagined yourself, for a moment at least, in the countryside. The trees and bushes and the bare earth had started to lose some of their winteriness as they put forth their first thread-like tendrils. When I first arrived in this greatest of cities and was affected by a longing for my native country, I had sometimes half-closed my eyes and blotted out the squares and straight lines of human habitation. If the trees were in leaf I saw only their green or gold, if the day was clear I saw the blue of the sky with its cloud-armada, and so was back in my own Somerset.

I am glad to say that these poetic fits passed quickly. If nothing else, the smell of the city will eventually bring you back down to dirty earth. And if that doesn't, and if you're unwise enough to walk round Southwark with your gaze fastened up in the air, you'll most likely tumble over a beggar or a boatman. Or tumble into a bog.

I was brought down to earth sharp enough now as I neared the Coven. The house where I lodged had lost something of its strangeness for me; familiarity had worked her reverse magic. But as I approached my 'home' at the end of this fine morning, the hairs rose on the back of my neck to hear the sounds of wailing and keening which issued from the interior. The noise was scarcely human, and I wondered for an instant whether some new breed of animal had been introduced into the household.

Nervously, I tiptoed towards the open door. Peering in, I could at first make out nothing except a huddle of shapes stationed around the cauldron to the rear of the ground floor. The room was thinly hazed with smoke. From the midst of this group emanated an unearthly whine interspersed with syllables, rising and falling, half a chant, half an outpouring of sheer misery. The outlines of the figures showed plain enough that the keening was produced by the sisters.

Considering that their business was none of mine, I slipped through the door and made to creep up the stairs. But they were not so absorbed in their troubles that they failed to notice my stealthy passage across their premises. With what seemed to be a single movement, three carbuncled and wizened visages turned towards me. Now more than the hair on my nape bristled. My scalp prickled and my guts seemed to coil around themselves. For, between the humped backs and bent shapes of these women and through the smoke haze, I saw a pair of legs protruding from the lip of the brewing cauldron. The syllables uttered by the women started to resolve themselves into short word-trains.

"Deadandgone."

"Beenandone."

"Drownedandfound."

Then they turned back towards the cauldron and resumed their wailing.

Unwillingly, I drew nearer to them. There was little light in the interior – and the smoke from the fire under the cauldron, now extinguished, made it harder to see – but the voices and the postures were sufficient to identify April, June and July. Where was May? I very much feared that the legs which stuck up straight from the edge of the cauldron were hers. For sure they belonged to no beast, as I had for an instant thought (and hoped). For sure there could be no other reason why these three should be making such a melancholy sound.

At the edge of the cauldron I peered over, as into a pit. There lay May, the least unwomanly of the quartet, curved like a spoon in the base. Her head was twisted sideways and partly submerged in the dark sloppy brew at the bottom. Her bare legs stuck out the top, the toes pointing heavenward. Like her sisters, she was wearing a dark smock which had, also like her sisters', probably not been removed for more months than there were in their names. Now this garment had fallen back and bunched about her waist so that her privities were dimly revealed. Turning my head away from this unwitting exposure, I felt dizzy and clung to the iron rim of the cauldron for support. April, June and July resumed their chanting and wailing.

"Drownedandfound."

"Beenandone."

"Deadandgone."

Tears trickled down from cloudy eyes, the water finding its way among their facial protruberances like a stream coursing in its several strands among boulders. My own eyes begin to prick, perhaps on account of the room's smokiness.

I started to tug at the edge of the cauldron, with some

notion of overturning it and retrieving the body from the interior. But impatient, scaly hands were laid over mine and I understood that the others wished May to remain where she was while they performed their wailing and chanting, their last rites.

So, as there seemed nothing further for me to do, I retreated up the stairs to my garret, thinking all the while that this dwelling-place was beginning to acquire an unlucky tincture. The death of Nat had now been followed hard by May's. My eyes pricked again; yet what was May to me, or I to May? Up in my little room – as the mild airs of the early spring blew through the gaps in the walls and blue sky might be glimpsed through the fitful thatch overhead – I sat on my low bed and wrapped my arms around my peaked knees. I thought.

Last time I'd stumbled over a body in this place I had leaped to the conclusion that murder was in question, and then made the self-centred assumption that I was the desig- nated victim. Now I was satisfied that Mistress Horner was no poisoner and that Nat had died natural, I told myself to take care not to arrive once more at a false destination. For it appeared that May too had died natural – or, if not natural, then accidental. I will leave it to schoolmen and philosophers to determine the degree of distinction between the two.

I tried to picture in my mind how it must have occurred. Often enough I'd seen the other women lying strewn about the floor of their sty, overcome by the cauldron's contents. They spent more time stupefied than awake and, even when walking and talking, seemed like creatures who were closer allied to beasts than men. Then I remembered the tears which I had just witnessed and thought worse of myself for not thinking better of them. How had this happened, then? May was a little different from her sorority. For instance she was often out and about, doing, doing, while her sisters were stay-at-homes; for instance she spoke whole sentences while they garbled and jumbled; but she also shared their life, tending to their fatal cauldron, selling its noxious contents to the unwise traveller.

What more likely than that, overcome by fumes as she was stirring the pot or disordered in mind from sampling too much of her own preparation, perhaps leaning forward to slip into the mixture some final ingredient (root of hemlock, gall of goat), she'd lost her footing and fallen headfirst into the cauldron? There was not much liquor in the pot – but a man may drown himself in a bucket or a river. Perhaps May had not even struggled to escape her fate but surrendered to the intoxication of her fumy death. Yet, had she died so easy? I recalled the awkward twist of her head, the bunched-up smock, the toes pointing sharp at heaven.

Well, her brew had finished her. I remembered Master Richard Milford shuddering and warning me against trying it. And a sudden thought struck me. I got up from the low bed and went to my chest. For the second time I was searching for a document.

This chest, the one which had harboured Mistress Horner's unfatal love-potion, was home to few possessions, as I've explained earlier. But I had placed there for safe-keeping not only the green bottle as well as the (incendiary, now incinerated) Phillips-Merrick dialogue, but also the few sheets of *The Courtesan of Venice*, the play which Milford appropriated and which was destined for imminent performance as *A Venetian Whore*. I checked most carefully through the sparse contents of the chest. The manuscript scraps, the only proof of Milford's plagiarising, had gone.

I returned to my bed, wrapped arms round knees once more and thought.

Nobody could have abstracted those sheets but Milford. Or

rather, no one but he would have a reason to do so. It was apparent that the prior existence of a text concerning a lady-whore and the fair city of Venice was known only to him and to me. Why, the very fact that the Chamberlain's were staging *Whore* was proof that the original had fallen into time's abyss. Milford had gambled on resurrecting the piece and claiming authorship, and the gamble would've come off had I not, by chance, been requested by Master Allison to catalogue the contents of the book-room trunk. And from the trunk I'd unearthed, again by chance, the first pages of *Courtesan*.

It was also in the book-room, on the same day, that I'd eavesdropped by chance on the dialogue between Augustine Phillips and Gelli Merrick (currently residing in the Tower).

Something snagged in my mind about that dialogue, about the way I'd just phrased it to myself. *Eavesdropped by chance.* How extraordinarily tidy and coincidental and convenient it all was: that on one star-lit night I should have been charged with a task by Secretary of State Cecil, warned of an approach to our Company by Merrick the Essexite, and then within a couple of days that I should hear first-hand evidence of exactly such an approach. It was almost as if I had been required to overhear that dialogue. It could not have been plotted neater in a tale. Master Allison had asked me to go to the book-room. But someone had suggested me for that job in the first place. Who was it? Ah yes . . . . Master WS.

But I put these nagging thoughts, these interesting speculations, to one side. I was still considering Richard Milford.

There could surely be no doubt that the plagiarising playwright had visited the Coven and crept up to my room – after all, he knew it well, he had lodged here himself – intending to recover the sheets of paper which would brand him a forger. Without the accusing manuscript there was no proof of his theft of another man's word-hoard. Only my own word against his. But it was the writing which was dangerous. I recalled the moment when I'd confronted him in the Goat & Monkey, how he attempted to snatch the papers from my grasp. I thought too of the sword of Damocles conversation, and of the anxious glances he'd thrown at me that morning during rehearsal.

He was a troubled man. Perhaps a desperate one.

Troubled enough to enter another man's room, rifle through his belongings and thieve a few sheets of paper.

Desperate enough to . . . ?

How had May really died? Natural like Nat?

I'd last seen her slipping back to the Coven at night. Both of us slipping back in the starfall. I was somewhat preoccupied, having recently deposited a dead man under a layer of leaves in a ditch. What had she been up to? More to the point, what had she seen? I recalled her words to me, her last words to me as it transpired: "I have something to tell you."

I should have listened.

It is strange how during that Essex season, everything happened or shaped itself by twos. Or so it seemed, looking back on it all afterwards.

In Shakespeare's drama of *Richard II* there are really two kings: the divinely appointed Richard and the usurping Bolingbroke. For certain, the supporters of the Earl of Essex planned to duplicate in real life what they saw played out at the Globe, hoped to unmake a queen by making a king. Or rather, they hoped that history would repeat itself.

The Earl himself had twice paraded through London. Once in premature triumph on his way to Ireland, when I witnessed his vainglory in Islington and the ominous black cloud which rose to the north-east. And once with treasonous intent, when he led his rag-tag army from Essex House to St Paul's, and when the insignificant figure of Nick Revill had again been present, something between a witness and a participant. And I had twice visited Essex House and twice encountered there Henry Wriothesley, the Earl of Southampton, to say nothing of the disagreeable gatekeeper Signor Noti.

And the other events with which I was involved also played themselves out in doubles.

There was, for example, the business of Master Milford, playwright and plagiariser, and of those two plays or, more correctly, of the one play with the two titles, *Courtesan* and *Whore*.

Then there was my double engagement with Isabella Horner and with Nell. Though not contracted to either woman – one being already another man's wife, and the other any man's for the taking (and the money) – I nevertheless regarded myself as a double man for carrying on with the one while persisting in visiting the other. Double in the sense of insincere, pretending. And to escape Mistress Horner's company had required a further pretence: to wit, that I preferred male bed-company.

Then there were bodies in the case, to the number of two. Both deaths occurred in the Coven. Nat the animal man's in my garret room and May's in the downstairs sty. The first I'd assumed was an 'accidental' poisoning, but my conversation with Isabella showed plain enough that she had no homicidal intent towards me and only intended to lure me back to her sheets with her potion. Therefore Nat died natural. The second death looked like an accident, with May drowning in a broth of her own making. But the disappearance of the fragment of play manuscript from my chest together with the fact that, at our last encounter, May had intimated she had something to tell me, caused me to wonder whether her death was as straightforward as it seemed.

And now I come to another example of this strange doubling of events. Early on in this story I recounted how I eavesdropped on a conversation that took place next door to the book-room. And how I was almost discovered, hiding behind the manuscript trunk, by Sir Gelli Merrick. It was only the intervention of Augustine Phillips which diverted Merrick from searching further for the sounds that alerted him. And now I came to think of it, it was most convenient – that word again! – convenient for me at any rate that Master Phillips had been on hand to distract Merrick with his talk of cats and rats.

Once again, I defer speculation on this question to describe what happened next.

We were three or four days away from our presentation of *Twelfth Night* at Whitehall. That we remained in good odour with the Queen and her court was evidenced by the fact that there was no interruption in our rehearsals at Clerkenwell, no hint that we of the Chamberlain's might suddenly find ourselves performing before an angrily vacated throne on Shrove Tuesday evening. Our seniors, like Master Phillips and the Burbages, must have played sufficiently well before the Council to ensure that we still sunned ourselves in the royal favour.

(The plight of the Earl of Essex was not so rosy. We knew – all of London knew – that he lay in the Tower under that sentence of death which it was in the Queen's power alone to remit. Myself, I wondered at the fate of Wriothesley.)

Now, we'd already performed at the Globe playhouse that day and were in the process of shifting to the Office of the Revels for a final – yes, final! – rehearsal of *Twelfth Night*. The piece we'd just performed had been a reprise of *A Merry Old World, My Masters*, the very play I'd been appearing in when I was introduced to Isabella Horner. After all the madcap action of that comedy, a slightly subdued mood settled over the company as we made shift to go to the Clerkenwell Priory. (And I've noticed before how a tragedy will give the players new heart while a comedy will leave them quiet and thoughtful.)

The crowd, not anyway a very large one, which had attended *A Merry Old World* was off home or on to their next diversion. Most of my fellows had already departed to cross the bridge or to take ferries to the north shore. Dusk was fast encroaching. Master Allison the Bookman called across to me.

"Oh Nicholas, could you do me a favour?"

He was holding bundles of schedules, presumably connected with the royal performance.

"If I can."

"I have left the plot in the book-room. The *Twelfth Night* plot. It is hanging up next to the trunk. I would go myself but . . ."

He gestured with his full arms.

"Of course," I said, with a modified willingness.

". . . and bring it across with you to the Priory. I must be on my way."

"Whatever you say, Geoffrey," I said.

I had grown a little wary over the last few weeks of undertaking 'missions', tasks and favours. Not only did a display of eagerness mark one out as a tiro – and by now I was feeling myself past the apprenticeship stage with the Chamberlain's – but the plain fact was that every recent little errand had landed me in trouble.

Nevertheless I did as I was bidden and made my way along the dark passage that ran past the playhouse offices. Here was the tiny room, scarcely more than a cupboard, where Mistress Horner and I had briefly consecrated our amour. And here was Burbage's room, where Phillips and Merrick had discussed the price of staging a play. And therefore next door to it was the book-room.

I went in, shut the door and cast my eyes about in the dimness for the plot. This is a significant item intended to hang on a backstage wall. Its real importance is not so much that it tells the story of the play in summary but that it contains details of properties and noises and the like. It was surprising, therefore, that Geoffrey Allison had forgotten such a vital scroll of paper or that he hadn't taken the precaution of having another copy over in Clerkenwell.

I was beginning to think that he must be mistaken in his belief that he'd left the *Twelfth Night* plot in his room. It wasn't hanging up near the open trunk. Other paper items were pinned to the wall, however, and by the time I'd found the plot amongst them the final remains of a grey daylight were altogether extinguished. I had no candle with me and, as on that earlier afternoon, a feeling of loneliness, almost of desolation, descended on me. By now the playhouse would be well and truly empty.

I listened, clutching the plot in my hand. Nothing or as good as nothing; just the random creaks of a newly emptied building and the thin pipe of the wind outside. I'd better hurry, otherwise I would find myself locked in overnight. It was the responsibility of one of our gatherers to secure the Globe at the end of each day's performance, and even now he must be working his way round the building, fastening the entrances and exits.

Yet I was curiously reluctant to stir from the dark of the book-room.

Then I heard the gatherer in the distance, at the far end of the passage. I opened the door of the book-room. And closed it fast again. For, whoever was coming along the passage was not Sam the money-collector. The steps that I was hearing now were steady ones, even ones. Sam, on the other hand (or foot), had a general lop-sidedness and, specifically, an un-evenness in his gait which gave him a walking rhythm like a string of Master Shakespeare's poetic feet – the short-long sound of di-daa, di-daa, di-daa – as he came down slightly heavier on the leg which was the shorter, whether left or right I couldn't remember. This was the reason why he liked his job of sitting at an entrance on a little stool and receiving the pennies of the audience, preferring to move about the play-house only after everyone had left.

It wasn't only the evenness of the footsteps which told me that this was not the sound of Sam doing his rounds. There was a combination of stealth and assurance in the tread – if such a combination be possible – which told me that the individual heading in my direction was not a regular member of the Chamberlain's. I think I'd have recognised my fellows, or most of them, from the sound of their approach. And this individual was not one of us. A late leaver from the audience? Someone who'd lost his way as he exited the theatre? But when you're not sure where you're going, your steps echo your mind, and this advan-cing tread sounded certain of itself.

Maybe it was the near-darkness in the book-room, maybe it was the sensation that I was indeed alone in the playhouse, maybe it was no more than the accumulated fears and terrors of the last few weeks, but I became convinced that the man approaching along the passage, with a pace at once stealthy and confident, was coming in search of me!

It took only a second to visualise the scene: an outsider asks to see me – such requests for players were sometimes made at the end of performances – and Master Allison responds by saying that he's sent me on an errand to the book-room. It's down that passage there, fourth on the left, you can't miss it.

But it was dark now. Would he send someone off to look for me in the dark?

My heart beat yet louder. The conviction struck as quick as lightning that I was not merely being looked for but *hunted*. There was no reason for this, I told myself; but there was every reason for this, I told myself. How many enemies had I made in the last few weeks, as if I'd gone round on purpose to gather them up!

This sequence flashed through my head in a tenth of the time it takes to read, and all the while the tread came on, steady and soft. Once again, the play-trunk looked to be my only recourse. An instant later and there I was tucked between trunk and plaster wall, tears of anger and frustration pricking at my eyes. Anger at myself for being so womanish as to fear a step in a passage, frustration at the ignominy of being compelled to play hide-and-seek for the second time in Master Allison's room.

And yet I was glad I did so. We should trust our instincts.

No sooner was I crouched in my nest than I heard the door opening and someone advancing into the room. On the previous occasion when I'd been forced into this position, Augustine Phillips had been on hand to usher out the suspicious Merrick. But this time there was no one to shield me from the enemy. And I was sure that it was an enemy who had entered the book-room.

He was carrying a dark lantern. There was a scraping sound as the shutter was slid back and what had been a mere gleam widened to a glow which illuminated the low ceiling. I was crouched down most awkwardly on all fours, but with my head turned sideways I could see from the corner of an eye his shadow swelling and swaying on the dirty white ceiling. He was standing in the middle of the room, casting his gaze about and holding his light aloft. The shadow of the play-trunk rose and fell at my side as the lantern swung slightly.

I prayed to the God of my father – and, believe me, at such moments He was my God as well – that the man with the lantern would not take it into his head to move a few feet to one side and peer into the gap between trunk and wall. My clothes were dark-hued, it is true, but he could hardly have failed to glimpse my white nape, my clenched fists. From close to he might smell my fear. Surely he could hear my heart banging?

Minutes seemed to pass. The light swayed across the ceiling. There was a short sigh. Then a single word, which sounded like "Bastard", but uttered without venom or any particular expression, followed by another sigh. The light was lowered and dimmed as the lantern shutter scraped once more and the intruder moved towards the door.

I waited while his footsteps passed down the passage with the same even, assured tread. I remembered playing hide-and-seek as a child in my father's parish of Miching. How, when you were being hunted, you would crouch, tense, almost quivering with the desire to be found. Because then the agony of waiting would be over. I remembered how I and my fellows would sometimes creep past a potential hiding-place – an abandoned hovel on the edge of a field, a hollowed-out space among the willows at the stream's edge – loudly declaring that we'd no idea where Tom or Dick had hid themselves. Only to go and hide our own selves behind a neighbouring wall or a sheltering tree, there to wait for Tom or Dick to emerge. Then we'd spring up and shriek out loud and chase and catch and pummel him, and all return home tired and happy at the end of a summer's evening.

I thought of that now, not the summer's evening and the innocence of boyish pursuits, but of the trick of waiting until the hider is comfortable that the searchers have gone off, and then the leaping up to surprise him as he comes out.

There was no sound of footsteps now. Had the stranger gone to another quarter of the Globe in quest of me? Or was I altogether wrong and fearful, and it was not me that he was looking for at all? Perhaps he really was an individual who had missed his way in the playhouse or someone who, for unknown reasons, wanted to scrutinise the interior of the book-room. I pondered these possibilties, reassured by none of them. Instinct told me that it was Nick Revill that was being sought. I was the 'bastard', though why anyone should refer to me in that way was baffling. Couched in the dark, I grew indignant. What had *I* done? It was more a question of what had been done against me.

I stayed in a half-crouch behind the trunk, delaying the moment when I'd have to exit the book-room. Eventually I judged it safe to shift. I straightened up and walked soft across the floor, my eyes accustomed to the dark. Only now did I suddenly remember that I was due at the Revels Office in Clerkenwell for our final rehearsal of *Twelfth Night*. I'd been clutching the plot tight in my right hand ever since plucking it from its hanging place and it was when I went to open the book-room door that I recalled the original purpose of Master Allison's errand. I transferred the plot to my left hand and eased open the door, which gave a tell-tale creak.

Wait. Count up to ten before moving out . . . no, twenty. Listen out for sounds. None. He'd gone for sure. Count another twenty for safety's sake, and all the while wonder why I am being forced to skulk and dodge about my own place of work. A faint light came through a casement at the far end of the passage. Since the playhouse would almost certainly be shut up by now, Sam the gatherer having made his limping departure, I decided that I'd have to make my own exit by the window. There was about an eight foot drop down into Brend's Rents, the alley that – if my sense of my whereabouts was correct – ran beside this stretch of the playhouse. I couldn't close the window after climbing through it but, with any luck, would be able to fasten it the next morning before anyone noticed.

My anxiety to escape the Globe was stronger at this point than any fear of the unknown intruder. By now my fellows in the Chamberlain's would have arrived at the Clerkenwell Priory – with its fire-warmed hall, its blazing sconces on the oak-panelled walls, with the familiar air of bustle and expectation – while I was trapped in a cold, dark, empty playhouse. An abrupt desire for their company seized my heart. I wanted to share their jokes and raillery, their good humour and disciplined excitement. Besides, there was a more practical reason for my attendance at Clerkenwell. Antonio doesn't appear for the first half-hour or more of *Twelfth Night* so I had a bit of leeway, but Burbage didn't look kindly on players who were late for rehearsal. I remembered his warning on the first occasion we'd met: a tardy arrival incurred a fine of one shilling, a day's pay.

So I turned in the direction of the window-glimmer at the end of the passage. And stopped – for, with eyesight now well worn to the shapes of darkness, I saw something shift under the sill of the window. And realised that, just as the boy searchers will sometimes wait for the hider, my opponent was waiting for me. Perhaps he'd worked out that the casement window was likely to be my means of egress from the building, and was ready to catch me by the legs as I tried to climb out.

I didn't stop to think what *his* intentions were. I didn't stop to consider anything. I spun in the opposite direction and made off towards the tiring-house, running so clumsily in this narrow, curving passage that I collided with the walls several times. It may be that my speed surprised the gentleman crouched underneath the window. It was a couple of seconds before I became aware of noises of pursuit behind me. That is, there was first a gasp and then some incomprehensible oath and then a stumbling and a crashing as he started to chase me.

I had the advantage of quite a few yards, and the advantage of knowing the playhouse better than he did (or so I assumed). I reached the tiring-house, slipped through the door, closed it behind me, and ran to one of the stage entrances. I knew where I was going to conceal myself but required a few moments' grace to reach it.

The stage was bare. The few properties from *A Merry Old World, My Masters* had been cleared straight after that afternoon's performance. In front of me yawned the groundlings' pit while the more expensive galleries were ranged in judgement above and to either side. It was very early evening but dark, especially under the overhang of the stage. If I'd had the leisure to glance up I would have seen the stars and figures of the heavens, depicted on the underside of the canopy. But it was down on the ground, or the bare boards, that my gaze was fastened.

There! Set more or less centrally in the stage was a trapdoor, wide enough for two men to enter at once. This was the counterpart of the 'heavens' up above, a universal hole to be used when a grave was required or a hiding place for treasure or an entry into Hell or Purgatory. It also gave access to the large area beneath the stage where some of the properties were stored and where, as in Master WS's *Hamlet*, a ghost may stalk and talk. The trap swung back easily and silently on its greased hinges. A little ladder led into the deeper darkness below. I half jumped, half slipped down the rungs, pulling the trap to behind me by the leathern strap nailed to its underside.

It was absolute night underneath the stage, appropriately enough since I had now descended into Purgatory – or worse. This was one Purgatory, however, which I hoped to make my salvation. It was possible that the individual who was close on my heels would come rummaging about down here. Whether he opened up the trap-door depended on how well he knew the geography of the playhouse. (And I could not at this time determine whether he was a real stranger to the premises or not.) He had the benefit of a lantern. Therefore I required a further hiding-place within my hiding-place.

Not long after I'd arrived at the Globe, Jack Horner had been generous enough to guide me round the holes and corners of the place. It is strange how you can think you know a building and then discover that you don't know the half of it. One room he failed to show me – perhaps because even he wasn't aware of it – was the tiny cupboard-like space into which Isabella Horner had enticed me (there to introduce me to her holes and corners). But one area Jack'd proudly taken me into was the underworld below the stage. He particularly wished to show off the largest of the properties stored down there.

"There. What do you think of that?" said Jack.

It was the middle of the day. Light spilled through the open trap and, in addition, Jack was carrying a lantern. Even so, all I could see was a black hole next to the ladder leading down from the stage.

"What am I meant to be looking at?" I said. "There's nothing to see."

"Well, I suppose that's right enough in a way, seeing nothing," said Jack. "Look more close."

I peered. The black hole into which I was looking was, I now realised, the empty middle section of a much larger wooden framework covered with painted canvas. This canvas was ornamented with flames, with devils sporting horns, with writhing worms and dragons rampant. White-faced individuals stood packed into cauldrons set above crackling fires.

Other hapless beings were being speared, lanced and tridented by grinning demons.

"Why, it's a hell-mouth," I said.

"Did you ever see a hell-mouth like it?" said Jack proudly. "It's the biggest in any London playhouse, they say. It only just fits through the trap."

"Hell-mouth will always fit through the trap," I said. "Where would we be without hell-mouth?"

This was true enough. There's perhaps been a falling-off in recent years of plays where one or more of the characters go to hell. I suspect that the modern shareholder and the more cultivated members of the audience consider such a purgatorial penalty to be a touch extreme, a trifle crude. Too reminiscent of those morality plays where hell is always lying underfoot, ready to gape. Nevertheless, there's nothing your average playgoer likes better than watching some wrongdoer dragged down into the sulphurous pit, via hell-mouth. Why, we were still playing Kit Marlowe's *Faustus* ten years after it first saw the light of day.

Any Company with a regard for its audience, and its profits, will ensure that it possesses a hell-mouth in good working order. They're generally on wheels so that they can be positioned above the trap. Now that I knew what I was looking at, I could see that the Chamberlain's was indeed a fine example: sturdy, wide and with some detailed work in the pictures that adorned the surround. There was a loving care in the painting, and it crossed my mind that there are many who take pleasure in the depiction of torment and misery (and I wondered too whether the craftsman who wielded the brush round the mouth of hell had also clambered aloft to paint the 'heavens' on our canopy).

So, after this excursion round hell-mouth, you can guess where I chose to secrete myself under the Globe stage. Feeling forward with my hands, I entered the infernal portals silently and willingly – unlike all those other souls who must be dragged through screaming. Once inside the little cave of wood and canvas, I felt oddly secure. Gauzy hangings, which fell from the roof of the hell-mouth to give the illusion that a new arrival had been swallowed up, brushed against my exposed hands and face and draped themselves about my shoulders.

So I huddled down in the back of this comfortable little cavern and waited. If necessary, I was prepared to stay here until dawn broke, my fellows returned to the playhouse and safety arrived. I listened out hard for the sounds of footsteps on the stage overhead and, at one point, thought I heard something. But nothing came of it. No one opened the trap-door to see what lay beneath, no one fumblingly descended the ladder, no one sought to penetrate the mouth where I lay, undigested.

The human mind is a strange thing, unaccountable in its workings. Though I'd been thoroughly frightened by the unseen stranger who'd pursued me through my workplace, I soon found my position in the gullet of hell-mouth to be as tedious as it was comfortable. I discovered in myself a wish to be out and about in the world again. Perhaps this is the reason why a ghost chooses to walk on earth: not *tedium vitae* but *tedium mortis*. I offer this only for consideration.

I had to hold myself back from strolling out of the underworld and clambering up to the surface of the Globe. Last time I'd come out of hiding the stranger had been waiting for me. Or had he? Was it possible that I had imagined the whole thing – not the entry into the book-room, I was sure enough about that, but the subsequent chase along the passage. Had the oath and the stumbling in the dark been my own?

I remained where I was for what seemed an eternity (apt enough considering my location!) but was probably a mere earthly half hour. Then I made a rapid exit from my hole, opened the trap, briskly crossed the stage and retraced my route through the tiring-house and down the passage to the casement.

Quickly, before I had time to grow frightened once more, before anyone might have the opportunity to seize me by the ankle, I unfastened the window, swung my legs over the sill and dropped to the ground. I took off like a hare down Brend's Rents. Found a late ferry to Paul's Wharf. Raced up to Clerkenwell. Arrived at the Priory to discover that the rehearsal hadn't even begun. Not even sure that my absence was noticed.

Also arrived at the Priory to discover that I'd lost the plot.

It hardly mattered, as it happened. Master Allison was quite apologetic when he told me that he did keep a spare copy in the Revels Office after all.

Some nights later we played *Twelfth Night* before her majesty at Whitehall. If that was an occasion to treasure, then what followed immediately afterwards was even more memorable – though not treasurable – as you shall hear.

But first to the performance.

I noticed that as we drew nearer to the hour of our commencement, even the more seasoned members of the Chamberlain's were exhibiting signs of excitement and fret. Strangely, I felt myself growing calmer, although I'd been unable to eat anything since early that morning. The fiftieth check was made of the properties, the hundredth inspection carried out on our costumes, the thousandth rehearsal of each man's lines took place inside his own head.

We were to enact *Twelfth Night* in the Hall, a great room

with many bays and buttresses and windows. I had never acted indoors before, although the many evenings of rehearsal at the Revels Office had taken away my initial sense of the oddness of being under a roof and playing by candlelight. Wooden seating had been erected around the walls of the Hall in tiers, an arrangement that was familiar enough although there was of course no equivalent to the playhouse pit in a royal palace.

There were other differences too. In the public theatres, we players are accustomed to being the cynosure of all eyes. (I say 'we' while really meaning the likes of Dick Burbage and Robert Armin; it is those individuals on whom the gaze of both the general and the gentry is fastened from the moment of their first appearance.) But in the court theatre it is, as it must be, otherwise. However brightly our stars shine, there will always be one who shines yet more brilliantly. And *She* will be found not on the stage but in the heart of her audience – as well as in their hearts. There the monarch is as much on display, perhaps more so, than her players.

So as we players waited – and there is a point before the performance begins when the player seems like the still centre, while all about him is rush and dash – I cast frequent glances at the imposing chair of state which was set up on a dais near the middle of the hall. This chair had a finely embroidered backcloth and a rich blue canopy. Earlier, I had daringly approached it. There, on that seat, in little over an hour, *She* would station her sacred self. I was sometimes conscious of referring inwardly to the Queen as *She*, with a reverential emphasis that was reminiscent of my friend Nell. I wondered how I'd recount this episode to her later, how I'd go about impressing her in bed with my great acquaintance. Would I catch Nell's habit of wrapping her majesty in a respectful indrawing of breath: *She*; or would I continue to allude to her casually in conversation: 'oh her'?

In the playhouse we start sharpish at two o'clock after the trumpet has sounded, and any latecomer may struggle both to find a place to stand or sit in as well as having to catch up with the plot. In the royal palace of Whitehall, by contrast, we were obliged to wait on our chiefest guest. Until *She* was established in her state, nothing could begin. I had heard that Elizabeth was, in fact, prompt enough in attendance, though whether out of real interest in the drama or because of her innate graciousness I did not know. Since it was the evening of Shrove Tuesday matters might be delayed because *She* first had to attend the usual banquet before arriving at the digestive of a drama. We players had been well enough supplied with food and drink by the officers of the household, although never so amply as to suggest that we were anything other than servants. Even so, I was still too anxious to eat anything and contented myself with sipping at a mug of ale.

On our improvised backstage, I wandered over to young Martin Hancock, he who played our heroine Viola-Cesario. He was deep in converse with Jack Horner, 'her' twin brother.

"So it is tomorrow," Martin was saying.

"So they say."

"Has she signed?"

"They say not," said Jack.

"But must do soon?"

"For certain she must, if it is to be tomorrow."

"What? Who?" I broke in.

"Why, don't you know, Nick?" said Jack.

"Obviously I do – that's why I'm asking," I said.

There was an unaccustomed seriousness about these two, which I didn't think was related to the imminent royal performance. Even Martin Hancock, now garbed as Viola, seemed to have forsaken his normal hinting and winking style.

"They say tomorrow that he goes to it," said Jack.

"*Who?*" I said with some impatience. But, as sometimes happens, the question had no sooner escaped my mouth than I realised what they were talking about. Jack's reply confirmed it.

"The Earl of Essex."

"He is to be executed?"

"Yes, Master Nicholas," said young Martin. "He must surely die."

"Not a traitor's death?" I said.

"No, she will not subject him to that, traitor though he be," said Jack, casting his eyes in the direction of the stage area, in front of which was, as we all knew, the still vacant chair of state. I shivered, wholly taken away in my mind from the warmth of the great Hall for an instant.

A common traitor's death provided a public show at Tyburn, with the condemned man sliced open while still alive so that the hangman could draw out his guts and flourish them in front of his tormented face. I had never seen the spectacle but was assured that the crowds spread about the scaffold would be the envy of any playhouse. But a well-born traitor enjoyed a less dreadful end: Essex might expect the privacy of the block in the Tower, and the merciful quickness of the axe. For sure he would have no common eyes trained upon him.

"And Wriothesley?" I said.

Now it was Jack's turn to ask who.

"Southampton, I mean," I said, feigning casualness. "He is closely associated with the Earl of Essex, is he not?"

"I don't know," said Jack. "I don't know what is to happen to him."

"The friend of Master Shakespeare?" said Martin Hancock, nodding towards one of the rooms which led off the Hall. Moments earlier we'd seen Master WS (who wasn't playing in his own *Twelfth Night*) go in there with John Heminges as well as Edmund Tilney, the Master of the Revels, and a clutch of court officials, presumably to discuss some aspect of the production.

"Is he?" I said, all ignorance.

"I saw them talking close together at the Globe after *Richard*," said the watchful Master Hancock. "I saw *you* talking to them too, Nicholas."

Fortunately, I was saved from having to respond to Martin's awkward observation by a great ripple and stir that now ran through the crowd of us players, assistants and shareholders clumped in threes and fours backstage. From the sussuration issuing from beyond the temporary divisions that separated us from the frontstage area it was evident that the court audience was assembling in the body of the Hall, and that we'd have to look sharp about our business. So I put to one side the melancholy end of Robert Devereux and the unknown fate of Henry Wriothesley, and turned instead to my *Twelfth Night* part, that of Antonio, the loving friend of Sebastian.

We had to wait several minutes longer until we were given the signal that we should process onto the stage. Because this was a royal performance – and I'd been told that the Queen herself had personally requested *Twelfth Night* – we were required to make our obeisances to the audience and principally to *Her* before the action commenced. Accordingly, led by Messrs Shakespeare and Burbage (costumed as Duke Orsino of Illyria) and Heminges and other of the shareholders, we walked out stately onto the dazzling stage. The Hall itself was also in full blaze, with candle-frames suspended from wires stretched from wall to wall and elaborate sconces on every buttress. I saw, for the first time, that one of the appurtenances of greatness and wealth is light.

Not for the first time, however, I was glad of my junior position in the Chamberlain's, since it meant that I, a tender sapling, could find shelter among the full-grown oaks and beeches of my elders. Together with the court audience, we remained on our knees until *She* had taken her state and indicated that we might all rise. Then we of the players continued to make graceful flourishes and bows until *She* signalled with a gracious wafture of her hand that we might begin.

It wasn't the first occasion I'd seen our great Queen. Soon after I'd arrived in London, I had glimpsed her in procession in the street, and *the very next day* I'd seen the royal barge on the river. This double sighting gave me the oddest, most vainglorious idea that she must be aware of my presence in the city and that I was destined to see my monarch every day. But of course I did not, until this Shrove Tuesday evening.

Not that I saw much now. I kept my head at a respectful angle, glancing up and round at the crowded Hall only momentarily. The great room was packed, with court-men and court-ladies standing at the edges and the more important seated and the most important of all nearest to Elizabeth. The fiery clusters of candlelight sparkled and spangled off brooches and clasps and rings, off pendants and necklaces, off gold-threaded stomachers and doublets. Everywhere, white lace waved and tossed like the spume I remember to have seen once on a stormy day in the Bristol Channel. Everywhere there was the subtler glow of silk. Players are used to being the finest dressed members of any assembly. Indeed, we are often reminded by the Tire-man of how much our costumes are worth in comparison to our insignificant selves, and how the audience has really come to see the clothes, to which our words and gestures are mere adjuncts. But in a royal palace the reverse holds. There we are outshone tenfold by the magnificence of the audience. And how could it be otherwise?

As for the Queen herself, I can report little at this moment. Rather than looking directly at her, I was conscious of a lavishly-decked figure shadowed by the canopy of state. To gaze straight at a monarch may be unwise, like gazing straight at the sun. Then again, all of us have heard stories of our lady's graciousness and directness with the common people, and of how she enjoins them to speak their minds to her. Even so, even as I was aware of being in *Her* presence, the main thought that floated through my mind was: if my father could see me now! A hater of plays, he surely would have modified his opposition if he had been able to witness his only son in the same room as the Queen. He surely might have allowed a grudging respect for the drama if he'd seen that scene! (But it may be that I'm imagining this.)

As we trooped off the stage to leave it clear for the first scene, set in Duke Orsino's court, I noticed a figure sitting on the front row only a short distance from the Queen. On the only previous occasion when we'd met, the light hadn't been so good, but under any circumstances I would have recognised the high white forehead, the candid gaze. To say nothing of the awkward posture which was produced by the man's hump back. Sir Robert Cecil, Master Secretary Cecil, caught my eye as I processed off stage. I thought that some signal passed from him to me, though I couldn't have said exactly what it was. Perhaps he was merely acknowledging my presence, acknowledging a small prior connection between a high statesman and a low player. Or perhaps it was something more. (But it may be that I'm imagining this too.)

So to the play itself.

Twelfth Night makes for fitting pre-lenten fare, even if it is a little adrift from its due calendar date. It raises our spirits before the days and nights of abstinence, and sends us out happy into the dark. And it cannot help reminding us a little of that dark by the humiliating ends of Malvolio and Sir Andrew Aguecheek. Not everyone in this world will conclude the day happy and married. Feste sings yet in the rain, while Antonio is forgotten by Sebastian.

Though a player usually wants a large scroll, a large part, I was again content to be in a subordinate position for this royal performance. I gave Antonio a kind of fervour in his declaration of love for Sebastian, I gave him bitterness in his denunciation of ingratitude – or at least I hope that I imparted these qualities to the role. I hope I spoke clear and full. But the weight of the play was borne by Dick Burbage and Armin, not to mention Martin Hancock as Viola or our other leading boy, Michael Donegrace, who assumed the mantle of wealthy Olivia.

Although noble patrons are not altogether strange to us, this Whitehall audience was different from the common run at the Globe. For one thing, they had been so well catered for at the banquet that wine filled their upper chambers and some were now more than halfway between satiety and stupor. Most of the rest took their cue from the Queen or would have done had they been easily able to gauge her response. But it was hard to see how *She* was reacting under the protection of her fine canopy. Her chair of state, though set up high on view, was also curiously insulated from her subjects. However, there was a not infrequent woman's laughter from that quarter at the antics of Sir Toby and Maria, at their fooling of Sir Andrew and Malvolio, followed by enough chuckles and snorts from the audience to indicate that what was good enough for their monarch was certainly good enough for them.

But it seemed to me that an air of reserve – even,

paradoxically, of sobriety – hung over the great Hall, for all the finery and intermittent jollity of its occupants. Now, there might be several reasons for this. For one thing, I had never experienced a performance at the palace before and, for all I knew, this might be the standard reaction to the Chamberlain's royal displays. There was none of the easy banter that obtains in the playhouse between those up on stage and those down in the pit. Whitehall Palace, as I've already mentioned, has no pit – but the *spirit* of the pit was also absent. And an absence of other things besides: no cutpurses, no whores, no swearing soldiers and boatmen, no vendors of nuts and apples and ale, no quicksilver gangs of apprentices. Without doubt, some examples of these types, of thieves and whores, were present in the royal court as they are in every human gathering but, if so, they were richly disguised in robes and lace.

But the principal reason for the *quietness* of the occasion I put down to one individual, someone who was both present and absent, someone whose fate had formed the pre-play conversation between Jack and Martin and me. If we humble players knew that the Earl of Essex was likely to die on the morrow then you could be sure that every last court-man and - woman in the audience knew it too. And, first and foremost in every sense, the Queen knew it. She, after all, was the one who would finally subscribe that fatal warrant. She alone could say where and when, and how, the Earl's soul would be sundered from his body.

Did this knowledge, this mortal responsibility, weigh heavy on her? How could it not? The closeness betweeen the Queen and the Earl had once been the talk of the town. It was commonly believed that he had escaped the ultimate penalty for treason after his return from Ireland because of a lingering fondness on her part. Now she was brought to the point where, all-powerful as she was, she was yet impotent to save him – and perhaps no longer wished to do so. She alone had to bring down the man whom she had once raised up.

So, as I say, there was a subdued tone to the event. Not my imagination, I think, because a brief moment in the play seemed to strike some hidden chord with the audience. When, as Antonio, I talk of the danger of being captured by Duke Orsino's men on account of having participated in a sea-fight against his galleys, I make mention of the penalty for resistance:

For which, if I be lapsed in this place,
I shall pay dear.

From some portion of the Hall, higher up near the top of the degrees, seemed to come a sigh which resonated as about a whispering chamber, broadcasting itself independently from different sections of the room. At the time I registered the effect but was puzzled. It was only afterwards that I connected the sense of Antonio's words – the notion of capture and paying the price – to my lord of Essex.

But I've no idea whether this intuition was correct.

After we'd exited the stage for the final time, after Feste had sung his little piece about the wind and the rain and we'd done our little closing jig and then made a fresh set of obeisances in the direction of the canopied state and returned once more to our knees as *She* made her own exit – after all of this, I say, we trooped back to our temporary tiring-house. There was some back-slapping and hand-clasping, with Burbage and Shakespeare being especially prominent in congratulating and thanking not only their fellows of the Chamberlain's but also the court people who'd assisted in the performance. I had noted before how assiduous these two were in paying their dues of thanks, and how their outlay was returned several times over in the quiet smiles or delighted grins of those they complimented. Even old Tilney, the Master of the Revels himself, and something of a dry stick – probably because he went right back to the days of Tarleton and must've shepherded dozens of productions past the Queen's eyes – even old Edmund wore a little expression of relief on his face.

As I was disrobing myself, I noticed a splendidly dressed courtier enter the tiring-area. He spoke to Jack and Martin, who happened to be standing together at that point, and all three turned to examine the scene. After a moment, Jack nodded and pointed me out to the courtier. This elegant gentleman preened across the floor towards me. Unaccountably, I felt myself going as hot and red as Richard Milford.

I was half out of my costume, a condition which always puts one at a disadvantage. Especially so when the other man was as finely adorned as this one. He stopped in front of me, removed a well-feathered bonnet and half-inclined his head. I wish I might have snatched his hat to fan myself cool again.

"Can I claim the inestimable pleasure of addressing Master Nicholas Revill of the Chamberlain's Company?" said this prim-mouthed figure. He was in the latest style, even down to being clean-shaven, a fashion which I'd observed among other courtiers. But his style of speech was as ornate as, contrariwise, his chin and upper lip were bare.

"You can, sir," said I. "I am Revill."

"Then may I make a further intrusion on that good gentleman's time, leisure and liberty as to entreat him to listen close while I impart a thing?"

"You may, sir."

Even as he spoke these long sentences, he was casting his critical eye up and down my person. My costume as Antonio was designedly rough and ready since I was just a faithful sea-dog. But I was hardly eager to crawl back into my street clothes while he looked on, for I feared that I would look no more significant in my own person than in another guise.

"Do please continue," continued this individual, "with your divesture . . . so that you may proceed to your revesture."

"Divest – ? Oh, you mean taking off my costume . . ."

The courtier looked pained at my low language.

"Only in order that you may the more speedily resume your customary habiliments," he said, as if he was making himself clearer.

"My day clothes, you mean. But surely you haven't come to talk to me about my *clothes*?"

I could sense two or three of my fellow players listening and sniggering nearby. Perhaps this gave me the nerve to talk plain. Here was your typical courtier. In fact, I wasn't sure that I hadn't earlier glimpsed him in the audience.

"No sir, the subject of your apparel is not within my compass—"

"Sir, I'm glad to hear it."

"—but the matter I have come to impart to you cannot be communicated until you have resumed your diurnal attire."

"Oh very well," I said, irritated and hurrying to change so as to remove myself from this man's company. As I shrugged myself into my street clothes, I said, "Would you do me the honour to acquaint me, sir, with the identity of the gentleman whom I am addressing?"

"I," said this important being, "am Sir Roger Nunn."

"Ah," I said.

"Of the Nunns of Northampton."

"Oh," I said.

"Your organ of hearing is perhaps not unacquainted with the nomination?"

"Are you related to the Knotts of Nottingham?" I said. "Or the Nevers of Nuneaton?"

He narrowed his eyes but did not condescend to reply.

"Well," I said, standing before him in my everyday garments. "I'm ready. Impart."

"Come with me," said Sir Roger, dropping his courtly manner. "Her Majesty wishes to see you."

He clapped his bonnet back on his head and spun on his heel. I followed him, without thinking. It was only when I'd gone a few paces that I realised what he'd said. Her Majesty? To see me? I must've misheard. Or this was his way of paying me back for my cheek. Nevertheless, I did as I was told, conscious that Jack and Martin were looking at us as we exited the tiring-house.

We left the Hall via a small side room and from there proceeded down a wide passageway. Then a warren of smaller passages interspersed with lobbies and more open areas. All the time, the bobbing, feathered bonnet of Sir Roger Nunn kept a few yards ahead of me. Occasionally he'd glance round to check that I was still in attendance. We seemed to be going deeper into the bowels of the Palace. I started to regret my gibes about Knotts and Nevers.

Eventually, we arrived at a much larger ante-room. And there I began to fear the worst for, seated to one side of a great fire, was Sir Robert Cecil. On the far side of the room four Yeomen stood at attention, in two pairs, grasping their halberds and gazing straight in front of them. Sir Robert must have signalled something to Sir Roger because the next I knew – not that I was truly aware of *anything* at that instant – the beautifully bonneted being left the room.

"Well, Nicholas," said Sir Robert, "you have done well."

"I – I – if you say so, sir."

"Yes, and now she wants to tell you so in person."

The warm room felt suddenly airless. The fire flared up. The shadow of Sir Robert's crooked back swelled and sank against the wall. I wanted to tear off my day clothes and to run screaming through the street. I wanted to hurl myself head-long into a pit of fire. I wanted to drown in the next pond. Anything but understand what he'd just said to me.

Sir Robert saw my quick misery and smiled.

"Be calm, Nicholas. She only wants to thank you. I say that you have done well."

"I – I – I have done nothing."

I could only think that he was referring to the business with Essex and the failed uprising. Considering the tiny role I'd played, it was not false modesty that caused me to say I'd done nothing. For this, I required no thanks, especially no thanks from *Her*.

"Perhaps it's also thanks for what you will do," said Sir Robert cryptically. "Go in now."

He gestured at a low door whose outline I now discerned in the oak panelling between where the splendidly uniformed guards stood in pairs. Like a creature deprived of the power to resist, like a beast being led towards the slaughter, I walked, walked as in a dream towards the small door.

This seemed to take hours – a lifetime – though it can't have been more than a few seconds. Once at the door, I raised my hand irresolutely and then lowered it again without knocking. Instead, the guard nearest the door leaned over and rapped gently with the tip of his halberd on the oak, presumably at some signal from Cecil. There may have been a response from within; I don't know, because my ears were suddenly filled with a roaring noise and I was conscious of my heart trying to batter its way out of my chest. Then the guard turned the handle and gently pushed the door open. Rather less gently, he prodded me in the back so that I found myself almost pushed through the entrance.

Once on the far side, I sensed rather than heard the door being closed behind me. Oh for a trapdoor like the one in the

Globe to open up at my feet so that I might disappear forever into the dark depths beneath! Oh to be pursued by my dearest enemy into wastes beyond the reach of man! Oh to be anywhere but here in one of *Her* privy chambers.

What do I do next?

How do I describe to you our Sovereign, and what it meant to be in *Her* presence?

The room was not over-large, and this was the first surprise, that Elizabeth our Queen, she who had the run of the whole land, should on occasion choose to confine herself in close quarters. There was a good fire going and sitting by it, tall, upright and alert, an old woman.

My first thought was: where is Her Majesty?

My second: perhaps this is one of her ladies.

My third: perhaps it is all a joke after all.

Then I realised, of course, that the old woman in the chair was the Queen.

I sank to my knees and let my head bow down.

"Get up, Master Revill. I can't talk with you in that position."

I rose shakily to my feet but still kept my eyes low.

"And look at me, man. Didn't your mother ever tell you that it was discourteous not to look someone in the face when you're speaking with them?"

"My father gave instruction in my household, my – your majesty," I said, a little surprised at the steadiness of my voice.

"And in mine," she said.

The Queen said! Said to me!

Then, "Sit down. You must be tired after your performance."

More by luck than by looking, I located a chair and positioned my buttocks on the edge of it. The room was ill-lit by the flicker of firelight and a handful of candles.

Nothing compared to the blazing illumination of the great Hall. Two other doors, apart from the one I'd come through, were set into the walls. I assumed that her ladies must be near at hand behind one of them. It struck me as strange – I mean not at the time but later – that so far I'd seen only men in the neighbourhood of the Queen.

I looked timidly across to where the old lady sat. If I describe her now, it's as a result of bringing together several tiny, quick impressions and forming them afterwards into a picture, however inadequate.

Firstly, she *was* old. Close to, there was no disguising it with face-paint and shadow. Old but very formidable; I mean formidable in herself, and not in what she was, if the two things can be distinguished. Even if she'd been an oyster seller in Eastcheap you'd have thought twice about crossing her. No, thought three times – and then you wouldn't have done it. Her straight posture in the chair emphasised her tallness. Her hair was red like the flickering fire but (I whisper ungallantly) not a quarter so natural. The most prominent features in her thin, pale visage were a high aquiline nose and her striking eyes. Ah, her eyes. What colour they were I couldn't have said. But they had opposing qualities: they seemed at once deep-set, almost buried, and also starting forward. For now, they were bent on me with an expression I couldn't determine.

"Not so tired, your majesty, as – as amazed to find myself here when my place would be better occupied by any other member of my Company."

"That is very modest for a player."

"But I mean it," I protested, forgetting formalities for a moment. And I did mean it. I wanted all my Company to share in the Queen's favour. Why wasn't Master Burbage here, or Master Shakespeare, or Jack Horner or Martin

275

Hancock come to that? Why had she requested a minor player?

"Did you like the play?" I said, greatly daring.

"Oh yes," she said absently. I noticed that her heavily beringed hands moved constantly in her lap. "How could one not like it? It is written to be liked. We were amused. Amused at the way Duke Orsino governs his realm of – Illyria, is it?"

"But he does *not* govern it, your majesty," I said.

"That is what is amusing," she said. "That he can devote himself to love rather than affairs of state, and yet come out of it clear at the end."

"Well," I said, not knowing what else to say.

"Well? Does he govern well? Perhaps he governs well because he does not know that he does," she said. "In truth, *fines principum abyssus multa.*"

"The designs of Princes are a deep abyss," I said, glossing her words automatically, almost without thought.

This seemed to delight her more than anything I'd said since entering the chamber. She leaned forward and, since she was wearing a low-cut gown, exposed a certain quantity of royal bosomry. Age had taken its inevitable toll here as well and the paps were somewhat shrunk and wizened.

"Master Revill, you are a scholar."

"My father was a stern schoolmaster, your majesty" I said. "I mean he wasn't a schoolmaster, he was a parson. But he insisted that I give many hours to the study of Greek and Latin."

"For which you ought to give him thanks every day," she said.

"I do, I will."

And at that instant, watching the Queen's hands shift unceasingly in her lap, I vowed to give daily thanks to the memory of my father and his severe regimen of learning.

"And you have other tongues?"

"Alas no."

"Never mind, you are young and have plenty of time to learn."

"I fully intend to, your majesty."

"It is good to expose ourselves to the variety of the world," she said, "and how better to do it than through a medley of tongues?"

"Of course, your majesty," I said, still surprised at the calmness of my responses.

"*Per molto variare la natura e bella*," she said, gesturing even more with her hands. "You understand?"

"Not entirely," I said, "yet I can catch the gist of it."

And at that moment my mind snagged on something else, and I did indeed begin to catch the gist.

"It is one of my favourite aphorisms. I have always loved the Italian music. Those are pleasures you still have before you, young man. French, Italian."

"Your majesty's learning is one of the wonders of her realm," I said, feeling that I'd got the measure of this courtly dance pretty quick.

"Yes, there are not many can best me," she said.

"None, madam, none."

"How old are you, Master Revill?"

"Er, twenty eight, your majesty." (Inexplicably, I added more than a year to my age.)

"Do you know where I was at your age?"

"You were – were our monarch then too," I said, hoping desperately that my guess was correct.

"I have outlived most of those who were my subjects when I first came to this place."

"And w-w-will live to – t-t-t-to outlive – t-t-to l-l-l-live for ever – t-t-t-to live longer—"

Tangled up in my stuttering expressions, I came to a stop. She half smiled but in a scornful way, as it seemed, and I remembered Master Secretary Cecil's words about the mortality of princes, and how the pious Elizabeth would subscribe to no blasphemous doctrine of divinity.

"*Non omnis moriar*," she said, and looked a question at me.

"The poet Horace," I said, hoping to please and make amends for my stuttering.

"And what does he mean?" she catechized.

"That – that – 'I do not die entire' – those are his words – and he implies, that no man dies entire if he has works that will survive him."

"Just so," she said, with satisfaction. "Tell me, Master Revill, since we were earlier talking of the designs of Princes, what is the supreme end of a Prince?"

"I am hardly in a position to say, madam."

"I will tell you—"

I leaned even further forward on the edge of my seat. It is not every day that the Queen imparts to you the secret of her reign.

"—it is to gain time."

"To gain time?"

I was not so much disappointed as baffled by her answer.

"Time in which her subjects may be born and grow up and grow old and die. To gain time for them to do that. Have I not done that for my countrymen these many years, done that handsomely?"

I bowed my head, partly because I could think of nothing to say.

When I looked up again, I saw that her eyes semed to have sunk deep into her head. Her hands writhed constantly.

"Yet not all are grateful. Especially those who have most reason to be grateful. I have discovered that ingratitude grows most abundant in the richest soil, in the best tilled earth."

She paused, then continued almost to herself.

"Wild and whirling himself, the ingrate seeks to infect all men with his dizzy condition."

I half nodded. I didn't know – but could guess – to whom she was referring.

"What is tomorrow?" she said with sudden fierceness.

"I – I—"

"Remind me of the morrow!"

Her hands opened and closed rapidly. Her encrusted, bejewelled fingers looked like chicken's feet. Fear entered my tones.

"W-W-W-Wed – no, A-A-A-Ash Wednesday, your majesty."

"Good," she almost barked, then in an insinuating tone, "Ash Wednesday will be a good day to finish all of this, will it not."

I grew frightened of this old woman or, to be precise, my previous fear of her returned two or three times over. I wished to escape her tight, hot chamber. I wished to rejoin my fellows and be nothing more than a small player for the rest of my life. Perhaps she sensed my fear and took pity on it or, what was much more likely, perhaps she had said all that she wanted to say.

"You may go, Master Revill."

I waited for a moment uncertainly, then half rose from the edge of my seat.

"Well, go, what are you waiting for?"

Head down, in a servile crouch, I proceeded backwards towards the door.

Then: "Master Revill?"

"Your m-m-m-majesty?" I half looked up.

"Secretary Cecil tells me that we owe you thanks, for helping to stem the giddy infection."

I made some deprecating movement of arms and shoulders and began to assemble in my mind the components for an answer, involving terms like duty and allegiance. But I don't think I would have got the words out. For some reason, any composure I'd had earlier now completely deserted me, and shivers and tremors ran through me like an aspen.

"And, Master Revill . . . ?"

"Y-y-y-yehyehyeh . . ."

My tongue was enormous and unwieldy. I shut my mouth to silence it. Fortunately the Queen didn't seem to notice; or if she noticed, she didn't care. Then she said, almost softly: "A handsome young man like you should have a fine future with the players. Now go and leave me alone."

I fumbled for the handle of the door, forgetting that it opened inward, and all the while kept an eye cocked on the fierce, upright woman in her chair near the fire. One of the Yeomen on the other side must have assisted in opening the door, an operation which appeared almost beyond my strength or wit at that point, and I edged around it and then out into the ante-room. The same guard, a tall heavily bearded individual, reached forward, shut the Queen in again and resumed his position.

The four guards stood stiff in pairs on each side of the entrance. They didn't look at me or say anything, for which I was grateful. Secretary Cecil had gone from his post by the fire. Discounting the guards, I was alone in the room.

After a time, deciding I'd get no help from the Yeomen, I wandered out through the main door and in the direction from which I'd first arrived with Sir Roger Nunn. Like Theseus in the labyrinth, I needed a thread to help find my way out of the deserted, ill-lit passages and lobbies which opened off one another. I had turned a few corners and paused at a handful of crossroads when the fearful nature of the interview which I had just endured with the Queen overcame me. This, together with some despair that I'd ever find my way out of her Palace, caused my legs to lose their desire to take me further. I sank to the floor and huddled there with my knees drawn up to my chin and my back resting against the panelled wall.

But I didn't merely sit.

I sat and I thought. And waited.

After a time, I spied the merry figure of Sir Roger Nunn approaching me along the corridor, his bonnet all a-flip and a-flop.

"Why, Revill," he greeted me like an old friend, seeming to have forgotten my rudeness towards him in the tiring-house. "I observe that your palatial peregrinations have brought you to the very borne of fatigue."

I grinned feebly, and stood up, using the wall for support.

"I wasn't sure of the way out."

"Then you must permit me the indulgence of acting as your cicerone and superintending your egress from this great edifice."

"If you're offering to guide me out of this place," I said, "then I gratefully accept."

He strode off down the passage and I moved to follow him. The gold and silver threads in his fine clothes were picked out by the intermittent candles that burned along the walls in sconces.

We turned a couple of corners. And a couple more. Climbed some short flights of stairs. Descended others. Ascended again. Resumed our long march down an interminable-looking corridor.

I chose my moment carefully.

"*Dove vai?*" I said.

Sir Roger affected not to hear me. The plumage on his bonnet crested and waggled, making him look like a species of exotic bird stalking the passages of power. Then suddenly he stopped and flung open a door to his right. I felt the breath of a cold night.

"We have achieved our terminus. This is the point at which you may consummate your quittance."

He ushered me ahead of him. I had half been expecting a lobby, a hallway, an exit – but only half. In fact, we were still quite high up in the palace. So high up that I found I was standing on a flat roof space. All about me were chimney stacks and roof pinnacles and tiled slopes. In between several of these I could see the black sheen of the river while above arced the burning stars. It was a clear, bitter night, like most of the nights during that Essex winter.

Sir Roger Nunn came through the door after me, turned about and shut it leisurely behind him.

"*Che cosa avete?*" he said, before striking me violently on the side of the face. I fell to the ground. Once I was lying there, he kicked me twice or thrice in the belly so that I near retched. Then he proceeded to walk round and round me in tight little circles, all the the while talking – though not in the polite and circumlocutory style he had adopted before.

"*Puttana*! You know what you are, Revill. *Puttana*! Whore! All players are whores but you are a whore in special. You sell yourselves, you show yourselves, you exhibit your bodies for the common delectation."

"I don't think – the Queen – would agree – she told me – she liked – the play," I gasped, and he gave me another kicking for my pains.

"*Non solamente puttana mai puttana e putto – insieme*! You understand, little fellow. You are a whore and a little lad together."

"Have it your way," I said, trying not to provoke him further.

He got down on his haunches and pushed his bare face into mine. His breath emerged in cloudlets.

"A little fellow playing out of his depth."

"As you say," I said.

"Now tell me how you knew."

"Let me up first. Or let me sit. I will not run."

"No, you will not. I am stronger and faster than you!"

"I remember your grip at Essex House," I said. "When you had me round the neck."

I levered myself into a sitting position and rested against the wall next to the door from which we'd emerged. I felt the chill of the brick through my clothes. The Whitehall Palace roof stretched away in every direction that I could see, as wide as a village but, with its strange peaks and slopes and pinnacles, a village built by a different tribe than any that lived at ground level. My face throbbed from his blow. My guts ached but I no longer felt sick. Sir Roger Nunn, alias Signor Noti, stood over me and slightly to one side. I'd no doubt that if I tried to make a break for it he'd be on me like a cat on a mouse. And I knew that he was as strong and quick as he boasted.

"It was something that the Queen said to me," I said, reckoning that now I'd reached this pass there was nothing to be lost by making the most of my royal connections.

"She will not save you. She has other things in her head than the fate of a little player fellow."

"Like the end of Essex?" I said.

"These are great affairs of state into which you have blundered."

"Was *invited* to blunder."

"What did she say to you?"

I was gratified to see that I'd pricked his curiosity.

"My knowledge of the Italian tongue is not like hers – or yours," I said, inclining my head towards him. "In fact it is hardly there at all. But, as you've so generously pointed out, I am a player and have a good head for words. Sometimes I can commit them to memory without knowing precisely what they mean. She said to me '*Per molto variare la natura e bella*' – or something to that effect."

"To that effect exactly. Your ear is good, Revill."

"She, the Queen I mean, told me that it was one of her favourite sayings. Something to do with variety in life and nature. And it came to me that I'd heard those very words a few days ago. On the river. While a certain Italian gentleman and I were being rowed to the safety of the south bank after my lord of Essex's rebellion started to split at the seams."

"Your *memory* is good too, Revill." There was a threatening undertone to his words. I hastened to resume my speech.

"The boatman had said something about Essex taking on all sorts, and then you added your groatsworth, '*Per molto variare*' etc. I remember thinking at the time that it was odd you should seem to be following the conversation because you hadn't shown any signs of being able to up to that point. That was before you allowed me to tumble into the water."

"Your *observation* is good as well, Revill."

"I am not yet finished. While I was sitting down in the passage from where you recovered me just now, I asked myself why one of Queen Elizabeth's favourite sayings should be known to an Essexite – not even an English Essexite, but a self-proclaimed foreigner. Wasn't it more likely, I asked myself, that the Queen's private expressions would be best known to her courtiers? Rather than to a foreigner, particularly one in the enemy camp. And then I thought that I'd seen you somewhere before and that it wasn't in the audience for tonight's play after all – but somewhere else."

"You must concede that I played the foreign part well, player," said Nunn-Noti.

"You played very well," I said, sensing that he sought approval if not flattery. "Even down to the disguise. Like a true player you used false whiskers. Noti's pencil beard and his ample moustache."

"A nice touch," said vain Nunn, stroking his naked chin.

"I was convinced."

"Say, fooled."

"Fooled then. Why did you choose to act the Italian?"

"You have heard of Niccolo Machiavelli the Florentine?"

"Of course. Any player – or politician – worth their salt knows the reputation of Signor Machiavelli. Some people'd say that he sported horns and cloven feet."

"That's a fable," said Nunn.

"And that his spirit still possesses the race from which he sprang."

"Well then. I choose the Italian."

I saw Nunn shrug his shoulders under the stars, as if no more explanation was required. Indeed, it wasn't. To be a Machiavel is to be crafty and cunning – and also clever, devilishly clever. I could see that, to a certain cast of mind, the Florentine's mantle would be a highly desirable garment.

"Go on," said Nunn. "I will decide when I have heard enough."

"So after that business of the Queen's sayings, I began to bring together the two names of Nunn and Noti in my mind, and to see that the one might be construed as the other. Because Nunn is None, that is nobody or nothing, and Noti is Not-I."

"Not quite construed," said Sir Roger Nunn, once again getting down on his haunches and putting his face close to mine. In his hand, I suddenly saw, was a dagger, perhaps the same one with which he'd threatened me at the gateway of Essex House.

"No not quite," I said as calmly as I could. "For Nunn is really closer to Nemo – or Nobody."

"Neatly done, Revill. I wondered how long it was going to take you."

"Now turn and turn-about. It is you who should answer some questions."

"Watch your tongue, Revill, or I will cut it out."

"I will be as respectful as you please, provided you answer me, Sir Roger Nunn – or Signor Noti – or Captain Nemo. How do you prefer to be called? Which of your four-lettered names do I choose?"

You will understand that I was talking to prevent his using the dagger which I could sense rather than see. He was resting easily on his hams, his hands dangling down, the tapered fingers of one clutching the dagger whose point grazed against the lead of the roof.

"As you please," said this strange individual. "But in truth I am Nunn."

Behind his hunched shoulders, I saw a meteor track across the heavens. Perhaps it was the clarity of the skies that February but there really did seem to be an inordinate number of them winging their ill-omened path.

"Whoever you might be, I thought you were surely a familiar at court."

I saw his shoulders slacken slightly in the shadows. He was pleased.

"Go on."

"To my first question. Why? What is your reason?"

"A more powerful reason than kings or princes. The god that we all worship, though some do it in secret. The god with an extra letter."

He ran the dagger point across his open palm.

"Gold?"

I felt, obscurely, disappointed. All this stir for – *that*? Also, I forbore to remind Nunn how disparagingly he'd spoken of the player's willingness to exhibit himself for money.

"Whose gold?" (Though I knew as soon as I spoke the words.)

"I was amused, Revill, when we were in that boat together and you denied that I was Spanish in front of our ignorant countryman. Amused too when he began talking about Spanish gold and the A-zores."

"But you are English!"

I was surprised at the indignation in my voice.

"Gold speaks in all tongues," said Nunn simply.

"So Essex and the rest were right. There really is a plot to put the Spanish Infanta on the throne."

"No such thing."

"What then?"

"Do you think Spain is happy to see a proud realm to the north of her? Do you think that she wouldn't prefer a confused, disheartened state? With a dying monarch, and a carcase eaten away by inward troubles? As in Master Shake-speare's dramas."

"You did this for lucre."

I was shocked to the core. All the stir and protest of an Essex seemed trivial compared to the cold-hearted treason of this individual.

"Can you think of a better reason?" said Nunn. "Gold – and the game. The parts I played. In this camp and that camp. I am to be paid for making mischief."

"And Master Secretary . . . Is he . . . ?"

My voice trembled.

"Oh he has his own game. It is called Save-the-Queen. In

his camp he practises surgery. An infected limb must be cut off before it poisons the whole body. To do that, a crisis may have to be induced. Matters provoked. Men must sometimes be whipped like tops to make them spin a little faster."

"So . . . if *you* wanted mischief . . . Master . . . [*Something restrained me from saying Cecil's name*] . . . he wanted trouble . . . he wanted *Richard* performed . . . wanted Essex to march . . . why, that Sunday morning summons to Essex to go before the Council was probably meant to elicit just the response it did . . ."

I was speaking more to myself than to Nunn. Faintly, like the glimmer of starlight overhead, I started to see several other things. Why, for example, the inquiry into the role of the Chamberlain's by the Council had been so half-hearted. For sure, the seniors of the Company and the Council had some tacit agreement together. I understood why it seemed that everything that happened was known to the authorities in advance. Essex, who now appeared a comparative innocent, was acting to a schedule penned by another's hand. I thought of that upstairs chamber where I'd first glimpsed Cecil, his hand ceaselessly weaving and unweaving a pathway across the strewn sheets of paper. And since, once you begin to discern conspiracy, you see its traces peeping out everywhere I applied conspiracy to small matters. I saw why I had been asked to be in the book-room on the afternoon when Phillips and Merrick met. To clear one side with the other: to be able to report back to Nemo, the slippery agent, that the Chamberlain's were fulfilling their part of the bargain.

But what were they – we of the Chamberlain's – getting out of it?

"Another question? Your last in all likelihood."

Sir Roger Nunn, traitor for the sake of Spanish gold, scraped the impatient dagger along the roof-lead. I drew a deep breath and sent out a white plume into the night. I wasn't as confident of my conclusions as I hoped I sounded.

"Why did you have to kill Nat the Animal Man – and May? They were harmless. What had they done to you?"

"Nothing," said Nunn-Noti-Nemo. "Nothing at all. Like the wise fox in the fable, I was merely covering my tracks. Nat Whatd'youcallhim took messages on my behalf to you, and to others. He had outlived his usefulness, never very great in any case. And as for the other person—"

"May was her name."

"She saw me slip into your quarters. She may even have seen me jerk this dagger into Nat's ribs up in your room. She had to go."

"I thought they died natural. As natural as a man falling in the water and drowning. An accident as he is disembarking from a ferry-boat."

"I took advantage of the moment there. If that boatman hadn't been on your side, you would have gone under. Looked at in the right way, all deaths are natural. When a hawk kills a vole or a shrew, is that not natural? These small people, Nat and the woman, they wandered into the arena where mighty opposites were engaged. They don't matter. I except you, Revill. You are worth a little more than the rest. You have been quick – for a player."

"I did not see the marks of violence on them."

"You were not meant to. I must say, young man, that I have one piece of advice for you. Not that you'd be able to act on it for you are not going to be let live."

"What is it?"

"Find yourself other lodgings. They are not safe. Why, two people have died there. Besides, you really should've been living in a more fashionable quarter. Too late now."

"I'm a poor player," I said.

"*Basta*," he said.

And another puzzle was solved.

"It was you who was seeking for me in the book-room," I said.

"*Bravo*."

"You must have been in your Italian guise. I heard someone come in and say 'bastard' but it *wasn't* 'bastard' – it was what you've just said, whatever that means."

"*Basta*!" he spat the word out. "I suspected you were there. I was relishing a chase but you eluded me, just as you had at Thames-side."

"I was in hell," I said, hoping that he would ask for explanation and so delay exercising the inevitable dagger. But Nunn was pursuing his own train of thought.

"It is more innocent than it sounds. It means 'enough', it means 'no more'."

"*Basta*," I said musingly.

"There is one more thing to do, one more trace to clear away," said Nunn, "and then I may go to earth again."

"Like the fox in the fable."

"Like enough," he said, flicking the dagger up.

"Yet the fox was not so wise after all."

So saying, I threw myself to one side. At the same time I lashed out with my right leg in the hope of striking the hand that held the dagger. I missed – or Nunn was too quick for me. He was as good as his boasting. Within a second he was on top of me, and our cloudy breaths mingled. He jabbed me in the left thigh. I saw his arm jerk out and in, but did not at first connect the movement and the searing pain.

"You see – the fox did not – did not—"

"Did not what, Revill?"

My assailant's face seemed to fill the entire sky, like a

malign tumbling planet. I spoke in short painful bursts, trying to hold his attention, to prevent his arm flashing out and then in again.

"—the fox swept away – the old traces – but he made new traces – even as – he swept away – the old ones—"

Nunn pressed heavy on me. If my thigh hadn't been so painful, I'd probably have been aware of the discomfort of bearing his weight.

"Different fable, Revill. I know another ending."

"—and new traces led back – to his earth—"

"Not my story, player."

He raised his dagger-tipped arm.

Behind him the door on to the roof creaked open and a weak light spilled over the roof leads. Nunn turned his head aside and his dagger hung irresolute in the frosty night. Through the door tumbled a rush of figures. Someone shouted. I twisted sharply and succeeded in shifting my attacker from his position atop me. Without thought, I half scrabbled, half rolled to the shelter of a nearby chimney stack, trying to put some solid obstacle between Nunn and myself. Once round the corner of the stack I was cut off from a view of what was happening. There were sounds of scuffling and muffled oaths. Then a shadow jumped across the gap that stretched between the tall chimney where I was lying and a steeply inclined section of roof. Two or three other shadows leapt after it and I heard thumps and gasps, and then a long-drawn sigh. Then nothing more.

Another shape came round the corner and, as it approached me, blotted out the stars. I may have screamed. I huddled into myself. Then yet another shape joined the first, and this one I knew. The hump back made an unmistakable outline.

"Wait!" Cecil commanded. "This one is a friend."

As the other man bent over me I recognised the heavily

bearded Yeoman who'd been standing guard outside the Queen's chamber.

"He wanted to kill me," I said. My thigh was throbbing and my leggings felt sticky. A strange lassitude filled me. I could have gone to sleep under the stars.

"He is hurt, sir, but it is not mortal," said the guard.

"Then he will be cared for," said Cecil.

"He attacked me . . . he would have killed me . . ."

"Who?" said Cecil.

"Nemo . . . nobody . . . Nunn . . ."

"Nobody attacked you? None was your assailant?"

"That's it. Nobody."

"Light-headed, sir," said the Yeoman.

"Hoist him up, Griffiths," said Cecil. "Be careful now."

And the giant of a guardsman lifted me up as if I was a baby and, cradling me in his arms, ported me across the roof and towards the door. In his wake, I was vaguely aware of other soldiers returning from the outer reaches of the roof. We went slow and Robert Cecil kept pace slightly behind us. His broad brow glimmered.

As they walked and I was carried down the long corridor Cecil spoke to me, low but urgent.

"Nicholas, you are hurt. We shall attend to you. But it is necessary that one thing be clarified first. You were hunting down nobody. You were exposing nobody, for which we thank you."

I was certainly light-headed. It sounded as though Robert Cecil was complimenting me. I must've been light-headed because his tone then changed.

"But that is over and done with. Nobody will never trouble us again."

"Good," I said.

"I mean," said Cecil insistently, his brow aglimmer, "you were attacked by nobody."

"Yes, Nunn. He wounded me here in the thigh."

I attempted to gesture with my head but wasn't sure that Cecil understood.

"No, you are wrong, Nicholas. You were wounded by nobody. Let us be clear on that before you are treated for your injury."

I tried to shake my head now, but only succeeded in inducing a wave of dizziness and nausea. There was a flaw in what Cecil was saying but I couldn't be bothered to identify it. It was only when we'd arrived at some room somewhere – this was a palace, there was no end to the chambers it contained! – and I'd been laid down on a daybed, that the contradiction struck me.

"If there was – nobody there – how was I wounded? For God's sake, sir, look. My thigh."

Blood had soaked through my hose and was starting to pool on the rough blanket beneath me. I turned in appeal to Griffiths the Yeoman but he was standing impassively by the door. The sleeves and front of his fine costume were smeared with my blood.

"You must have fallen on your own dagger," said Cecil. "Either that, or you have given yourself a voluntary wound in the thigh."

I lay there gazing up, as the low ceiling seemed to hover and swoop and tremble before my eyes.

"You must choose how you came in harm's way, Nicholas. Then we can get physic for you."

Cecil was standing awkwardly beside the daybed, looking alternately direct at me and then at my gory thigh, from which all sensation was starting to depart. With his hunchback, he did not show to advantage standing up.

"After all," he said with a trace of asperity, "you have already declared that you were attacked by nobody. So it must follow as the night the day that you did this to yourself – either by accident or design. Please choose which, Nicholas, so that your wound may be staunched and a cataplasm applied."

"I – I – must have fallen on my own dagger somehow," I said, and sighed, and hung my head back.

"Good," said Cecil. "So let us hear no more nonsensical references to none and nobody."

He said something to Griffiths which I didn't catch. I didn't catch very much from that point on, in fact, as I slipped in and out sleep. I preferred being asleep anyway. It took me away from the buzz of voices in the low-ceilinged chamber, it took me away from the pain and discomfort of having my leggings cut away and my (apparently self-inflicted) wound being cleaned up and poulticed. These things I still felt or saw or heard intermittently but, as I say, I really preferred to sleep through them.

Epilogue

Spring 1601

"So," said Nell.

"So," I said.

"It's not *that* bad here. Though these blankets have a stench."

"I must be used to them, I hadn't noticed."

We were lying in a post-coital tryst in my execrable bed in the Coven attic. It was a mild late afternoon. Spring was about to make good on her promise. The holes and gaps in the walls and roof still admitted air but it was almost balmy compared to the bitterness of February. As you can see, I hadn't quite got round yet to taking the advice of Sir Roger Nunn – or Captain Nemo – or Signor Noti – that I should shift to more fashionable quarters. Not that men who never existed can give you advice, of course. No, I was still living in the lodgings of that witchy trio, April, June and July.

I hadn't enquired what had happened to the corpse of the unfortunate May, last seen stuffed in her own cauldron. Tact or guilt prevented my asking. I assumed they had disposed of her with appropriate rites and ceremony. I hoped that she had been given, if not a Christian burial, then one that God in His infinite mercy might find acceptable. I liked May, and held myself not a little responsible for her death. And for Nat's death too, another hapless victim buried hugger-mugger, not dignified with Christian obsequies. Obviously, Nunn – if he ever existed, which of course he didn't – had decided that all those involved in his treacherous double dealing with the Essex enterprise should be wiped from the slate. He had picked out the small detail, Nat and May, and all that remained was to erase the final figure, one N.Revill.

And when I asked myself who Nunn was doing this for, I had no clear answer. He was working for Cecil and working for Essex and, ultimately, working for gold and the game, as he had expressed it. He was a foul traitor, deserving of that foulest of punishments, hanging and drawing and quartering.

Yet much of the affair could be laid at Cecil's door. In order to forestall a dangerous threat to an ailing Queen, he had actually set out to encourage the very rising which the country feared. This had a double advantage. Essex's actions, if provoked by Cecil and his agents, remained to an extent under their control. It was the Secretary's schedule which the Earl followed or, to vary the figure, it was the Secretary who was piping the tune to which the Queen's favourite jigged and pranced.

There was a further benefit, too – by provoking a head before it was truly ripe and ready, Cecil and the authorities had to deal with a threat that was essentially unformed. Not yet the full-grown serpent, it was merely the snake in its shell. But the wary statesman does not show mercy to the snake on that account; only the fool gives him the time to grow fangs. I remembered the confusion and uncertainty that attended the Sunday morning march of Essex and Southampton and the rest, the dithering over which direction to turn, the shut-up city houses, the fear in the faces of the onlookers. Oh, how ingenious Cecil and Nemo and the unseen others had been!

How hot-headed and short-sighted were Essex and South-ampton and their acolytes!

"What?" I said.

"I said," said Nell, "does that hurt?"

She was pressing, gently but quite insistently, on my dressed thigh.

"Not much," I said, undecided whether to solicit her sympathy for my pain or her admiration for my stoicism. "Not too much, that is."

"Things must be better if you were able to do what you've just done."

"*We've* just done."

"I told you that my preparations and simples would help," she said, ignoring my comment.

The moment she'd seen my wound, Nell had at once decided that the remedies applied by Cecil's physician were inadequate. Telling me that that ignorant gentleman'd gone wrong straightaway by not placing two periwinkle leaves between my teeth so as to staunch the flow of blood, she then washed out the raw gash all over again with juice of Saracen's root ("you'll know it better as comfrey" she explained comfortingly) before applying some poultice of her own devising. What I knew all too well was that she had obtained her herbal lore from Old Nick the St Paul's apothecary*, herbal lore and much else beside, I used to fear.

It may be that the wound wasn't as bad as it first felt or appeared. Nunn had given me a fleshy stab prior to the fatal stroke he was about to inflict when interrupted. I owed my life to the arrival of Cecil and the guard. So, although I was most angry that the Secretary had used me to unmask Nemo and his madness and then compelled me to turn my ordeal into a dream or a delusion ("You were attacked by nobody. You were

* see *Sleep of Death*

wounded by nobody."), I couldn't but acknowledge that he had saved me. Saved me to lie once again flank-to-flank with Nell, to enjoy the company of my compeers in the Chamberlain's, to breathe the spring air through the rents in my rented wall.

Within a few days I was able to get about without too much discomfort, though I pleaded incapacity to get Nell to visit me at the Coven rather than have to find my way over to Holland's Leaguer, her place of work. Fortunately, we of the Chamberlain's had just entered on the lenten period when companies had to obtain official dispensation if they wanted to play anything, so there wasn't much doing at the Globe now. In any case, after our unfortunate involvement with the Earl of Essex – although it had almost certainly been foreseen, even planned, by the Council and the Company together – it might have seemed politic to lie low. Not that we were out of favour, as far as I could see. Hadn't we just presented that melancholy but diverting comedy *Twelfth Night* to the Queen, and hadn't she told me with her own lips that she'd enjoyed the play?

I fervently hope that *Twelfth Night* distracted her for a couple of hours on that Shrove Tuesday night. On the next morning, Ash Wednesday morning, Essex was beheaded in the Tower yard. They say he made a good end.

As for Southampton . . . that gentleman I will come to in a moment.

Oddly enough, I hadn't been able to impress Nell with my personal account of meeting our Queen. Prompted by her at one of our earlier encounters, I'd run through the performance, described the appreciative laughter that issued from the canopied chair of state, catalogued the interior of the great Hall ("How many candles, Nick? I don't believe you."), even mentioned how, as I thought, one of my own lines had elicited a sigh from the depths of the chamber. But when it came to Sir Roger Nunn's summoning of me to her majesty's presence, Nell flatly refused to believe a word of it.

"I'm telling you the truth, Nell," I protested. "She asked to see me specially. The Queen asked for me."

"I suppose *She* admired your black hair – or your playing."

"Neither." (Though the suggestions were flattering and not entirely beyond the bounds of possibility.)

"Why did *She* want to see you then?"

"I cannot speak of it."

"Oh, we're back to that again."

"But I did see her nonetheless, and speak to her and she to me."

"Very well. What is *She* like then?"

"She is . . . she is an old lady now."

"There, Nicholas. And you wonder that I don't believe you. How can *She* grow old like other mortals?"

"Because she is like other mortals," I said. "Because she is not a goddess."

But Nell was clasping her hands to her ears, unwilling to listen to another sacrilegious word from me. I didn't mind her adopting that position, at least when she was naked, since it caused her breasts to swell as the billows do in the Bristol Channel. However, I soon saw that if I wanted to avail myself of what was on offer, I would have to drop any pretence of meeting the Queen, let alone trying to present a truthful portrait of that great lady.

Similarly it wasn't worth even beginning to describe to her the story of Nunn-Nemo-Noti, even had I not been bound by some notion of silence. Why, Secretary Cecil himself refused to accept what had happened – and he'd been there! Accordingly, when Nell inquired how I'd received the wound in my thigh I had to adopt the lie which Cecil had forced on me, that I had been careless and stabbed myself with my own dagger (the tiny one which I kept buried in my clothing and which was more suitable for nail-paring than flesh-gouging). This was also the story which I retailed to my fellows in the Company, and although they laughed at my clumsiness and although one or two of them looked askance as if they thought I was hiding a deeper tale, it was soon accepted that Nick Revill was not a man to be trusted with his own knife – or another man's wife, as the saying goes.

Which brings me on to a final detail from my dialogues with Nell. On the spring evening mentioned earlier, I eventually got round to the subject of Isabella Horner. I hadn't forgotten that I'd left her and Nell discussing – *things* – in the Goat & Monkey. I was eager, though fearful might be a better word, to discover what had passed between these two women. Judging that Nell was preoccupied with the smell of the blankets or with the efficacy of her remedies for my wounds, I saw an opportunity to mention casually what was on my mind. I contrived to drop Isabella's name in the conversation, and was surprised to see Nell smirk.

"You are a fool, Nicholas," she said, though not unkindly.

"How so?"

"That you think I do not know."

"Know what?"

"And still to keep up the pretence like this."

"What pretence?" I said with a faltering heart.

"I know that you and Mistress Horner have shared a bed together."

"I – we – once—"

"*Once?*"

"A handful only."

"A small handful no doubt – like this handful," she said,

grasping my member, which had suddenly developed a desire to run for cover. She shifted her hand and squeezed my cullions hard enough (but I was aware that she might have done it much harder).

"I have talked with Isabella, see," said Nell. "And she has told me how matters stand."

"Matters? Stand?"

"With you and with her and with her husband too. Her husband Jack."

"Oh God."

"He knows all."

"Say you so?"

I felt myself going hot and cold at once, and blushes breaking out all over my face, and the wound on my thigh throbbing fiercely.

"I do say so."

"He has not said anything to me."

"Is there a law that says the cuckold must speak to the cuckolder? Should he not rather run him through?"

She removed her hand from my privates and jabbed me in the belly.

"Oh God," I said. "Jack is a peaceable man. He is my friend."

I buried my face in the stinky blankets and rugs that were piled on the narrow bed.

"The more shame for you if he is your friend," she said remorselessly.

"I know," I said, feeling very sorry for myself.

"But I can tell you why he has kept silent."

"Because he means to stab me instead?"

I visualised Jack waiting in some dark corner and then leaping out to complete the work which Nunn had begun. No, the scene did not convince.

"I think we can leave you to stab yourself, Nicholas. You do that well."

"I know the proverb about a knife and a wife," I said.

"But that isn't the reason that your friend Jack does nothing."

"What is it then?"

"Because it suits him that you should occupy his wife."

"What?"

"Though it does not suit me," said Nell.

"What?"

"You are a parrot today, Nicholas, with your beak gaping in surprise and the same sound emerging. I say that it suits him because he is more interested in another member of your Company. Mistress Horner says."

"Who, Jack is?"

At this point my mouth must have been gaping even wider.

"He is on most friendly terms with a boy player – I forget the name—"

"Martin . . . Hancock, it must be," I said slowly as light began to dawn.

"It is possible that was the name she mentioned."

"They are often together, it is true. But I thought it was only . . . friendship."

"So it is too. Friendship and other things besides. And Isabella tells me that her husband has not done her a good turn for, oh, eight months now."

"A good turn?"

"What you did me some time ago now."

"What *we* did together," I said, though my mind was on other things. Jack and Martin . . . so.

"Therefore Isabella Horner was glad enough to turn to an energetic young player for a good turn . . ."

"Oh."

". . . and now she has her eye on another in your Company. Someone senior to you. A poor player was all *you* were, was what she said."

"Perhaps she will give him some of her potions," I said, inwardly relieved to have this confirmation that Mistress Horner was aiming her arrows in a different direction and brushing aside her dismissive description of me. Well, almost brushing it aside.

"Oh, I think she hopes to be fed on *his* potions," said Nell. "She is enchanted by his words. They weave a spell about her. And it is someone who you admire, I believe."

"I wonder who it is," I said, not wondering at all. "Don't tell me."

Then I did a very childish thing and clapped my hands over my ears so as not to hear my friend Nell name the new suitor of Mistress Isabella Horner. Of course, with hands thus occupied, I had left open the rest of myself to attack. And attack me Nell did – but in a loving way, a way which showed (without words) that she had forgiven me for my dalliance with Isabella and showed furthermore what she meant by the expression 'a good turn'.

A couple of mornings later I was lying at my ease in the spring sunshine and gathering my strength on a turf bank outside the Coven. I'd taken a scroll into the fresh air so as to get acquainted with my next role which, as it happens, was in Master Richard Milford's *second* play. His first, *A Venetian Whore*, in which I'd played the Duke of Argal, had been staged in the brief interim between our last rehearsals for *Twelfth Night* and that Shrove Tuesday presentation before the Queen.

Whore had been a modest success, though somewhat over-shadowed by the Company's royal affairs and, in my own mind, by the dramatic sequel to that evening. The playhouse audience was pleased by this bawdy comedy, and Messrs Burbage and Shakespeare and the rest were pleased that the audience was pleased, and Master Milford, he was very pleased with life in general. No doubt relieved too that I had not unmasked him as an unscrupulous plagiariser and sneak thief. I was fairly sure that he, like a number of others, had made free with my room at the Coven and searched through my chest for those damning sheets which would link him to *The Courtesan of Venice*. As a result I'd suspected him of foul play in the matter of May and the cauldron, as well as pursuing me down to hell in the netherworld of the Globe. Now, as I should surely have intuited, Master Milford might have stolen some scraps of paper, but he was no murderer, no hunting hell-hound.

In fact, by comparison with the other things which people had been perpetrating around me in the last few weeks – murders, both attempted and accomplished; treason and insurrection; gross lies of state and a politic duplicity – a spot of plagiarism and the theft of a few pages appeared positively innocent.

So, following the success of his first piece, Richard Milford's second play was already in hand, to be staged by the Chamberlain's after the lenten season had finished. It was titled *The Murder in the Garden*, and appeared to be a domestic mystery or tragedy. I had his own word that it was all his own work, and perhaps it was this time. Of course, I didn't have the full story, only the scroll of my role. I was pleased to note that my scrolls were slowly growing bigger as I too grew up into my place with the Globe players.

I'd taken my part to the turfy bank outside with the best intentions of committing to memory a hundred lines or so of *The Murder in the Garden*, but the soothing warmth of a watery sun and an inclination to fall asleep at odd times (I was still a little weak from the thigh wound) tugged at my eyelids. I was enjoying the red play of light on the underside of those same lids when a sudden shadow fell across them. I blinked, to see an individual blocking the sun. I assumed that it was a passer-by, come to purchase some of the sisters' brew. As far as I could tell, May's death had made no difference to their business, and they were still using the fatal cauldron to mix their noxious messes. I hoped they'd scoured it after they'd removed her corpse, while knowing perfectly well that they wouldn't have done.

I gestured with my thumb in the direction of the Coven.

"They're in there," I said.

"Who?"

"April and the rest of the sisters in the Coven."

"How do you call it?"

"The Coven."

I sat up fast then because I recognised the voice of Master WS. Sure enough, it was the playwright and no common wayfarer who was standing in my light.

"I – I'm sorry, sir – I thought you'd come to buy their brew—"

"Later perhaps. I have come to see my wounded fellow. How are you, Nicholas?"

"Well enough, sir – William."

"And your wound?" He gestured at my dressed leg.

"I am mending fast."

"I am pleased to hear it. So it is not a case, Nicholas, of 'Thigh no more, ladies, thigh no more'?"

I did not dignify this 'joke' with a response (there are limits), and after a time Master Shakespeare cast his eyes about in search of fresh material.

"So this interesting-looking place is where you lodge."

"For the moment."

I resolved to move as soon as I could properly walk again.

"Learning your part, I see."

He sat down beside me on the bank of turf and took the scroll.

"Richard Milford's new thing?"

"Yes. *Murder in the Garden*."

"I enjoyed his *Whore*. More to the point, our congregation did too. A nice, light piece for the middle of winter, to distract our minds before the royal performance."

"I thought it – it was – a little like . . ."

"Yes? Like what?"

WS turned his large, curious gaze on me.

"Like . . . your own *Merchant of Venice*, William."

"Of course it was. All plays are made out of the scraps and fragments of other plays."

"Of course," I said.

"But I have come not to talk about Master Milford, Nicholas, but to commiserate with you."

"Thank you."

I felt myself growing warmer under the wintery sun.

"And to congratulate you. I hear that the Queen herself summoned you at the end of the performance."

I had not made a great noise about this in the Company, perhaps fearing that (as with Nell) I would not be believed.

"I will not ask what you talked of," said WS.

"She liked the play," I said.

WS seemed gratified by this, but only slightly.

"And then afterwards you had that regrettable accident. Fell on your own dagger, or some such thing."

"Oh yes," I said, looking away and now feeling that the sun had grown altogether too warm. "I was careless."

"You were not the only individual around the Palace to come to grief that night."

"No?" I said, supposing that he was referring to Essex.

"No. There was a gentleman discovered on the ground near the Court Gate. It appeared that he had fallen from an upper window – or the roof."

"Did he—" – I swallowed – "—do they – who was it?"

"It appears that he was a courtier, though his name slips my mind," said WS. "A fine gentleman but they say that, like many of his kind, he lived beyond his means. He was heavily in debt."

"Death cancels all accounts," I said mechanically (while remembering Nunn's words about gold speaking in all tongues).

"Yet few are indebted to it on that account," said WS.

I winced at the word-play. WS must have noticed for, clapping me on the shoulder, he made to rise. "Well, Nicholas, I will leave you to learn your lines or to enjoy your sleep in the sun."

He stood up, again casting his shadow across me.

"Sir?" I said tentatively.

"Yes."

"I recently ran an errand for you to a certain gentleman, who was lodging temporarily in Essex House."

Shakespeare said nothing, and I could not tell from his sun-limned outline whether he was willing to listen to me or not. However, I ploughed on.

"And I wondered . . . whether all was well with that gentleman?"

I knew that Wriothesley, the Earl of Southampton, had, for the time being, avoided the fate of his friend and cousin, Essex. I knew that he was incarcerated in the Tower. But I knew no more.

307

"He has lost his liberty and will not regain it for the moment. How can it be otherwise? But, do you mean, will he lose any more? will his life be forfeit?"

"I – I – think that was my meaning, yes."

"The answer is no. I believe that the gentleman is safe from the extreme penalty."

"It may be presumptuous in me to say it . . . William . . . but I am glad."

My heart hammered. I thought of Wriothesley's touch, his brilliant gaze, his designation of me as Mercury.

WS lingered for a moment.

"Not presumptuous in you. After all, I sent you to him with some small reminder," he said. "That he should be mindful of himself."

(I thought of WS's lines, the ones which I'd carried to Wriothesley at Essex House – *'For shame deny that thou bear'st love to any Who for thy self art so unprovident.'*)

"He chose to ignore it," he continued.

"But you still saved him," I said, recklessly perhaps but wanting to establish once for all *what was the case*. "By keeping a foot in both camps, by listening to the overtures of the Essexites and staging *Richard* and by letting the Council know everything that was happening in advance, you saved your friend. It was an arrangement. The Council knows everything, and in return Southampton is allowed to live."

"There is nobody to say so."

"Didn't you tell me that you had contemplated the story of Damon and Pythias? The friends who would lay down their lives for each other."

"A play is not life," said WS.

"There was a bargain struck," I said excitedly.

"Nicholas, I think you've been lying overlong in the sun,"

said WS. "Either that or you're still weak from that wound which you inflicted on yourself."

"Of course," I said.

At that moment there was a great clatter and a shouting and wailing from inside the Coven. Shakily, I stood up. Out of the house rushed the pig and the dog and the chickens and the cats, followed by the three sisters, my joint-landladies, April, June and July. Much flailing of limbs as they pushed through the entrance. There'd apparently been some upset in the witchy interior. Once outside, and ignoring altogether the presence of a distinguished stranger on their turfy bank, they shouted and screamed at each other. By now, I had grown slightly skilled in their strange tongue, and from the accusations and counter-accusations that were flying to and fro, I understood that the cauldron had been upset and a quantity of valuable ingredients (powdered unicorn's horn, essence of dead toad, ground dogs' tongues and so on) lost to the world.

As the screeching and the screaming continued, I grew more and more embarrassed. *I* was used enough to the antics of April, June and July, but was very unhappy that they should expose themselves in all their witchy wretchedness and squalor to the sharp eyes of Master Shakespeare.

What would he think of these howling hags? More important, what would he think of Nick Revill for lodging with such she-devils? I was about to say something about my intention to shift lodgings soon, very soon, when I observed that *he* was observing this scene of the squabbling women, the fleeing animals, the smoke-filled entrance – observing all this with a pondering eye.

He tapped his forefinger to his lips.

"What did you call this place, Nicholas?"

"The Coven, William."

"And these three women, they have names?"

So I told him, expecting him to laugh or express disbelief.

But Shakespeare did neither of these things. Instead he simply stood there, gazing at the three quarrelling witches, tapping his lips.

"Hm," said WS finally. "Hmm."